THE BLOOD KING

WITHDRAWN

THE BLOOD KING

Book Two of the
CHRONICLES OF THE NECROMANCER

GAIL Z. MARTIN

SOLARIS

First published 2008 by Solaris
an imprint of BL Publishing
Games Workshop Ltd, Willow Road
Nottingham, NG7 2WS
UK

www.solarisbooks.com

ISBN-13: 978 1 84416 531 5
ISBN-10: 1 84416 531 0

Copyright © Gail Z. Martin 2008

Map by Kirk Caldwell

10 9 8 7 6

A CIP catalogue record for this book is available from the
British Library.

Designed & typeset by BL Publishing
Printed in the US

For everyone who believed in my dreams and helped to make them happen.

ACKNOWLEDGEMENTS

This book was made possible by the loving indulgence of my family, who were used to sharing me with Tris and now has been kind enough to share more of my time with readers and the obligations of publishing. To my husband Larry, a wonderful first editor and muse. To my daughters Kyrie and Chandler, who read rough drafts and told their friends about the books. And to my son Cody, for being patient while I write! Thanks also to the crew at Solaris—Mark, Christian, George, Vincent, and Caroline. And of course, for my agent Ethan, who got the ball rolling.

THE WINTER KINGDOMS

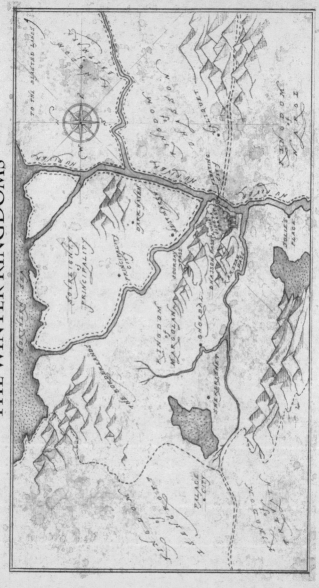

CHRONICLES OF THE NECROMANCER

I T SHOULD HAVE *been an evening of feasting and court merriment. But on the night of the Feast of the Departed, nineteen year-old Prince Martris Drayke's life is changed forever when his half-brother, Jared, kills their father and seizes the throne. Aided by his dark mage, Foor Arontala, Jared murders the royal family—all except Martris, who barely escapes with the help of a handful of friends.*

Tris is now an outlaw, hunted by Jared's assassins. As danger and grief push Tris to his limits, he discovers that he is the mage-heir of his sorcerer grandmother Bava K'aa, a powerful sorceress whose spirit magic made her a Summoner, able to intercede among the living, dead, and undead. In a world where ghosts walk freely and where the undead vayash moru walk the night, this wild and powerful magic may be the advantage Tris needs to win back the throne—if he can keep his newfound power from destroying him first.

Tris flees the palace Shekerishet with three good friends: Carroway, a master bard; Ban Soterius, captain of the king's guard; and Tov Harrtuck, a loyal officer. Desperate to find sanctuary in one of the neighboring kingdoms, the four are pursued by bounty hunters hired by Jared to kill Tris. Harrtuck leads them to Jonmarc Vahanian, a mercenary and smuggler who can guide them through the dangerous mountain passes to reach sanctuary in Principality. Taking cover with a traveling caravan, they meet the healer Carina and her brother Cam, who are on their own quest to find a way to heal King Donelan of Isencroft from a mage-sent illness.

When slavers sent by Jared destroy the caravan seeking Tris and his friends, Cam, Soterius and Harrtuck are presumed dead. Only Tris's half-harnessed power is able to save him in the Ruune Videya forest, where malicious ghosts take their long-overdue revenge. Tris and his friends take with them one of the slaver's captives, a young girl named Berry, who helped them escape. Two of the undead vayash moru, Gabriel and Mikhail, join the group along the way.

On the road, Tris meets Kiara, daughter of King Donelan of Isencroft, who has gone on a dangerous coming-of-age Journey to evade a long-ago arranged betrothal to Jared of Margolan. Kiara believes that Arontala is behind the wasting spell that is killing her father. She pledges herself to Tris's cause. Hounded by the king's troops, Tris and his friends find sanctuary at the legendary Library at Westmarch. The Library is a repository of ancient magical lore run by the eccentric Keeper Royster. At Westmarch, Tris's training begins with the Sisterhood, a reclusive group of powerful sorceresses.

Tris learns from the Sisterhood that Arontala has stolen the orb in which Bava K'aa once trapped the soul of the Obsidian King, a dark and powerful Summoner who nearly destroyed the Winter Kingdoms fifty years ago during the cataclysmic Mage Wars. Arontala plans to free the spirit of the Obsidian King on the night of the summer solstice—the Hawthorn Moon—and permit it to possess him, making that ancient evil incarnate and assuring Jared's power over Margolan and the entire realm of the Winter Kingdoms.

In spite of the danger, Tris and Kiara fall in love. When they leave the safety of Westmarch so that Tris can continue his mage training with the Sisterhood, they are ambushed by Margolan assassins. Fighting their way free from one ambush, they are captured by the guards of King Staden of Principality. Expecting to be sent back to Jared in chains, Tris and the others discover that their capture was Staden's way of bringing them safely to his court, where Soterius and Harrtuck have won the king's support. Berry, Staden's daughter Berwyn, urged her father to support Tris's quest. Now, as the last month of the year approaches, Tris finds himself in exile, struggling to master powerful spirit magic that has the potential to destroy him. Tris must find a way to take back the throne from Jared and defeat Arontala in order to free Margolan and keep the dark magic of the Obsidian King from rising again.

CHAPTER ONE

MARTRIS DRAYKE, MARGOLAN'S exiled prince, looked up sharply as the door to the war room swung open and King Staden of Principality strode into the council chamber.

"Today, we talk of war," Staden said as those assembled rose in deference. With him were a stiff-stanced man whose military bearing made plain his vocation, and another nervous man whose eyes constantly scanned the room.

"I gave you my word that you'd have access to my best strategists, Prince Drayke," Staden said proudly. "Here they are. This," he pointed toward the tall man who, even at rest, stood at attention, "is General Darrath, and this," he gestured toward his other companion, "is my chief rat catcher, Hant. If a successful campaign can be planned, they can do it."

Tris Drayke bowed in acknowledgement. "Thank you, Your Majesty," Tris replied. "I'm in your debt." Only a day had passed since Tris and his companions had been brought to Staden's palace. They had been captured by the king's guards at the border as they fled an ambush by assassins sent from Jared of Margolan. At the time, with their weapons confiscated and transported under heavy guard, Tris was sure they would be turned over to Jared, like bargaining chips in a high-stakes game of *contre* dice. Instead, Staden welcomed them as heroes, grateful for the return of his daughter, Berry. The past evening was spent at a banquet celebrating the princess's safe return and honoring Tris and his friends. They were richly rewarded with gold and gems, and Jonmarc Vahanian was named Lord of Dark Haven for his heroism. The reward money would be enough to help Tris raise an army of mercenaries to take back the throne. Undeterred by Jared's threats, Staden openly welcomed Tris and his companions. And so Tris found himself seated at the table with Principality's leading military strategists, beginning the task of waging war to free Margolan from Jared's rule.

"Nonsense," Staden boomed. "Let's not get into that again. I'll have your meals sent to you. Take as long as you like. I've got work to do elsewhere," he bustled, heading for the massive wooden doors. "Do join me for supper," he invited over his shoulder as he left, pulling the door closed with a bang behind him.

"So you are Martris Drayke?" Darrath said in a voice rough enough to sand wood.

"I am," Tris replied.

"Come closer, boy." Darrath beckoned with a long finger. "I want to see you." Tris stepped closer, but the general beckoned once more. "Close enough to look in your eyes. I want to know what you're made of."

Tris stood a head taller than the sharp-featured general. Darrath regarded Tris coldly through eyes that seemed as if they could see down to his bones, and for a long, uncomfortable moment, Darrath's eyes met his. Tris felt as if he were being measured. "You realize," General Darrath said finally, "that if we support you, Principality will be at war with your homeland."

"I realize that."

"And you realize," Darrath continued, "that many men will die to put you on Margolan's throne. Some might say that's none of our affair."

"It's already Principality's affair," Tris replied. "Jared sent his troops across your borders to hunt down Kiara, persecute the Sisterhood, and look for me. He bargained with slavers who kidnapped your princess, and who took prisoners a day's ride from the Principality border. Margolan refugees crowd your borders. What Arontala hasn't taken already, he'll take once The Hawthorn Moon is past. Margolan's troubles are already Principality's concern."

Darrath regarded him silently for a moment, then nodded. "Well said, Prince Drayke. Yet you ask an enormous favor. I wonder: do you have the mettle to stand against King Jared and his dark mage? You're barely twenty summers old."

"I'm not a boy," Tris replied. "I'm a mage—and a Summoner. And by the will of the Lady, I'll rid Margolan of Jared and his sorcerer or die trying."

Darrath nodded once more. "You're willing to give your life. Are you willing to offer up your friends' lives too?"

"I'd give my life willingly to save theirs," Tris replied. "I haven't asked them to go with me. They have reasons of their own to wish Margolan free of its darkness. It's their choice."

"Tris speaks for all of us," Kiara Sharsequin put in. The Isencroft princess, dressed as she had been on the road in the tunic and trews of a soldier, was unmistakably a warrior in her own right. "He hasn't asked us to follow him. But none of us can let Foor Arontala gain the power of the Obsidian King." From beside her, Jae, her hunting gyregon, hissed. Tris exchanged glances with his companions. Jonmarc Vahanian, a fighter whose escapades—and lawbreaking—were legend. Ban Soterius, former captain of the late King Bricen's guard. Tov Harrtuck, Bricen's armsmaster. Carroway the bard, who together with Soterius and Harrtuck spirited Tris out of Margolan after Jared's coup. Carina Jesthrata, sworn to Tris's cause to break Arontala's mage-born curse on King Donelan of Isencroft. Their faces and their murmured assent made their solidarity clear. They were unlikely rebels, each brought into the quest for their own reasons, and now, bound by shared danger and fierce friendship, they were preparing to wage war against Jared the Usurper to destroy the Obsidian King.

Darrath remained silent for a moment, as if considering Kiara's words. "Very well," he said finally, motioning them to sit. "Let's get to it."

***

EVENING FOUND THEM still so deeply engrossed in their discussion that Staden joined them, and bade the servant fetch them dinner. Mikhail joined them at sundown.

"I trust our kitchen was well-stocked with fresh deer's blood?" Staden asked Mikhail.

Enough faint color tempered Mikhail's usual pallor to indicate that the *vayash moru* had recently fed. "Your cook has been most generous. I dined very well."

Although his face and form were that of a young man in his early twenties, Mikhail, one of the undead, had been liegeman to Tris's ancestor, King Hotten, two hundred years before. Now, Mikhail pledged his allegiance to the effort to unseat Jared Drayke.

By the evening bells, the group had reviewed the qualifications of every mercenary company in Principality. Famous for the paid companies that operated within its borders, Principality more than compensated for its own relatively small army. Small but wealthy, Principality's northern gold mines were known for their rich veins. A spoil of war in conflicts among Margolan, Eastmark and Dhasson over generations, Principality seized its independence three hundred years before, when the squabbles of the major powers distracted them as a local warlord rose to power.

Back then, Algor the Tall nurtured relationships with the best mercenary companies, augmenting the modest army raised from Principality's own sparse population. In return for the ability to operate freely, the mercenary companies swore their intent, if not quite their allegiance, to protect the small country and made an oath that their swords would never be purchased against Principality. It was an arrangement that served the kingdom well. The mercenary companies that operated from a Principality base were among the most trustworthy in an uncertain business, and the major powers considered the land more trouble than it was worth.

For more than a candlemark, Harrtuck and Vahanian heatedly argued the merits of one company over another, punctuated by Soterius's strong opinions and Mikhail's more moderate views. Kiara chimed in more than once, revealing a knowledge of the mercenary groups and their fighting tactics which impressed Tris. Carina and Carroway sat at the far end of the table, insistent in their wish to be present but silent, watching intently. Royster, the librarian from the Sisterhood's stronghold in Westmarch, chronicled the debate for history's sake.

Tris leaned forward to catch every word, acutely aware of how sheltered he had been as King Bricen's second son. Tiredly, he smoothed back a stray lock of white-blond hair that fell into his eyes. Anxious to learn, he willingly ceded the discussion to the professional soldiers. Darrath presided over the arguments with seasoned tolerance, adding his own impressions of the companies wintering in the area.

They determined that Harrtuck would command the mercenary troops, and ate their meal embroiled in debate over how best to contain Jared and his army. Hant said little, observing the discussion with an uncanny silence, as if he were analyzing the essence of each of the people at the table. His dark eyes darted from speaker to speaker. Finally, Hant held up his hand for silence.

"Have you considered," Hant began in a tone that clearly said he knew that his suggestion had not, in fact, occurred to them yet, "that there is an alternative to taking Margolan by force?"

Harrtuck frowned and sat back in his chair, crossing his arms. "How do you propose to do that? March in and ask Jared to kindly step aside?"

A cold smile flickered at the corners of Hant's mouth. "Something like that, only perhaps less civilly. I suggest," he said, "that the armies be engaged, but not cross into Margolan."

"And just what good will that do?" Soterius demanded, running a hand back through his short-cropped, russet hair.

"You were the captain of the king's guard, were you not?" Hant turned his cold stare on Soterius, who nodded. "Were your troops cold-blooded killers?"

Soterius looked troubled. "Margolan's army was a disciplined fighting force. But they weren't monsters."

Hant templed his fingers in thought. "Do you know these men personally?"

Soterius nodded. "Many of them. I'd recognize even more by sight, although I couldn't put a name to the face."

"Then if they aren't bewitched, might some of them accept the chance to stop the evil that grows in your homeland, if they thought they had a chance of winning?" Hant asked.

Soterius paused as he thought, his dark eyes sober. "I believe so," he replied, "unless Jared's killed the good men and replaced them with his own ilk." He was silent for a moment. "One of the hardest parts will be figuring out which soldiers have done the killing and looting—either on their own, or on Jared's orders."

"Orders or not, every soldier is responsible for his own choices," Vahanian's tone spoke of bitter experience. "The soldiers you want will be outlaws by now—if they haven't been hanged. The ones still in uniform are the enemy."

"I have no desire to see Principality and Margolan locked in a war that may last for years," Darrath said. "I believe I see where Hant is leading. If you were to slip into Margolan and recruit its troops against Jared, we may never have to march paid soldiers against your people. Are you willing to take that risk?"

Once again Soterius paused, then looked at Tris and looked back to Darrath. "I am."

"I'll go with him," volunteered Mikhail to everyone's surprise. The *vayash moru* seemed unperturbed at their reaction.

"I'd be glad for the company," Soterius replied.

"And what of the mercs?" Harrtuck demanded.

"The mercenary companies would hold the borders as a second line of defense," Darrath replied, leaning forward as he caught the spirit of Hant's proposal. "You can contain Jared between Margolan's northern border and the river, and patrol the border." He paused, looking at the map. "The magicked beasts Arontala sent to keep Tris from reaching Dhasson should cut Jared off to the east until they're dispelled."

"We don't know what is going on in Isencroft," Kiara added. "Carina's brother, Cam, would certainly have asked father to support Tris, but there's no way to know what father will be able to do."

"Perhaps there is," said Staden from the doorway, where a page had urgently beckoned for his attention. He stepped aside to reveal a tattered and dirty messenger. "This rider arrived from Isencroft not half a candlemark ago. Whatever news he carries must be important, if it was worth so hard and dangerous a ride."

Eagerly, Kiara and Carina sprang from their seats to meet the exhausted rider halfway across the room. From a pouch under his tunic, the messenger produced a sealed parchment which Kiara took with trembling hands. "Look," she said to Carina, "it's in father's handwriting."

"Read it!"

Kiara read the missive in silence, her auburn hair falling around her face, framing an expression growing by turns more serious and then relaxing, until she looked up, her dark, almond-shaped eyes shining. "The potion the Sisters sent with Cam made father able to bear up under the wasting spell," she announced excitedly. "He's taken back some of his duties. And he's sent the army to the Margolan border to aid the defeat of Jared Drayke, given the limited resources of Isencroft."

"There's more. He sends his greeting to King Staden," she said, glancing at their host, "and wishes to give his official recognition to Martris Drayke, son of Bricen, the rightful king of Margolan." She looked to Tris with amazement.

"Then we have him!" Mikhail said, rearranging the small wooden markers on the map of the Winter Kingdoms that stretched across the table.

"Mercs to the northeast, the river and Dhasson to the east, Isencroft to the west. Trevath, to the south, has reason to be wary of interference. Jared will be bottled up on all sides, while we turn his own army against him."

"Aye." Harrtuck's voice was sober. "And no small number of refugees will take up arms as well once they know what's up, I wager. More than once I've seen a well-trained army fall to a mob of farmers with a cause and a sickle."

"What you're proposing makes sense," Tris said slowly. "But what would you have me do? Wait behind the lines until Jared is defeated?" He shook his head, his green eyes worried. "That won't work."

Darrath regarded him once more in silence, and Tris thought he glimpsed the faintest flicker of approval in the hard-bitten man's eyes. "What is it you would do, Prince Drayke, if not wait?"

"I have to confront Arontala," Tris replied, meeting Darrath's unyielding gaze. "I have to return to Shekerishet and finish the matter."

"Alone?" Darrath mocked.

"Not alone. I'll go with him," Kiara replied.

"So will I," Carroway added.

"I've got an old score to settle myself," Vahanian drawled. "Count me in."

"Me too," Carina said.

"Assuming you could cross Margolan alive," Darrath said. "What then? Will you march up to the doors of the palace and demand to be let in?"

"No," Tris said, shaking his head. "I've gone over this time and again since we left the palace, and there's only one way in." He paused. "From above."

Vahanian raised an eyebrow. "You can fly?"

Tris grinned. "No. I don't need to. Shekerishet is built out of a steep cliffside. No one has been able to attack from that angle, so Jared won't expect it now."

Darrath cleared his throat. "I don't doubt your prowess as a Summoner, Prince Drayke," the older man said. "But if no one has scaled Shekerishet's cliffside walls before, how will you do it now?"

Tris exchanged knowing grins with Soterius. "Well, it would be a little more accurate to say 'no one at war with Margolan' ever climbed the cliff successfully. I once bet Ban that he couldn't do it, and he took the bet on the condition that I climb with him. He's from the highlands, and they're half mountain goat out there. We made it to the top and dropped in on the highest parapets, all before lunch. Neither Jared nor father ever knew, and we didn't say anything about it ourselves, since father frowned on that sort of thing." He chuckled. "In all its history, Margolan never was at war with the highlands."

"And you believe you can do it again?" Hant asked, leaning forward.

Tris shrugged. "It's the only way in. I'll have to."

"I've never really liked climbing," Vahanian commented. Kiara elbowed him in the ribs and glared at him. He rolled his eyes. "I guess I could learn."

"I'm up for it," Kiara said gamely.

Carina looked uncertain until Carroway spoke up. "I didn't really picture Carina and me taking the castle by storm," the minstrel said. "But if we could find some sympathetic hedge witches and my minstrel friends, I think we could make a diversion, stir up the mob, incite a riot, that sort of thing. Keep the guards distracted from the real action."

Hant nodded, deep in thought. "It might just work. Yes, it just might," he repeated.

"It's much too risky," Darrath said, shaking his head.

"Of course it is," Hant replied with contrary glee. "That's why I like it. Only a fool would try it."

"I'm not sure I like the way that sounds," Tris murmured to Kiara.

Hant looked up sharply, his keen hearing picking up Tris's comment. "That isn't what I meant." He chuckled at the audacity of the plan. "They'll never expect it. Too bold. Too risky. They'll be looking for armies on the border, and while they're busy fending off our phantoms, you'll be dropping in like so many spiders." He rubbed his hands together. "Oh yes, this does have promise."

"Easy for him to say," Vahanian said under his breath. "He's not going."

"Hush," Kiara admonished.

Darrath nodded. "I have no better plan," the general admitted. "And there is an element of surprise that I must admit I find intriguing."

"Intriguing," Vahanian commented dryly. "I'd feel better if you said 'promising' or 'brilliant.'"

Darrath ignored him. "How long until you plan to depart, Prince Drayke?"

Tris had debated that question with himself the entire evening. "We have to reach the palace before the Hawthorn Moon," he said. "That's when Arontala will try to free the spirit of the Obsidian King."

Darrath frowned. "Is such a thing possible?"

Tris nodded. "The Sisterhood believes so. I can't take the chance."

Darrath rubbed his chin. "That's half a year from now."

"Mikhail and I can start with the refugees. If we can get a few clusters of fighters in position, we can make sure Jared doesn't send more soldiers across the border. The mercs can sweep up after us. The snow is bad here, but it shouldn't be quite as much of a problem once we get a little further south into Margolan. And we're moving small groups, not a full army," Soterius said. "We'll need time to train the rest of you to climb. It will take more than two months to get from here to the palace in Margolan without taking the main roads."

"It'll also take time to raise the mercs," Harrtuck added. "They're wintering here, not looking for hire. They'll need to get provisioned."

It would also take time, Tris knew, for him to complete even a fraction of his training, to learn to channel the wild power that was only just beginning to come under his control. At the Library at Westmarch, Tris had learned that his grandmother, the great spirit mage Bava K'aa, had given him as much training as she dared, and then buried those memories deeply to protect him. With the help of the Sisterhood, Royster the head librarian and the other Keepers, Tris had accessed those memories and added what training time permitted.

Though he had been in Principality City for only one full day, word had already come from the Sisterhood, the shadowy council of high mages that Bava K'aa once led, that Tris and Carina were to journey to the Sisterhood's citadel in the city for further training. That summons, and the implication that his own training would require the services of an expert healer, weighed heavily on Tris's mind. In the short time before the Hawthorn Moon, Tris knew he must master what the Sisterhood had yet to teach him. And in that same few months, Kiara and Vahanian would need to gain the skills of climbing a sheer rock cliff, Soterius must find and contact the refugees and Margolan defectors, and he himself had yet to take his fighting skills to the level which he knew he must reach in order to hold his own. It would all take time, Tris fretted, time they did not have but could not do without.

Hant nodded. "It can be done."

Darrath nodded his assent. "Good." He placed his palms on the table as he stood. "Hant and I will provide anything you require in terms of weapons or armor. Your horses will be the finest in Principality. And you will have gold enough for your mercenaries," he nodded to Harrtuck, "sufficient to stir them from their winter sleep, I think."

"Thank you," Tris said.

Darrath's met his eyes evenly. "Make no mistake, Prince Drayke. I am not supporting this out of a love of Margolan. But what you say is true. For Principality to rest safely, we must put down the evil in Margolan, or lose everything." He paused. "I don't doubt that if Jared were to secure Margolan and invade Isencroft, he would eventually turn his eye toward the mines of Principality to replenish his treasury."

Hant nodded. "I agree. For now, Margolan's cause is our own."

"Then it's settled," Staden said from the chair where he had watched the debate for more than a candlemark, his burly arms crossed across his chest. "Until then, you and your companions are welcome in my home."

Tris inclined his head in acknowledgment. "We are in your debt."

Staden waved his hands in dissent. "Now none of that, or you'll be thanking me and I'll have to turn around and thank you again, and we'll be here all night. Now that the decision's made, who'll have a glass of port with me?"

CHAPTER TWO

TRIS PULLED HIS cloak tighter around himself as the king's carriage carried him to the citadel of the Sisterhood. Beside him, Carina looked equally cold. "I'm still wondering—what kind of training requires a healer?" Carina asked, pulling her lap robe closer and rubbing her hands together.

Tris managed a wan smile. "I've been asking myself the same thing. And I can't come up with any good answers."

Carina frowned. "Tris—how sure are you that the Sisterhood is on our side?"

Tris shrugged. "Grandmother always said the Sisterhood was on its own side," he replied. "I got as much out of Royster last night as I could—he's been the Keeper of their Library at Westmarch for almost fifty years. What he said—and he was damn cagey until I pushed him—was that since grandmother's death, there's been a split in the

29

Sisterhood that goes back to the war with the Obsidian King.

"According to Royster, there were so many of the great mages killed in that war that the ones who lived through it were either badly wounded or very frightened. The Sisterhood took very heavy losses. Grandmother was nearly killed." He sighed. "Even after grandmother recovered and became the head of the Sisterhood, Royster says that the Sisterhood split into two groups: one that thought the Mage War proved that the Sisterhood shouldn't intervene, and one that thought careful intervention was the only way to keep the peace."

"What about your grandmother?"

Tris looked out the carriage window at the cold winter dawn. "Grandmother always said that power of any kind—physical, magical, or political—was a gift from the Goddess to be used for the good of all."

"That's a hard balance to strike," Carina said, burrowed so far into her cloak and lap robe that only her face showed.

"What I could pry out of Royster makes me think that there have been some heated arguments about what to do with me," Tris said. "For now, apparently, the mages who sided with grandmother are winning, and so the Sisterhood has agreed to train me. But I'm not sure that's the same as giving us their full support. I don't think we can count on them to come to the rescue if anything goes wrong."

"But we've heard that Arontala is hunting down mages! Doesn't that make this war the Sisterhood's business?"

Tris shrugged. "Not every mage is one of the Sisterhood. They're a rather elite group. And the impression I got from Royster was that some of them think that the Sisterhood shouldn't be involved in the outside world at all. They want to study magic and let the rest of us be damned." He paused. "Although Royster didn't say as much, I wondered whether the mages who run the Sisterhood now are as powerful as the Sisters who fought the Mage War. Perhaps they're turning inward because they're not what they once were," Tris speculated. "Maybe they don't think they can go up against Arontala—let alone the Obsidian King reborn—and win, so they don't even want to try."

"But they'll send you? That's not making me feel any better about this training." Carina shivered.

Tris chuckled mirthlessly. "You're not the one being trained."

Carina's concerns only made him more nervous. Though Bava K'aa said little about the Sisterhood, what little she did say was usually about Sisters taking sides or pursuing competing agendas. Now, as the carriage headed for the citadel, Tris wondered whether, in the Sisterhood's game, he was the king or the pawn.

"You said Sister Taru sent the message?" Carina's question stirred Tris out of his brooding.

He nodded. "That's the one bright spot. After training with her at Westmarch, she's someone I trust."

"She knew your grandmother?"

"Taru was grandmother's assistant."

"I trust Taru," Carina agreed. "The others, I'm not so sure about."

* * *

THE CARRIAGE TURNED and Tris saw the citadel, a large gray walled area, almost a city within the city. The cut stone that made up its outer walls looked older than the buildings around it, which seemed to keep their distance, giving the citadel a wide span of open area despite the crowding of the rest of the city. Only a few high narrow windows broke the citadel's façade, which rose several stories above the ground. A portcullis opened to admit the carriage, and Tris felt his stomach knot at the thud of the iron gate falling shut behind them.

A robed figure waited for them in the snow as Tris helped Carina down from the carriage. "Welcome," Taru said, pulling back her hood. Taru's chin-length dark hair framed a round face, and her cloak covered an ample frame. Her broad smile was a sincere welcome. Tris felt himself relax, just a little.

Tris gave a courteous bow, and Carina embraced Taru. "Thanks for meeting us," Tris said as they headed up the broad, snow covered steps that led into the citadel. The façade of the citadel was as imposing as any palace, and the archway over the heavy, iron-bound doors was carved with intricate runes and interlocking designs.

Even before the doors opened, Tris could sense old, strong magic. Power seemed to radiate from the stones of the walls, as if they retained the imprint of the workings done within. Tris hoped to pick up the lingering sense of his grandmother's magic, the sense that her rooms at Shekerishet held like old perfume. But there was no familiar resonance, and Tris found that its absence heightened his nervousness.

A footman gathered their bags and followed behind them. "You've come prepared to stay for at least a fortnight?" Taru questioned.

Tris chuckled. "We've learned to travel light," he replied dryly. "Since I left Shekerishet with only the clothes on my back, a whole pack seems like a luxury!"

Carina shrugged. "I brought my herbs and powders—and some of the books Royster and I brought from Westmarch. Cam and I lived on the road for so long, I've learned to make do." She managed a grin. "You weren't expecting us to dress for court, I hope!"

Taru smiled. "No dear. We have robes to spare—what you wear underneath them is your business," she added with surprising mischief.

Inside the great doors, a high-ceilinged entranceway made an imposing first impression. Around the grand entrance room, eight larger than life size marble figures of the Goddess—four light and four dark—encircled the room on pedestals. Tris looked to the statues of the Mother and Childe, Margolan's patron Aspects, but in the kindly gaze of the Mother and the mystical eyes of the Childe, he found no assurance. It was Istra, the Dark Lady, who drew his attention. Istra, patroness of the *vayash moru* and the outcast, the champion of lost souls. Tris could not shake the feeling that the eyes of Istra's statue seemed to follow him.

Carina seemed preoccupied as they headed deeper into the massive building. Tris looked around. Tapestries covered the walls from floor to ceiling, and Tris could tell at a glance that they were even older and more finely woven than any he had seen in Staden's palace or in his own home at Shekerishet. Everywhere he looked—at the furnishings, the finely wrought candelabra and torch sconces, at the scrying basins and leather-bound books—Tris saw evidence of wealth and power that would impress any king in the Winter Kingdoms.

For a group that isn't supposed to be involved in mortal affairs, the Sisterhood has done well for itself, Tris thought.

"This citadel was built over five hundred years ago," Taru said as they headed deeper into the building. "It's older than Staden's palace. We can comfortably house over two hundred Sisters, although only about fifty live here at most times. Many come and go, staying for a few months and then moving on to one of our other holdings."

They climbed a broad, curving staircase that cantilevered from the walls, seeming to rise of its own accord. Down through its center hung a massive candelabrum easily as large as the carriage that brought them to the citadel, and Tris wondered if its dozens of candles could be lit by means other than magic. The stairs narrowed as they reached the upper floors, and Taru led them down a long corridor. Tris felt engulfed by the remnant of old power, as if the lingering tingle of magic would smother him. Even Mageslayer seemed to respond to the magic that surrounded him; the ensorcelled blade drew his attention as if awakened.

Taru stopped in front of two doors that opened off the right side of the corridor. "I've put you in adjoining rooms—I hope you don't mind," she said. "There's a sitting room in between. I thought it would give you some privacy—and make it easier if Carina needs to check in on you."

Tris frowned. "You seem to be taking it for granted that I'll need serious healing. What kind of training—exactly—do you have in mind for me?"

Taru motioned them inside, and gestured to the footman to leave the bags in the sitting room. A fire already blazed in the large stone hearth, and the sitting room, while less lavish than the entranceway, was still the equal to the guest rooms in any palace. A pot for tea and another small cauldron of water simmered in the coals, and several chairs plus a small couch offered ample seating. There was a broad study table with a four-candle candelabrum, and one wall was covered with shelves of books. One glance gave Tris to guess that they were healing tomes, and his uneasiness increased again.

Taru closed the door behind them with a quick glance in either direction down the hallway to assure they were alone. Carina moved to warm herself by the fire, and Tris stretched their cloaks over two chairs near the fire to dry. "There's only one kind of training that can build the skills you'll require in the short time available," said Taru, and Tris could hear concern in her voice. "Simulated battle—both physical and magical."

Carina gasped. "Against whom—the entire Sisterhood?"

Taru met Tris's eyes. "Yes. You'll be led through a series of tests. Some will be quests past the traps in the labyrinth beneath the citadel. They'll test your cunning and your ability to use your magic with precision. Others," she said, "will test your battle skills and your magic for defense and for attack." Taru watched him, gauging his reaction. "In some tests, you'll face a Sister—or two—in person. In other tests, you'll face avatars—golems animated by magic—controlled by Sisters."

Tris looked at Taru. "There's something you're not saying. Something important."

Taru nodded. "When you fight the avatars, they will have the face and form of others. Jared, perhaps. Arontala. And you may find allies—like Vahanian, or Kiara." She paused again. "The magic and the weapons will be real. In the most extreme simulations, wardings will be set that cannot be broken except by completing the task. In the case of a confrontation with Jared's avatar, for example—"

"It's not over until one of us is dead," Tris finished tightly.

Taru nodded.

"Taru, you can't be serious!" Carina protested. She moved away from the fire to join them.

Taru met Carina's gaze. "If he can't stand up to the Sisterhood, what chance has he against Arontala—or the Obsidian King?"

"And so you thought to do Arontala's work for him?" Carina demanded.

Taru looked down, and began to pace again. "There's been a great deal of debate—heated debate—about whether the Sisterhood should involve itself at all in your training," she said with a glance at Tris. "I suspect the decision to bring you here was made more out of fear that some of us would do it, regardless."

"From the Sisterhood's perspective—and I'm not saying it's my view—the only thing that matters is keeping the Obsidian King from rising again, or at least, containing the damage if he does." She looked to Tris and Carina. "The Sisterhood is not concerned with the kingship of Margolan, or with undoing Jared's damage—or with healing King Donelan by destroying Arontala." Taru shook her head. "The Sisterhood tends to take a historic view of such things which can be damnably impersonal."

"What could be worse than the Obsidian King rising and taking over Arontala's body?" Carina burst out. Even before Taru spoke, Tris knew what she would say, and that knowledge chilled him to the bone.

"It would be worse if he arose in the body of a great Summoner," Taru said quietly. "The Sisterhood agreed to train you because they need to assure themselves that you will not fail. Above all, they don't wish to face the Obsidian King again as he once was, with a Summoner's power."

"Then grandmother was correct—Lemuel was possessed?" Tris said. Taru nodded. "So if I'm not strong enough to succeed, they want me to fail here, even if it kills me?"

"Yes."

"I see."

"You don't know how much they fear the Obsidian King," said Taru. "You passed one small test when Alyzza found you in the caravan—"

"Alyzza was a Sister?" Carina exclaimed, remembering the disheveled old woman who had traveled with their caravan in Margolan.

Taru smiled. "Did you really believe she was a hedge witch? Many years ago, Alyzza was a great sorceress. When Bava K'aa was taken prisoner by the Obsidian King, Alyzza and King Argus used their magic to enable Lord Grayson to rescue Bava K'aa from the Obsidian King's stronghold."

She shook her head. "The effort killed King Argus, and badly injured Alyzza. Her mind was never the same afterwards. Bava K'aa barely survived. Elam was Bava K'aa's healer, and Elam wouldn't let anyone else near your grandmother, even though it took a long time to heal her. Elam performed the marriage between Grayson and Bava K'aa when your grandmother was barely recovered from her injuries. And Elam delivered Bava K'aa's child—your mother, Serae," Taru said with a glance toward Tris.

Outside, the bells tolled eight times. Taru looked at Tris and Carina apologetically. "I know you've barely had a chance to get warm and put down your things, but we're due in the council chambers," Taru said. "You'll be formally introduced, and Sister Elam will present your first trainers. Your challenges begin today."

Carina took a half step forward. "Who will be in the council chamber?" Tris had the sense, as he had often felt at Westmarch, that Carina and Taru's acquaintance stemmed from somewhere before this present quest.

Taru gave a half-smile that did not reach her eyes. "Some friends—and others I'm not sure about." She paused. "Sister Elam was the same age as Tris's grandmother. She took over the leadership of the Sisterhood after Bava K'aa's death."

"Sister Landis will be Elam's successor," Taru said neutrally, but Tris saw a shadow of distaste color Carina's face. "She was one of the younger mages at the time of the Mage War, and she often clashed with Bava K'aa over the role of the Sisterhood. Landis' assistant, Alaine, may have recently given her reason to reconsider. Alaine was staying with another of our citadels when it was overrun by Jared's troops. She barely escaped."

Taru drew a deep breath. "And then there's Theron."

Carina muttered something that Tris did not catch.

"Theron will be one of your trainers," Taru said. "She comes from Eastmark, and so her style may be similar to what you've learned from Kiara and Jonmarc." Taru frowned. "You may find that compared to Theron, Jonmarc's training style is merciful."

Merciful, Tris thought wryly. *An odd word to use. Considering the pounding I've taken in the salle from Jonmarc, that doesn't bode well.*

Tris drew a deep breath, fighting his fear. *Sweet Chenne, what have I gotten myself into?* He knew that his real enemy was time. It was less than a fortnight before the Crone Moon, the last month of the year. The Hawthorn Moon at mid-year was just seven months away. There was very little time to prepare.

Tris knew what his failure would mean. Kiara delivered into Jared's control, a thought that made his blood run cold. Jonmarc and the others hanged for treason. No relief for Margolan, and no justice for the wretched souls under Jared's yoke. War, as Jared and Arontala sought to expand their boundaries among the Winter Kingdoms. If he could prevent that future, Tris was willing to risk the confrontation—even if it cost him his life. But Taru

raised the thought that death was not the worst out-
come, and the possibility that he might be
possessed, his power used against his will, hardened
Tris's resolve. He felt a coldness wash over him that
had nothing to do with the chill in the corridor.
Taru was right—there was no alternative.

The citadel smelled of candle wax and herbs, with
the musty scent of long-unused rooms. Taru
stopped in front of two iron-bound double doors.
The sound of raised voices carried through the
heavy doors. While the words were not clear, the
passion of the women's voices was evident. One
voice, higher in pitch, sounded angry. The other
voice, low-pitched and measured, seemed resolute.
Taru grimaced and rapped loudly at the door. The
voices stopped abruptly, and Taru gestured for the
doors too open.

Creaking heavily on their hinges, the doors slowly swung backward. Inside, the council chamber
was hung with heavy tapestries, lit by a bank of
torches and two fireplaces which were each the
length and height of a tall man. Above the long
table of dark wood hung two multi-tiered candelabra, each holding dozens of candles. Even that
light did not seem to completely dispel the shadows.
Despite the roaring fires, Tris shivered as he stepped
into the room.

Four robed Sisters were seated at the table. At the
center, facing Tris, was an old woman, cadaver-thin
and very wrinkled. He guessed that she was Elam.
At her right was an empty seat, and Tris assumed it
was for Taru. To the thin woman's left was another
Sister in her middle years with a determined expression. *Landis?* He wondered. With gray short hair

and a serious expression, she looked as if an inner dialogue continued the discussion they had overheard from the hallway.

At Landis's left was a younger woman who watched Tris intently. With dark blonde hair pulled back into a plain braid, she looked haggard. Tris guessed this was Alaine, Landis's assistant. To the right of the empty seat was another young mage, a woman perhaps ten years Tris's senior, whose lean form and strong arms seemed more fitting for a fighter than a sorceress. Her dark hair was cut short so that it stood up, brush-like, on her head. She seemed to be sizing Tris up like a sergeant-at-arms appraising a new recruit. He had no doubt that she was Theron. The Sisters did not seem to be concerned with Carina. She stepped behind him, as if relieved to be overlooked.

"Worthy Sisters," Taru said when they stood before the table. "I bring to you Martris Drayke of Margolan, and with him, Carina Jesthrata."

"Welcome," said a figure at the center of the table. "I am Sister Elam," the old woman said. Her voice was strong, at odds with how she looked, and Tris knew better than to judge a sorceress by her appearance.

"Do you accept our offer of training?" Elam asked.

Tris steeled himself. "I accept."

Elam smiled mirthlessly, showing yellowed teeth. "As you may know, the Sisterhood does not lightly involve itself in the affairs of kings."

At least, not openly, Tris thought.

From the stony expressions and stiff postures of some at the table, Tris surmised that Elam had greatly understated the amount of discussion that preceded the Sisterhood's offer of training. He guessed that, at least for some at the table, the argument was not yet over.

"Taru told me of your training at Westmarch. When you won Mageslayer from the ghost of King Argus, you passed one test." A "test" Tris had barely survived.

"If you are to be ready to face Arontala—and possibly, the Obsidian King himself—by the Hawthorn Moon, there is little time," Elam said. "We don't train from books. You'll face a series of trials, not unlike what you encountered with King Argus. Real magic, sent against you with the full strength of our mages. Traps and obstacles that will push your body to its limits. We'll see just what you're willing to pay to win back the crown."

"If I die here at the citadel, it seems rather pointless," Tris countered.

Elam's smile chilled him in its ruthlessness. "It would be worse for all of us should you confront the Obsidian King and fail. Pain is often the most powerful teacher of all. Your training begins today."

AFTER THE MIDDAY bells, Tris was taken to a salle deep in the lower levels of the citadel. Despite Carina's protests, Taru took the healer in a different direction, promising that Carina would be close at hand if needed. Carina gave Tris a wad of rope vine to hold in his cheek, a way to lessen the effect of the wormroot poison that could push his magic out of reach. Tris was dressed to skirmish, with a studded leather cuirass and Mageslayer in the scabbard at his belt.

Theron was waiting for Tris in the windowless salle. She was nearly his own height. No longer dressed in her council robes, Theron wore the studded leather armor of a fighter. She carried herself like a seasoned soldier.

"I wish to see you fight."

"Very well," Tris's hand fell to Mageslayer's pommel.

Theron launched herself at him, moving so quickly that Tris barely had time to draw his sword. Their blades clashed; Theron's strength was easily equal that of any man Tris had fought. Parrying took all of his concentration as they traded blows that could cleave a man shoulder to hip.

Theron swung into an Eastmark kick, and seemed surprised when Tris blocked her, although the force of her kick almost knocked him off balance. Sweating hard, gripping Mageslayer two-handed, Tris saw the ensorcelled blade flare a brilliant green as Theron's lips moved in the words of a spell. A streak of fire blazed from her left hand. The blade's warning was all the time Tris had to summon his shielding, while deflecting another sword stroke that nearly tore the sword from his grip. Theron's fire bounced away, only to be replaced by darkness so complete that only Mageslayer's glow enabled Tris to see Theron's attack.

He thought he saw a glint of approval in Theron's eyes as he cast away the darkness, and before it cleared he swung into an Eastmark kick of his own, almost knocking her sword from her hand. As Theron's lips moved once more, Tris felt blinding pain sear through his body. For an instant, he thought Theron had run him through.

He staggered, and Theron scored a gash on his forearm. Reeling, Tris held on to Mageslayer, gasping as he struggled to counter her magical assault. As he focused his power to dull the pain, the gash on his forearm began to burn. *Wormroot!* Tris thought, managing to deflect the worst of another thrust from Theron's sword. This time, she scored his thigh, a deep cut that burned with the poison on her blade.

Tris nearly fell, swinging his blade wildly to keep Theron at bay as he drew on Mageslayer's power to neutralize the effect of the poison. Even with the rope vine, the wormroot was beginning to take effect. Another wave of pain swept over him, as if he were being burned from the inside with hot coals, and his eyes stung. But he kept his grip on the sword, battling Theron's press.

The tip of Theron's blade opened a deep cut on Tris's shoulder and he fought to retain control of his magic. His heart hammered and his palms sweat as he countered her blows, slowly losing control of his magic. Theron murmured another spell, and this time the pain seemed to be crushing his skull. Tris cried out, resisting the urge to drop his weapon and clasp his head in both hands.

Focusing all of his remaining power on Mageslayer, Tris saw in his mind an image of blue fire streaking from the sword's tip, engulfing Theron and ending the pain. A heartbeat later Mageslayer blazed with light, fire streaking from its tip. He heard Theron gasp, her shields barely snapping up in time to deflect the attack.

Tris stumbled. The wormroot was making it difficult for him to stay on his feet. With a predator's smile, Theron whispered another spell. Mageslayer was torn from his hand by an irresistible force. With the blade's magical protections gone Tris fell, unable to counteract the wormroot. As the wormroot pushed the magic beyond his reach, Tris felt his power fail him. Another wave of excruciating pain swept over him, and he nearly blacked out. Theron kicked Mageslayer beyond his grasp.

"Is that the best you can do?" she taunted, standing over him. "Without your magic, you're just a man, and a mage can break a man with a thought." She whispered and the pain came again, worse this time. Tris's screams echoed in the stone vault. The wormroot burned in his veins, and his magic was far out of reach.

Theron raised her sword over his neck like an executioner, and Tris rolled, scything his legs and bringing Theron down with him. She hit the ground hard and gasped. Tris dove for Mageslayer, barely able to keep his concentration against the pain. But as he struggled to his feet, his wounded leg folded under him. Theron rolled to her feet and swung her sword at his neck. For an instant, time seemed to stand still. Tris knew that her blade, if it connected, would kill. It stopped just short of its mark as he collapsed to the floor.

"That's nothing compared to what Arontala can inflict," she hissed, laying the blade across his neck for emphasis. "And with the power of the Obsidian King, he can torment you past the point of death, past madness, and strip your soul to shreds."

She might have said more, but the pain and the wormroot overwhelmed Tris, and darkness took him.

* * *

TRIS AWOKE IN a darkened room, utterly spent. He could still feel the wormroot in his blood, and knew that his power was out of reach. The void it left was unsettling to the point of discomfort. He remembered Carina telling him that a mage could be killed or driven mad by constant dosing with wormroot. He did not doubt it.

Tris shifted, and revised his assessment. While the torment of Theron's spell was gone, his body ached of its own accord. Where Theron cut him the deep gashes were expertly bandaged, but even Carina's healing had not completely removed their pain. He wanted to retch, and gauging from the taste in his mouth and how sore his stomach muscles felt, he ruefully gathered that he had probably already brought up anything he could, and more.

He sank back against the bed, angry at himself for his failure. *I'm sure by now they've reconsidered training me,* he thought. *I'll be lucky if they don't just decide to kill me before Arontala does.*

He heard a rap at the outer door to the sitting room, and the rustle of someone moving to answer.

"You can't go in there," Carina protested. "He's not ready."

From the sound of the approaching footsteps, their visitor was undeterred. Tris forced himself to open his eyes and turn his throbbing head. Theron was approaching in the dim light. She wore her council robes, and her expression was of sincere concern.

"How long did it take for him to come around?" Theron asked Carina, who was clearly unhappy with the intrusion.

"Three candlemarks," Carina clipped. "Most of the time, I was busy keeping him from choking on his own vomit. Just how much of this 'training' do you think he can take?"

Theron looked closely at Tris. "Just three candlemarks?" she asked. "And he's only been hit with wormroot once before?"

Tris thought Carina might explode with the anger that seethed in her voice. "Three candlemarks is an eternity," she said between gritted teeth. "And compared to how much wormroot you managed to get into his system, what he had before was hardly anything."

Theron nodded. "Exactly. He's adapting. Learning to work around it. The last time—how did he react?"

"We'd just been attacked by soldiers. He barely stayed on his horse, and he collapsed when we got to the cell."

"Um hum." Theron moved to take Tris's pulse and look into his eyes.

"I'm awake and alive," Tris managed through parched lips. "You can speak like I'm here."

"You kept fighting, after three doses of poison," Theron remarked. "Your Eastmark kick needs some work, but given your condition, it wasn't bad. Not bad at all. We've got to work on your control. You didn't effectively counter the pain spell."

"I know."

"And your magic got wobbly after you lost Mageslayer."

"Wobbly?" Tris echoed hoarsely. "It was out of reach."

"Not immediately. For an untrained mage, you hung on to it—at least a little bit—for quite a while." Theron managed a smile. "I'm glad you weren't at full strength when you sent that blast my way, or we might have needed a new trainer."

"I can teach you to counter that pain spell—and some other nasties that you might encounter." She chuckled mirthlessly. "You may not choose to use them on someone else, but it can be damn handy knowing how to deflect them. And we've got to build up your tolerance for wormroot."

"Build up a tolerance!" Carina exclaimed angrily.

"We know Arontala uses it on other mages. As a *vayash moru*, it has no effect on Arontala himself. It's likely he and Jared will take some kind of precautions, and wormroot could be part of them." She gave Tris a crooked grin. "It's going to get worse before it gets better."

Tris swallowed hard and nodded. "I thought you might say that," he said, surprised at how spent his own voice sounded.

Theron spared a glance at his bandages. "Looks like Carina's got you patched up."

"Even with deep healing, he's not going to be good as new overnight," Carina replied tersely.

Theron met her eyes. "Whatever he's got will have to do," she said matter-of-factly. "We don't have time to wait." She looked down at Tris. "See you at the salle tomorrow morning. We'll work on that kick." Without another word, Theron turned away. Carina followed her to the door and might have said something more to Tris, but as the healer closed the door behind Theron, Tris felt the world waver around him. He closed his eyes as consciousness once again slipped out of his grasp.

CHAPTER THREE

"You held your own today." Sister Theron offered Tris a hand up from where he lay on his back in the salle floor. He smiled ruefully and accepted her offer.

"If you mean that I managed to stay on my feet longer and I didn't lose my breakfast right away, then thank you." He steadied himself, fresh from a dosing of wormroot and a bad gash on his shoulder. Warm blood trickled down his arm underneath his sleeve, and the leather cuirass he wore seemed to weigh him down as he fought the poison in his system. His right leg throbbed from a bad wrenching after Theron pushed him to practice his Eastmark kick. In all, Tris could not recall ever feeling worse.

Theron seemed to guess his thoughts. "Your kick is getting cleaner," she said. "For a prince, you've picked up some interesting street fighting techniques."

Tris managed a chuckle. "Thank Vahanian." He tried to take a step and staggered. Theron caught him, getting under his left arm for support and draping it across her shoulders as he limped toward the door.

"I know you won't believe me, but you're learning to handle the wormroot," she said. Nothing about Theron was coddling. Tris knew that any praise he wrested from the skilled fighter was hard won.

"It's hard to remember that when I'm puking my guts out." Tris was leaning far more heavily on Theron than he wanted to admit.

"I don't think you understand," she said as they made their way toward the salle door. "A mage of middling power would be unconscious from the dosing you've had. Many strong mages take longer to recover their power after they've been poisoned. In between dosings, your power came back at full strength. And you've hung on to more control for longer each time."

"I still feel like shit," Tris muttered as they began the painful climb to the top of the spiral stairs.

When they reached the upper floors, a brown-robed sister ran past them, sobbing. A knot of robed mages huddled in conversation along one wall, and a small crowd had gathered around the doorway to one of the bedrooms. Tris and Theron exchanged worried glances.

"Go ahead," he said, leaning against the wall as she removed his support. "I'll get there. Looks like something big is going on."

Theron nodded and made her way through the crowd. Tris limped behind her through the cluster of Sisters, some of whom were weeping. At the doorway he saw that Carina and Taru were both already in the room, which was a bedchamber. With a shock he recognized Elam slumped at a table near the fire.

Carina ran to him. He waved off her assistance, finding that he could stand if he leaned against the wall. "What happened?" he asked, trying to take in the scene through a throbbing reaction headache.

"Elam's dead." There was a catch in Carina's voice. "Her heart—" She shook her head. "She was almost seventy years old." Carina moved past him to close the door, bolting the door to assure their privacy.

Landis was already in the room. Alaine was cleaning up Elam's spilled tea. Landis and Taru were deep in conversation. From their expressions, Tris could see that the two Sisters were not in complete agreement.

Something familiar tugged at the frayed edges of his power and Tris closed his eyes, struggling to control his magic through the fatigue and the poison. Carina laid a hand on his arm, but he shook his head, focusing all his will on the spirit that was trying to reach him through his fogged mage sense.

He opened his eyes. "It's Elam," he said, and the others in the room turned to look at him. "She's quite insistent—but the wormroot is making this difficult..." He closed his eyes again, willing his power past the poison in his veins. What should have been a simple working took all of his concentration, but he brought the spirit closer, and then, with effort, made the revenant visible to the others.

Carina gasped. Elam's ghost stood before them.

"I was murdered," the spirit said in a voice audible to all. "We have a traitor within the Sisterhood."

Taru stepped forward. "Elam—who did this?"

"I don't know. Something I picked up had a triggering spell. It stopped my heart. Every mage in this citadel has the power for such a spell. And many had the access to place the trigger." Elam looked at Tris. "Someone does not wish you to succeed in your training."

The image of the spirit wavered as Tris felt the wormroot unravel his control. Theron pushed a chair under him as he began to fall. Tris's power slipped beyond his grasp, and the visible image of Elam's ghost disappeared. In his mage sight, Tris could see Elam standing at a distance, her expression serious.

"Beware the avatars," she warned in a voice that only he could hear. "Whoever killed me will come for you next." Her spirit faded completely as the wormroot pushed even mage sight beyond his control.

Tris opened his eyes and took a deep breath, willing himself not to pass out. Landis crossed the room and stood before him, her arms folded. Carina took a half step forward protectively, putting herself between Landis and Tris. Landis, easily ten years Elam's junior, looked haggard, and her eyes were tired.

"Elam and I often disagreed," Landis said quietly, "but I respected her. This is a great loss."

Alaine stood quietly near the fireplace, awaiting Landis's instruction. Taru walked back to where Tris sat and looked at Landis.

"What now?" Tris knew that it was his training, and not the future of the Sisterhood, which was uppermost in Taru's mind.

Landis drew a deep breath. "We will complete what Elam began." Her sharp gaze fixed on Tris. "Before you came to us, I found the stories difficult to believe—that a mage so young and untrained could survive the spirits of the Ruune Videya, let alone dispel them. Elam was correct in sensing the promise—and the danger—in that power."

"How can he train here?" Carina gasped. "He's not safe."

"I wasn't exactly 'safe' here before." Tris let his head rest against the wall; the room swam dangerously if he tried to sit upright. "Continue my training and you'll find your traitor."

"You offer yourself as bait?" Landis asked with a raised brow.

"I have no choice. There isn't time to delay the training. Elam believed that whoever killed her did it to stop me. So train me. The killer will have to strike."

"It's too dangerous," Carina protested. "Bringing down Jared and Arontala are more important—and if you don't survive your training, there's no one else to do it."

"Elam was right," Tris said quietly. "If I can't hold my own here, I won't defeat Arontala, either. And if I can't do that—the Winter Kingdoms are better off with me dead."

Landis looked at Tris in silence for a moment, and he thought he saw approval in her hard gaze. "All right. Say nothing of this to anyone else. If the killer doesn't know we've heard from Elam, she may be overconfident. Let Taru and Carina help you back to your rooms before you need a stretcher. I will see to making Elam's arrangements."

BACK IN THEIR suite of rooms, Tris waved off further assistance, refusing to go to bed.

"I've been flat on my back for half of the last week," he grumbled. "I'm tired of passing out and I'm tired of retching and I'm tired of feeling like shit."

Carina went to the hearth for a pot of hot water, from which she poured both of them each a cup of healing tea. She rummaged through her bag, cajoling Tris to sit forward so that she could bind up the gash on his arm. She was unusually quiet, and Tris knew she was upset.

"You haven't been yourself since we arrived at the Sisterhood," Tris said quietly.

"It's not important."

"It's important to me."

Carina was silent.

"There's something bothering you," Tris ventured, "and I don't think it has to do with my training."

Carina let out a deep breath and nodded. "Do you remember when we were captured as we entered Principality City?" Although it had been little more than a week ago, so much had happened that it seemed like forever.

"Of course."

Carina looked down at her hands. "The general who took us prisoner was the older brother of a man I was engaged to marry, almost seven years ago. Ric and Gregor were mercenaries, running one of the most successful merc companies in Principality." She bit her lip.

"I was sixteen when Cam and I hired in. The next year, Ric and I fell in love." Carina spoke just above a whisper, and her eyes filled with tears. "Before we could marry, Ric was injured in battle—run through, like Jonmarc was back with the slavers. I didn't have anyone to help me with the healing, and I went too deep, hung on too long. When he died, I couldn't pull back." A tear streaked down her cheek.

"Cam told me later what happened. When he found me, he couldn't get me to wake up. He panicked. He took me to the Sisterhood—here in Principality City—because he didn't know what else to do. They told him to leave me here, that they would find him if I recovered.

"Cam knew we were distantly related to King Donelan. He was so panicked that he rode to Isencroft. Kiara says he practically burst in on the throne room. Donelan took him in, and in a year, the Sisterhood sent for him." Her eyes were dark with old memories. "They brought me back from the arms of the Lady. I don't remember much about what happened, only that Ric was gone." She bowed her head, and Tris reached out to take her hand.

"I never wanted to come back to Principality City," Carina murmured. "I know that what we're doing is more important, but by the Dark Lady! I never wanted to remember those days. It's been on my mind since we crossed the border. In another two months, it will be seven years since Ric died. Being back here just makes it all much harder to forget."

"I'm sorry," Tris said. He had wondered about Cam's skill with weapons and Carina's knowledge of mercs. Now it all made sense. It also explained Carina's skittishness around Vahanian, Tris thought, and why she fought the attraction that was so apparent to everyone else.

Carina wiped away her tears with the back of her hand. "It doesn't matter. We have a job to do," she said, swallowing hard. "And you're the one in real danger."

She dug into her bag again, pulling out a small velvet pouch. "I almost forgot." She handed the pouch to Tris, and managed a smile. "Carroway let slip to Kiara that it would be your birthday on the first of the Crone Moon. Kiara wanted me to give that to you."

Tris shook the bag over his palm. A silver pendant on a chain poured like liquid moonlight into his hand. Two stones, one fiery red and the other a shiny black, were set into the symbol of the Lady.

"Berry sent them with a servant yesterday," Carina said as Tris turned the piece in the light. "The note said it was Isencroft silver. The stones are onyx to speed healing and purge poisons, and garnet for safe journey—and love." She pulled out a sealed envelope and passed it to Tris. "That's from Kiara, too," she said with a grin. "I'll let you read it in private."

Tris closed his hand around the talisman. "I never thought I'd be in exile for my twentieth birthday," he said quietly. "Mother wanted me to joust this year at the Winterstide tournaments. Kait was going to fly her falcons. Now everything's turned upside down. And if I don't make it through the

Sisterhood's trials at the end of this week, I won't see Winterstide this year."

"Don't say that. You've got three days to recover. No more training until then—and no wormroot. You'll be back at full power—like you were in the Ruune Videya, only stronger."

"I don't know if it's enough."

Carina laid a hand on his forearm. "You can do this, Tris."

He opened his hand to look at the pendant. "I've got one more reason to make it back, don't I?"

"Kiara's counting on you," Carina replied. "We all are."

ALL TRIS'S PREPARATION could not dispel his nervousness three days later as he and Theron made their way into the lowest levels beneath the citadel. The last traces of wormroot were gone, and a few days' rest had done much to restore his strength. His hand fell to the pommel of his sword. Mageslayer tingled at the edge of his senses, not quite sentient, but no mere steel, imbued with a power of its own. Neither he nor Theron spoke as they descended the steps to the maze of rooms where the trial battle would take place.

If he survived this encounter, Tris's battles would be fought alone against the avatars. Now Theron came with him, and he was grateful for her support. They would face one or more avatars whose motions—and magic—would be controlled by other Sisters outside of the encounter room. Taru promised Tris that this battle was not warded to the death as future trials would be. Those battles would come after Winterstide—if he survived.

They entered the chamber, and Tris stifled a gasp. The chamber's appearance had been magically altered to resemble the great room at his home in the palace Shekerishet, its details exact in every way. The tapestries along the walls, the carving in the mantle of the huge stone fireplace and the inlay in the furniture around the edges of the room were perfect. Tris wondered who among the Sisters was so well acquainted with Shekerishet, and he fought down his emotions at being back in the familiar surroundings of home.

The door closed behind him, and Tris and Theron moved forward slowly.

"Guards!" Theron shouted. Tris turned to see soldiers streaming in from two side doors. Six soldiers, coming at a dead run. Tris drew his sword, knowing that Theron was at his back. Tris parried the first soldier's strike, wheeling to deflect a second guard. He heard the clash of steel behind him as Theron engaged her attackers. Tris landed a solid Eastmark kick that sent the third soldier sprawling. He assumed that the soldiers' blades would be tainted with wormroot.

Tris barely deflected the second soldier's press, but his blade caught the first soldier unprepared, and cut him down. The third soldier scrambled to his feet and ran at Tris as the second soldier moved forward. Tris held them off, swinging Mageslayer with a two-handed grip as the soldiers' blows jarred him hard enough that his teeth ached. A moment's inattention was all he needed to get inside the third soldier's guard, and sink his blade deep into the soldier's side.

"Behind you!"

Tris wheeled, his blade sliding down his attacker's sword until they stood nearly guard to guard. Tris heaved the man clear of his sword and palmed the dagger from his belt in his other hand, circling warily.

Theron dispatched two of her attackers, but her third assailant dove toward her relentlessly. Tris took the offensive, surprising his attacker with a loud cry and a head-on run, their blades clashing so hard that it nearly tore the sword from the soldier's grasp. Tris dropped to a crouch, brandishing both knife and sword as Vahanian had taught him. The soldier, taken off guard by Tris's boldness, gave Tris the opening he needed. He struck first with Mageslayer, using the blade to push back the soldier's sword. Then he let his momentum carry him forward, sinking the dagger into the soldier's chest. The soldier groaned and sank to his knees, a look of surprise on his face as he fell.

Tris cried out as a dagger buried itself deep in his left arm. He wheeled, blade raised, as the soldier he had fought slumped to the ground, dead, his objective accomplished. Already, Tris could feel the wormroot tingle as warm blood spilled down his arm. From the initial jolt, he knew the dose was sizeable. He chewed harder on the rope vine wad in his mouth, hoping that the anise-flavored juice would buy him a few precious moments of control.

Winded, Theron joined him. The six "soldiers" lay still on the floor. Tris knew that they were golems animated by magic, but the detail, down to the blood that flowed from their death wounds, made the simulation deathly real.

"Welcome home," a voice said from the shadows of the far corner. A chill went down Tris's spine.

The voice was a flawless imitation of Arontala's. A thin red-robed figure stepped forward, and Tris felt his mage sense tingle a warning.

Something was very wrong, Tris thought as the figure approached. A crystal pendant around the mage's throat burned a bright red, and the fire captured within that small orb seemed to seek Tris, glowing more brightly as it fixed on him. He knew the imprint of the power that radiated from the figure just as surely as he knew the danger of the fire's red glow.

"Theron—shield!" Tris cried out in warning, snapping his own shields up in defense. A blast of red fire streamed from the robed figure's hands, sizzling against Tris's shields and catching Theron unprotected. Before Tris could move in defense, the fire hit Theron squarely in the chest, slamming her back into the wall. Tris heard Theron cry out in pain, smelled the stench of burning flesh, and saw Theron slump to the floor, dead.

Behind him, Tris felt a sudden, wrenching shift in the wardings that protected the training room, and he knew with a sick feeling that a death warding had been set. Tris turned to face an avatar that had suddenly become dangerously real.

"SOMETHING'S WRONG." TARU'S head snapped up abruptly from where she and Carina waited in a parlor near the encounter room.

Carina looked worried as Taru sprinted for the door, and ran to catch up. "What do you mean—wrong?"

"I mean the magic is wrong," said Taru.

"But you said Landis was running the trial—that you trusted Landis," Carina countered, needing to run faster to catch up with Taru.

"I do trust Landis. But it's not Landis's power—not any more."

Taru and Carina burst into the room where the training simulation was controlled. Landis lay in a pool of blood with a dagger in her back.

Carina gasped and dropped to her knees beside the mage. "She's been dosed with almost enough wormroot to kill," Carina diagnosed, "and she's lost a lot of blood. She's barely breathing."

"Can you help her?"

Carina was already digging in her pouch for powdered rope vine. She grabbed a pitcher and a glass from the table nearby, then dissolved the powder in a glassful of water. Taru held Landis upright while Carina carefully dripped the liquid into Landis's mouth so that she would not gag. Carina bandaged the wound to stop the bleeding as Taru carefully set Landis back down on the floor.

"It's all I can do. The knife didn't hit anything vital—thank the Lady. There's no real cure but time for either the wormroot or the blood loss." Carina wiped Landis's blood off her hands and onto her robes. "We can't leave her alone."

"I'll get help," Taru replied, disappearing for a few minutes and returning with one of the other sisters, a plain-faced woman Carina knew was one of the citadel healers. They moved Landis to a couch near the fire, and Carina gave terse instructions to the healer. Once Landis was safely settled, Carina looked back at Taru.

"If Landis isn't running the trial—who is?"

They headed out at a dead run for the encounter room, but at the doors, Taru stopped abruptly. She raised her hands, palms out, and slid them above the doors, a hands' breadth away from the wood, and then swore.

"What's wrong?" Carina asked.

"The wardings are wrong," Taru replied. "Landis promised me she wasn't going to set death wardings. Not yet. But that's what's in place—and they weren't set by Landis." She paused. "This warding is tainted with blood magic."

"Arontala," Carina breathed. "Could he be here—within the citadel?"

Taru shook her head. "Unlikely. The citadel is warded against magical intrusion—we can't just 'pop' in and out, even if such a thing were easily possible." She closed her eyes, stretching out one hand toward the encounter room doors. "There is no avatar. And only two mages are alive inside."

"Theron's the traitor?" Carina asked. Taru began to stride down the corridor.

"Unlikely. Although she had the skill to set the spell that killed Elam, she didn't have an opportunity. She was with me, and went directly to train with Tris—remember? And she was with Tris again just now, when Landis was attacked. Landis couldn't have been stabbed long before we arrived, or she would have been dead." Taru slammed open the doors to a small library, lighting the torches around the room with a word. She strode over to a large crystal basin filled with water that sat on a bronze pedestal.

Carina caught up to Taru, breathless, as the Sister raised her hands over the scrying basin and held them, palms toward the water. Gradually, a mist appeared within the basin. As the mist cleared, an image emerged, as if from a distance, shrouded in fog. Carina gasped. "It's Alaine."

"It is Alaine's body—but not Alaine's power," Taru said. "We've made a grave mistake."

"What do you mean?" Carina asked, unable to take her eyes off the image unfolding within the scrying basin.

"Alaine was hand-picked by Landis, and her loyalty was absolute," Taru said quietly. "But a few months ago, Landis sent Alaine to one of the other citadels within Margolan, before we understood the extent of Jared's treachery. While Alaine was at that citadel, Jared's troops attacked. She was the only survivor." Taru sighed. "We were relieved that she came back to us—now I see it was a trap. Arontala must have broken her and embedded his own triggers, hoping that she might encounter Tris. Maybe he has spies in each of our citadels, on the chance that you'd seek sanctuary."

"What's that around Alaine's throat?" Carina asked as the image wavered in the scrying bowl.

"That must be the portal for Arontala's power," Taru said. "It's not something easily made."

Carina cried out as fire streamed from the red gem, blasting against Tris's shielding. "We've got to help him!"

Taru shook her head. "No one can enter or leave until one of the mages within the room is dead. The warding cannot be broken. Tris is on his own."

WITHIN THE ENCOUNTER room, Tris bit down hard on the rope vine, clenching his teeth as he struggled to hold his shielding against the blast of mage fire that burst from the red-robed figure's talisman. The hood fell back, revealing not Arontala's face, but Alaine's, her features twisted in an agonized grimace, her eyes desperate.

Tris knew the power of the red fire, and the searching presence that accompanied it. That fire had nearly killed Kiara in the scrying at Westmarch, and it had sought and found him when he had attempted a scrying with the caravan.

The fire battered his shielding, draining his strength as he struggled to hold his protections in place. Tris felt the presence find him. The glow in the talisman at Alaine's throat pulsed a deep carnelian.

"See your future," a voice rasped from Alaine's throat, contorting her features. Images flooded into Tris's mind, searingly clear. Within Shekerishet's corridors Tris saw Vahanian lying dead in a pool of blood, pierced through the chest by a crossbow bolt. The image flickered, and Tris saw a courtyard of gibbets, and hanging lifeless, Carroway and Carina, their faces blackened, their bodies twisting. Another image replaced that, of a forest of pikes set into the ground. Fixed on the stakes, impaled alive, Tris saw Soterius, Gabriel, and Mikhail, saw the dawn break and saw the agony of the *vayash moru* as the daylight burned them, saw Soterius writhe in pain that did not end with the light of day. Once more the sending pulsed and the image shifted. This time Tris saw Kiara, battered and drugged, given to Jared for his pleasure.

"This is Margolan's future," the voice hissed, seeming to come from both around him and inside his own head, deafeningly loud, impossible to shut out. The sending shifted once more, and Tris saw the orb Soulcatcher in Arontala's chambers pulsing with the same bright fire, saw the maw of the abyss open and the terrible power of the Obsidian King stream forth, freed from his prison, descending on the red-robed mage who stood with arms upraised, awaiting his possession.

The power of the next image nearly drove Tris to his knees. He saw himself in Arontala's workshop at Shekerishet, saw the Obsidian King in Arontala's body send a massive blast of power toward him. In the vision, Tris saw his own shields strain and buckle, saw his body contort in agony, and felt the Obsidian King strip away his protections and break his will. Tris saw himself, tortured to the point of death and revived, pushed far past mortal endurance. In the vision, broken in spirit and body, he begged for death. And he saw himself, scarred and crippled by Arontala's tortures, blank-eyed, without the will to resist, his power used as a resource for Arontala's blood magic.

"You have failed," the voice rasped, deafeningly loud. "And your failure will be the destruction of all those whom you loved."

The visions were overwhelming and Tris strained for control, feeling grief and hopelessness wash over him even as the wormroot threatened to push his power beyond his reach. Then at the edges of his mage sense, Tris felt something else. As the air turned cold around him, he realized that he and Alaine were no longer alone.

"Take your shot!" Tris heard Theron's voice in his mind as the spirit of the fallen mage-fighter streamed from her burned corpse. With her was an older presence, and Tris knew it was Elam's spirit.

Reeling from the onslaught of the fiery blast and the sending, Tris saw the spirits howl toward Alaine. As they descended on Alaine with the fury of the ghosts of the Ruune Videya, Tris gathered all his remaining power.

With a murmured word he dropped his shielding and sent an answering blast, drawing on Mageslayer's power to keep the poison at bay. Sighting down Mageslayer's blade like an athame, Tris directed his power, borrowing from the blue glow of his life thread.

Distracted by the vengeful spirits, Alaine's attention shifted for an instant and Tris sent the full blast of his power toward her. Alaine screamed as the blue fire lifted her into the air, slamming her against the rough stone wall and pinning her against the rock. Unlike the blast that killed Theron there were no real flames, no charring flesh. The blue mage fire struck at the spirit and the life force within Alaine's body, evaporating that life force like water beneath a flame. Alaine screamed once and her body writhed, and then Tris felt the tortured spirit wrest free of her prison. The orb at her throat, deprived of a life source on which to draw, went dark.

Tris fell to his knees, completely spent. Alaine's body tumbled to the ground. He felt his own life force waver as he fell face-forward onto the bare stone floor. The illusion of Shekerishet's great room disappeared, leaving him in an empty salle as the wardings that held the doors winked out. Tris heard the doors slam open, heard footsteps running in his direction, but the ones who reached him first were the spirits. Theron and Elam and Alaine swirled around him on the Plain of Spirits. From Alaine he felt gratitude for ending her torment, and he knew her soul bore the guilt of the murder that her body was forced to commit. From Theron and Elam Tris felt approval and commendation, as the ghosts were stronger here on the far side of the line between light and darkness.

Tris stood on the Gray Shore of the Shadow Sea, further into the spirit plains than he had ever before ventured. There was a figure coming toward him along the water's edge. Even from a distance, Tris could feel the power of the Lady. He fell to his knees, his head bowed. *I have failed.*

The figure stopped in front of him, and Her power overwhelmed his senses. He dared not raise his head.

Rise. The voice sounded in his mind, in his heart, and in his soul. Able to do no other, Tris slowly stood. He expected that it would be the Mother Aspect of the Goddess who came for him, Margolan's patron Aspect, and the Aspect to whom he had paid tribute all his life. But the face he dared to look upon was framed with wild long hair the color of midnight, breathtaking in its dusky beauty, with eyes that glowed amber. The Aspect smiled, revealing its long eye teeth, and Tris knew that he stood in the presence of Istra, the Dark Lady. Numb with shock and grieving from the images of the sending, Tris felt no fear.

Istra opened her arms, spreading her heavy cloak. Tris's mage sense could feel the spirits clustered in the darkness beneath that cloak, spirits that clung to the power of the Dark Lady like frightened children, sheltered beneath an intricately woven pattern that shifted as he stared. He knew without a word that he must step into that embrace, though in the mortal world, fear would have frozen him in place. Drawn by Her power, Tris stepped forward, wondering what would become of his soul with no Summoner to make his passage. Istra's cloak folded around him, smelling of leather and sweet grass, and Tris felt a power beyond words stream through him as he fell into her embrace. Strong immortal arms closed around him and the darkness of the cloak covered him.

My soul is forfeit, Tris made his confession. *I've failed my family, my friends, and my people.*

Not yet. Istra's voice sounded in his mind, impossibly sweet, defying mortal description. *You must return.*

Tris felt the spirits that clustered beneath the cloak enfold him as his own strength failed him entirely. Borne up by the spirits, supported in the arms of the Dark Lady, Tris surrendered to the darkness.

TRIS WOKE TO find himself in his own room, the darkness lit only by a bank of candles. At first he wondered if he had truly returned to himself, or whether he might find himself a witness to his own funeral. But the bed beneath him felt solid, and the bandaged wound in his shoulder throbbed. When he turned his head, the pain nearly made him lose consciousness.

In the near-darkness, Tris could make out two figures near the fire, and realized that both Carina and Taru were keeping a vigil. He wanted to call out, but he found he lacked the strength even to do that, and his power felt out of reach entirely.

Maybe this is the Lady's judgment, Tris thought, closing his eyes. *Maybe She won't take me until I've lived the visions, until I've lost everything, and felt the pain. Maybe I'm damned.*

Three days later, after the chills and fever of the wormroot left him and he was able to leave his bed, Tris sat by the window of his room, huddled in the deep window frame, looking out at the snow-covered city below. The food on the table beside him was cold, untouched. Carina had pleaded with him to eat, but he felt no hunger, and while the gash in his arm was nearly healed and the poison in his system was gone, the images of the sendings haunted him. He had not slept.

Carina, worried because he would not speak to her, had finally left him alone. Tris was too numbed by his own grief and failure to find the words to answer her questions. He could not look into her eyes without seeing the noose and the gibbet. He was resolved to neither share his visions nor allow them to come to pass, but how to stop them from happening he did not know.

The door behind him opened. Tris did not turn. *The worst that can happen is that someone sinks a shiv in my back,* he thought. *Perhaps it would be for the best.*

He sensed Taru's power before she spoke. "Carina asked me to come," Taru said, moving toward him in the darkened room. Tris neither waved her away nor bid her closer, never taking his eyes off the falling snow beyond the window.

"Something else happened in that room that Carina didn't heal."

Tris didn't move. "I don't want to talk about it."

"You have to."

"I said I don't want to talk about it!"

"I don't think Arontala expected to kill you through Alaine. Oh, he could have gotten lucky—and he certainly came close. But he can sense your power. You've turned him back before, without training. No," Taru said, "he didn't really expect to kill you. And at a distance, he couldn't possess you. So it had to be something else. Something to break your will, make you question your purpose, lose heart."

Tris kept his back turned, so that Taru could not see the tears that filled his eyes.

"You saw something in that room, didn't you?"

Tris nodded wordlessly, unable to trust his voice.

"A mage of Arontala's power could project a vision through a vessel like Alaine," Taru went on quietly. "A dark sending can take the heart of a strong man," she said. "Once, I saw a great general throw himself off a cliff because a dark mage convinced him that his wife, his children, had been slaughtered."

"Jonmarc, Carina, Carroway—I saw them die," Tris whispered. "I saw Kiara taken—" his voice failed him and he bowed his head.

Taru moved to stand behind him, and placed a hand on his shoulder. "Wormroot poisons the body," Taru said quietly. "But a dark sending poisons the soul. Tell me—were the images you saw clear, as if they were happening in front of you?"

Tris nodded, swallowing hard as the images came again to him, real and overwhelming.

"Real scryings of the future are not so clear," Taru said. "A real scrying sees a future that is always in motion. To see what's happening at the same instant is one thing, but to see into the future with certainty—that is for the Lady alone. A clear future vision is not even given to seers, whose gift is the magic of foresight. Even they get fragments, not sharp images. That's part of their gift of divination, to know what those pieces mean.

"Arontala meant the sending to break your will," Taru said gently. "It's a soul poison, pulling from your own fears. As long as you hold it inside, it will do its work."

"I can't tell Carina. I can't—"

"Carina is a powerful healer, but she's young in her gift," Taru said. "And she has scars of her own that, until they are healed, limit her power. She isn't the only healer at the citadel." Taru drew up a chair to sit behind him. "She is also not yet a mind healer. I am."

Tris wondered if she saw madness in his green eyes. "I can't sleep," he said, choking back tears. "I can't close my eyes without seeing the visions. Last night," he confessed, his voice a tortured whisper, "last night I reached for Mageslayer. I thought that I might save them if I didn't come back. I thought that I might end the dreams." He held out his hand that was clenched against his body, and Taru gasped at the blistered burn on his palm. "Mageslayer knew. It wouldn't let me draw the blade."

"Show me the visions." Whatever she saw in his eyes, she did not turn away. "I've seen more than you can imagine, both of battle and of death. Open your mind to me, and let me see."

She held out a hand to him and Tris grasped it in both of his, heedless of the pressure against his scalded palm. He felt warmth as Taru placed her free hand on his head, felt that warmth move from her hand into his scalp, through flesh and bone into his mind, and deeper into his being. Tris could feel Taru's presence in his thoughts as he could feel the presence of the ghosts on the Plain of Spirits. He shut his eyes and let the images of the sending wash over him, hearing himself weep as if from a distance. His shoulders shook and he gasped for breath. He held back nothing, sparing her none of the details of the deaths he saw, nor of his vision of the Dark Lady.

Tris felt Taru's presence shield him, her power absorbing the dark sending, as if the images were pulled into the light that was her magic. As the images faded he felt the dread and grief recede, leaving him raw and spent. When the darkness was gone, Tris felt Taru's power like a balm, washing over him, healing the wounds of memory. Then he felt the presence fade, until he became aware that he was rocking back and forth, Taru's hand clasped in a desperate grip.

"I still remember," he whispered.

"But you remember a nightmare—not a reality," Taru said. "The danger still exists—but not the certainty of their fate, or of your own. The poison of the sending is gone. What remains you can handle without being consumed." She paused. "The other image, of the Dark Lady—that came after Alaine's death?"

Tris nodded.

"You weren't breathing when Carina and I reached you," Taru said quietly. "For a moment,

Carina thought you were dead. She pushed against your ribs and breathed into your mouth, and you came back to yourself. Truly, I hadn't seen the like, though she swore it wasn't magic, that it was like pushing on a bellows, something she learned from a battle healer, long ago." Taru paused again, longer this time. "What you saw of the Dark Lady, that was a true vision. I can feel the remnant of Her power. And I believe that you've glimpsed Her before."

Tris swallowed hard and nodded. He dragged his sleeve across his red-rimmed eyes. "Some hero, huh?"

He could not read the look in Taru's eyes, but her expression softened. "Only madmen are unafraid. Even the dead—and the undead—feel pain. Arontala knows that your love for your friends is your weakness—as your grandmother's love for Lemuel was hers. He can't understand that it's also your strength."

"I refuse to believe that I have to sacrifice Kiara and my friends in order to defeat the Obsidian King," Tris said, raising his head. "I refuse to go into battle, willing to let them die. I might as well put a knife to their throats. I'd make Istra's Bargain myself before I'll do that."

Taru smiled. "That won't be necessary. I believe you are already the Dark Lady's own." She was quiet for a moment. "Arontala will try to use your fears against you. Darkness always does. It's as if we're each followed by a dragon, Tris, made up of those fears and those old wounds. And if you don't turn and face your dragon and call it by its true name when you're young and strong, then when you're old and weak, it comes by night and devours you in your bed. You've faced your dragon," she said quietly. "You know the price of your worst fears. You know now that the future isn't certain. And as a Summoner, you know that death itself can't sunder love."

Tris nodded, feeling his throat tighten. "I know." Tris caught at her sleeve as she stood and turned away. "Thank you."

Taru nodded in acknowledgement. "Tomorrow night, you and Carina will return to Staden's palace until after Winterstide. Then your training will resume."

CHAPTER FOUR

THE WOMAN'S PIERCING scream ended abruptly as she slammed against the stone wall and slid limply to the castle floor. Jared Drayke stood, panting and sweat-soaked, his fists balled and ready to strike again.

"You ought to know by now that the human neck is a fragile thing," Arontala's comment sounded from the doorway. Jared wheeled.

"Shut up." When Arontala made no reply other than a shrug, Jared strode over to the battered body and hefted it in his arms, then crossed the room with his burden to fling wide the curtains to the garderobe and dump the body down.

"That's the third in as many months," Arontala observed acidly. "Not counting the ones you've given to the guards for their sport when your use is over. At least *they're* buried in a trench behind the barracks."

"I don't want to hear it."

"The common folk think you're sacrificing maidens to the Crone," Arontala continued without pause. "Or that you've conjured a demon."

"I'd need a mage for that, wouldn't I?" Jared shot back. "A real mage, not just one that promises everything and delivers nothing."

Arontala shrugged again. Beneath the voluminous red robes that marked him as a Fire Clan mage he was slightly built, standing a head shorter than Jared. The undead pallor lightened the duskier complexion of his native Eastmark. He crossed his arms, and the long, thin fingers of his right hand tapped with boredom. "You wear the crown. Margolan is yours."

"For now. My brother's still out there, and everything you've tried to do about it has failed." Jared began to pace, running a hand through his long, wavy dark hair. He had his late mother Eldra's black eyes and an olive complexion that was a mixture of Bricen's fair skin and Eldra's darker tones. But the high cheekbones and angular features were all Bricen's, and the family resemblance between Jared and his hated half-brother Tris was as near as the reflecting glass. "He slipped right through your slavers' fingers. And Staden of Principality welcomed him like a hero! You heard the spies." Jared fingered the null magic charm that hung around his neck. Although it limited any magical control over him that Arontala might try to wield, Jared did not trust the charm completely against the dark mage, nor did he underestimate the power of Arontala's abilities as a *vayash moru*.

"There's no cause as romantic... or hopeless... as an exiled prince's," Arontala said. "There are no Principality troops at the border, and your guards have burned a swath through Principality to make Staden pay for his indiscretion."

"You forgot to mention the Isencroft bitch. The spy said she was with Tris in Principality. She's defied me, and joined him in treason."

"Then you can watch her hang for it. You'd most likely have killed her before you could have sired a brat by her."

"I want more than promises!" Jared's face was only inches from the *vayash moru*. "Summon your great spirit. Secure my throne!"

"Patience is a virtue." Arontala turned away. "Anyway, it's not mine to decide. The working can only be done at midnight on the Hawthorn Moon. The spells won't break before then. It's been tried."

Arontala didn't flinch as Jared hurled a metal pitcher past his head. It clanged against the wall. "Then try it again. The Hawthorn Moon is months away. I can't wait forever."

"You can't wait at all, that's the problem," Arontala observed. "Your army is deserting because they're sick of burning down their own villages. Your nobles are close to revolt. I handed you the throne of Margolan on a platter and you've destroyed it before you've worn the crown a year."

"My only mistake was trusting you."

In the blink of an eye, Arontala was across the room, and the display of power only served to darken Jared's mood further. "A little late for second thoughts, my king," the *vayash moru* said in a voice as smooth as brandy. "Our fates are joined until we've seen this through." Jared repressed a shiver, unwilling to let Arontala see how much the undead mage unsettled him. He was glad that he had reinforced his amulet's power with other null charms hidden around the room. Arontala never spoke of them, and if he noticed an effect on his magic, he did not seem to care.

"Once the snows are gone," Jared said, "and the roads are firm enough to ride, I want to strike against Staden so that the Winter Kingdoms know that *I* am the true king of Margolan."

Even the firelight could not add color to Arontala's features. "I advise against that."

"Of course you advise against it!" Jared raged, dashing a platter to the floor. "You care nothing about my throne. The only thing you care about is that damned orb and your pitiful spirit king."

"Your troops are needed here, to keep your loyal subjects from slitting your royal throat," Arontala continued as if he had not heard. "And as for the 'pitiful spirit king,'" Arontala added with a trace of irony, "he can assure you the kind of power you crave to hold Margolan *and* the Winter Kingdoms for as long as you live. Perhaps longer." He tasted his sharp eye teeth with his tongue.

"What is that supposed to mean?" Jared felt a tingle of fear as his anger waned.

"You could reign as an immortal, with the greatest wizard the kingdoms have ever feared at your side, reborn to an immortal's body," Arontala said, his eyes alight.

Jared hand went to the amulet at his throat. "I want no part of your perversion."

A mirthless smile touched Arontala's lips. "No? You've already learned that it is the blood, and not the act, that satisfies." He glanced pointedly toward the garderobe.

"We have spies among the Sisterhood, within the families of *vayash moru*, and soon in Staden's court," Arontala said smoothly. "A little patience, my king, and you'll have what you desire."

Whatever Jared might have said was silenced by the rapping at the door.

"What now?" Jared shouted.

The door edged open to reveal a pale guardsman. "Sire, the Nargi emissaries have arrived."

Jared cursed. "Seat them in the audience hall. I'll attend when I'm free." He turned to Arontala. "If I can't have results from you, I'll find an ally who can honor a promise." He rinsed the last traces of blood from his hands in the basin near the bed and pulled his stained tunic over his head, shouting for a valet to assist him. Arontala said nothing during the process, standing in the shadows near the doorway. When Jared had inspected his image in the looking glass and called for his circlet crown, he met the *vayash moru's* eyes for a moment, then cursed and turned toward the door, giving tacit permission for the wizard to follow. Four Nargi priests wait-ed in the audience hall, watching impassively while Jared ascended the throne.

"You may address the throne," he said with a trace of ennui.

"Why have you called us?" The speaker was the eldest of the priests, a bent, lined figure whose face looked more mummified than aged.

"I have a proposition for your king."

"Go on."

Jared felt his mood grow darker at the priest's complete lack of intimidation. "Half a century ago, your people swore allegiance to the Obsidian King. On the Hawthorn Moon, he will rise again, and I'm prepared to help Nargi regain the territories it once held... if," he held up a finger, "you'll prove to me your good faith and raise your army against one who would usurp the throne."

"How can this be?" The priest's dry voice was like the death rattle of a corpse. "The Obsidian King was destroyed."

"Not destroyed. Bound. What's bound can be loosed. At the Hawthorn Moon he will be free again, and his power can make Margolan a powerful ally... or a formidable foe."

"You would invite the armies of Nargi into Margolan?"

"Help me crush the usurper, and I'll reward your king richly."

"We will carry your terms to our king," the priest agreed. His companions whispered among themselves, their cowls shrouding their faces. "It is his to decide. Our armies cannot move before the snows melt. The worst of winter is now upon us."

"I understood that in Nargi, your king rules at the pleasure of the Crone and those who speak for Her. Can we not make an agreement now?"

Once more, the priest turned to his whispering companions, ghostlike in their hushed voices and hidden features. Finally, he returned his attention to Jared. "We will convey our endorsement to our king. But even for an ally, the king will not sacrifice his army. We cannot move until the snows melt."

Jared barely restrained his anger at the delay. "Then we shall ask the Goddess for an early spring," he said between clenched teeth.

The old priest regarded him for a moment. "Our days are in the hands of the Crone. As are we all."

When the emissaries had been escorted from the hall, Jared turned to Arontala. "Come the thaw, the Nargi army will show everyone the full power of my crown." He rose from the throne. "I don't need the soldiers of Margolan."

"As you wish, my king," he said, moving for the doorway. He paused, turning once more toward Jared. "But are you *quite* sure of your bargain?"

"What do you mean?"

"You've asked them to stop the usurper," Arontala explained. "In the most literal terms, only one man has usurped the throne of Margolan. You, my king." He was unconcerned at the rage that filled Jared's face. "Perhaps you should learn to be more precise in your wording. One should always be careful what one wishes."

CHAPTER FIVE

I N THE PALACE of King Staden, the winter days quickly fell into routine for Jonmarc Vahanian. Most days, Vahanian was up before dawn, training in the salle with Kiara. The sessions ran late into the night when Mikhail was there, and sometimes Gabriel joined them.

In the few months since Harrtuck had hired him as the group's guide, Vahanian had seen his world turned inside out. He'd been skeptical at first, unwilling to believe in Tris's power as a mage and distrustful of nobles in general. But Tris had seemed unconcerned with rank, willing to accept Vahanian on the merit of his skill alone, and Vahanian had been grudgingly impressed. After the battle with the slavers, Tris and Carina had saved his life.

At Westmarch, Tris had helped Vahanian make peace with his grief and guilt over the death of his wife. And when Tris went to fight the ghost of King

Argus for Mageslayer, Tris had entrusted his own signet ring and the vouchsafe from King Harrol into Vahanian's keeping—a small fortune by any standards. As the weeks passed, and Vahanian came to see that Tris's offer of friendship was real, his objections to throwing in his lot with the others gradually waned. He had come to genuinely like Tris. Ten years older and with more combat experience than any of the others save Harrtuck, Vahanian held no illusions about the odds against them. He had his own reasons for wanting to see Arontala destroyed. The Fire Clan mage had been the reason for the death of his wife and for his own rigged court martial.

But something else had stirred deep inside him as Vahanian heard the refugees' tales about plundered farms and murdered villagers. Although he'd proudly been liegeman to no king before Staden made him lord of Dark Haven, Vahanian was born in Margolan. And while he was cynical about appeals to flag and kingdom, a love for that land was in his blood. He'd survived the plunder of his own village, when marauders had come years before. Those memories would forever haunt his dreams. Now, the tragedies of his past made the stories of the refugees real to him, and the chance to help stop the killing was more compelling than he expected.

And then there was Carina. Back in the caravan, he'd enjoyed riling Carina, although he rapidly came to respect her healing talent and her stubborn dedication to her patients. When they were taken by the slavers and Carina was almost killed, Vahanian admitted to himself that he cared about the healer. Time on the road had only deepened his resolve. While he was unsure whether Carina returned those feelings, his new lands and title made him bold enough to pursue her. On saner days, he chided himself for undertaking two hopeless quests at once. Most of the time, he put those doubts behind him, surprised that he could believe in anything again.

Vahanian wiped away the sweat from his forehead with his sleeve as he and Kiara wrapped up another round.

"You're good—damn good." Vahanian took a long draught of water from a bucket at the edge of the room. "I can see why Tris's Eastmark kick has improved, if he's been training with you on the side."

Kiara, her tunic wet with sweat, grinned. "Thanks. But the way you put those moves together still throws me for a loop. My armsmaster in Isencroft wouldn't have known what to do with you!" The princess's auburn hair was pulled back in a functional single braid, and she was dressed, as she preferred, in a tunic and trews. Her dark almond-shaped eyes and the dusky hue of her skin spoke of Eastmark blood.

Vahanian chuckled, and held out the dipper. "Alleys and battlefields are a different kind of salle. Points don't count—just blood." Kiara was the first real challenge he'd encountered in the Eastmark style of fighting since his days as a Nargi captive, and he found the purity of her technique an interesting counter to his own, battle-won skills. They were well-matched. Jae, Kiara's gyregon, perched high in the salle rafters where he had an excellent view of the sparring, and hissed at the action.

"Sun's up. The others will be here soon." Kiara replaced the dipper after a long drink.

Soterius hailed them as he and Carroway entered the salle. "Who won today?"

"A tie, as usual," Kiara laughed. "I beat him once, he bested me once, and we did enough damage to each other on the third round to agree to disagree!"

"Have you started yet?" Berry—Princess Berwyn—called from the doorway. She was dressed in a simple shift and slippers. "Did I miss anything?"

Vahanian sighed in jest. "Don't you have lessons or something?"

Berry fixed him with a dour look. "Of course I have lessons. I've finished my lessons for today. And I think we've all seen the need for a princess to defend herself." The mischievous twinkle in her eye showed how much she enjoyed her verbal jousts with Vahanian. "Carroway has graciously agreed to continue my knife throwing lessons." She twitched her right hand, and a blade fell out of her sleeve into her palm. "Besides," she complained, sounding every bit the ten year-old princess that she was, "lessons are boring. *You're* making history."

As they day wore on, they trained with swords and in hand-to-hand combat. When darkness fell, Mikhail joined them. Mikhail made a challenging sparring partner, combining the speed of a *vayash moru* with battle skills of a style two hundred years in the past.

What Carroway lacked in strength he made up for in agility and a true eye for aim. With his blue-black long hair and his long-lashed, light blue eyes,

Carroway was a favorite of the ladies, with good looks that were almost beautiful. That made his dead-on aim with a dagger even more unexpected. Jae fluttered down to join Kiara in a practice round, feinting and flying at her opponent, but careful to draw in his razor-sharp talons. When the little gyregon tired, Berry was happy to welcome him onto her lap, where he curled up, satisfied with the treats she always seemed to have in a pocket of her robe. Although Jae could be mistaken at court as a pet, Vahanian had seen gyregons in battle, and knew that they were as fast as a falcon and more dangerous.

"You're improving," Vahanian said to Soterius as they lowered their swords, sweating hard after a practice bout.

Soterius grimaced. "You know, every time you say that, I really want to punch you."

Vahanian raised an eyebrow. "You can try. But I've won the last three rounds."

Soterius was the same height and had the same reach as Vahanian, but where Vahanian was lean and muscular, Soterius was stocky. That difference gave Vahanian an edge with agility and Soterius an edge with strength. Vahanian, ten years older and with more battle experience than either Soterius or Tris, was a master of practical tactics. Soterius, like Kiara, was largely salle-trained, without Vahanian's rough-and-tumble experience. Unlike Kiara, Soterius had difficulty leaving behind the rules.

Soterius grinned. "Don't forget—we've got climbing practice after this. Your favorite."

"Don't rub it in."

The group ate a cold supper before they undertook the second part of their training. The lower regions of Principality were gently rolling hills, so they made do with the tallest thing at hand: the inside of the great bell tower in the castle yard, and riggings affixed to the tallest beams in the high-ceilinged salle.

Given the snows that blanketed the countryside nearly thigh-deep, they trained in the salle. The rough salle walls served for practice, and the rigging that secured Vahanian across his chest and looped between his legs was attached to a rope that ran through a pulley affixed to the high beams of the salle ceiling. The rope was fastened to a winch of Soterius' devising so that they could be secured as they climbed up or hoisted to the roof and left to climb down with some assurance that a misstep would not be fatal. Vahanian cursed under his breath as he secured his riggings, working the stiff rope into tight knots.

"Curse louder, and it can count for both of us," Kiara groused, struggling to secure a foothold on the rough wall. It made her fingers bleed, and seemed to defy a solid toe hold for her boots.

Carroway and Berry cheered from the floor as Mikhail and Gabriel climbed effortlessly alongside them, clinging to the wall or hanging in midair with the *vayash moru*'s unsettling ability to levitate.

"Tell me again why you can't just fly us wherever we need to go," Vahanian grumbled as the rough rock opened another cut on his calloused fingers and he struggled for a grip.

"For one thing, it's possible that Arontala has spelled Shekerishet against other *vayash moru*." Gabriel stayed in place without any apparent effort as Vahanian's arms ached from holding onto the wall. "It's more likely that he has his own fledglings standing guard, and that I'll be needed elsewhere, for defense." He smiled, showing his eye teeth. "And I'm told that mortals find such transport unsettling."

"Try me." The rock to which Vahanian clung slipped from his grasp and he nearly lost his footing.

Vahanian heard a rush of air, saw a blur faster than sight could follow, and then felt two impossibly powerful arms close around his chest in a crushing grip. Without warning, they rushed upward so fast that Vahanian felt his rope snap like twine. They reached the highest peak of the roof and then descended with equal speed; he fought a primal fear of falling and felt his stomach lurch into his throat. His feet touched the ground with a gentle thud, and Gabriel released him.

Soterius and Kiara barely hid their snickering as Vahanian tried not to be sick. "You've made your point," Vahanian said thickly, his knees suddenly unsteady. "I'll take my chances on my own, thank you."

Kiara looked at Gabriel. "The *vayash moru* have the strength, the speed, and the means to kill beyond any war machine. Yet I can't recall hearing of a battle where the *vayash moru* fought—except against the Obsidian King. Why is that?"

Gabriel answered. "Four hundred years ago, a truce was formed between mortals and Those Who Walk the Night. Mortals feared us because they knew that although we were few in number, we had superior strength and speed. Because of that fear, mortals often turned against us, burning our day resting places and destroying us at our most vulner-able. We were hunted and murdered, and when the *vayash moru* defended themselves or retaliated, it got even worse. So we agreed to allow mortals to fight their own battles. The mortals agreed to stop trying to destroy us. Part of that bargain was that we would not intervene in wars of plunder or expansion. Only for the survival of the Winter Kingdoms, and not the power of a mortal king, have we set aside that agreement. Such was the peril in the Mage Wars, when we helped to defeat the Obsidian King. Among ourselves, the terms of that truce are stringently enforced."

Gabriel went on. "And so Mikhail and I believe it is again, should Arontala succeed in raising the Obsidian King from the abyss. But not all of our kind are in agreement."

Vahanian met Gabriel's eyes. "So you break the truce. What are they going to do? You're already dead."

Gabriel's eyes held something Vahanian could not read. "Death is not the worst punishment. Pain can continue after death. The penalty for breaking the truce is destruction. At Winterstide, I must make our case before the Blood Council, the ruling body of our kind. If we can persuade them, we may gain powerful allies. If not," he exchanged glances with Mikhail, "we'll deal with those consequences as they arise."

Under Soterius's energetic urging, Vahanian and Kiara grew more confident with their climbing, practicing ascents and descents. They practiced until they had memorized the other's individual rhythms and skills, and then they rehearsed even more, with Soterius devising increasingly difficult trials. On occasion Carroway joined them for fun. The bard's natural agility annoyed Vahanian, whose own dislike of heights made the exercise grueling.

After another candlemark, Carroway took a seat next to Berry to cool down. "Sorry to leave early, but I promised the court minstrels that I'd help plan the Winterstide festivities. I'm due there before the evening is completely gone."

The bard grinned as the others dished out good-natured ribbing for his departure. "Sure, sure, you say that now," he grinned at their teasing. "But when you're enjoying a glorious Winterstide spectacular with the finest music in the Winter Kingdoms, you'll realize I had my priorities straight!"

Vahanian and the others wrapped up their practice in time for a late snack. Berry's lady in waiting came looking for her, and hustled the princess off for bed against her strident objections. Although Vahanian and the others were exhausted from the day's training, they had little time to rest. Staden had sent word of a war council meeting at the ninth bells, and so while Gabriel took his leave, Kiara, Soterius, Mikhail, and Vahanian did their best to look presentable before heading for the war room.

"I have to admit, I enjoy the salle time more than the strategy sessions," Kiara said as she and the others made their way toward the war room. "Sometimes I think we'll talk ourselves to death!"

Vahanian shrugged. "I'd rather hear the arguments now, when there's time to change the tactics, than later when we've got troops in the field."

Mikhail nodded. "I agree with Jonmarc. Much better to know your strategy—and your enemy—going into war than to change directions with troops on the ground."

Some days, Staden sent military experts from his army to consult on difficult scenarios. The rest of the time, Vahanian and the others met with leaders of the mercenaries Tris retained for the war against Jared. Tonight, Staden's spy chief, Hant, promised to bring them a leader from among the Margolan refugees who crowded Principality's makeshift border camps.

"Good night for a warm mug of ale," said Harrtuck as he met them at the door. "Miserable weather out there."

Vahanian looked askance at Harrtuck. "Missed you at practice today."

"Yes, well. Might have stayed up a wee bit too late last night, and had a tad more ale than I recall," Harrtuck said, rubbing his neck.

"The war hasn't even started yet, and you're already acting like a merc."

Harrtuck chuckled. "I'm a bit out of practice. Had a nice comfortable palace job for too long."

Vahanian, Kiara, and Harrtuck bantered with Soterius and Mikhail in the war room as they waited, jokingly taking bets on Soterius's ability to climb a local landmark. The door opened, and all joking stopped as Hant stepped briskly into the room, followed by a cowled stranger.

"It's nasty outside," Staden's spymaster remarked, shaking off the snow from his cloak as he set it aside. He gestured toward the man beside him. "I'd like you to meet Sahila." His companion, a thin man, was wraith-like in a dark cloak. The hood fell back, revealing Sahila's badly scarred face.

"You!" The gasp of surprise came from both Sahila and Vahanian at once.

"We were told you died," Sahila said to Vahanian, falling into Eastmark's guttural language.

"I nearly did," Vahanian replied, in heavily-accented Markian.

"How is it you're here?"

"Long story."

Kiara cleared her throat. "Although Hant and I are following this, perhaps you'd like to switch back to Common for everyone else?" she prodded in perfect Markian. Vahanian glanced at Kiara. It was the first time he had heard her speak Eastmark's language. She spoke it fluently, without an accent.

"What mystery is this, I wonder," Sahila said, "to have a high-born swordswoman in Principality who looks and speaks like a daughter of Eastmark?"

Kiara met his eyes evenly. "I'm Kiara Sharsequin of Isencroft. Daughter of the late Queen Viata, who was sister to your king."

Sahila bowed low, making a gesture of deference. "A thousand pardons, m'lady. We could never forget the beauty of Princess Viata, nor the tragedy of her loss. May your days be long, m'lady, and may you favor her in both beauty and skill."

Kiara inclined her head in acceptance, then returned her attention to Vahanian. "You two know each other?"

Sahila spoke first. "He saved my life, ten years ago, at great cost to himself." Vahanian shifted uncomfortably as all but Harrtuck leaned forward to hear the unfamiliar story. Harrtuck exchanged glances with him, and Vahanian drew a deep breath, then shrugged.

"I'm Eastmark born," said Sahila, addressing first Hant, then the others. "I was hoping to live out a quiet life as a farmer in a village called Chauvrenne. A bad harvest left nothing to pay taxes with. The first time I saw Jonmarc Vahanian, he brought a troop of Eastmark soldiers to our village, demanding payment for the king.

"We had nothing to give, and he went away. But there was a shadow over the land in those days," Sahila said. "A blood mage named Arontala." He paused to spit and grind the spittle under his heel as a warding against evil. "Arontala corrupted a great general among my people, and turned his head against the king, father to King Kalcen, who now reigns.

"The general sent the soldiers back, and told them to burn us out. But this man, their captain, refused." Sahila looked at Vahanian, whose expression had become unreadable. "The soldiers warned us to flee, so disgusted by their orders that they buried their uniforms and fled in farmers' clothes with us."

"What happened?" Soterius asked quietly, looking at Vahanian as if taking his measure anew.

"The general sent more troops to hunt us down," Sahila said in a bitter voice. "Many were killed. Vahanian and his troops were run to ground and brought back in chains, as were the villagers, to make an example of us." He met Vahanian's eyes, sharing an old, painful memory. "They locked us in a barn, but we could see what they did outside. The general and his mage hanged the soldiers for treason—all but their captain." His voice became quieter. "They locked him in the barn with us, and set it afire. I bear these scars." He turned his head to show the puckered and discolored skin along one side of his face, and slid the loose sleeve of his robe up to show an equally disfigured arm.

"Together, he and I kicked out a portion of the floor, into the caves below. We saved as many as we could, but there were so many, and the fire was so fast." He shut his eyes, remembering.

Vahanian looked down, aware that the others were watching him, uncomfortable with the telling of the tale, the scenes that had replayed themselves too often in his dreams. He clasped his hands, sweating.

"When the fire was out, and the general was gone, those of us who survived dug our way out," said Sahila. He turned to Vahanian. "You left us, headed south toward Margolan. We heard you were taken by Nargi. Then we heard no more."

"Wasn't much to tell," Vahanian said, with a glance toward Harrtuck that quieted anything the other might have added.

"For a while, I fought with the resistance in Eastmark," said Sahila. "We were ten to their hundred. We took a heavy toll and, I believe, stopped Arontala. I grew tired of war, and made my way to Margolan, perhaps more luckily than you." He directed a faint smile toward Vahanian. "There I raised a family and found a living with my plow. Then Arontala returned, and the fires began again." The pain was fresh in Sahila's voice. "This time, I was able to get my family to safety, but many could not. And so, I laid down my plow and raised a sword.

"There are rumors, among the refugees, that Prince Martris survived the coup. General Hant tells me the rumors are true. I've seen what Arontala has done in Margolan, and I've seen how King Jared rules. Hant tells me that Prince Martris intends to destroy Arontala and win back the crown. If you believe that Prince Martris can do this, my friend," Sahila said, "then I'll give you what help I can."

"Believe," said Vahanian. "If there's anyone who can defeat Arontala, it's Tris."

Sahila took his place at the table, and Hant cleared his throat. "I contacted Sahila because he has done on a small scale what Soterius and Mikhail plan for Margolan. Sahila recruited and organized the farmers and townspeople in Eastmark against Arontala's general. They were able to harry him enough to stop him from gaining more power." Hant paused. "Sahila can advise you, connect you to the refugees, guide you through the camps."

"If you wish to raise an army against Jared and his mage, you'll find a legion waiting among the refugees," Sahila promised. "I'll take you to the camps and the hiding places, and they will show you where the others have fled. I'll show you how we fought in Eastmark, from the forests and marshes, in the mountain passes and the caves, so that we moved as shadows, and couldn't be driven out by armies a hundred times our size." He took in Soterius and Mikhail once more.

"You're both soldiers?" Sahila asked, and they nodded. "Are you willing to forget the rules, to think like a stawar that stalks his prey, or a falcon that strikes like lightning? There are no rules in this combat, save honor. Can you fight like a predator without becoming an animal, without hurting your enemy the way he has hurt you, and thus becoming him?"

Soterius met Vahanian's eyes, and for the first time, Vahanian thought he saw true understanding in the soldier's gaze. "Yes, I believe so," Soterius said.

Sahila smiled wolfishly. "Good. Then bring me your maps."

LATE THAT EVENING, after the eleventh bell, Vahanian slipped out onto one of the small balconies that overlooked the courtyard. Even now the bakers and grooms bustled back and forth, their torches and lanterns bobbing in the darkness. For the season the night was mild, and although Vahanian was glad for his cloak, the brisk night air was refreshing. He brushed the snow from a stone bench and leaned back against the wall, drawing a wineskin from beneath his cloak. The wine warmed him but did little to relax his tired muscles or lift his mood.

Seeing Sahila again, hearing his recount of the rout at Chauvrenne, brought back old memories Vahanian preferred to avoid. While Sahila's story seemed to have further increased Staden's esteem, and possibly won him grudging regard from Soterius, Vahanian knew it was also likely to replay itself in his dreams for nights to come. Though eight years had passed, Vahanian doubted he would ever be free of those memories. The thud of a gallows

trap door—common enough since hangings doubled as public entertainment—or the smell of
burning hay could bring the memories back in full
and twist his stomach into a knot. Memories,
Vahanian knew, were just another type of scar.

The sound of footsteps made him reach for his
sword. To his surprise, Kiara stepped out onto the
balcony, raising her cowl around her head once he
had a chance to recognize her. "Mind if I join you?"

Vahanian offered her his seat, and walked over to
the railing to look out over the night fires of the
city. "Be my guest. But if you want another go in
the salle, you're out of luck. I've had it for tonight."

Kiara chuckled, but it sounded forced. "No
thanks. I just came out to get a breath of fresh air
and hoped it would clear my mind."

"Something bothering you?"

Kiara drew her knees up and wrapped her cloak
more tightly around herself. "Homesick, mostly.
I've never been away from home for Winterstide. I
miss father."

Vahanian offered her his wineskin and she accepted, taking a draught of the warm wine and handing
the container back to him. "I have to admit, before
I met you and Tris and Berry, I never really thought
about a king having a family. Kings were—well,
kings. You served them and you paid taxes to them
and you died for them, but I guess I never realized
that anyone loved them. It hadn't crossed my mind
they were someone's father." He lifted the wineskin
to take another drink.

Kiara gave him a mischievous sideways glance.
"Or father-in-law?" she asked. It was worth it, she
thought, to see him choke on his wine.

"You know, since Cam and Carina came to Isencroft, father took them in like they were his own," Kiara went on. "Mother nearly died bearing me, so I don't have any brothers or sisters. Don't worry," she said with a wicked grin. "The last letter I got from Cam said he was putting in a good word for you with father." She leaned forward conspiratorially. "I think he's afraid that Carina might make good on her threat to be the spinster sister who moves into his back room when he settles down. Even so, it must mean he likes you. He wouldn't try to marry her off to just anyone."

Vahanian cleared his throat. "Nice to know. Somehow, I can't imagine her taking it well to have Cam matchmaking for her."

Kiara chuckled. "Someone has to. You know, until this journey, Cam and Carina were never apart, except for the time she got sick. When Ric died. Cam always let her do the talking, and she always hid behind him."

"Hell, two or three people could hide behind Cam."

"You know what I mean. So in an odd way, maybe this journey has been good for both of them. Cam has to navigate on his own at court, and Carina is learning to stand on her own."

They were silent for a moment. Vahanian looked out over the courtyard. "Ric—was Gregor's brother?"

Kiara nodded. "I figured you picked up on that, when Gregor captured us." Vahanian listened in silence as Kiara told the story. When she finished, neither spoke for a few minutes.

"That explains a lot," Vahanian said finally, looking away. "But there's one other thing I wondered about—how come you aren't at the citadel training too? After all, you're a bit of a spook yourself—aren't you?"

"If you mean the scryings, like the one that went badly at Westmarch, it's not quite the same as the type of power Tris has. The kings of Isencroft have a regent magic that's inherited through the royal line. It's not sorcerer-caliber power—never has been. It's more for personal protection, and some handy skills to help protect the kingdom. Like the ability to do scryings."

"Pardon my saying so, but after what happened at Westmarch, I can't say that it works well on either count."

Kiara chuckled dryly. "I have to agree with you. And I've no desire to try another scrying, maybe not ever. It certainly didn't protect father from Arontala's wasting spell. Perhaps it wasn't meant to hold off a full mage. I can shield and scry, and sense the weather, which can be helpful in battle. Certainly not anything like Tris can do!"

She burrowed further into her cloak as the wind swirled the snow around them. "I'm worried about both Tris and Carina," Kiara confessed after a long silence. "About what kind of training the Sisters are going to put them through. Father never really trusted the Sisterhood. He said they were too in love with their grand theories of how the world should be, and didn't mind how many people died putting those theories into action."

"We've only got a few months left until the Hawthorn Moon," Vahanian said, looking out at the clear night sky. "That's not a lot of time. Barely enough to hire troops and plan a campaign. Tris is going to need everything he's got to do that. We only get one shot."

"I know," Kiara replied. "It's just a feeling I've got, that something's wrong." She grew quiet again. "Last night, I had a dream." Her voice was barely above a whisper. "Tris was fighting a mage in a red robe. And even though I couldn't see the red mage's face, I heard his voice. I knew that voice—it was the same voice from the scrying. It was Arontala." She looked up at Vahanian, and knew he could see worry in her eyes. "In my dream, Tris destroyed Arontala, but then I saw Tris fall—" She swallowed hard, trying not to cry.

Vahanian was completely at a loss for what to say. "Look, you said yourself, magic doesn't work for you. Maybe you just had a bad dream."

Kiara was unconvinced. "Maybe. I hope so." She stretched and stood. "It's almost twelfth bell. I guess I should at least get back to my room." She paused at the door. "I'm afraid to go to sleep. I'm afraid to dream."

"I know the feeling."

Kiara considered his comment, and nodded. "Any suggestions?"

"Well, you can try getting drunk or staying up all night, but it doesn't work for long. Everyone's got to sleep sooner or later. Time helps. But not as much as the healers tell you it does."

"Good night," she said, heading inside. "Thanks for the wine."

"Sleep well," Vahanian murmured. When she was gone, he opened the wineskin and took a long drink. Though the evening had grown colder, Vahanian did not go inside right away, waiting until he had finished the wine and was too exhausted to stay awake. Between the wine and the fatigue, he counted on being too tired to dream.

The dreams still found him.

THE CONSTANT TRAINING and strategizing could not quell Vahanian's growing concern. Tris and Carina had been at the citadel of the Sisterhood for two full weeks. No one—not even Staden—had heard from them. As the days wore on, he could tell that Kiara was worried as well. Her training lost focus and she drew away from them, into her own thoughts.

There was little comfort he could offer. While Kiara and Tris were open about their involvement, his relationship with Carina was much more tenuous. And while Vahanian finally admitted to himself that he was in love with the dark-haired healer, he remained unsure about the extent to which Carina returned those feelings.

So it was with carefully guarded reserve that he greeted the late evening news of Tris and Carina's unexpected return from the Citadel. They arrived in a closed carriage, under the king's guard. Only the companions from the trail and Staden met the carriage. Vahanian hung back, willing to let the others take the foreground. His concern deepened as Tris and Carina stepped from the carriage.

Tris's thin frame was gaunt. When Tris's cowl fell back to expose his face, Vahanian could see the marks of battle wounds, recently healed. For a moment, Tris's green eyes met his, and Vahanian felt a shiver go down his spine. Tris's gaze reminded Vahanian of the look he'd seen before, in the eyes of returned prisoners of war, men who had endured the unspeakable and would never sleep well again.

Carina leaned heavily on Tris's arm. Her slight frame was nearly hidden by her heavy cloak and her face was haggard, with dark-circled eyes and a weary expression. Kiara rushed forward to greet both of them, and while Vahanian could not hear the words that were spoken, it was clear from Kiara's expression that Tris had asked her to look after the healer. Carina nearly stumbled as Kiara took her arm. Carina looked over her shoulder, and Vahanian thought she looked his way. Reluctantly, he watched her disappear toward the stairs with Kiara as the others crowded around Tris.

"I promise, I'll tell you everything I can—tomorrow." Tris managed a wan smile that did not reach his eyes. "We've been to the Crone and back, and I'm afraid I'm a good bit worse for the wear, in spite of all Carina's help."

"You look tired, m'lad," said Staden. "Best thing for you is to get some sleep. Tales will wait until morning."

Tris nodded, and grinned wearily at Carroway. "I have some more grist for your stories," he said, clapping the bard on the shoulder. "But I don't know if anyone will believe them."

"The drunker they are, the more that sounds reasonable," assured Carroway, but Vahanian could see the worry in Carroway's face.

"Give me a day or two to rest, and I'll be back in the salle," Tris said to Vahanian.

"Yeah, sure thing," Vahanian agreed dubiously.

Early the next afternoon, Vahanian chanced to encounter Kiara in the upstairs passageway, bearing a tray with two teapots and plates of cold meats and cheeses. "Filling in for the kitchen help?" he asked, raising an eyebrow.

Kiara blushed. "Yes, I guess so. Tris asked for some tea, and I volunteered to bring it up. It's just—"

Vahanian chuckled. "I understand." He nodded toward the two pots. "You must expect him to be thirsty."

"I planned to stop by and check on Carina." She shot a sly glance toward Vahanian. After the conversation on the balcony, he was sure that Kiara both recognized and endorsed his interest in her cousin. "Carina said she'd be working in the study. I'm late getting up to Tris—would you mind taking the tea to Carina if you're going that direction? I wouldn't want it to get cold."

"Glad to help," Vahanian deadpanned, taking the teapot and cup from her tray.

Kiara's eyes grew serious. "I'm afraid for them, Jonmarc. Both of them looked like they'd been to battle. I'm not sure how much more either of them can take."

Vahanian nodded. "I wondered that myself. I'm the wrong one to ask about magic. But remind Spook that if he gets his royal ass fried, the rest of us hang. And personally, I'm counting on doing some damage to Arontala. So... he needs to stick around for the party."

Kiara smiled at his irreverence. "I'll remind him— in so many words," she chuckled. "Go on now, or the tea will be cold. Let Carina know it will be

tomorrow before the court healer can see her—
there was an outbreak in the village and Staden sent
the healers to help."

"I'll tell her," Vahanian replied, heading for the
study.

AT THE STUDY, Vahanian knocked lightly at the
door. When no answer came, he frowned and
knocked again, more insistently. "Carina?" he
called quietly. "Kiara asked me to bring up some
tea. It's Jonmarc."

When there was still no answer, he tried the door.
It was unlocked, and swung open at his touch.
Carina lay sprawled on the floor, her book fallen
beside her.

Vahanian rushed inside, and the door swung
closed behind him. The tea was forgotten on the
table as he knelt beside Carina, turning her over
gently.

Carina was pale and feverish. A fresh gash bled
on her upper arm, and Vahanian guessed that she
had fallen against the edge of the table. From the
lump on her forehead, it was obvious that she had
hit the floor hard.

Gently, Vahanian lifted Carina into his arms and
carried her to a small couch. Although he possessed
none of Carina's healing magic, Vahanian had seen
enough battle—and enough battle healers—to
make a fair assessment of her injuries. Carina's
breathing was steady and her pulse was strong.
Vahanian spotted Carina's healer's bag near the
fireplace, and rifled through it with a practiced eye.
He selected a few herbs and a stretch of cloth, and
brought the small iron pot of water that simmered

on the fire. Within a few minutes, he had fashioned a rough bandage from part of the strip and made a poultice from the herbs to bind up the gash on her arm. He mixed some powders with the tea to bring down Carina's fever, and made a compress with a rag and the water on the washstand.

Carina began to stir as he patted the cool water against her face.

"Take it easy," Vahanian instructed. "You had a nasty fall."

"How—"

"Kiara asked me to stop off with some tea on my way by," Vahanian said, helping her sit to sip the tea. "She said to tell you that none of the palace healers could come by until tomorrow—some kind of plague in the village has them all busy."

"Then where did the poultice—"

He chuckled. "As you love to point out, I've been in more than my share of fights. Just a little battlefield healing, to return the favor."

Carina gingerly touched the fresh bandage on her arm, and sniffed the air. "Acycla leaves and cass root, with featherwort. Not a beginner's mixture."

"I spent a few years helping a hedge witch gather herbs," Vahanian said off-handedly. "You learn things."

Carina looked at Vahanian, meeting his eyes as if she were trying to read his thoughts.

"Who are you… really?"

Vahanian recognized the question. It was the same loaded query he had tossed her way after the slavers' rout in the Ruune Videya. Something in her eyes made him take the question seriously. He ran a hand back through his long, dark hair.

"Why do you care?" he asked quietly, refusing to look away.

"Because the answer matters."

"It's a long story."

"I don't think I'm going anywhere." She closed her eyes and sank back against the couch. "I saw you once, when we were at Westmarch, down in the forge. You handled those blacksmith's tools like you were born to them. For a merc, you've been a lot of strange places. So I'll ask you again—who are you, really?"

Vahanian took a long breath and looked toward the fireplace, unsure how to answer. Finally, he drew up a chair and sat down. "My mother was a weaver and my father a blacksmith, up in the Borderlands, near enough to the Northern Sea that the ship captains and the traders gave us good business. I started working in his forge from the time I was old enough to carry the tools. We made a good living."

"But you didn't stay."

"When I was fifteen, raiders came. We made too good of a living, I guess. My father died trying to help hold the gates. I grabbed his sword and tried to protect the forge, but I was just a kid. First time I got stabbed," he said ruefully. "When I came around, it was over. The village was looted, half of it burned. My mother and brothers were dead. I tried to get help in the next village, but I didn't make it through the woods."

"What happened?"

"The hedge witch's daughter was out gathering herbs. She found me and dragged me home. Guess I gave them a scare," he chuckled sadly. "After I healed up, they apprenticed me to their village blacksmith. A few years later, I married the hedge witch's daughter."

Carina said nothing, but her gaze made him look away, back to the fire. "There was a late spring that year, and the sea captains didn't stop at our port. Money was tight. I started pulling old relics out of the cave tombs—gold and jewelry and rare wood—and selling what I could find to traders just to get by. Then one night, after Shanna and I had been married about six months, a mage showed up, and wanted me to find him a relic."

"Arontala?"

"Yeah," Vahanian said. "Offered a year's wages if I'd bring him back a talisman. So I went up there, and I found it. Put it on a strap around my neck to keep it safe."

"The charm we saw at Westmarch—the one that keeps the magicked beasts away."

Vahanian nodded. "All these years, I thought that damned thing called the beasts." He paused for a moment, swallowing hard, until he could find his voice once more. "The beasts came that night and there was nothing to stop them. Nothing I did made a difference. They couldn't kill me, but they gave me this." He tilted his head so that the scar showed from beneath his collar, a jagged line that ran from his ear down under his shirt.

"Everyone died—everyone but me," he said quietly. "All these years, I thought I brought the beasts." He dared to meet Carina's eyes, knowing that she struggled with her own ghosts. "I didn't believe Royster, didn't believe Tris. But Tris summoned Shanna's spirit, and I believed her."

His voice caught, and he looked away. "That's what I meant when I told you that the dead forgive us. That's how I know.

"I got as far away as I could, which was Eastmark. Only thing I had to sell was my sword. I was barely eighteen—younger than Tris is now by a couple of years. Met Harrtuck there, in a merc troop. He taught me the basics, kept me from getting killed. But I learned fast, got field promotions, and a general in the Eastmark army asked me to join them. He was a hero, and I was flattered." Vahanian's voice was bitter. "Made full captain by the time I was twenty. It was nice, for a while."

"Kiara told me... about Chauvrenne."

Vahanian nodded. "I figured she would. After that, I had the bad luck to get captured by the Nargi as I was trying to get back to Margolan. Almost drowned in the Nu River when I escaped. Washed up on the river bank, and a lady named Jolie took me in, gave me a job, taught me to smuggle on the river. And that's what I was doing until Harrtuck hired me as a guide."

Any chance I had with her probably just disappeared, Vahanian thought with a sigh, looking down at his hands. *Why should someone with her gift, her connections, look twice at someone like me?*

Vahanian looked up, startled, as Carina's hand slipped over his in a weak clasp, warm with fever. "Thank you." For once, her green eyes did not seem so guarded. She did not let go of his hand. "Stay with me, please." Her voice was barely above a whisper, and he daubed her face once more with the cool cloth.

"As you wish, m'lady," Vahanian said, lightening his tone with a smile, and daring to kiss the back of her hand. Carina smiled as she closed her eyes.

Vahanian watched her relax, until her breathing was deep and measured, and she finally fell asleep. He looked down at her hand, small against his, in amazement.

Maybe, just maybe Vahanian thought, *an outlaw turned noble has an outside chance with a noble turned outlaw.* He shifted in his chair, careful to make sure that his sword was clear to draw and that he had a good view of the door. Then he settled in for the rest of the evening, lost in thought, standing guard until dawn.

CHAPTER SIX

SOTERIUS RUBBED HIS newly-grown beard, a reddish brown complement to his darker brown hair. He brushed back his hair, usually cropped short for a battle helm, now also grown long. "This is going to take some getting used to," he said with a glance toward Mikhail.

Mikhail chuckled. He had also grown a beard and let his dark hair grow long. "I don't know, it's something of an improvement. Hides your face."

Soterius gave him a sour look. "You should talk. Took you one night to grow both beard and hair. And I bet your beard doesn't itch!"

"Being undead has its rewards," Mikhail commented. "Actually, it's a bit of a relief. To keep the hair short and beard gone, I had to cut both each evening. Goes with being *vayash moru*."

"Let's just hope that it fools some of the guards we run into. I'd just as soon not be recognized by every soldier we pass."

"According to Carroway, you're in more danger being recognized by the ladies," Mikhail joked. Soterius grinned. He stood a hand's breadth shorter than Mikhail, with a trim, muscular build suited for soldiering. Before the coup, both Soterius's good looks and his position as captain of the king's guard made him a sought-after companion for the ladies. And while both Tris and Carroway did their best to elude the marriage-minded young women at court, Soterius managed to juggle multiple relationships without entanglement.

By contrast, Mikhail was as tall as Tris and Carroway, with dark brown hair. He was solidly built, and even after death his posture and stance made clear his military background. Like Soterius, Mikhail had been a younger son of a Margolan noble who took to military service since his father's lands and title went to his eldest brother. Two centuries and a shortage of heirs meant the lands finally reverted to Mikhail, another benefit of immortality. Those lands, like the estate of Soterius's father, were in Margolan's northwestern corner, in the Borderlands near Isencroft.

Soterius laughed. "You're just jealous, being dead and all."

Mikhail shrugged. "You assume that such attractions end. But immortality isn't as lonely as you seem to think."

Soterius gave him a sideways look. "You're kidding me—right?"

It was Mikhail's turn to smile. "On the contrary. Liaisons among my kind can last for several lifetimes. And mortal loves—while necessarily brief and always tragic—aren't uncommon."

Soterius thought about that. "How is that possible?"

Mikhail was silent for a few moments, until Soterius thought the other might not answer. "Mortals' lives are urgent and passionate because they are brief," Mikhail said finally. "There's a jadedness that comes with knowing you have all the time in the world." His smile was sad. "Some among our kind never look back. Others leave behind a mortal lover and don't want to let go. Nearly all of us, I think, at one time or another, are drawn back to the warmth."

"It works better than you might think—no more difficult than those who overcome a difference in religion or who fall in love from opposite sides of a war. But for us, your days are so short—just a few seasons—and the life and light fade. Afterwards, the cold is worse for having been near the flame."

"I never knew that being dead had quite so much in common with being alive."

"Being 'dead' doesn't. Being 'undead' is something else entirely."

TADRIE, THE FARMER Kiara had rescued on her trek across Margolan, met them at the entrance to the refugee camp. He was as tall as Soterius and lean, with broad shoulders and calloused hands that spoke of hard work. Soterius guessed that Tadrie was past his fortieth year, although he looked older. "Good, you're here." Tadrie bustled toward the two men. "I have a crowd for you."

Soterius brightened. "You found volunteers?"

Tadrie chuckled. "Oh, I found volunteers enough. Had to keep the women and boys from volunteering, that's the Lady's truth. Everyone in this camp wants to see that demon Jared off the throne."

"I feel the same way," Soterius said. "Let's see what you've pulled together." He gestured to the wagon behind him. "We've brought supplies for the camp—food and firewood from Prince Martris and King Staden, and weapons to help with the training."

"And blankets?" Tadrie asked excitedly.

"And blankets."

Tadrie whistled, and the refugees pressed forward. Soterius and Mikhail helped unload the precious cargo and smiled uncomfortably as the displaced farmers and trades people thanked them over and over again.

"They're Margolan people," Soterius said with a lump in his throat, looking at the ragged refugees. "Our people. Look what Jared's done to them!"

"It will be better if we can give them hope and purpose, and a share in reclaiming their lands," Mikhail said. He patted the pommel of his sword. "As refugees, they have no hope. As soldiers, they have the chance to make a difference."

Soterius repressed a sigh of complete hopelessness when he surveyed the "arms" the refugees bore. Sickles and staves, hoes and rakes made up the bulk of the weapons. Most of the volunteers carried a knife or two, dull things barely useful enough to peel a potato, hardly the weapons of an army. They were completely unready for the swords and quintains in the wagon. It took lesss effort than Soterius expected to convince the refugees that Mikhail was on their side. Soterius realized that in the farmlands, extended family remained close—whether living or *vayash moru*.

With a resolution born of desperation, Soterius and Mikhail organized the commoners into two bands and drilled them on how to swing, parry and fight. Children too young to join the fray cheered and played as they watched, dueling with sticks.

Looking into the determined faces of the refugees, Soterius knew that they, too, were aware of how much preparation was required.

At the end of the first night's practice, Soterius saw three young men pushing through the crowd. They were as ragged as the other refugees, but they held themselves like soldiers.

"Captain!" one of the men shouted as they grew closer, and Soterius brightened as he recognized the men from the barracks at Shekerishet.

Handshakes and hearty backslaps followed as Soterius introduced the three soldiers—Andras, Tabb and Pell—to Mikhail. As the crowd dispersed for the night, Andras invited Soterius and Mikhail to their camp, and the five men picked their way through the crowded refugees to reach the small square of bare dirt where the soldiers made their home. They had an army-issue tent, better shelter than most of the refugees. A neatly-built fire warmed them as they sat on logs around the fire pit.

"So it's true, what they say?" said Andras excitedly. "That you helped Prince Martris to escape?"

Soterius nodded, and accepted a warm mug of watered ale with thanks. "Harrtuck was with us, and the bard Carroway."

"Lady be praised!" Tabb exclaimed. "We were afraid that it was just a rumor, spread among the refugees."

Soterius leaned forward. "Tell us what happened in the barracks that night, and how you came to be here."

Pell took a long breath, and ran a hand back through his filthy blond hair. "That's a hard tale, captain." He glanced at the others. "We were on patrol that night, and we knew something was very wrong when we reached the city gates. Guards were everywhere, checking everyone. It was chaos with the parades and the pilgrims, and all of the drunks celebrating Haunts. But when we reached the barracks, they said the king was dead."

Andras jumped in. "The story we heard at first was that Prince Martris had killed the king—and his family—and that Jared only barely drove him off. They said that you and the others were traitors, and Jared put a huge bounty on all of you."

Soterius swore. "Jared paid slavers to hunt us. They almost got us."

"Even then," Andras said bitterly, "we didn't believe it for a moment. Oh, Jared had his friends in the barracks, that's for sure. You know how he used to come down and talk to the men, filling their heads with dreams of an empire. So some of them didn't think about it too hard when he blamed the murders on Prince Martris."

"We knew better," said Pell, anger coloring his tone. "And as the next days passed, we saw our worst fears confirmed. Jared sent squadrons out to the manors of the loyal nobles. He put them under house arrest, or worse. Palace staff began to disappear. Those who could fled as soon as they realized what had happened. Jared hanged a dozen of the servants, on charges of aiding the conspiracy."

"He declared martial law," Tabb said. "Told us that to protect Margolan, we needed to help him build a war chest. So he sent soldiers in twos and threes to shake down the merchants, the tradesmen and the farmers."

"That's how we escaped," added Andras. "We agreed among ourselves that we wanted no part of Jared's army. But we were fond of saving our necks. Then the order came to go to the farms outside the city and collect second taxes. No one questioned when we packed for the road. Once we reached the farmlands we warned the farmers, who gave us clothes and burned our uniforms. They helped us pass from farm to farm, and we protected the refugees who went with us." He spread his hands to indicate the camp. "We came here, and here we've been, without hope until now." He looked up at Soterius and Mikhail.

"If you plan to cross Margolan and recruit troops, you'll find an army waiting for you, captain. We heard tell of other soldiers who also went missing, from outposts and garrisons, hidden by the people. And we heard tell of others, who didn't flee, who either did the demon's bidding or were hanged for refusing orders." He shook his head. "It's been bad, sir, since the coup. When Prince Martris returns—and I pray to the Lady that he does—he'll have a mess to clean up."

Soterius nodded. "That's what we were afraid of." He paused. "By any chance, did you hear what happened to Lila? I was supposed to meet her after the celebration at the palace the night of the coup. She promised to save me a seat down at the Bristle Boar. I stood her up to save Tris."

Andras, Pell and Tabb exchanged glances and fell silent for a moment. Finally, Andras spoke. "Aye, we heard. A few days after the murders she came to the barracks, looking for you. Unfortunately, she didn't come to one of us. She went to Aeron, and he took her to Jared. No one saw her again."

Soterius looked down at his hands. Although he had not loved the tavern owner's daughter, Lila was a lively date and a good dancer. Knowing that she had died because of him filled him with regret and shame. Mikhail laid a hand on his shoulder.

"You didn't know, Ban. There was nothing you could have done."

Soterius felt his regret harden into anger. "It's just one more reason to see Jared hang."

"Whatever you need from us, we're your men," Andras said, uncomfortable with the silence. "We'll help you train the volunteers, and we can help lead the practices when you can't be here. When you're ready to cross back into Margolan, we'll go with you. These farmers know the land. We can stay to the caves and the swamps and forests. Jared's men will never know what hit them, and they'll be afraid to move."

Pell cast a look at Mikhail. "If more of your kind are on Prince Martris's side, Jared's men will even be afraid to sleep."

Mikhail smiled, his long eye teeth discomfortingly apparent. "That's the idea."

* * *

AFTER TWO WEEKS, Soterius and Mikhail were ready to test the skills of their best recruits from among the refugees. Sahila's scouts brought news of a small squad of Margolan soldiers camped just over the border, and gave eyewitness accounts of the Margolan soldiers making night raids across the Principality border to harry the refugees. It was good enough provocation for Soterius.

For this first strike, Soterius chose his best men: Mikhail, Pell, Tabb, Andras, Sahila, Tadrie, and five others who had shown promise with the sword in training. Soterius spent a portion of his part of the reward money to buy weapons and leather armor for the group. He had black woolen outfits and cloaks made that would allow them to move unobserved in the dark.

Sahila led them through the low brush toward the border. It was obvious to Soterius that Sahila knew the land well, and that he had a tracker's instincts for cover and direction.

"They cross here—look," Sahila motioned toward the blurred tracks in the snow where a recent snowfall had not yet obscured the passage of a group of men on foot. Sahila, Soterius, and Mikhail had conferred at length before heading out as to the best place for an ambush. Now that they had reached Sahila's recommended spot, Soterius looked around in the dim light. From the flat area where the Margolan strike force was camped, the land became hillier the closer one got to the refugee camps on the Principality side of the border. This trail ran along the edge of the forest, between the trees and a ridge. The trees and the rocky outcropping could provide cover for Soterius's refugee-soldiers. With Mikhail, Soterius was less worried about wolves or other predators in the forest should they have to run for cover.

"It's good," Mikhail said of the ambush point.

"Let's get in position, just like we practiced." The small band of refugee fighters gathered around Soterius. Within minutes his men were in position, careful to cover their tracks in the snow. Soterius smiled. Most of these men had been hunting—or poaching—all their lives, and the same skills that enabled them to feed their families would now make it possible for them to strike back at the soldiers who had taken those lands from them.

"You're sure the soldiers are going to come tonight?" he asked Mikhail under his breath.

"They were getting ready to move when I scouted the camp. Looked like they meant to take prisoners. They had a large box on skis that they could pull behind a horse team."

Soterius frowned. "Then all the better we strike tonight."

They did not have long to wait.

When the moon was high in the sky, the Margolan soldiers made their move. Mikhail was the first to hear them, and he gave the silent signal to the watching fighters. The soldiers moved over the rise and down along the forest's edge. Soterius pursed his lips. Behind the soliders was a man leading two cart horses through the snow, and pulled behind the horses was the large box on skis.

"What the hell is that box for?" Soterius murmured to Mikhail under his breath.

They waited for the target to move into the most vulnerable point along the ridge, where they were fully exposed to both the fighters who waited above them hidden in the brush along the outcropping, and the archers who lurked in the shadows of the forest.

The Margolan soldiers were armed and alert. They could have no other purpose than to strike at the refugee camps, the only cluster of habitation close to the border near this point. The soldiers were already on Principality soil, an act of war in itself. Still, Soterius's heart beat faster when he saw the insignia on those uniforms. He was about to begin the war against his own homeland. He waited to give the signal for attack until the Margolan troops were in the middle of the pass.

"Now." He lifted a branch above the brush where he hid, so that the archers in the forest could see.

A hail of arrows burst from the cover of the dark trees, taking down three of the lead Margolan soldiers before they knew they were under attack. Soterius's fighters swarmed down the hillside, swords glinting in the moonlight, with a battle cry that echoed in the night. Soterius realized Mikhail was no longer beside him. He glimpsed the *vayash moru* at the rear of the doomed soldiers, already discarding a body.

The Margolan soldiers regrouped quickly, and soon Soterius was parrying blows with the group's captain, a man he did not recognize, who looked to be only a few years older than himself. Around him he could hear arrows striking the deep snow. Out of the corner of his eye he could see Sahila and the other refugee soldiers wading into the fight.

The Margolan captain struck hard and Soterius parried, feeling the jolt of the strike down his arm.

Soterius turned the momentum into a strike of his own, scoring a deep gash on the soldier's shoulder. He let his knife fall from its wrist scabbard into his hand. He circled the soldier warily, his second blade ready.

"We have no gold for you, brigand." The captain struck again, landing a good blow against Soterius's sword and leaping back as Soterius nearly scored again with his knife.

"You're on Principality land, here to harm your own people." Soterius took the offensive, landing a series of hard blows that the captain was hard-pressed to deflect. "And you serve the Usurper."

"We serve King Jared, the rightful king of Margolan." The captain's strike went wild. Soterius's left hand slashed with the knife, cutting the soldier's forearm to the bone.

"You serve the demon." Soterius doubled his press, forcing the captain backward. The snow shifted beneath his feet, and Soterius gained the advantage he sought, using his sword to deflect the captain's blade while he sank his own knife deep into the man's chest. "Prepare to meet the Crone." Surprise spread across the captain's face as blood spread across his tunic.

"Behind you!" Soterius heard the warning and wheeled, barely parrying the wild attack of a young soldier who made up in ferocity what he lacked in technique. Around them, Soterius's refugee fighters were holding their own, and the archers joined them, trading their bows for swords now that the fighting had begun.

As the horses shied and whinnied, the soldier nearest to the large wooden box brought his sword

down on the lock, cutting through the rope that secured it. He wheeled too late to meet the sword of one of Soterius's refugee fighters, and the sword took the lieutenant through the chest.

"Sweet Chenne," Soterius murmured as the box door flew open, pushed from within. Bursting from the box were a half a dozen wild-eyed fighters swinging sledgehammers and axes. With incoherent cries, the ragged fighters streamed from their prison, as the Margolan soldiers scrambled to get out of the way.

Soterius wasted no time on his inexperienced opponent. He ran the man through, turning to face this new threat. He heard a cry from Tadrie to his left; the refugee seemed frozen in place, a look of horror on his face as one of the rag-tag fighters advanced. "Pell, Andras, Tabb—I need you!" Soterius cried out as several other refugee soldiers seemed to lose their focus, staring at the wild-eyed fighters as if they were spirits from the abyss.

Dimly, Soterius realized that the few Margolan soldiers who were still alive were running for the forest, and that Mikhail was nowhere to be seen on the battlefield.

"By the Whore, what are they?" Pell cried out. Soterius tackled Tadrie to get him out of the way of the attacking creature's hammer. Now that he was close enough to see their new opponents, only Soterius's battle training kept him from staring in shock like the refugee fighters. There was something very wrong with the fighters who streamed from the wagon, who waded into the battle heedless of whom they hit, striking as indiscriminately against the Margolan soldiers as against Soterius's stealth fighters.

"Find out if they bleed!" Soterius shouted as he dragged Tadrie to his feet. Pell and Andras closed ranks in front of him. "Stand your ground!"

"Back from the dead," Tadrie was murmuring, staring uncomprehendingly at the fighter who was striking so ferociously that both Pell and Andras were hard pressed to keep him at bay.

From the forest, Soterius heard a man's scream, and guessed that Mikhail was cleaning up the Margolan soldiers who had run for cover beneath the trees.

"*You* won't come back from the dead," Soterius shouted at Tadrie, shaking the man. "Fight!"

Soterius heard one of the rag-tag fighters approach and turned, still shielding Tadrie. Now up close, Soterius knew these fighters were no common back-up troops. There was more than rage in their eyes—there was a complete lack of humanity, as if the soul itself had been replaced with blood madness. Unkempt and unshaven, smelling of sweat and waste, the rag-tag fighters fought with insane ferocity. The fighter's wild blow broke Soterius's sword, and Soterius dove aside, feeling the axe graze his shoulder. Blood streamed down his left arm but he could still move it, and he had no time to triage his wounds. Snatching up a sword from one of the fallen Margolan soldiers, Soterius swung two-handed, knowing that a madman wielding a battle axe could easily best a swordsman before too many blows were traded.

The wild-eyed fighter swung again. He was a burly man with the look of a farmer, wide-jawed and broad-shouldered, built like a bear. He roared in attack, and Soterius could see no reason in the man's eyes. There was nowhere to run. Soterius threw his knife, catching the big man in the thigh. Blood streamed from his leg and into the snow, but the axe-wielding fighter did not slow, as if pain meant nothing to him.

Sure he was about to die Soterius braced himself, looking for an opening. As the man lifted his axe to swing he stiffened and his head jerked up, blood spurting from his mouth. With a death rattle, the big man keeled forward, Tadrie's sword through his back. Soterius realized he was shaking as he met Tadrie's eyes, and saw the farmer's look of complete horror and revulsion.

There was no time to ask questions. Snatching up the dead man's axe, Soterius lifted the heavy blade and went running at full speed toward the attackers that were driving Pell and Andras back to back. With a wild cry he swung the blade, cleaving one of the madmen practically in two. Tadrie seemed to have snapped from his trance, dropping his sword and grabbing a sledgehammer from one of the dead men. He swung the hammer in wide swaths, closing on Pell's attacker. Soterius could see that tears glistened on the farmer's face and he could hear Tadrie murmuring a prayer for the dead. Andras and Soterius made a frontal strike, rushing at the rag-tag fighter with a ferocity that matched his own madness and striking with sword and axe. Tadrie's hammer fell from behind, taking off the back of the man's head.

"I want one of them alive!" Soterius knew as he said it that he was asking a lot from his own men, who, having neatly routed the Margolan troops, were barely holding their own against these berserker fighters. Three of the madmen were still standing, and Soterius could only count half a dozen of his own men on their feet. The trampled snow was red with blood, and bodies littered the space between the hillside and the forest.

There was a rush of air beside him, and a blur of motion. Soterius glimpsed Mikhail as the *vayash moru* struck at one of the madmen attacking Sahila and another fighter. Soterius jerked his head, and Pell and Andras fell behind him at a run, stopping only for Pell to snatch up the axe from the dead madman's hands.

Sahila swung his heavy two-handed sword in wide swaths, trying to keep his distance from the madman who was advancing, completely heedless of the blade. As they grew closer it was apparent that Sahila's companion was badly wounded, but he attempted to back up Sahila nonetheless. Soterius watched in horror as Sahila's blade connected with the advancing fighter, severing his arm at the shoulder. Still the madman came on, with no hint in his expression that the pain even registered. Soterius, Pell, and Andras charged from behind. Soterius let his axe fly when he came into range. The heavy weapon spun handle over blade, until it hit with a sickening thud in the middle of the madman's back. The big man dropped to his knees without a sound, and fell face-forward into the snow.

To his left, Soterius saw Mikhail engage another of the madmen, while across the way, Tadrie and one of the other refugee fighters were holding their own against the last of the attackers, keeping him at bay until a third refugee hurled a large rock at the madman's head. The madman fell and lay still.

Soterius looked around. From the position of the moon, barely a candlemark had passed since they attacked the Margolan soldiers. "Check the bodies!" he shouted. "Don't leave any of our own!" Grimly, the men still on their feet began to check the fallen, dispatching one or two of the badly wounded Margolan soldiers who had not yet died with a merciful sword strike.

One of the fighters was already calming the horses, and after carefully checking the box that was still hitched to the harness, he waved for his fellows to begin the grim work of bringing the dead and those too badly wounded to walk into the wagon.

"A little assistance, if you please." Mikhail did not even sound winded, although he pinned the last of the berserker fighters in his grip. Soterius, Pell, and Tabb ran to help him, grabbing rope from the soldiers' packs. They trussed up the struggling madman from shoulders to ankles, taking no chances. The man struggled and bucked with his full might, but where Soterius should have expected a captured soldier to curse them and spew profanities the berserker raged incoherently. Up close, the madness in the captured man's eyes was even more disturbing, as if his humanity had been stripped away, leaving something feral in its place. Soterius noted as they bound the man that the prisoner was badly wounded, with deep gashes that would have disabled a normal soldier.

"Let's get them to the healers," Soterius sighed, wiping the blood off his hands in the snow. Mikhail lifted the trussed-up madman with immortal ease;

the wagon shuddered when Mikhail dropped his cargo in. Pell counted as they loaded bodies and wounded men into the wagon, while Sahila took roll among the surviving fighters. Three of their own were dead. Three more, including Tadrie, were too badly wounded to walk back to camp.

"Let's get that arm bound before you need the wagon, too." Mikhail stood next to him, with strips of cloth Soterius bet the *vayash moru* had torn from one of the dead men's shirts. As usual, he had not heard his friend approach. Soterius let Mikhail bind up his arm, just now becoming aware of how much it throbbed, and that he could no longer feel his feet in the bitter cold.

"We lost too many," Soterius sighed, looking over the bloody snow.

"They fought well against the regular soldiers," Mikhail observed. "But what came out of that wagon—we didn't train for that."

"What *were* they?" Soterius did not expect an answer.

"*Ashtenerath*." It was Tadrie who spoke, from where he sat huddled in the back of the wagon-box, as Pell did his best to dress the farmer's wounds. Soterius frowned, recognizing the term from old tales.

"Awakened dead?" Soterius replied, meeting Mikhail's gaze. "Those are just stories told to scare children."

"Not necessarily," Mikhail said quietly.

"That man... was my brother-in-law," Tadrie said haltingly, shivering with the cold. Andras stripped cloaks from the dead soldiers and distributed them among the wounded and survivors. "He was taken by Margolan troops six months ago. We thought he was dead. Better for him if he had been," Tadrie said, still obviously shaken by the encounter. "The Lady forgive me. I had no choice but to kill him, although I don't know how to tell my wife." He shook his head. "Then again, that... thing... wasn't really him, at least, not in his right mind."

"What do you mean, 'not necessarily?'" Soterius looked from Tadrie to Mikhail. Pell finished binding up Tadrie's wounds and stepped back, closing up the wagon doors for the slow trip back to the refugee camp. Soterius and Mikhail, two of the least wounded, led the group. Andras guided the horses with Tabb as guard, and Sahila and Pell brought up the rear.

"During the Mage War, the Obsidian King was able to reanimate corpses on the battlefield," Mikhail said as they walked. "I didn't see it myself, thank Istra, but I knew men who saw it first-hand. Such fighters were of little use other than to terrify their comrades."

"So such a thing is possible?" Soterius remembered the story Carroway had told him, about the vengeful woman's ghost who had tried to possess Carina as Tris and the others were fleeing toward Principality. And while Soterius knew that Carroway was often given to exaggeration to make a tale better, the bard had sworn to him that in this case, the truth needed no embellishment. In Carroway's recounting, Tris had fought the dead woman's ghost for control of Carina's body. In throwing clear the vengeful spirit, he had accidentally cast it back into the woman's corpse, momentarily reanimating her until Vahanian struck her down with a sword.

Mikhail nodded. "But I don't think that's what we fought tonight. The man I captured was alive. Although... there was something that didn't feel right. I suspect that we're dealing with blood magic."

"Prince Martris is a Summoner," Andras said from behind him. "Perhaps he could raise us a whole army from the dead."

Mikhail turned. "I don't doubt that Tris is strong enough to do just that. But no Summoner who serves the Light would do so, on peril of his own soul."

"But we need everything we can get to defeat Jared!" Andras argued.

Soterius shook his head. "I think I know what Mikhail means. And it's the same reason Bricen forbade his troops to torture, even when we fought the Nargi, and even when we knew they tortured our captives. Bricen knew that you can't use the means of the enemy without becoming them. Tris wouldn't do it—and I won't ask him to."

"Arontala isn't a Summoner," Mikhail said. "He doesn't have the magic to reanimate corpses. But if, with his magic and his drugs he could break a man utterly, tamper with his mind, leaving only pain and anger—then I think it would be possible to create such a monster."

The unbroken snow of the countryside was serene in the moonlight. It did not take much imagination to envision what would happen if more Margolan troops returned, with greater numbers of *ashten-erath*.

"How do we train to fight those things?" Soterius wondered aloud.

"We tell the refugees that such an enemy is likely. We warn them that it may be their own family members, enslaved to Arontala, tortured and broken into submission, doomed to a living hell. We let them know that to kill an *ashtenerath* is to free it from torment. It will be worse to encounter a friend or relative who willingly serves Jared. That will also happen."

"It was even worse when you fought the Obsidian King, wasn't it?" Soterius asked.

Mikhail's eyes were haunted. "I saw things that I can't speak of. And it will be like that again if Tris can't stop Arontala."

Soterius shivered. "Then we'd better prepare the fighters to come up against their worst nightmares."

IN THE REFUGEE camp, Esme the healer waited for them. Blue-eyed, red-haired Esme was one of the court healers. Soterius had known her for years. Willowy and tall, Esme was just a bit shorter than Soterius. She was the daughter of a tin trader, who had risen to a court position on the merits of her talent alone. Many times, she had come to the barracks to attend the soldiers' wounds, and Soterius had discovered the way to win Esme's friendship. Esme respected commanders who kept their soldiers from preventable injury. Her disdain for those who did not, who considered their enlisted men to be disposable, could be scathing. Finding her in the refugee camp was an unexpected boon. After one of Soterius's trips back to Staden's palace, Carina had gladly helped Soterius provision Esme for battle healing, to ease the suffering among the refugees.

Esme waited at the edge of camp for Soterius and the others to return. A cry went up from some of the waiting refugees as they realized that their loved ones were not among the soldiers walking back from the encounter. Frightened family members clustered around the soldiers and the cart, making it difficult for the group to reach the clearing in the center of the camp. When they stopped, Soterius and Mikhail went back to unload the wagon, while Tabb and Andras helped Esme prepare pallets in one of the larger tents and Pell kept the horses still amid the confusion.

Mourners keened as Soterius and Mikhail carefully bore the dead to their relatives. Soterius watched the three men's widows embrace each other, weeping, as frightened children wailed, clinging to their skirts. And although he assured them that their husbands died with valor, the words tasted of ash in his mouth.

Soterius followed to where Esme and her small group of hedge witches and healer trainees attended the wounded fighters. Already, the healers had made a noticeable difference in the men's injuries. Soterius waited patiently as the healers worked, lending a hand as Carina had often required of him, and stopping to speak to each of his men who was conscious to praise and reassure. Mikhail stood watch at the makeshift hospital's doorway, keeping the gawkers and family members at bay until Esme and the healers were finished.

When the last of the fighters was healed and out of danger, Soterius guided Esme to the back of the tent.

The trussed-up *ashtenerath* lay still, but when he saw them approach, he began once more to buck and cry out unintelligibly. Esme's eyes widened and she backed up a step at the ferocity of the man's response.

"Tadrie called him '*ashtenerath*,'" Soterius said. Esme gasped and put a hand to her mouth.

"Truly?"

"I'd like you to confirm what he is. And while we don't dare let him loose, he is wounded. We need to patch him up."

"I'll do what I can."

Mikhail moved to secure the *ashtenerath* fighter, holding him by the shoulders. The man's eyes glinted with pure madness, and his face was twisted in animal rage. Esme knelt next to the bound man and laid her hand across his forehead. Almost immediately the fighter slumped, unconscious.

"That 'trick' comes in handy with drunks and guys who are spoiling for a fight." Esme let her hand linger on the man's forehead and frowned, then brought her hands down over the trussed man's body, assessing his injuries. For nearly half a candlemark she worked to heal the worst of his wounds. Then she sat back on her heels.

"Well, that's a new one." She shook her head, looking at the still unconscious prisoner.

"What did you find?" Soterius bent lower, on alert.

The red-haired healer chewed her lip as she mulled over what her healing senses had told her. "Mikhail's right—this man isn't dead. There's no decay. And he's not undead. A *vayash moru* feels... different. There's actually nothing different about his body from you or me. But his mind—"

"What?"

Esme stared at the *ashtenerath* fighter. "I tried to treat a man once who was bitten by a dog with the foaming disease. He was like a wild animal, willing to strike at anything that came near, kill anyone in reach. Almost got myself killed, and did no one any good," she added ruefully. "That's what he reminds me of."

"Is it a disease?" Soterius asked.

"No. That's not what I meant. I could sense the changes in the brain of the man with the foaming disease. It had been changed by the sickness—damaged so badly that I couldn't put it right. That's what's happened here, but it's not a disease that did it. It was blood magic—I can feel the traces of it."

"So Arontala did this?"

Esme nodded. "When I was healing him, I could tell that there were fairly new injuries that hadn't healed right. He's been tortured, probably to the point of breaking. Traces of drugs, too—the kind that never really leave the body completely. There are some strong potions—some of the mystics use them—that can give a man visions or horrible nightmares that seem real, down to every sense and smell. But there are also the changes in his brain. Changes somebody meant to put there."

"I've tried to heal enough patients with head injuries to know that if you get hit hard enough in the right places, different things happen. Get hit just so and you remember what you did ten years ago, but you can't remember what you ate for breakfast. Take a lump somewhere else, and the sweetest old lady will become a screaming shrew." Esme looked at the prisoner for a moment, tight-lipped in anger.

"Someone's deliberately damaged him, trying to create just what you see—something that looks like a man but acts like a crazed beast. At least he won't suffer for long."

"What do you mean?"

Esme looked up at Soterius, and he could see in her blue eyes that she was upset. "The changes are too great to last for long. He's burning himself out. I can feel him dying—and it's not the injuries from the battle. Those, I healed. But all the same, he'll be dead by morning." She laid a hand on the madman's forehead once more, and her lips moved quietly. After a moment, the man's form relaxed, just a little, though he still tensed and twitched from time to time.

"I've done what I can for his pain," Esme said. "Part of the madness that made him attack you was sheer agony from the ways he's been altered. The human part of his mind is gone—what's left has no more reasoning ability than a stampeding bull." She looked to Soterius again, and her eyes hardened with anger. "If this is what Arontala can do—and what Jared permits—then sign me up as a battle healer. I'm with you."

Soterius managed a smile. "Carina's shown me what an advantage it is to have a healer with you in a fight. But you're needed here, Esme. These refugees won't stop taking sick and having babies just because there's a war on. And the men will fight better, knowing their kinfolk are as safe as we can make them."

Esme sighed. "You're right, of course. But just knowing that someone did this to him deliberately makes me want to knock some heads together!"

Soterius laughed. "I've seen Carina in a fight. Never underestimate an angry healer with a quarterstaff!"

The laughter quickly faded, and Soterius and Mikhail sat down with Esme next to the unconscious prisoner. "Can you tell how long ago the changes were made to him?" Soterius asked with a nod toward the *ashtenerath* fighter.

"The scars from the torture are several months old. And from the amount of the drugs left in his system, I'd say he'd been drugged for quite a while. But the changes in his brain were new—about a month old, no more."

"At that rate, Arontala can't afford to make too many of these," Mikhail observed. "Tadrie said his brother-in-law disappeared six months ago. If it takes five months to capture and break a prisoner and they only survive for a month after they're turned into a weapon, then we're unlikely to face whole armies of these things—at least, for long."

Soterius nodded. "It's like the mage monsters that Arontala called along the Dhasson border, and the ones that Tris ran into the night they found Kiara. Those things are horrible killing machines, but Tris says it takes so much magic to raise them and control them that even a mage as strong as Arontala can't keep it up for long. And they can't breed on their own. Thank the Lady, or we'd probably be overrun with the things!"

"Could Arontala have help?" Mikhail asked.

Soterius frowned. "In all the years we put up with that cursed mage at Shekerishet, I never saw him in the company of other magic users. I can't imagine him sharing any of his power or secrets with anyone. I've heard tell of other dark mages from time to time. Maybe they're taking advantage of all the havoc to cause some problems of their own. But I just can't picture Arontala working with anyone."

"I hope you're right," Mikhail said.

Soterius looked back at the prisoner, who twitched and moaned even in his sleep. "Can the *vayash moru* help to keep the *ashtenerath* at bay? You were able to subdue him a whole lot easier than we could have."

"Had his axe taken off my head or cut me through the heart, I'd be as dead as the rest now. We may be undead, but we can still be destroyed. So it's not without risk. But you're right—assuming we can get close enough, our strength and speed should give us an advantage in restraining one of these things long enough for someone else to make a strike. I'll let the recruits among my people know, and we'll prepare."

Soterius looked over his shoulder, toward the wounded men who lay on pallets in the makeshift hospital tent. "We'll have to prepare the fighters as we recruit them. At least now that we know that the *ashtenerath* are in pain and won't live long, maybe our men will see it as a kindness to kill them, especially if it's someone they knew." He sighed. "By the Whore! This war hasn't even started yet, and it's already a nightmare."

Mikhail jerked his head toward the refugee camp outside the hospital tent walls. "When they find out what Arontala does to his captives, you may have the most motivated troops in Margolan's history."

"By Chenne, we're going to need it."

CHAPTER SEVEN

TRIS RESUMED HIS lessons with Royster within a day of his return to the palace. Although not fully recovered from his training with the Sisterhood, Tris was driven by the knowledge that time was passing quickly. It was already the Crone Moon, the last month of the year, and Winterstide would soon be upon them. And while he had begged off of a return to the salle and climbing practice for a few days, even that could not be postponed for long. There was far too much to learn, and too little time.

Tris and Royster continued their lessons in the palace library. A huge fireplace, easily the height of a tall man and twice a man's length, held a roaring fire that barely warmed the room. Royster focused on history and legend, and on the complex wording of powerful incantations. Tris was physically and mentally weary, but he knew he could not allow himself the luxury of rest.

"What do you know of Winterstide?" Royster's voice shook Tris out of his thoughts.

Tris searched his memories. Bricen had not been overly devout, and Margolan's celebrations had lacked some of the pious observances of other kingdoms.

"Winterstide is the winter solstice," Tris said, trying his best to remember. "The longest night of the year. The spirit realm is closer then, as it is at the Hawthorn Moon, on the summer solstice. On those nights, the division between the realms is fragile." He paused. "At Winterstide, the spirits are closer because the realms are out of balance, and the scales in the hand of the Lady tip toward the realm of the dead. After the night of solstice, the days grow longer again, until the balance is restored again in the spring when day and night become equal. Then, the balance tips once more, until the Hawthorn Moon."

Royster nodded. "What do you know of the role of a Summoner on Winterstide?"

Tris tried to remember the celebrations of his childhood, when Bava K'aa played a prominent role in his father's court. From the night of the solstice for a fortnight, Winterstide was one of the most glittering feasts of the year, filled with candles and torches, banqueting and processions. He had vague memories of his grandmother welcoming the ghosts of the kingdom to the palace, but for what purpose, he could not recall.

"I don't know," he admitted with embarrassment.

"In the days leading up to the solstice, Summoners help to ease the imbalance created between the realm of the living and the dead," said

Royster. "It is very important when the fabric between the realms is thin. You must learn to hold court for the spirits and ease the imbalance."

"Why?"

Royster closed his book. "As with the cycle of the rains and the movement of the winds, the natural way of magic is a balance among the currents of force, and between the living and the dead. As the gift of Summoning became rarer, so it became more difficult to maintain that balance.

"When Arontala works his blood magic, the currents of magic become tainted. You—like all mages—must draw upon those currents of magic, the river of power that the Sisterhood calls the Flow, when you confront Arontala. Anything that can be done to remove the taint and balance the energy of the living and the dead will strengthen your power. You will confront Arontala when the fabric between realms is once again thin."

Tris closed his eyes, feeling a headache coming on. "I used to think that all a mage had to do was learn a few mysterious rhymes and 'poof,' it would be done." He ran his hands back through his hair wearily.

Royster gave him a dry look. "Shows what you knew, doesn't it?" he said irreverently. "Oh, there are little rhymes a mage might use to remember the sequence of what must be done, but the words themselves don't do a thing. You could write every magic 'spell' as high as a man on the barn wall, but if you don't have the power to start with, all you'd have is a strange rhyme. And a bad one at that."

"You and the Sisterhood have told me what a Summoner may and may not do. You've listed for me every kind of ghost and spirit and made me memorize all the things that can bind a spirit to this world. And between me and them stands only death," Tris said quietly. "But what is death?"

Royster pulled a coin from his pocket. "What's on the front?" He held the gold up in the firelight so that it glistened.

"The image of the king."

"And on the back?"

"The crown of Principality."

"Can you cut the coin to separate the front from the back?" Royster handed him the coin.

Tris took it and turned it in his fingers, then finally shook his head. "How could I tell where one stopped and the other started?"

Royster nodded. "Exactly. So it is with death. On one side of death, a person is alive. And on the other, only the spirit remains. But death itself? It's only the somewhere between awake and asleep. For those without your gift, it's a line that can be crossed only once, and in one direction. But for a Summoner, it's a doorway that can be entered and exited at will."

Tris turned the coin thoughtfully in his fingers. "The dead aren't really at rest, are they?"

"That's the true purpose of a Summoner," Royster said. "To give rest to spirits that would otherwise wander, or who cannot find their rest. And to defend them against those who would hold them against their will, or snuff out their energy for power's sake, or bind them for evil.

"A land mage knows the secrets of the world around him, the stories of the birds and animals, the voices of every living thing. An air mage speaks to the winds and the weather. The sea itself answers a water mage, and all the things that live in it obey his commands. And a fire mage knows the mysteries of the depths of the world," Royster said. "But only to a spirit mage is it given to summon the dead and ease their pain and to know the mysteries of life itself. That's why the Lady permits so few to share the power, and why so often the power corrupts."

"How can I know if I'm being corrupted, too?"

"You can never know for sure. The heart has a hundred ways of telling you all is well. Power used in anger is already corrupt. Guard against that, and you may be safe."

Tris looked toward the fireplace, staring into the embers. "To know what Jared has done, and the evil Arontala has caused, and not feel angry…"

"There is a difference between anger and justice," Royster said. "It appears the Lady's hand is on your quest, and if you reach your goal, it may be that She is using you as the instrument of Her judgment. But if you go to Arontala with hatred in your heart, no matter how justly deserved, he will own your soul."

"I'd rather be destroyed."

"Pray the Lady it does not come to that. Bava K'aa couldn't bring herself to destroy the Obsidian King, and so she was nearly destroyed by him." Royster met Tris's eyes. "How far are you willing to go to destroy the Obsidian King?"

Tired as he was, Tris felt his anger rise. "I'm willing to sacrifice myself, and I've proven that," he snapped. "But if the Sisterhood is looking for me to offer up Kiara and the others as some kind of loyalty test, then no, I won't do it. There has to be another way."

"And if there is no other way?" Royster asked, watching him carefully.

"Then I'll do what I must, even if I go to the Crone."

TRIS WAS PLEASED to find Kiara waiting for him in the hallway when he concluded his lessons with Royster for the evening.

"Royster promised he'd let you off by the tenth bell," she said conspiratorially. "I didn't even have to bribe him."

Tris smiled tiredly. "I'm glad to see you—but I'm hardly up to sparkling conversation."

Kiara took his hand. "That's all right."

He took her in his arms and kissed her. She reached up and touched the pendant on the chain around his throat, her gift for his birthday. "I didn't get the chance to thank you," he said, letting his fingers toy with her dark hair.

"I thought it might be a bright spot in your training." She tilted her head so that her cheek brushed his fingers.

"The only one," Tris sighed.

"Since neither you nor Carina is talking about it, it must be grim."

Tris fought down the memories of the dark sendings, and the horror they foretold. "The Sisterhood isn't much for half measures."

They walked out onto a loggia overlooking the courtyard. Servants and merchants bustled across the dark cobblestones, their way lit by the small fires and torches that gave the guards a measure of light and heat in the cold evening. Kiara shivered. Tris wrapped his arms around her, letting her lean back against him and enjoying the moment.

"Do you think that Jared and Arontala know where we are?"

Tris remembered the red fire that pulsed from Alaine's orb, and the battle at the citadel. "I'm sure of it."

She leaned her head against his shoulder. "How is it that two brothers can be so different?"

"We're half-brothers, really. Same father—different mothers. Father was younger than I am now when he married Eldra—it was an arranged marriage, to keep the peace with Trevath. I understand that they hadn't even met before their wedding day. But they fell very much in love.

"Remember that all this happened before I was born, and it wasn't often spoken of openly, since father had remarried by then. But Eldra didn't make a good impression. The ladies at court thought she was aloof and demanding. Her mood could be so dark that some of the noblewomen said she had a demon. And she had difficulty producing an heir."

Tris looked out over the darkened courtyard. "Through it all, father loved her. And when she died bearing Jared, father was devastated. Bricen had just taken the throne—my grandfather died suddenly on a hunt—and he had no idea what to do with a baby. So Jared was left for the servants to raise and father retreated into his grief for ten years—until he met my mother."

He smiled, remembering Serae. "Mother was like a spring wind, full of life and energy. And even though there was talk because she was the daughter of a sorceress, she gave father a son within the first year they were married. Me. Kait came along seven years later—they lost three children in the years between.

"I always thought Jared hated Kait and me for having a mother—and for getting father's attention. Jared was an awful bully, and he had a pack of noble trash that did his bidding and liked the way he took whatever he wanted. Jared had Eldra's temper, and her dark moods. It got worse once he found Arontala—or Arontala found him."

"I don't know whether father realized the mistakes he'd made with Jared or whether he just didn't know what to do about it, but he wouldn't crack down on Jared, and Jared knew it. Mother and grandmother did their best to keep Kait and me out of Jared's way, but I don't think they ever realized how often he thrashed us." He gave a sad chuckle. "I got rather good at stealing herbs out of the kitchen to mix up poultices to patch us both up. Since Jared had a penchant for beating the servants, I always wondered whether the kitchen staff knew what I was doing, and made sure to leave what I needed where I could find it."

"I'm sorry," Kiara said, turning in his arms to face him. "I didn't mean to bring up bad memories."

Tris shrugged. "Everything we're doing is about unseating Jared. It's hardly as if I can keep from thinking about him." He closed his eyes and the memory of the dark sending came again. He struggled to push the thought of Kiara with Jared from his mind.

She raised a hand to touch his cheek. "What is it?"

"Nothing," he said tightly. He met her eyes. "I want to keep you safe, Kiara. I know what Jared is like. I'd die before I'd let him hurt you."

"The Oracle sent me on my Journey for a purpose," she said, and let her right hand fall to the pommel of her sword. "I fight as well as you do—maybe even better." There was a hint of challenge in her voice and Tris chuckled at the dare. "And until Arontala is destroyed, father—and Isencroft—are in danger. It's my fight too. Don't you dare try to make me into one of those cosseted noblewomen, spending their days playing tarle and embroidering handkerchiefs!"

After all the tension of the last week, it felt as good to laugh as it did to hold her near him. "I wouldn't dream of it," Tris promised. "I love you," he murmured, bending to kiss her. *More than you can imagine*, he added silently as she returned the kiss. *More than life itself.*

MUCH LATER, WHEN Tris found his way back to his own quarters, he found a warm fire and a fresh bottle of Cartelesian brandy waiting for him. He kicked off his boots and sprawled in a chair in front of the fireplace. The brandy, a belated birthday gift from Vahanian and Soterius, made his aching muscles relax. He let the fire warm him as he drifted off to sleep in his chair.

Tris, help me! He could hear Kait's voice in the darkness all around him, and Tris sat bolt upright. The cry rang in his mind, not from a dream, but from the netherworld itself. Tris closed his eyes and tried to concentrate.

Focusing his power, Tris cast his circle and drew his wards, plunging into the darkness after Kait's cry. In the gray world where only his spirit could travel, he slipped among the dead and the undead, steeling himself against their cries and petitions. With all his strength, he focused on the sound of his sister's voice. As he drew closer he could feel her pain, her fear, even as the image of her face, trapped in a glass prison, grew clearer in his mind. But before he could reach her, a wall of cold darkness drove him back.

Free her! Tris shouted to the darkness, but there was no reply. His feeling of dread grew steadily stronger. Kait's image grew dimmer, though her hand was pressed against the glass and her eyes begged for his help.

Show yourself! Tris demanded, but again, no answer came.

He found himself blinking at the light of Royster's candle as the librarian bent over him worriedly. The fire in the hearth had died, and Tris knew the night was far spent.

"You saw Kait again, didn't you?"

Tris realized that his hands were shaking. His shirt was wet with sweat, and his heart pounded. "It was so real. I could see her face pressed against the glass. I heard her crying for help." Haltingly, he found the words to recount the rest of the contact. Royster listened intently, frowning.

"It was real. I'm not a mage, but I'm sensitive to the working of magic. I felt the magic myself, that's why I came. You say that Arontala laid a spell over the palace to drive out the ghosts that protected your father?" At Tris's nod, Royster thought for a moment, then moved to the books that lay on a table in Tris's room. He set down his candle and paged through the yellowed volumes, muttering to himself. Finally, he motioned Tris to join him, and ran his finger beneath a passage in the diaries of the Obsidian King.

"Look here," Royster said. "This tells about how the Obsidian King, who was a great Summoner, started to draw on the spirits of the dead for power. At first, he drew from them to work magic that helped them. But later, as he turned to the darkness, he drew from unwilling spirits to enhance his own magic. At the end, he slaughtered captives, and then bound their spirits so that he could draw on them for a reserve. He fashioned a great crystal orb in which to capture souls and hold them until he could draw from their life force for his power."

"The Soulcatcher," Tris murmured, remembering the glowing red orb in Arontala's library that he glimpsed the night of the coup; the same red fire in the crystal pendant around Alaine's neck in the Citadel.

"When your grandmother fought the Obsidian King, the Mages of the Light opened a doorway to the abyss, so that Bava K'aa could drive him into the void, and he would be trapped in the abyss forever."

"But she didn't."

"No. Because of her love for Lemuel, for the mage whose body the Obsidian King possessed, Bava K'aa could not bring herself to destroy the orb. That orb is what you call Soulcatcher. Bava K'aa gave it to the sons of Dark Haven—the *vayash moru*—to guard. The currents of magic run strong below Dark Haven, and the Flow runs through the foundation of the great house itself. So the Obsidian King remained trapped in the orb, in Soulcatcher, on the edge of the Abyss all these years, waiting to be freed."

"Then Kait's spirit is in the orb, for the Obsidian King to feed on when he breaks free?" Tris asked, the horror of it dawning on him as he framed the words. "The spirits he's trapped in there with him, he's going to feed on them to get the power he needs—"

"To make the transfer," Royster finished. "Yes. That is why you must reach Margolan before the Hawthorn Moon. The Obsidian King was bound on the night of the Hawthorn Moon, and only on that night can he be set free. And may the Lady go with you."

CHAPTER EIGHT

"Go on and have your fun—we'll hold the border." Harrtuck grinned and slugged Soterius in the shoulder. As the time came closer for Soterius and Mikhail to leave Principality, Harrtuck moved the mercenary companies to the Principality border. The refugee fighters and the professional soldiers regarded each other warily. But Soterius's stories of fighting the *ashtenerath* fighters had been enough to get the interest of the mercenaries, who doubled their evening guard.

"Just wait to open the new casks of beer until we get back!" Soterius rejoined, making an effort to cover his apprehension.

"Once the *ashtenerath* showed up, Staden's council certainly didn't mind deploying the mercs along the border." Harrtuck said, with a nod toward the mercenaries who were now camped between the refugee settlement and the Principality border.

"I'm still hoping we don't need your troops to move onto Margolan soil," Soterius said.

Harrtuck quickly sobered. "I'm with you, m'boy. If those fighters of yours kick ass they way you say they will, then I've got a cozy job coordinating the merc commanders. While Jared's expecting an attack, we'll keep his troops from 'wandering' into Principality territory."

They both knew the other half of the "if." If Soterius did not succeed in raising a large enough band of strike-and-hide fighters from among the deserters and discontented in Margolan, then it would be up to the mercs to engage Jared's army, and the effort to put Tris Drayke on the Margolan throne would move from stealth attack to open war. Should the Principality mercs be needed, Soterius knew that Isencroft would also deploy its troops, now held in readiness along its border. Dhasson, bottled up by Arontala's magicked beasts for months, had its own reasons to wage war against Jared the Usurper should the beasts be dispelled. Eastmark was unlikely to remain neutral when Kiara was the niece of Eastmark's king, daughter to his favorite sister. Nargi and Trevath were likely to enter any war as Margolan's allies. If the gambit to destroy Arontala and depose Jared by stealth failed, the alternative was war—and the specter of unrestrained blood magic through the power of a reborn Obsidian King.

In the two weeks since the last strike, Soterius had trained his refugee fighters hard. Tadrie and Sahila had recounted the attack of the *ashtenerath*. After all they had witnessed of the murders and atrocities committed by Jared's troops, the refugees believed

Sahila's account of the *ashtenerath* without question, and with less terror than Soterius expected. Esme backed up Sahila's story, and when the healer was through explaining how Arontala created his *ashtenerath*, the shift in the refugees' attitude was palpable. Through their tears and grief at the thought of missing loved ones being tortured and altered into beast-like weapons, Soterius had felt a hardening of purpose. Almost overnight, the refugee camp became a base camp for the war. Any men healthy enough to train—as well as the strongest and most fit women—came forward to add to the numbers of Soterius's fighters.

The rest of the camp organized itself with the help of Sahila's and Tadrie's wives. The two women, already leaders among the refugees, used their skills to marshal the refugees. Old women and children mended the armor, tents, and packs Sahila purchased from the mercs. Others sewed the black tunics, trews, and cloaks that would provide camouflage. Blacksmiths set to honing the blades of sickles and knives, or to producing hundreds of razor-sharp arrowheads. Boys too young to fight made arrows, filling quiver after quiver, or willingly stuffing and restuffing the targets that the fighters-in-training used in their dawn-to-dusk training.

"As strange as this sounds, I think this has been good for the camp," Harrtuck observed, looking over the bustling tent city of refugees. "Look at them—they've got a purpose. They're not waiting to die, the way they were when we got here. By the Whore! All but the suckling babes have something useful to do—and the hope of going home. That's no small gift you've given them, Ban."

"If it's a gift, it's a bitter one. We've got to keep a full scale war from happening, Tov. I've no desire to see your merc army waging war on Margolan soil."

"Aye, you're right there," Harrtuck agreed. "I'm happy as anyone to be the back-up plan. And I hope to the Lover and Whore that we're not needed to step foot across the border. On the other hand, many a barroom brawl's been prevented by having the biggest, burliest guards stand where everyone can see them. That's something I've seen with my own eyes!"

Soterius grimaced. "You and Vahanian. Spare me the details. My question is: now that they're paid for and outfitted, can you keep your mercs from spoiling for a fight?"

Harrtuck nodded. "Principality mercs are the best disciplined, best led mercenaries in the Winter Kingdoms. Nothing like the moth-eaten vermin you'll find elsewhere. Several of the commanders are from Margolan themselves, and no small number of the troops. They're taking this personally.

"Hell, I found a couple of the men Vahanian and I fought with ten years ago who have managed to keep their heads on their shoulders and the rest of themselves in one piece. Didn't hurt that they remembered Jonmarc and knew what happened at Chauvrenne. He's a bit of a legend in some quarters. So having Jonmarc on our side won us points.

"The mercs who knew us then are commanders now, every bit as sharp as you'll find in the armies of the Winter Kingdoms, and sharper than a few generals, I'd wager. They understand the stakes. You won't have any problems with them."

Soterius couldn't resist a grin as he looked at his old friend. Harrtuck was trimmer than he'd been in years, having lost some of the girth that came from too much ale and a comfortable palace job. He was dressed like the mercs in a quasi-uniform of wool, but where each merc company's heavy cloak bore its insignia on the shoulders, Harrtuck's sported Tris's coat of arms, the insignia of Bricen's second son, and now, the mark of the Margolan rebellion.

"Ready to start the night's work?" Sahila and Tadrie joined them, and down the hillside, Soterius could see the rest of his fighters finishing their preparations.

"More than ready," Soterius replied, and knew that it was true. Despite the stakes, he loved the work of soldiering, and the physical exertion of the task at hand kept him from brooding overmuch about the future.

"Keep a lantern lit for us," Soterius joked, slapping Harrtuck on the shoulder.

"Aye, and a warm mug of ale, too!" Harrtuck replied. He grew serious. "The Lady's hand be on you tonight, Ban."

Soterius nodded. "We'll need the luck of all eight of the Lady's Faces before we're through."

THEY SET OUT two candlemarks later, in the light of the waning afternoon sun. Mikhail would meet them at sunset, at the inn that was the rendezvous point for their contact. Soterius and Sahila rode in front. Tadrie, Pell, Tabb, and Andras each rode with their pods of four fighters. Under their cloaks they wore the leather armor Sahila had bought from the merc units. Each man carried a sword or a battle axe, but after the encounter with the *ashten-erath*, Soterius had insisted on more distance weapons. So the men now also carried an assortment of crossbows and long bows, bolos, and heavy-duty sling shots.

"Who's this contact of yours at the inn?" Soterius asked Sahila as they rode.

"Alle's from Margolan," Sahila said. "Came east following the rumor that Prince Martris had survived, dead-set on joining up with a rebellion. Brought out a group of bards when Jared tried to kill them. The story I heard said Alle slit a couple of guards' throats when the group was ambushed. Won't say a word about family, but I'm guessing there's some blue blood, wrong side of the blanket or not. Joined up with Lemus, the tavern-keeper. The innkeeper's been running a regular ghost carriage for the last several months."

"Ghost carriage?"

"It's a Nargi term." Mikhail's appearance, moments after the sun set, startled them all with its suddenness. "In Nargi, the Crone's priests persecute and destroy any who get in their way, or who stray from their idea of 'purity.' Those with a gift for magic, or for music or art, can find themselves taken for the Crone's service or dead. Worse if they're found to be *vayash moru*, or any of the other things that the priests have decided for the Lady should not exist," he said with distaste.

"Over the years, brave souls have taken it upon themselves to spirit away as many of the persecuted as they can save. It's only a fraction of the ones who are imprisoned or die, but it's a remnant at least. They operate in secret, using false names, hiding their identities even from each other. It's said that they have way stations all across Nargi, inns and caves and farmers who look the other way. And so a lucky few disappear from under the noses of their persecutors, as if they stepped aboard a ghost carriage and vanished into thin air." Mikhail smiled. "It's another case where the Blood Council chooses to stick to the letter of the truce and not mind the small details. And more than one of the Blood Council has been known to fund such things privately."

"So this Alle is helping the fighters?" Soterius asked.

"Alle is one of our best spies," Sahila said with a grin. "Overhears plenty from the troops that like to get their ale at the tavern. Never supplies a bad bit of information."

It was barely a half-candlemark's ride to the inn. Tadrie and the others secured their horses in a barn behind the inn rather than in the stable to stay beyond the prying eyes of guests. Sahila and Soterius scouted both the stable and the front of the inn before they approached the tavern's back door. They could hear raucous singing in the front room, and the smell of venison and potato pies carried on the cold winter air.

Cautiously, Soterius and Sahila approached the back door. Soterius knew that Mikhail watched from the nearby shadows, ready should there be trouble. Sahila gave a coded rap on the door, three quick knocks and two slower knocks. The door opened, and a blonde barmaid stood framed in the light. She motioned them inside quickly.

"We're looking for Alle," Soterius said.

Sahila and the barmaid began to laugh. "You've found me," the barmaid said. She was close to Soterius's age, with a figure that Soterius did not doubt guaranteed her good tips from the inn's male patrons. Her blouse was low-cut, offering a tantalizing view of an ample bosom, and her full skirt fell just to the calf above low-heeled leather boots. She had shoulder-length dark blonde hair framing a pleasant face, and Soterius allowed that she might be quite pretty if she cleaned up from the sweat and stains of the kitchen. He looked at her blue eyes, and paused. There was something almost familiar about Alle's face, but whatever association he could make flitted at the edge of his memory and was gone.

"You're Alle?" Soterius asked as Sahila and Alle continued to laugh.

"Alyssandra," she replied, tossing back her hair. "Alle for short."

Alle gave Sahila a peck on the cheek in greeting and Sahila elbowed Soterius. "Now you see what I meant about being our best spy. A few beers, and most men will tell Alle anything as long as she keeps on smiling!"

Alle sobered and looked to Sahila. "You've got your fighters in the barn?"

"Just as we planned."

Alle nodded. "Let's go then." She reached for a cloak from a peg near the doorway.

Soterius looked from Alle to Sahila. "She's going to lead us to the target?"

In one smooth movement, Alle wheeled, and Soterius found the business edge of a large knife close to his throat. "My home's been burned. My friends are dead. I slit the throats of two of the king's guardsmen the night I brought the bards from Palace City. And every night, I keep the drunks at the bar from getting what they think they're entitled to. I can handle myself."

Soterius raised both hands. "Calm down. I get the point. Let's go."

It seemed to Soterius that both Sahila and Alle were still chuckling as Alle led them back to the barn where the others waited. Covered by the heavy cloak and hood, Alle was less of a distraction for the fighters, who stood aside when she told them to move away from a corner of the barn and directed two of the men to lift away a heavy stone slab that covered a dark entrance leading down into the ground.

Sahila lit a lantern and gave it to Alle, who partially shuttered it to dim the light. "Follow me," she said, descending the wooden stairs.

The men followed her in their marching order. Mikhail brought up the rear, pausing only to move the heavy stone back into place.

"Where are we?" Soterius whispered.

"Caves beneath the barn," Alle replied without glancing backward. "The barn's pretty old. We figure that the settlers found the caves to hide from raiders. Since then, they've been used by smugglers, bootleggers, you name it." She flashed a conspiratorial grin. "Useful thing to have."

The caves were bitterly cold, and icicles glistened along the cave walls in the dim light of the lantern. The trail through the cave was well-worn, broad enough in most places for two men to walk abreast, and in some places, opening into larger rooms of inky darkness. In the distance, water dripped. From time to time, something skittered past their boots, and Soterius had the distinct impression that something—or someone—was watching them.

"Careful," Mikhail warned, his *vayash moru* senses serving him well in the dark. "There are sheer drops not far on either side—I wouldn't like to bet on how far down they go."

Soterius's fighters stayed close together, following the path. After about half a candlemark, Alle stopped.

"It's safer to cross the caves than to go through the forest at night," Alle said. "We have an arrangement with the local *vayash moru*. They keep the caves free from squatters and wild things, and they can take refuge here any time they want."

"A reasonable bargain," Mikhail replied. "That explains why the *vayash moru* we passed didn't try to stop us."

"When we come up to the surface you'll be in the foothills, behind some trees. Just beyond the tree line is a camp. I scouted it earlier today. There are twenty-five Margolan soldiers, plus captives. We think they're the ones who looted a village about a day's ride from here. Burned most of the houses, ran off the livestock, and killed the villagers who wouldn't run. From the sound of it, they've taken a couple of the village girls with them."

"*Ashtenerath*?" Soterius asked.

Alle paused. "We found half a dozen of those things dead in the village. Haven't seen any in the camp since."

"Fair enough," Soterius said. "What about getting back?"

"I'll wait here," Alle said. "Can't be any more miserable than scouting them earlier." She looked sideways at Soterius as if she anticipated an objection. "Don't worry—I won't try to be a hero. You can do all the fighting. I stashed some bandages and supplies when I came earlier. Just get your wounded back here."

Soterius was impressed by Alle's matter-of-fact manner. "We'll do our best not to need them."

He turned, and Alle grabbed his arm. "Bring the village girls with you," she said. "We've got a couple of healers standing by back at the inn. If they're still alive, they've got nowhere else to go."

Soterius exchanged glances with Sahila. "That's a big 'if,'" he said. "But if they're alive, you have my word we'll get them out of there."

"Then the Lady go with you," Alle murmured. She gestured for silence and led them around a bend, shuttering the lantern completely as moonlight lit the mouth of the cave. Alle stood aside, motioning for Soterius and Sahila to pass, melting into the shadows.

Mikhail made a quick scouting foray, moving silently down through the trees along one side of the camp. The soldiers had found a small clearing, far enough from the road not to be bothered. It was bitterly cold, and Soterius's breath steamed in the night air. He was glad for his heavy woolen uniform and an equally heavy cloak, and wished for the milder weather of the Margolan plains. He glanced at his fighters. The professionals—Pell, Tabb, Andras, and Sahila—had an expression of anticipation, but did not look fearful. The refugee-fighters were doing their best to hide their fear. They looked grimly resolute, firmly gripping their weapons. Within a quarter candlemark, Mikhail had returned. Soterius knew that the *vayash moru* not only moved more silently than a human scout, but could complete his mission without leaving foot-prints in the snow.

"It's as Alle said," Mikhail reported in a whisper. "Two dozen soldiers, plus some horses. I didn't see any *ashtenerath*, and I couldn't smell any, either. Wouldn't be surprised if they can only deploy those once—how do you get them back in the box wagon?" He paused. "I found the bodies of three of their captives in the latrine trench. We may be too late for a rescue."

"All the more reason to kill the bastards," Sahila murmured.

"If there are any captives left, they're in the far tent, over there," Mikhail added.

"Get them out and bring them here, then come join the party," Soterius instructed. Mikhail nodded, and disappeared into the night.

Soterius gestured, and the fighters spread out to find their assigned positions. Whether or not there were *ashtenerath*, Soterius had decided that striking first and hard from a distance was the best way to reduce his casualties, and so swords and axes were sheathed in favor of the bows and thrown weapons. Soterius heard the owl call that was Mikhail's signal. The soldier on night watch was dead.

"Let's go!" Soterius whispered, giving his own signal, a creditable imitation of a wolf's cry.

Before the echo of the howl faded, arrows rained down on the camp. The long bows and slingshots picked off panicked soldiers, while flaming arrows set tents ablaze and forced their residents to run, half-clad and unarmored into the snowy night.

Soldiers who veered too close to the forest fell to the crossbows, or heard the 'snick' of flying bolos around their neck. Soterius watched his fighters with pride. Swords were unfamiliar to farmers and herdsmen, but these men had used bows and sling-shots all their lives to hunt vermin, and bolos to round up errant herds. Striking from the cover of the forest, Soterius's fighters exacted a hefty price before ever showing their faces. Instead, they echoed Soterius's wolf cry, until the moonlit clearing rang with the eerie call of the predator.

"Ghost fighters!" one of the hapless soldiers cried, trying to pull his pants up as he ran, fleeing his burning tent.

The captain of the fighters had been drinking with his men around the fire when the attack began. He called for order as his panicked troops fell, with arrows piercing their chests or bolos straps strangling their throats. Half of his men rallied to him, falling into a defensive formation, swords ready.

"Now! Soterius cried. His best hand-to-hand fighters slung their bows and hefted their swords or axes, running from the darkness of the forest as they shrieked a battle cry.

"Demons! *Ashtenerath*!" Soterius's fighters waded into the fray. Spurred on by their anger over the lost village and the dead girls, the refugee-fighters fought like the blood rage was upon them, giving no quarter and needing none. Any soldier who ran for the forest was met with a deadly hail of arrows, or was sure to encounter Mikhail once he reached the darker shadows beneath the trees.

The Margolan captain and a handful of his soldiers held their positions, launching themselves at their attackers with desperation born of mortal fear. They set about with their swords, still sober enough to stay toward the center of the camp, furthest from the archers.

Close enough now to see the Margolan captain's face, Soterius startled with recognition. "Aeron," he hissed. The captain's head jerked up. For an instant, their eyes met; Aeron recognized him as well.

"The captain is mine!" Soterius headed at a dead run, sword raised, for the Margolan leader.

Aeron's face twisted into a sneer as he met the attack, and their swords clanged loudly as they parried. All of Soterius's anger and frustration found an outlet in his sword. He no longer felt the cold of the bitter night.

"Soterius!" Aeron made the name a curse. "Traitor! What kind of brigand are you?"

"Prince Martris's brigand!" Soterius wheeled to parry one of Aeron's wild strikes. Aeron had been drinking. The ale made his strikes less predictable, but the random blows delivered at full strength were as dangerous as any planned attack.

"Your girlfriend's dead." Aeron dealt a sideways blow that almost got inside Soterius's guard. "Took her to King Jared myself."

Soterius set his jaw, focusing all his skill on besting Aeron. He scored a deep gash on Aeron's thigh, and the tip of Aeron's sword opened up a cut on Soterius's forearm. Aeron dropped and rolled, slicing low, a street move Soterius knew wasn't taught in the army salle. Vahanian's training served Soterius well. He evaded the blade, anticipating

Aeron's momentum and delivering another deep cut, this time to Aeron's thigh. Limping, Aeron made it back to his feet. Blood coursed down his leg. Soterius closed for the kill, his sword ready. He brought his sword down two-handed, and the blow shattered Aeron's blade, knocking him off balance. With one forward thrust, Soterius sank his blade deep into Aeron's chest, feeling it scrape against bone and then slide free out the other side of the soldier's body.

"That's for Lila," Soterius said with a brutal twist of the blade. Aeron's mouth opened as if to reply, but nothing sounded except a bloody gurgle. The Margolan captain was dead.

Soterius wiped his blade clean on the snow and looked around. In the light of the burning tents, he could see bodies in the snow. The camp was quiet. The snow was trampled and blood stained. Sahila and Pell moved through the camp, counting the dead. Tabb and Tadrie set the surviving fighters to stripping the soldiers of anything useful. Andras sprinted toward him.

"Report."

"Got them all, sir. Mikhail took out two that ran for the forest, and the archers got about half. We finished the rest."

Soterius nodded. "Captives?"

"One girl. She's in pretty bad shape. Mikhail took her to the cave entrance."

"Casualties?"

"Better than last time, sir." It was Pell who answered, with Sahila a few steps behind him. "Two with serious wounds, a few more with minor injuries, none dead."

"I found this in the captain's tent," Tabb reported, as he and Tadrie lugged two burlap sacks behind them. Soterius knew at a glance where the Margolan captain had acquired such a collection of odd coins, jewelry and small trinkets.

"Spoils from the village they looted." Soterius felt his anger rise once more. "Bring it. We'll use it for provisions for the refugee camp. Since we can't return it, it's as close to recompense as we can make." Tabb and Tadrie nodded soberly, tying off the bags and slinging them across their shoulders.

The refugee-fighters scoured the camp, bundling up the dead soldiers' cloaks and weapons. Distasteful as looting the dead would be under normal circumstances, Soterius had seen the conditions in the refugee camps. Even the gold that Tris and Staden had sent would not fully tend to the needs of so large a crowd. This time, there were horses to gather as well.

"At this rate, we're going to need storehouses and stables," Soterius said under his breath to Sahila, who clapped him on the back.

"A good problem to have!" Sahila said with a sharp laugh. "You'll need both horses and weapons if you mean to ride to Shekerishet."

"True enough."

Alle was waiting for them at the entrance to the cave, tending to a battered girl who looked just a few years younger than Soterius. The girl's bruises and torn clothing left no question as to the soldiers' actions, and when her dark eyes met Soterius's he saw pain verging on madness. Any guilt he felt about the raid on his own colors died at the look in the girl's eyes.

"Can she walk?" Alle shook her head.

"I'll carry her." Tadrie stepped up. He was old enough to be the girl's father, and he squatted down to look her in the eyes. "You've nothing to fear from me; I've a daughter of my own. Will you let me help you?" He held out one of the pilfered cloaks, and Alle helped the girl wrap it around herself.

The girl paused for a moment, but her injuries won out over her fear, and she nodded. Gently, Tadrie lifted the girl into his arms. Behind him, Alle murmured a string of curses, angry at the abuse the girl had taken at the hands of the Margolan soldiers.

Soterius, Alle, and Sahila field-dressed the worst of the injured fighters' wounds. One man had taken a bad cut to the bone on his forearm and a deep shoulder gash. Another was limping badly from a sword stroke that had sliced his hip and thigh. The other injuries required only splints or minor bandaging.

"There're healers at the inn. We figured someone would need them," Alle said, finishing up the bandaging.

"I'd better stay with the horses." Mikhail's voice broke Soterius from his dark thoughts. "They're too valuable to drive off, and if we leave them here, they wolves will get them."

"Lemus is the innkeeper," Alle said. "He can send his hired men back in the morning to help with the horses. If you stay up here near the caves, you'll have shelter before dawn comes, and Lemus's men can be here at first light."

"Much obliged, m'lady." In the moonlight, Soterius could see that his friend's complexion was almost ruddy, a testimony that he had fed well on the soldiers who had run for the forest.

Alle lit the lantern and led them back through the twisting cavern passages. The caves seemed even colder than when they had set out, and Soterius's hands and feet were numb.

It took two men to lift the stone slab that hid the entrance to the passageway. The barn, warmed by the horses that waited there and sheltered from the wind, was a haven from the brutal cold outside. When the last of the soldiers had climbed from the passageway and the slab was again in place, Alle stood with her hands on her hips and looked at the group.

"There's not room for all of you in the inn, so Lemus said he'd send out blankets. We'll take the girl and the worst injuries inside for the healers, and I'll send a boy out with some warm food and ale. Mind that you stay quiet. We don't use this barn for customers, but the inn still gets some guardsmen, and you don't need their attention!"

Sahila stayed with the men in the barn while Tadrie, still carrying the injured girl, followed Alle into the inn. Soterius helped the fighter with the leg wound, while the other refugee, gingerly supporting his injured arm with his good hand, declined help.

Lemus met them in the kitchen. He was a short man with the look of a clerk, whose long face and brown eyes appeared guileless. A perfect spy, Soterius thought.

"And?" Lemus asked.

"A rout!" Alle grinned. She slipped out of her cloak and ran a hand through her long hair. "Need a room for this one," she said with a nod toward the girl Tadrie carried. "She was the only one they could save from the captives. Have a couple of other injuries to tend, too," she indicated with a glance toward the wounded fighters.

Lemus nodded. "Take the back stairs. I kept the third room on the left for you. Keep your head down. We've got a couple of Margolan guardsmen in the common room tonight, and one of them took a room upstairs for the night."

"Lovely," Soterius murmured.

Alle went ahead to scout the hallway; the others moved as quietly as they could up the back stairs. She checked to make sure their room was empty, and then waved them on. Inside the room, Tadrie set the girl down on the bed. With a whimper, the girl curled into a ball, wrapping her arms around her knees. Tadrie took a blanket from a peg on the wall and gently tucked it around her. The two wounded soldiers found seats on a chair and a bench. Alle lit two lanterns and then she smoothed down her skirts and straightened her hair.

"I'll send the healers right up. And I'll bring up some stew and ale. I'd best go have a look at who's in the common room, so that we don't have problems later. Wait here. Don't go wandering around."

"I'm too cold to wander anywhere." Soterius leaned back against the wall and ran his hands up and down his arms to warm himself. Despite his heavy cloak he was chilled through. It would take time, even in the warm inn, for him to feel comfortable again.

"Aye, everyone but Mikhail was feeling the wind tonight, I wager!" Tadrie replied.

Alle returned before long with a thin, hawk-faced woman, a pot of stew, and a pitcher of ale. Tucked

into her belt was a large napkin filled with hard
rolls. Alle laid the food on the small table as the
hawk-faced woman looked at the girl and the two
injured men.

"This is our healer, Kae. She'll take good care of
your folks. Help yourself to the food—it's warm.
Lemus has sent more of the same out to the barn,
so your men should be warming up!"

Kae quickly triaged the wounded, and started on
the two soldiers first. Alle motioned for Soterius to
step to the side.

"The Margolan guardsmen downstairs," she
whispered. "I don't like the look of them. Lemus
says they've been throwing their weight around,
bullying the servers and threatening some of the
customers. They've taken a room for the night, just
a few doors down. Keep your head down—the
older one talks like he's spent time at Shekerishet.
You don't need to be recognized."

Soterius looked at her, startled. "Oh, I know who
you are, Ban Soterius. Captain of Bricen's guard.
And I'll wager I wouldn't be the only one. No one's
where they're supposed to be these days. And even
fewer are who they pretend to be. That beard's not
much of a disguise."

Alle moved to help Kae with the healing, dutiful-
ly fetching hot water and whatever ingredients the
healer needed for her poultices. Soterius tore strips
of cloth for bandages from a clean sheet Alle thrust
into his hands. Tadrie stayed close to the village
girl, talking to her in low, reassuring tones, like a
father with a sick child. Soterius guessed that
Tadrie's wife would find herself with a new charge
once the girl was well enough to travel.

After a couple of candlemarks, Kae finished her healing. The wounded fighters rested on pallets on the floor. After much coaxing and reassuring, the wounded girl permitted the healer to tend her wounds, and drank a mixture of herbs and warm wine that guaranteed her a peaceful sleep. When Kae finished, she washed her hands in the basin Alle provided and looked from Alle to Soterius.

"I've been to the village that girl came from," Kae said sadly. "They were honest tradesfolk. They did nothing to deserve what happened to them. What she's been through... I've healed her body, made sure she wasn't with child, but there are scars I can't fix. She needs a mind healer." Kae's hand tightened to a white-knuckled fist and shook against her skirt. "I'm glad you killed the ones that did that to her—saves me from breaking my healers' vows."

"I killed their captain myself," Soterius assured her. "He had it coming."

"I'll be back to check on them before dawn. They should all sleep well tonight, and feel no pain," Kae looked back at her three charges. "On the other hand, they're in no shape to flee if we get raided tonight."

"I'll stand guard," Tadrie volunteered, patting the pommel of his sword.

"Come downstairs with me," Alle said to Soterius. "Lemus has information for you from what he's heard in the common room the last few nights."

They were halfway down the narrow hallway when a loud voice sounded on the front stairs. The speaker was well into his ale.

"Margolan officer!" Alle hissed. The door behind her was locked, and they were too far from the back stairs to run without being caught. As the footsteps approached the top of the stairs, Alle fell backward against the wall, grabbing a handful of Soterius's shirt and pulling hard against him. He lost his balance, bracing himself against the wall with one hand on either side of her shoulders. Alle reached up and pulled his head down, crushing his lips against hers. Her leg slid up and wrapped around his hip. She gave a shrug, letting her blouse fall provocatively from one shoulder.

"Someone's lucky tonight!" the drunken man chortled as he and his companion started down the hallway. "How about coming to see us when you're finished?"

Alle thrust out her hand, rubbing her fingers together as if to ask for coin.

"Poxy whore!" the man's companion spat as they shoved past. The two made ribald remarks, laughing at their own jokes, until they reached their room at the end of the hall and the door closed behind them.

Alle pushed Soterius away, straightened her blouse, and smoothed her skirt. "Don't let it go to your head," she warned, and then flashed him a wicked grin. "I figured it was better than killing them and having to clean up the blood. And we've all got to make sacrifices for the war—right?"

Soterius gave her a sour look that made her laugh. "C'mon. Lemus is waiting."

After another candlemark in the kitchen, Soterius was finally warm once more. His mind buzzed with the bits of information Lemus shared: overheard troop movements, rumors about Jared's interest in an alliance with Nargi, and unsettling tales about soldiers in the cities sent to round up and eliminate dissenters. It was almost dawn when Soterius finally made his way back to the barn, and while he thought he might be too full of thoughts and worries to rest, exhaustion won out, and sleep found him quickly.

CHAPTER NINE

STADEN GAVE HIS whole-hearted permission for Tris to set up a Court of Spirits in the weeks before Winterstide. Word spread quickly, and Tris was aghast to see how many petitioners, living, dead, and undead, lined up to receive the blessing of the first Summoner to pass through the kingdom in years. Tris began the Court of Spirits just a few days after he returned from the citadel. Within a week, the court was so crowded that Tris could not see all of the petitioners in a single day. Many camped outside the palace wherever the guards would permit, awaiting their place in line. As Winterstide grew closer, both petitioners and spirits seemed to be filled with a new urgency to make things right before the solstice. Staden often watched from the back of the great room, shaking his head in awe at Tris's ability to intercede between the living and the dead.

Inside the great hall, many of the revenants could not be seen by anyone except Tris. These spirits lacked the power to show themselves except on the night of the Feast of the Departed—"Haunts" as it was called. Other, stronger spirits made themselves visible throughout the year. The people of the Winter Kingdoms expected their loved ones to remain with them after death. In Margolan, most households set out a plate with a token amount of food at the evening meal, inviting their departed loved ones to join them. Some of the more devout households even had a "spirit room," a small box with miniature furnishings and tiny replicas of personal items to entice family spirits to dwell alongside them in comfort and respect.

In the Winter Kingdoms, living with the dead was a daily occurrence; most gave it no more thought than they gave to fixing their meals or minding their trade. Ghosts and the undead were a part of life, though it rapidly became apparent to Tris that many of life's complications and tangled relationships extended even beyond death.

Women came to seek the favor of a departed mother or grandmother for advice. Husbands, sons, and brothers sought to make peace, beg forgiveness, or have a troubling spirit banished. Ghosts asked Tris to bear messages to their families, or carry word of some important thing left unsaid before the spirit's death. Restless spirits sought redress and the help of a Summoner to make the final passage to the Lady. Even *vayash moru* came, seeking the spirit of someone from their mortal past. Living, dead, and undead, they filled the audience chamber and the hallway beyond, waiting for Tris's help.

It was a good thing that most spirits did not require the intervention of a Summoner to pass over, Tris thought. Most of the time, only those souls who wished to stay or were bound by tragedy or the guilt of the living remained behind. Among the living, those without an urgent need were content to wait until Haunts to communicate with the dead. Most made offerings of ale and honey cakes around the small altar kept in every home, no matter how poor. Tris knew that the petitioners who were willing to wait for days to see him now were desperate in their need for reconciliation.

The next petitioner stepped forward, a man who was very much alive. He was in his middle years, with work-worn hands. Despite his weathered appearance, the man had a plain dignity about him as he tugged uncomfortably at his home-spun coat. "Your Highness," he said awkwardly, attempting a deep bow.

"What is your need?"

"My name is Kelse, and I'm a freeman. My family owns a bit of ground a day's ride from the palace. Please, sire, I need to speak to the ghost of my father."

"And what is it you seek?" As the man spoke, Tris extended his mage sense, trying to gain not only the measure of the man, but also to sense whether any spirits lingered near him.

"My father was a cautious man. He put away some coins in a safe place, against a bad year. He was also a stubborn man. Last year, during the troubles—" Kelse's voice caught. He took a moment to compose himself. "Last year, during the rains, our village flooded. Father died. We managed to save some of the barn and all of the livestock, but our planting stock is gone, and there's naught to replace it. I need to find those coins," he begged. "I've looked everywhere. Please, sire. I've nothing to feed my family with. If I can't find the coins I'll have to sharecrop, and I swore to my father I'd never be any man's servant."

As Tris stretched out his senses, he felt the tug of a spirit, and used his magic to enable the spirit to travel to him. Tris reached out his hand to where the farmer stood and concentrated on the dim pulse of the wraith, focusing his power to bring it closer and make it visible. Kelse gasped and Tris knew that he had succeeded.

There in front of him stood a thin man with a set jaw and a hard-bitten glint in his eye. Kelse sank to his knees, sobbing. "Your son wishes to ask for your help," Tris said to the apparition. The old man's ghost looked from Tris to his son.

"I'm sorry, Kelse. I should have told you long ago, but I was always afraid someone would fritter it away." The ghost's voice was distant. Kelse lifted his head, silent as the tears streaked down his cheeks. "Take the logs out of the fireplace. Sit where the logs would be, face the hearth, and lift a candle up above your head. There is a ledge above the fireplace opening. Reach all the way to the back. You'll find five pieces of gold. It's all I had. The Lady bless you, son. I didn't plan to leave you like this."

"I know, father. I know." Kelse rocked back and forth in his grief. "Thank you," he whispered, both to Tris and to the ghost. "Thank you."

Tris turned toward the old man's ghost. "Would you go to your rest now?"

The old man looked at his son, and then back to Tris. "I can do no more to help him," the ghost replied. "And I've worked the fields since I could walk. I'm tired. It's time."

Kelse stood slowly, and took a step toward the wraith. "We didn't get to say goodbye," he said in a strangled voice. "The Goddess bless you, father, and hold you in Her arms." He made the sign of the Lady in blessing.

The ghost turned back toward Tris, who nodded, and began to murmur the passing over ritual. As he spoke the words of power, he felt the threshold open, although no one else but the old man's spirit could see it. In the distance, Tris heard a voice; the words were beyond his grasp but the sweetness pulled at his soul. He closed his eyes and felt, not saw, as the old man turned toward that voice and squared his shoulders, crossing the threshold. When Tris opened his eyes again he found Kelse staring, wide-eyed, at the place where the apparition had been.

"Thank you, Your Highness." Kelse backed away, still bowing in respect as one of the bailiffs led him to the door.

Carroway and Royster showed up at lunchtime bearing a plate of cheese and meat for Tris, and pitchers of warm ale. The two retreated to seats near the back of the room, and Royster withdrew a leather volume from the folds of his heavy robes.

"What brings you here?" Tris was glad for a momentary reprieve.

Carroway grinned. "When we heard what was happening, we didn't want to miss it."

"As I've told you, your grandmother didn't have a decent chronicler in the lot," Royster said. "We intend to fix that. I've already begun your history—I'm calling it the *Chronicles of the Necromancer.* Catchy, isn't it?"

"And since music travels faster than the wind, I figured that I'd get the inspiration for some tavern songs, the kind that stirs the ladies to tears and make strong men rise up to arms." Carroway smiled conspiratorially. "Musicians make the best spies."

Tris chuckled. Carroway had always seemed to know what was going on anywhere in the kingdom. Jared viewed traveling bards with distrust; he sought to silence or imprison those he considered a threat. Since most of the farmers and many of the villagers could neither read nor write, song, skit, and story were the most reliable ways to transmit news. Even in matters of faith, the acolytes of the Lady depended on pictures and symbols to share the rudiments of belief. Kings and the Sisterhood and the temple priestesses had their libraries, but most of the people cared only enough about history to share a sense of tribe or have an excuse to hate their enemies, and about faith to find a good luck charm for warding off monsters, real and imagined.

"I'm open to all the help we can get." Tris thought of the ghosts he had seen earlier in the day. "But if you're going to stay, prepare yourselves. The tales aren't always easy to hear."

The next petitioner was a tall, angular woman who smelled of fish. Although she might have been in her third decade, her face was creased from worry, and her eyes were troubled.

"By your leave, m'lord." The woman made an awkward curtsey.

"What is it you seek?" Tris asked.

"My only son is dead a year," she said. "We quarreled over a small matter, but the quarrel became bitter, and my tongue got the best of me. In his despair, he hanged himself." Tears welled in her eyes. "I'd give all I possess to have him back with me."

"That power is not given to me."

"I know that. But if you can summon him, my lord, please—I wish to beg his forgiveness, and to tell him that I love him."

"What is the boy's name?"

"Tabar. His name was Tabar."

Tris took a deep breath and let himself slip into the Plains of Spirit. He called for the ghost of the woman's son, waiting until an answer came. A young man appeared, bearing the red scar of a noose. Tris used a little more magic, and the spirit became visible. For a moment, he thought the woman might swoon. She clutched at her heart and dropped to her knees.

"Forgive me!" she cried, prostrating herself at the ghost's feet. "Tabar, I never meant for our quarrel to go so far. I wish you had put a knife through my heart instead of leaving me this way!"

The young man's ghost stepped toward her and knelt, taking her into his insubstantial arms. "I was foolish and angry," the ghost said. "I didn't mean to die; I wanted to worry you and win my point. When the breath left me and you found my body, I saw your pain. Every day I've been with you, although you couldn't see me. I was wrong—both in the quarrel and for taking my life. I know it can't be undone. I need your forgiveness before I can rest."

The woman reached out to touch the dead boy's face. "I didn't know that you were with me," she said, as tears streaked down her cheeks. "I want you to stay with me, but I know it's wrong to keep you from your rest. I just couldn't let you go without telling you how sorry I am, without saying goodbye." She embraced the spirit, wrapping her arms around the wraith, soaking up one last moment of contact. She moved as if to kiss the boy's forehead, although her lips met only air, and the boy returned the kiss.

"I thank the Lady that you came to us," the woman said to Tris, standing beside the ghost. "M'lord, will you see him across, so that I know he is safe on the other side?"

Tris stretched out his hands and spoke the words of power, feeling the young man's ghost fade before him and grow stronger on the Plains of Spirit. As Tris made the passing over ritual, he felt the ghost's turmoil subside, replaced by a sense of peace, tinged by regret. Then the spirit was gone, and only the woman stood before him. She bowed low.

"Thank you, m'lord," she murmured. "May the Lady favor you."

As he waited for the next petitioner, Tris sipped some of Carina's headache tea. It did little to ease the throbbing behind his eyes that came with candlemarks of using his magic. He could see a line of supplicants that wound out of the room. Those were the living who waited for their chance to speak with the dead. In a room that had become cold even for the season, spirits milled among them, awaiting their turn. Some of the spirits were strong enough to manifest on their own, but many were visible only to Tris, until he acknowledged them and lent them the energy to take form. It had been the same every day since he began to hold court for the spirits, and he was certain that the demand for his help would last until he left Principality.

There was bitter irony in knowing that he could lay to rest everyone's ghosts except his own. While he could intercede on behalf of all of his petitioners, the spirits of his mother and sister remained beyond his reach, trapped in Arontala's orb, in torment.

Tris looked at the desperate faces of those who came to beg his help. For him, the inability to reach Kait and Serae was an aberration, as all the other spirits responded to his call. But Tris knew that for those who came to seek his intercession, the silence was unbearable. Try as he might to distance himself from the emotion of the crowd, his own loss was too fresh for him to be objective. And so he drove himself to exhaustion, giving closure to others that he could not find for himself.

He had seen at least fifty supplicants since morning, and Tris knew he could not go on much longer before he was exhausted. Tris motioned to the bailiff. "Please—close the doors and bid them come again tomorrow. I'll hear this spirit's request, but then I've got to rest."

The spirit who awaited his attention was the ghost of a man in his fifth decade, with the tight-jawed look of a merchant. He bowed when he was brought to stand before Tris. Tris willed for the spirit to become visible to the others in the room, and the man's spirit took form.

"My lord Summoner," he said formally. "A petition, if you will."

"What do you seek?"

"Justice, m'lord," the ghost replied. "I'm Hanre, the silversmith. For twenty years, my partner Yent and I built a profitable business. I did not know that Yent was seducing my wife and that he wanted all the profits of the business for himself. He put poison in my cup, and told the doctors that it was a weak heart when I collapsed at my work bench. Within a few months of my death, Yent married my widow. He stole my life from me. My lord, I beg of you. Let there be justice done!"

Tris stretched out his mage sense, but read no falseness in the spirit's words. He gestured, and one of Staden's guards approached. "Tell your story again to this guard," Tris instructed. Hanre repeated his tale, and the guard listened solemnly.

"Bear the news to King Staden," Tris told the guard. "It's for him to determine how to deal with the murderer. You can witness that you heard the story yourself."

"Yes, Your Highness." The soldier bowed. Hanre watched solemnly as the soldier departed.

"No punishment can return my life," Hanre said sadly. "It grieves me to know that all the work I've done these many years is now to the profit of a murderer!"

Tris blinked, trying to focus. His head was pounding so badly that it was becoming difficult to see. "Would you have me help you make the passage?" he asked Hanre's ghost.

The silversmith shook his head. "Not yet, my lord Summoner. I would stay and see justice be done. Then, perhaps, I can truly rest. Thank you, m'lord. I'm in your debt." The spirit made a deep bow, and departed. Tris signaled to the bailiff to close the doors. He hoped that he could make it up to his rooms before the headache grew any worse.

A HOT BATH and a good supper eased both Tris's headache and the stiff muscles he had from sword practice. He'd wrenched his neck climbing, and he had still not completely recovered from his injuries at the citadel. The warm fire sent him to sleep. He dozed in a chair in his rooms until a sharp knock at the door roused him. A page stood in the hallway.

"Begging your pardon, Lord Wizard," the boy said nervously, "but the king wishes you to meet with him in his sitting room."

"I'm hardly dressed for an audience," he said wearily. "Please give me a few minutes to get ready." Moving as quickly as he could, Tris tried to ignore his headache as he dressed to meet with King Staden. The page waited until Tris emerged. They walked the short distance to the king's doors, and the guards stood to the side to allow Tris to enter.

Staden took in Tris's condition. "How long do you think you can go on like this, before you have nothing left?" Tris gave a courteous bow that made his head pound.

"Just long enough, I guess," Tris replied. With Staden was another man, and Tris frowned, struggling to place the unexpectedly familiar face. The man had white hair and was dressed well without ostentation. His bearing spoke of nobility. Tris finally connected the face with a memory, and he recognized Abelard, Bricen's ambassador to Principality.

Tris stepped forward to shake Abelard's hand, but the older man bowed low. "Greetings, my prince," the ambassador said, accepting Tris's hand as Tris bid him rise. "We thank the Goddess for your safe passage to Principality."

Staden motioned for them sit near the fire. A servant brought them each a mug of warm mulled wine.

"Abelard has been here in Principality City, under my protection, since the coup," said Staden. "With your comings and goings to the Sisterhood, I haven't had the chance to present him before this. I imagine you two have much to discuss," he said, rising. Staden bustled out of the room before either man could reply.

"Is this official business?" Tris watched the older man closely.

Abelard chuckled sadly. "There's been no *official* business since I declined Jared's demand that I return to Shekerishet. Word of the coup reached me just before Jared's orders. I was a friend to your father for many years. I could not serve his murderer. And so I'm an exile, kept by King Staden's kindness, for which I'm grateful."

"What of the other ambassadors?" Tris asked. He sipped at the wine, which eased his pounding headache.

"Much the same. Cattoril is dead. Drawn and quartered, I hear, for his failure to bring Princess Kiara back with him from Isencroft."

"And the others?"

"All, like myself, are in exile. We remain in touch, hoping that there might be some way to serve our homeland, not daring to believe the rumors that you had survived.

"We had no man in Nargi, so from that kingdom I have no news," continued Abelard. "You've met Mikhail, who brings news from my counterpart in Dhasson now that magicked beasts have closed the border."

"The beasts were sent by Arontala to keep me from reaching King Harrol's court."

"That may well be," Abelard said. "I believe Jared's coup was long-planned. From Trevath, I hear little, but the last message gave me pause. Their king is concerned about the events in Margolan, and fears being drawn into war."

"Why?"

"Are you familiar with Lord Curane?"

Tris nodded. Curane held lands on Margolan's southern plains. Bricen had considered Curane self-serving, and of dubious honor.

"Curane's wife is from a powerful family in Trevath, one that wields much influence at court. Trevath's king is concerned that Lord Curane's family ties may compromise Trevath, and bring Jared's army against them."

"Why would Jared care?"

"Because it is said that Curane's granddaughter bears Jared's child."

"By rights, half of Margolan should be Jared's bastards," Tris said dryly. "But if that's true, it bodes darkly for the future."

"Aye, my prince. Although you've more pressing threats to deal with, and there are years before the throne is in danger. The situation will bear watching.

"From Eastmark, King Kalcen is taking a personal interest in Margolan's troubles. Princess Kiara's mother, Viata, was his older sister. So Jared's threat to Viata's daughter is worthy of Kalcen's regard." Abelard smiled knowingly. "Or perhaps, he thinks history might repeat itself."

"How so?"

"A little more than twenty years ago, Donelan of Isencroft met Viata of Eastmark at a court ball, here in Principality. Eastmark does not give its daughters to wed outlanders, but the two fell very much in love. They eloped, keeping their wedding a secret until Viata was with child and the bond was irrevocable.

"Viata's father, the late King Radomar, was furious. Rumor said he planned to take his warships across the Northern Sea and strike at Isencroft from its coast. Then your father stepped in. Margolan, as one of the oldest and most powerful kingdoms, has always been able to be heard among the rulers of the Winter Kingdoms. Bricen didn't want war. He offered a betrothal contract to Donelan, matching the two heirs. His action showed Margolan's support, and King Radomar backed down. There was no war."

"The betrothal contract between Kiara and Jared," Tris murmured. "I wondered how that came to be."

"I have an awkward question, my prince, but one I must ask, with your permission."

"Go on."

"Your interest in Princess Kiara—is it genuine, or is it a calculation to embarrass the usurper?"

Tris felt himself color, and struggled to keep his voice neutral. "I fell in love with Kiara before I knew of the pact. She didn't know who I was when we first met. While I'd die before I'd see Jared touch her, that 'calculation' never came into my thinking."

"So I hoped, and so I believed knowing what I do of you, Prince Drayke. You received King Donelan's recognition as the rightful heir to the Margolan throne. Do you realize that he has, in that recognition, declared you to be Kiara's betrothed by the terms of the covenant?"

Tris's mouth went dry.

Abelard chuckled. "I thought not. That's why your intentions matter. I should hate to see you gain the throne and begin a war."

"If I survive the battle for the throne," Tris replied, regaining his composure, "I hope to ask for Kiara's hand. But there's so much that must happen, between now and then—"

"I understand, my prince. These are your judgments to make. But should you choose to wed in exile, and secure the succession—"

"Out of the question. Kiara intends to accompany me to Margolan. She's an excellent swordswoman, and was sent on her quest by the Oracle herself. To do as you suggest would place her in even greater danger."

Abelard held up a hand. "I meant no disrespect, my prince. Merely an option."

This is exactly why I never wanted to be king, Tris thought. Yet he knew that Abelard would not be alone in wanting a stable line of succession. There would be pressure to produce an heir, especially if there was truth to the rumor about Jared's bastard. Tris had cherished the relative freedom of the road. They had been hunted and in danger for their lives, but these past months had been free from the politics of court. That would end if he succeeded in winning the crown.

"Thank you," he told Abelard, anxious to work though this alone. "You've given me a lot to think about."

"Walk carefully, my prince." Abelard bowed low, leaving Tris alone with the fire and his thoughts.

As THE DAYS grew shorter, Staden's court prepared for Winterstide. While Staden welcomed Tris's participation as Summoner, many at court were curious as to what such participation might add to the feast day. Tris knew that most residents looked forward to a week of revelry.

Carroway was thoroughly enjoying the chance to entertain once more at court. When he was not practicing in the salle, he was rehearsing with the minstrels. His skills gained him the respect of Staden's musicians, who, knowing his stay to be temporary, did not see him as a rival. Carroway commented dryly that perhaps Staden's minstrels eyed his odds of surviving the return to Margolan, taking this opportunity to learn his songs and stories in the event of his untimely demise.

Even Tris couldn't resist the lure of the festivities. Winterstide was a festival of light at the year's darkest month, glittering with candles, stuffed with traditional delicacies, and brimming with ale and merriment. Staden kept the feast in high style; balls and jousts marked the weeks leading up to the feast night itself. In Margolan, Tris had often excused himself early from the revelries, to keep his distance from Jared and the nobles' predatory daughters.

Now, the prospect of accompanying Kiara heightened his interest tremendously.

Tris had to admit that his record with the ladies was every bit the disaster Soterius joked it was. He was realistic enough to know that his title and rank alone would have gotten him almost any young woman he set his eye on. He'd been told often enough that he was handsome, though he privately had his doubts. A few early crushes had gone badly; the girls he'd trusted with his heart had been more interested in becoming a princess than in the particular prince it took to achieve that goal. And then there was Jared.

Jared's reputation for promiscuity was legendary, but beneath that lust ran a fondness for violence. There were too many retainers at the palace eager to cover Jared's indiscretions, either to save Bricen from embarrassment or to court favor with the heir apparent. Perhaps they knew Jared's rages and learned to fear him. Even before the murders of the coup, Tris had formed a loathing for his half-brother. He'd vowed to never take after Jared. So while courtiers bedded each other without a second thought and trysting became the favored sport of the young nobility, Tris held back. It wasn't piety, and it certainly hadn't been for lack of interest. He had no intention of having his heart toyed with, or being a prize for the winning. And while the warmth of a bedmate would have been pleasant, he had no desire to callous his heart to the casual partings.

There had been beautiful girls aplenty at court, though few cared to talk about anything but tiresome gossip, and fewer still could engage in a discussion of ideas, with convictions and opinions of their own. Tris had despaired of ever finding a soulmate. He'd witnessed the loveless marriages at court, the travesties of name and residence that held a tattered mask of propriety over sordid schemes and affairs. Being alone seemed better than that. Kait, knowing that the blows she'd taken at Jared's hand were not uncommon even in noble marriages, had resolved to never marry. Tris often dreamed of the day when he might be permitted to escape the scrutiny of court and move to Bricen's lodge.

Jared's coup ended those plans.

The constant danger of fleeing from Margolan should have pushed any thought of romance from his mind, but Tris never expected his reaction when he met Kiara on the road to Westmarch. Before that night, Tris dismissed love at first sight as one of Carroway's exaggerations. But from the first time he had looked on Kiara, his heart had been forfeit. She was everything he had hoped to find: smart, strong, confident, and able to make her way in her own right. He hadn't cared about her birth or rank, or even that she came from beyond Margolan's borders. All he had wanted was to gain her favor.

Then reality hit. While he might unseat Jared and destroy Arontala, surviving was asking a lot of fate. Worse, there was the old betrothal contract, promising Kiara to the heir to the Margolan throne. He could not bear to think on that, to imagine Kiara given to Jared. He would have been willing to fight Jared to the death just to prevent that from happening, even without so much else at stake. Many a night he'd been unable to sleep, wrestling with the fear that he would not survive to marry Kiara.

He'd underestimated her. Kiara knew enough of war to realize that their gambit to unseat Jared was up against the odds. But it had been impossible to deny the attraction they felt for one another, even though Tris knew he should hold back. Kiara did not seem to care that their romance might cause a scandal, and she shared his loathing for Jared. And so, in the brief sanctuary of their stay in Westmarch, they had declared their love. Nothing about his feelings had changed since then; if anything, the peril at the citadel of the Sisterhood had deepened his resolve. But at the same time, between the dark sending and his own brush with death, Tris was torn, not wanting to cause Kiara pain.

Abelard's revelation forced Tris's hand. While the shift in the betrothal contract removed the scandal from their relationship, declaring their engagement would enrage Jared even more. Tris had no illusions that Jared wanted anything beside Isencroft's lands and satisfaction of his own lust, but he knew his half-brother well enough to be sure that Jared would see their alliance as a challenge. Jared would be merciless in his revenge.

Tris rejected out of hand Abelard's suggestion of a wedding in exile. The phrase "secure the succession" rang of all the things that made him never want the crown. He knew that to be the heir meant to be brokered off like a prize race horse for breeding stock. It was one of the many things he was not looking forward to if he survived to gain the throne. He could not in good conscience put a wife and child in that kind of danger. And so he had not slept all night, arguing with himself over what to do, his heart aching at every option.

Since the conversation with Abelard a few days before, Tris had found no private moment to talk with Kiara. This evening, she lingered after dinner, as Carroway offered a preview of the music for the feast. When the music ended amid enthusiastic applause, Tris noticed that Vahanian offered to walk Carina back to her rooms. Carina had accepted with a blush and a smile.

Tris took Kiara's hand, deliberately falling behind the others. Knowing what he had to say left him dry-mouthed, and he decided that when it came to talk of marriage, both princes and plowboys were alike in finding themselves tongue-tied.

The great hall was garlanded for the feast It was empty for the moment, though the torches and candles that burned warned that its decorators might return before too long to finish their chores.

"You've been quiet," Tris said.

"Just thinking of Isencroft at Winterstide," she said. "It was always my favorite time of the year. I thought father knew how to throw a feast, but I'll admit that Staden puts our feast to shame."

"Kait always loved the falconing trials that came before the feast. Father kept the feast well, and I know Carroway is happy to have a real audience once more." Tris paused. "I've missed you, the weeks I've been at the citadel."

Kiara turned to him, lifting a finger to touch a newly healed scar on his cheek. "Carina won't tell me much about what happened there, but I can see it troubles her. You look so tired. I'm worried about you."

Tris drew her into his arms and kissed her, taking comfort from the moment, enjoying her nearness.

She leaned against him, her arms wrapped around his waist. After a moment, she drew back, looking at him questioningly.

"What's on your mind?"

Tris tangled his fingers in her auburn hair. "I swore to you, back in Westmarch, that if I take the throne, nothing will be required of you—or Isencroft—by force."

Kiara kissed his hand. "I know."

"Abelard says that when your father sent the letter recognizing me as Margolan's rightful heir, that it changed the terms of your betrothal contract." The words just tumbled out. "He says it means that we're already betrothed."

Kiara gasped.

"I love you, Kiara. And I am willingly your betrothed." He swallowed hard. "But I can't—not now, not when it's so unlikely that I'll even live to take the throne. I can't ask you to be bound to me like that. I don't want to hurt you."

Kiara stood completely still. "And that will save my heart? To be betrothed in thought but not in deed?" The same pain that filled his own heart was in her eyes. "The weeks you've been at the citadel—every time I heard footsteps outside in the corridor, I was afraid that Staden was coming to tell me you'd been killed in the training. It's too late. I love you. It has nothing to do with that damned covenant, and it never did. My heart's already bound to you.

"If you... don't take the throne... I won't have time to mourn. Don't you see? I can't—I won't—let Jared use me to gain Isencroft. I've seen what he's done to Margolan. And I swear by the Lady, I won't be captured. So we'll be together—one way or another."

Tris's vision blurred. "Kiara, I—"

"We have this time, these days," she said fiercely. "Father and mother thought they had all the time in the world. They were wrong. Today is all we ever have. It's too late to protect me. We can deny the covenant, we can pretend that what's between us isn't here—but it's not going to spare my heart. I love you, Tris. If these next few months are all we ever have, then so be it. Just don't make me lose you twice."

Her voice was firm, although her whole body was shaking. Tris reached for her and she fell against him, sobbing. He laid his face against her hair, knowing that she saw his own tears. "I didn't dare to hope that you would feel that way," he murmured, stroking her hair, holding her until the shaking stopped. "I want to marry you, Kiara. I want you with me always."

She pulled back far enough to look in his eyes, and she raised a hand to touch his tear-stained cheek. "I accept. And Istra damn the consequences!"

CHAPTER TEN

VAHANIAN FELT HIS spirits rise as the preparations for Winterstide bustled around him at the palace. Principality's Winterstide celebrations were opulent, and Vahanian was impressed despite himself. Carroway had already won an esteemed place among the court musicians and entertainers, letting slip with a wicked smile that he planned to try out a song about their journeys. Vahanian could only hope that his part would be omitted.

His years of smuggling had never made him rich, but they had earned him more than a few enemies. Some of those enemies had the means to settle the score through bounty hunters. Once the struggle to win back the throne in Margolan was over—assuming he survived—Vahanian intended to use some of his reward money from Staden to pay off his remaining debts. He resolved to start fresh with his new holdings in Dark Haven. Between now and then, he was content to keep as low a profile as possible.

Vahanian was also well aware of just how close Principality lay to Eastmark, where he had disastrously crossed paths with Arontala ten years before. Although he had escaped a wrongful court martial and the royal death sentence that claimed his squadron, Vahanian suspected that the death warrant remained on the books. He was unwilling to find out, and leery of providing a target to anyone who thought to claim a bounty by delivering him across the border.

By the eve of Winterstide, Staden's palace was aglow in banks of candles. Velvet and brocade pennants with the four light faces of the Goddess fluttered in the cold night air, and bonfires lit the courtyards. Tempting smells of baking bread and roasting meats wafted from the kitchen, over the scent of mulled wine and warm cider. Before the feast came the day of fasting, from sundown the night before Winterstide through midnight on the evening of the solstice. Staden's court did not neglect the fast in preference for the revelries to come.

While the castle prepared, Vahanian sought out Carina. It was more difficult than he expected. When she was awake, she spent most of her time studying healing lore with Royster. Even with Kiara Carina seemed withdrawn, and Vahanian wondered again about the terms of Tris's training with the Sisterhood.

He had glimpsed Carina in the crowd earlier that evening, when Tris had presided with Staden over the initial rites of the festival. Tris's presence as a Summoner made it possible to acknowledge parts of the liturgy that had gone unspoken and ignored for years, and the crowd was thicker than usual in anticipation. With Tris's help, Staden accepted the fealty of long-departed nobles whose loyalty or desire made them remain near the court. Tris stood with Staden as the king gave a benediction over those who had fallen in battle—no small number given Principality's popularity as a mercenary haven. Thanks to Tris's power, the war dead gained the power to make themselves visible, to receive the blessing of their king and his dismissal, freeing them from their oaths of honor and sending their spirits to rest. Other spirits whose tie to the palace outlasted life itself came to the ceremony, drawn by Tris's power. Staden was shaken to receive the blessing of long-dead members of the royal family, who had chosen to remain and watch over their descendents.

At the tenth bell, a large crowd gathered in the courtyard. Staden had ordered his servants to build a dais, and on the dais there were life-sized statues of the Lady, one for each light Aspect, and on its reverse, its dark face. In the center of the dais was an altar covered with a cloth of midnight blue, decorated in a complex pattern of silver embroidery. Banked high around the large dais were rows of unlit candles. Vahanian waited in the throng, near the front but slightly to the side, out of old habit so that he might have the best view of any approaching trouble. He spotted Kiara in the crowd, and Carroway with the bards. Carina was with Kiara, in the front row. Vahanian wondered if Carina's position was out of reverence, or if she was on hand should Tris collapse from the exertion.

A red carpet defined a walkway through the crowd. Staden sat on a throne in a tall viewing box with the queen and Berry. But here, everyone had come to see the Summoner.

A hush fell over the crowd, and Vahanian turned. Tris stood at the far end of the walkway. He was dressed in gray with a heavy gray cloak, looking the part of a Summoner and, Vahanian had to admit to himself, every inch a king. Tris's long blond hair stirred in the wind as he strode toward the altar on the dais. Slowly, Tris climbed the steps and knelt in front of the altar. Vahanian saw Tris's lips move. The banks of candles burst into flame, lighting the night. From beneath the altar cloth, Tris removed a large honey cake and a tankard of ale, the traditional gifts to the Lady. And, on behalf of the *vayash moru* which were more numerous than usual in this night's crowd, he also set a flagon of goat's blood on the altar.

"Lady of Many Faces, hear me!" Tris began in a voice loud enough for all to hear. "Tonight, the veil is thin between our world and the next. Accept these gifts from your children, the living, the dead, and the undead, and show your favor."

The night seemed to grow even colder. All around Vahanian spirits gathered, far more numerous than before. Many found a place with someone standing in the crowd: an elderly man's ghost next to an old woman, a young mother's ghost beside a harried-looking young man holding a small child. Some of the *vayash moru* stood apart, while others were joined by the spirits. Tris was making it possible this night for the spirits that had chosen to remain with the living to be seen and to take part in the festival. In the crowd,

Vahanian saw a *vayash moru* man who looked to be his own age in mortal years standing with an elderly woman who was very much alive. They were holding hands, and the woman inclined her head against the man's shoulder. Vahanian realized with a start that it was the gesture of a wife, not a mother. He could not look away. If they had been together when the young man was brought across, then decades would have passed, during which the young man remained unchanged and the years did their slow damage to his wife. Vahanian did not realize that Gabriel had slipped up beside him until the *vayash moru* spoke.

"Some of us choose to remain among mortals much longer than others," Gabriel said.

"I just never thought—"

"Here in Principality, and especially in Dark Haven, such things may be done openly. In many other places we must watch over our families from a distance, to protect them from those who fear us."

Vahanian realized that Kiara was no longer alone. The spirit of a beautiful, sad-eyed woman stood with her, a woman whose unmistakable resemblance to Kiara must mean she was the late Queen Viata. With the king stood the spirits of several men, each clad in the formal robes of bygone days, the dead kings of Principality. Vahanian saw Carina startle, and noticed that she had gone quite pale. He followed Carina's gaze toward a spirit on the edge of the crowd. Hanging back in the shadows stood the ghost of a young man in his mid-twenties, dark-haired, in the uniform of an Eastmark mercenary. Vahanian knew by the resemblance to General Gregor that it was Ric, Carina's lost betrothed. He felt a stab of jealousy. Ric's memory, and Carina's guilt over Ric's death, were implacable rivals for her affection. The ghost stepped back into the shadows and vanished.

On the dais Tris stood, his arms outstretched toward the four figures of the Lady. "Thank you, Lady Bright, for the bounty of the fields and the vineyards, the health of our livestock, and the rains that sustain us. We ask your blessing on this kingdom, and we beg you to give succor to the spirits who do not rest and to Those Who Walk the Night, showing your mercy on us, the living, dead, and undead."

Tris lowered his arms. The candles dimmed, but did not go out. Around them, some of the spirits lost their distinctive form. Tris bowed his head as he turned toward the crowd. The cowl hid his face from view, but Vahanian could tell his friend was near exhaustion.

"He can't keep pushing himself like that—not if he's going to live long enough to challenge Jared," Vahanian murmured to Gabriel.

Gabriel followed Tris's exit. "He feels the burden of the Lady," the *vayash moru* replied. "There's nothing heavier."

VAHANIAN HOPED FOR a chance to see Carina alone. He decided that the chapel was the place to wait after the ceremony in the courtyard, as the twelfth bells approached. As guests of the king, the palace's chapel was opened to Tris and his friends. It was there that Vahanian waited, expecting the opportunity to encounter Carina.

Vahanian staked out a shadowed corner of the chapel, watching as a steady stream of courtiers brought their gift of honey cakes and ale and lit candles in remembrance of a loved one. Finally, near the twelfth bells, when most in the castle assembled in the great hall in anticipation of the feast, he spotted a lone figure in green. Carina brought her offering to the crowded alter, made the sign of the Lady, and murmured the words of dedication, lifting a wavering taper to light a candle.

Vahanian fell into step beside her as she left the chapel. "Heading up to the feast?"

Carina shook her head. "Not tonight. Maybe tomorrow."

"You've been pretty busy helping Spook with the witch biddies at the citadel."

Vahanian's irreverence made Carina smile. "You really are incorrigible," she murmured.

"Completely," he said, grinning. From a distance, Vahanian could hear the music begin in the great hall. "Come on. At least get some food. And who knows—Carroway said he was going to try out a new song he'd written about the last couple of months. You might be famous."

Carina blushed. "I hope not." She let Vahanian steer her toward the great hall, where they found food and ale set out to break the fast. She seemed to relax. From where they stood near the back of the room, they could see the succession of musicians, jugglers, acrobats, and parlor magicians begin the all-night revelries.

Although Carina demurred when the dancing began, the music seemed to lift her mood, and she did not press to leave. For his part, Vahanian enjoyed the long-overdue opportunity to talk with her. He had no doubt that Berry's endorsement had won him his initial acceptance in Staden's court, and that Tris's friendship along with his new title and lands made him more acceptable to the purists. But as the weeks wore on, he found himself included in the plans for battle and the preparations for war. He credited Staden with the rare genius to create a court where talent and ability counted at least as much as bloodlines. Some of that success emboldened him now, as he attempted to draw Carina out in conversation.

Carroway did debut his song, a spirited ballad about the caravan and its valiant defense against weather, bandits, and raiders. The crowd loved it, even as it became a moving lament. Vahanian saw emotions flicker in Carina's eyes that hinted at a more melancholy reception.

"I think it's really time for me to go," she murmured, stifling a yawn.

"Let me walk you back," Vahanian offered. "There's quite a crowd here tonight," he added before she could turn him down. "Staden can't know all of them personally. I'd feel better if I saw you safely to your room." His hand fell to the sword at his belt. At Berry's request, and in acknowledgement of their unusual circumstances, Staden permitted Vahanian the great honor of wearing his sword in the presence of the king.

Carina looked as if she might refuse, and then smiled. "Thank you. I'm a bit too tired to bash anyone with my staff tonight. Besides, I left it in my room," she joked.

The outer corridors were nearly empty as they worked their way from the public chambers of the palace. Carina slowed as they crossed an outdoor palazzo. Below them in the courtyard burned one of many huge bonfires that were part of the evening's celebrations. They could feel its heat and smell the rising smoke.

Carina was beginning to shiver, and he offered her his cloak. "I miss Winterstide in Isencroft," she said quietly. "It was always wonderful. I don't know if it will ever be like that again."

"Maybe not." Vahanian looked out over the courtyard, where the songs and merriment from within the palace were beginning to spill outside. "Things change. Sometimes, maybe even for the better."

Vahanian reached out and gently tipped Carina's chin up. Her expression was open, unguarded. "Something's been bothering you since we got here. Whatever happened, happened a long time ago. Forgiving yourself is hard. But the people who care about you would like to help you try." Her eyes filled with tears and she turned away, but she did not shrug off his arm from around her shoulders as they walked the length of the palazzo in silence. They stopped at the door to the rooms she shared with Kiara, and Carina slipped out of Vahanian's cloak.

"You'll need this; it's cold outside." Carina handed the cloak back to him. "Thank you."

"I enjoyed the company. I haven't celebrated Winterstide in years." He reached out for her hand and kissed the back of it. To lighten the moment, Vahanian made an exaggerated bow and clicked his boot heels together. "Sleep well, m'lady."

He could not read her smile or her expression, or the emotion in her eyes. "You too, m'lord," Carina slipped through the doorway and closed the heavy door behind her.

CHAPTER ELEVEN

O N THE FEAST day of Winterstide, Staden's court outdid itself with merrymaking. Through Tris's efforts with the Court of Spirits, some of the balance between the restless spirits and the living had been reconciled. Tris could sense a change in the currents of magic. Even after the festival was over, Tris suspected that his Court of Spirits would remain in high demand for as long as he stayed in Principality.

A highlight of the feast was Staden's announcement of Tris's betrothal to Kiara. Tris wondered whether any of the nobility at court knew of the old arrangement between Donelan and Bricen; wags would quickly discover a hint of scandal. On the other hand, there was scandal enough for the gossips in Tris's status as an exiled prince, in Vahanian's reputation, and in the friends' journey unchaperoned for months on the road together.

After the death mark Jared set on his life and on Kiara's, Tris cared less about the loose talk of court than ever before.

This night, Tris was resolved to push aside any forebodings and enjoy the moment. Kiara seemed equally determined to enjoy the evening, and Tris was happy just to have her beside him. He looked around at the greatroom, bustling with guests. At the far end of the room, Royster was surrounded by a cluster of adoring ladies, who indulged the white-haired librarian and his tales of the chivalry of ancient heroes.

Soterius and Harrtuck, resigned to appearances at court, joined Tris and Kiara in good spirits, well into their ale. Berry, seated nearby, was radiant in her gown of midnight blue Mussa silk, her hair twisted into a high braid. Berry's appearance made it difficult to remember the tomboy they had rescued on the road north. She was Carroway's most enthusiastic patron, and beamed at the announcement of Tris and Kiara's betrothal as if she had brokered it herself.

Once again, Staden's palace staff had outdone themselves in outfitting Tris and his friends. Tris's tunic and trews were in charcoal satin, with a contrasting wine-colored brocade doublet and a matching dark gray velvet cloak. Kiara's gown picked up the dark claret of Tris's doublet perfectly; Tris was sure Berry had had a say in the choice of their wardrobe. The rich dark hues complemented Kiara's complexion and her auburn hair, with a headpiece of fine gold chain that matched the thin gold collar on Jae's throat. The little gyregon preened and posed on Kiara's shoulder as if he knew he was on display.

Soterius wore a simple but elegant ensemble of hunter green, with straight, almost military lines that complemented his bearing. Harrtuck looked chagrined but resigned to his dark brown outfit, with a velvet vest and a finely spun shirt that did not strain at his broad, barrel chest. Carroway, as usual, was resplendent in a fashionable mix of silks, with deep plum, bright green, and gold accents. Seated at the front of the greatroom with the other musicians, Carroway was reveling in his return to giving court performances.

Mingling among the crowd, a mix of mortals and *vayash moru*, Mikhail wore a steel-gray doublet of opulent brocade. Mikhail moved through the crowd comfortably, and Tris wondered how many lifetimes it might take to feel so at ease. Across the room, Tris spotted Gabriel wearing an exquisitely cut dark blue doublet, his flaxen-colored hair loose around his shoulders, every inch an aristocrat.

Tris nudged Kiara as Carina and Vahanian entered, with the healer lightly taking Vahanian's arm. Carina's gown was of emerald silk, with a high waist and a slim fit that accentuated her petite frame and set off her dark hair. At her throat, a necklace of green turquoise and onyx glittered, and Tris wondered from where Berry had procured such a beautiful complement to Carina's dress.

Beside Carina, Vahanian seemed in exceptionally good spirits, dressed head to toe in black as was his preference when ceremony demanded that he dress for court. The outfit set off Vahanian's dark brown hair and brown eyes. He wore no other adornment than his sword belt with its expertly-forged and well-used blade.

"Still taking bets?" Tris whispered.

Kiara chuckled. "Now that Berry has us taken care of, I'm sure she'll double her efforts to match them up."

"They might not need her help," Tris observed, grinning as the others joined them. "Glad you could make it," Tris greeted Vahanian, who seemed quite pleased to have Carina as his companion for the evening.

"Nice to know the witch biddies let you have the night off," Vahanian quipped. "I understand congratulations are in order." In the busy greatroom, the press of guests jostled them as a new group of musicians took the stage.

Kiara's smile was wistful as she took Tris's arm. "There are a few technicalities to take care of," she murmured, "but thank you."

"Good evening to you all," a familiar voice greeted, and they turned to see Gabriel behind them, though there was no noise at the *vayash moru*'s approach. The flaxen-haired *vayash moru* bowed to Kiara and Carina, then greeted Vahanian and Tris with a nod.

He turned to Tris. "Are you ready for our appointment with the Blood Council?"

Vahanian looked askance at Gabriel, then at Tris. "Call me superstitious, but coming from him, that doesn't sound good."

Gabriel regarded Vahanian with faint amusement. "You're welcome to join us," Gabriel said smoothly. "As Lord of Dark Haven, it would be appropriate. At some point, you must also meet the Council."

"Why me?"

"Because Dark Haven is the traditional sanctuary for the sons and daughters of darkness," Gabriel's faint smile showed his disquietingly long eye teeth. "And you are the Lord of Dark Haven."

"That was something Staden didn't exactly make clear when he gave me the title," Vahanian replied. Carina giggled.

"Nonetheless, the matter does, in a way, concern you directly. The members of the Blood Council are the ruling noble houses of Dark Haven."

"Just how, exactly, can you have a hereditary nobility among *vayash moru*?" Vahanian asked, raising an eyebrow.

"It would be more accurate, perhaps, to say there is an aristocracy of age and wealth, more by the dark gift than by mortal birth," Gabriel replied. "Many have served on the Council for well over two hundred years."

"So you're planning to walk Tris into a room full of *vayash moru*. And you want me along for what—an appetizer?"

"When the Obsidian King fell, the orb that held his soul on the edge of the abyss, Soulcatcher, was given to the sons of Dark Haven to protect. It was secured beneath Dark Haven, where a great river of power runs. When Arontala wrested the orb from its resting place, the last Lord of Dark Haven died, and the great house itself was damaged. The river of power has been tainted, and not even the Sisterhood has been able to purify its flow. That history makes the present problem Dark Haven's concern. Tonight, we meet with the Council to present Tris as Summoner and the rightful king of Margolan."

"Why does this Blood Council care?" Vahanian asked warily.

"Because Arontala is *vayash moru*," Gabriel replied. "There are old and binding rules among my people that govern how we may act—toward mortals and toward our brethren of the dark gift. This is necessary to keep the truce. It's forbidden for *vayash moru* to side with mortals to destroy another *vayash moru*. I believe I can receive the Council's permission to make an exception.

"Before this is over," Gabriel continued, "we'll likely need the assistance—or at least the forbearance—of those *vayash moru* who remain in Margolan. Such things are better done through proper channels."

"As much as this doesn't sound like my kind of party," Vahanian said grudgingly, "maybe I'd better come along to watch Spook's back."

"As you wish," Gabriel said with a low bow. "I'll return for you at the twelfth bell. Until then, I'll take my leave. There are preparations to be made."

The *vayash moru* seemed to vanish into thin air. "I hate it when he does that," Vahanian muttered.

"Thanks for the support," Tris said. "I have to admit, the whole idea makes me nervous."

"You hold court for ghosts all day and a couple of *vayash moru* make you nervous?" Vahanian joked. "Aren't you officially Lord of the Dead and Undead?"

"In the case of the *vayash moru*," said Tris, "I have the distinct impression that the title is ceremonial."

Partygoers jostled as the guests, crowded shoulder to shoulder, moved for a better view of the musicians, who struck up a lively tune. Vahanian turned toward the music. In that instant, he saw torchlight glint off steel behind Tris.

"Get down!" Vahanian shouted, pushing hard against Tris as the dagger fell.

The dagger struck just below his shoulder as he shoved Tris out of the way. He staggered, reaching for his sword. Carina screamed. Jae gave a shriek, diving toward the assassin. A streak of blue mage fire burned past Vahanian, striking the attacker. Vahanian heard the whirr of a blade flying through the air. The attacker fell to the ground, a small blade lodged between his shoulders. Vahanian glanced up, expecting one of the guardsman, and instead saw Berry, standing on her chair, a look of surprise and self-congratulation on her face.

"You're hit," Carina said, guiding Vahanian to the floor as the room began to spin. Guardsmen shoved their way through the screaming crowd, forming a circle around Vahanian and Carina. The guards tried to whisk Tris and Kiara out of the room, but Tris jerked away and Kiara would not be moved. Vahanian could hear Carroway shouting above the screams of the crowd, attempting to shift the partygoers away from the incident.

"Coming through!" he heard Soterius shout as he and Harrtuck barreled their way through the guardsmen's line.

"How bad?" Harrtuck asked, taking in Vahanian's condition with a practiced eye.

A servant handed Carina a fistful of rags. She applied pressure through Vahanian's bloodsoaked shirt and felt around the wound. "Not as bad as it could be," she appraised, looking worriedly at

Vahanian. "The knife hit a rib, or it might have had you in the heart." Blood stained her green gown and covered her hands. "We've got to get it out."

Vahanian felt the room swim around him. He turned to one side, and retched.

"I'm betting the blade was poisoned," Carina assessed. "Wormroot, to disable a mage." She laid a hand on Vahanian's shoulder, steadying him. "Since you don't have magic, it's just going to make you throw up." She looked up, and saw Berry, ashen and scared, just within the circle of guardsmen. "Nice aim," she said, and Berry nodded, too concerned to smile.

"Problem is, we won't know who sent the assassin, because he's dead," Soterius clipped.

Vahanian saw Tris glance past the guardsmen, to where the assassin lay. "Not necessarily," said Tris. "Let's get Jonmarc taken care of, and then we'll deal with the assassin."

Vahanian became aware of a growing stiffness that started in his legs and rapidly worked its way up his body. It was getting harder to breathe, as if iron bands encircled his ribs. He grabbed Carina's wrist.

"Can't… breathe…" he rasped.

"Tris—I'm going to need help!" Carina shouted, and Tris knelt beside them.

"There must have been another poison on the blade," Carina said. Vahanian fought his own rising panic and pinpricks of light danced before his eyes. "He's not breathing—Tris, I need time to counter the poison!"

Vahanian had the disquieting sensation that he was watching from outside himself, Tris clutching his arm,

Carina trying to push a wad of rope vine between his own clenched teeth. He felt disoriented, as if he were drunk with strong wine, and then a familiar presence brushed against his mind, something that he knew was Tris's power, closer than thought.

Abruptly, Vahanian felt himself back in his body, starved for air. Panic filled him in the darkness, the memory of nearly drowning in the cold water of the Nu River, his lungs burning. And then Vahanian felt his chest rise, awkwardly at first, then in smooth, regular rhythm. He gasped, and his lungs filled with sweet, fresh air.

Carina, her face wet with tears, struggled with the knife. Berry stood behind her, clinging fearfully to Kiara. "Please don't die," Carina whispered as she tried to free the knife. "Please don't die."

"I've got him," Tris said. "And at least for now, his heart and breathing are stable."

"By the Dark Lady!" It was Staden's voice, somewhere behind them. "How is such a thing possible?"

"I could bind soul to body because he wants to live. That is permitted to a Summoner." Tris replied, and Vahanian guessed that Tris was also supplying Carina with energy. "As for the heart and the lungs, they're like a bellows and pump—if he can't move them, it's a small thing to make them move on their own."

"A small thing," Staden replied, awestruck.

Vahanian felt a sharp pain as Carina pulled the knife free and pressed a rag into the wound to staunch the blood. Two grooves marked each side of the blade. "I've never seen a knife like this," she mused, holding up the blood-covered weapon.

"It's a Mussa knife," Vahanian heard Gabriel say, as the *vayash moru* walked up behind Carina. "The grooves hold thin vials of poison that shatter when the blade enters the body."

Carina looked at Tris grimly. "There was even more wormroot on the knife than what the Sisterhood used on you. If the assassin had hit you—"

"My magic would have been out of reach, with no one to do for me what I did for Jonmarc. I'd be dead."

"How long does the poison last?" Staden asked. "You can't breathe for him forever."

Carina shook her head. "There are antidotes I can try, but I don't know—this poison works so quickly, the victim is usually dead long before it can wear off." She looked up sharply. "Tris—what will you do? You were to meet with the Blood Council tonight."

"The Council does not reconvene lightly," Gabriel observed. "From their perspective, being dead is not an excuse."

Tris looked down at Vahanian, who was unable to so much as nod in recognition. "Call for Taru," he said. "The soul-binding will hold. I've set the breathing spell so that a mage of her power could monitor it, even add to the magic if necessary." He looked at Gabriel. "We won't be long, I hope."

Staden sent a servant to the citadel for Sister Taru. Carina finished her makeshift bandage. "Let's get Jonmarc off the floor and somewhere quieter," Carina ordered She wiped the blood and tears away with her stained sleeve. Soterius and Harrtuck picked him up, one at his shoulders and one at his feet, and hefted him onto a couch in a nearby sitting room.

"T'will have to do—he's too blasted heavy to carry up the stairs!" Harrtuck exclaimed.

"What about him?" Kiara asked. The assassin still lay in a pool of blood on the floor of the great-room.

"Let me get Jonmarc settled," Tris said. "Then, with your permission, Your Majesty, I'd like to interrogate the assassin and see if we can get some answers."

"But he's dead," Staden began to protest, letting his voice trail off as he realized the implications. "Yes, yes, interrogate him. I have to see this. I'll bring Hant with me. He's the best one for this if we've rats to catch."

"I'll sit with Jonmarc," Carina said, and looked to Kiara. "Please, can you bring my bag from my room? And water—I'll need a kettle and a basin, along with fresh rags. He's lost a lot of blood." Kiara nodded, but before she could move, Berry bolted for the door.

"I'll get them," the princess assured Carina as her running footsteps grew distant.

"I'd best leave you to your healing," Staden said, turning for the door. "I'll see you in the greatroom at the tenth bell, to see what you can make of the assassin."

"Tris," Carina said quietly, her voice faltering, "are you sure... sure he's alive? Your power is so strong... I was thinking about that time, by the well—"

Tris shuddered. Vahanian remembered the ghost who tried to possess Carina and how in throwing the spirit free, Tris accidentally reanimated her corpse. "I'm sure," Tris said. He sounded exhausted. "Although we'd better hope the poison wears off before too long, since he'll have to eat."

Vahanian could not see Carina's face, but her voice was ragged. "There's an insect, in the forests of Eastmark, whose sting can make a man lose the feeling in an arm or leg for a day if he's bitten. I'll start with that antidote, see if I can concentrate it. Royster will help me. There has to be something."

Tris laid a hand on Carina's shoulder. "If anyone can figure it out, it will be you and Royster."

Carina found the pulse in Vahanian's neck. Her fingers lingered on his skin, and her eyes had a haunted look. Although Vahanian called out to her with his thoughts, he could not force his lips to form the words, or his body to make any movement at all.

There was a knock on the door. Sister Taru entered. Berry and Royster followed, bearing Carina's satchel, clean rags and both a large kettle and a basin. Tris and Taru conferred in low tones for a few minutes, casting glances in Vahanian's direction, but he could not hear their conversation.

"Show me what you've done," Taru said as she moved to stand beside Vahanian.

"I thought about what you said, back at the citadel—how Carina got me to breathe again," Tris replied. "She said the lungs were like a bellows. And I thought about the spell that stopped Elam's heart. If it can be stopped, it can be kept going." Tris took Taru's hand. The Sister shut her eyes, and Tris moved her hand above Vahanian's chest. "Can you feel the spells I've set? Those don't require a Summoner's magic."

"I can also feel the soul-binding, although I can't make such a working myself."

"It will hold." Vahanian was not sure that the look in Tris's eyes matched the certainty of his voice. "As for the other spells, now that they're set, you should be able to make sure they remain. I should only be gone for a few candlemarks."

"I can do that," Taru replied. She looked at Tris with concern. "Be careful, Tris. Very few mortals are called before the Blood Council. Few that are, return."

"Gabriel believes he can protect me. I hope he's right." With a worried glance in Vahanian's direction, Tris left to interrogate the assassin and ready himself for the Blood Council.

Taru stepped closer to Vahanian, and touched his forehead lightly with her fingertips. She closed her eyes in thought, and then looked over to where Carina watched worriedly from the fireplace. Berry had appointed herself Carina's apprentice. Royster set out two worn leather volumes he withdrew from under his coat.

"Whatever you need, Carina, we're here for you," the white-haired librarian promised.

Carina squared her shoulders and drew a deep breath. "Then let's get started. It's going to be a long night."

CHAPTER TWELVE

A LONE IN HIS rooms, Tris leaned back against the door and closed his eyes. He was far more spent than he had let on to Kiara, perhaps even more than Carina realized. Blinding headaches came less often in reaction to strong magic as Tris grew more adept with his power, but Tris resigned himself to a continual dull throb behind his eyes. His body ached from the grueling pace of sword practice and climbing drills. Although the night's commitments made it likely he would be awake until dawn, Tris wanted nothing so much as a long soak in a very hot tub and an uninterrupted night's sleep.

Giving up that fantasy, he pushed away from the door. A fresh outfit lay on his bed. His own shirt and doublet were stained with Vahanian's blood. *Not something I want going into a council of* vayash moru, Tris thought as he loosed his ruined vest and pulled his tunic over his head.

He was too tired to pick up the discarded items. He moved wearily to the pitcher and basin at the bedside, steeling himself for the splash of cold water as he washed Vahanian's blood from his hands. *My own blood will be distraction enough for the Council.*

Tris poured a glass of port, and realized his hands were shaking. It was the first opportunity he'd had to think about what happened. Saving Vahanian's life had crowded out everything else in the moment. Now, Tris realized that the knife had been meant for him. Clearly, the attacker had considered how best to strike a mage. Tris did not relish the task of interrogating the assassin.

He remembered Abelard's warning. Even here, amid Staden's protections, neither Tris nor his friends were completely safe. *Yet another reason I never wanted to be king. No one tries to kill second sons. Normally, we're not important enough to assassinate.*

Tris sat for a moment beside the fire, letting it warm his chest and shoulders as he sipped the port. *Oh, Kait,* he thought, *how did we ever get so far away from home?* Her spirit did not answer him. He remembered the glitter of Winterstide in Bricen's court, with Bricen and Serae presiding over the well-feasted crowd of nobles, and Kait, showing off shamelessly at the falconing trials. Serae had been pressuring Tris to enter the jousting competition. Now they were all dead. Even if he succeeded in taking back the throne, Margolan's celebration would never be the same again.

Tris stared into the fire, watching the dancing flames as the port warmed his blood. Vahanian's injuries worried him. Tris had been able to anchor his friend's spirit and compensate for the paralysis, but all would be in vain unless Carina could purge the poison before lasting damage occurred. His own gratitude was tempered by guilt. *I've got to be on guard, all of the time,* Tris chastened himself. *I can't depend on Jonmarc or anyone else to watch over me. It's my risk, my responsibility.*

Reluctantly, he set aside the empty glass and stood, stretching to ease his tired muscles. He dressed in the fresh clothing and tried to smooth his hair into a reputable queue. There was a knock at the door just as Tris finished adjusting his collar. With one hand near his sword, Tris opened the door, relieved to find Gabriel outside. While Gabriel maintained that *vayash moru* could not truly read mortals' minds, Tris found that their enhanced hearing often gave the illusion of telepathy. The trait was unnerving.

"King Staden and General Hant will meet us in the greatroom, my prince," Gabriel said. "After that, by your leave, we'll go to the Council."

Tris fell into step beside the *vayash moru*, who slowed his stride to accommodate mortal speed. The evening's merrymakers had fled the palace after the attack. In the greatroom, only the king, Hant, and a half dozen guards awaited them.

Apparently Staden is feeling a bit vulnerable too, Tris thought.

The dead assassin lay in a pool of congealed blood on the floor. His back bore a burn from the blue mage lightning Tris had cast, and Jae's talons had left six long tears where the gyregon had struck the assassin's shoulders. The hilt of a small dagger protruded from the man's chest, testimony to Berry's aim. Tris motioned for the others to give him more room, and they all stepped back respectfully.

"So it's true... you intend to summon this brigand for questions, even now?" Hant asked, his eyes narrowing.

"Have the guards determined anything from the body?"

Hant shook his head. "By the look of him, he could be from Margolan—or from Isencroft or Dhasson, for that matter. No identification on him, but he had Margolan gold in his pocket, and these." Hant nudged the body with his boot to reveal a variety of short darts.

"He had a Mussa knife," Gabriel observed. "Not a common weapon."

Tris bent closer, and pulled the dead man's shirt to one side. Around his neck on a strap was an amulet. Tris sensed its dark power. Tris pushed Hant's hand aside when the general moved to touch the talisman. "It was spelled by Arontala, I'm sure of it. Don't touch it."

"What does it do?" Hant asked, fearlessly crouching closer for a better look.

"I won't know without probing it, and I don't want to probe it without wardings set. But I have a few suspicions."

Staden looked at Tris. "While this one is beyond punishing, if you can summon him and find who sent him, Hant can take it from there."

Tris took a deep breath and closed his eyes, finding his center. He raised a warding, first around the body on the floor, and then a second one separating himself from the group of onlookers. Finally, he raised a third warding over the entire group, remembering the way Arontala had sought and found him on the spirit plains during the ill-fated scrying at Westmarch.

Tris was aware of the living men in the room, of the curious emptiness that signaled a *vayash moru*, and of the body on the floor. It was toward that corpse that Tris stretched out his power, seeking its soul on the Plains of Spirit.

The spirit rushed up at him, rising so quickly that Tris took a step backward, raising his hands to keep the angry ghost at a distance. The spirit lunged at the wardings, trying to tear through with both teeth and nails, wild-eyed in its ferocity. When it found it could not break the wardings, it keened a high-pitched wail of sheer frustration.

The guards cried out and pointed in frightened awe. Staden drew back a pace. Hant did not move, his thin body coiled as if to spring, his flinty eyes narrowed and intent on the target.

"Why have you called me?" The spirit spoke with the accent of the Margolan plains.

"Who are you, and why did you try to kill me?" Tris countered, adding power to his wardings.

"I am Hashak, and I serve King Jared!" The ghost drew back, no longer charging at the wardings but still wary, his fists balled at his sides.

"Who sent you?" Tris pressed. "Someone acquired the knife and the poisons for you. Who was it?"

"I thought you were a Summoner," the ghost taunted. "If you want that information, take it from me. Why should I tell you?"

"No Light Mage will harm a spirit, although perhaps your master's mage won't be so forgiving. But no, I don't need your statement. A Summoner of power can read the last thoughts of a fresh corpse. From that, we'll know who sent you."

The spirit looked surprised, and his bluster tempered. "Then why call me here?"

"I can offer you something Jared can't. I can pass you over to the Lady." Tris gestured to the amulet around the corpse's neck. "When Jared gave that to you, did he tell you what it does?"

"He said it would protect me. Obviously, he lied."

A slight, bitter smile reached the corners of Tris's lips. "Of course he lied. His blood mage made that amulet. In the palace, Shekerishet, there's an orb that is the portal to the abyss itself. In that orb, the spirit of the Obsidian King waits to be reborn. Before he can be reborn, he must feed. On souls," Tris added, watching the treachery of Jared's gift dawn on the spirit.

"You mean he plans to pull me into his bloody orb?" the spirit shouted. "Feed me to his monster?"

Tris nodded, feeling the amulet gather power as they spoke. Any moment now it could trigger, and if it sensed Tris's magic close at hand, Tris was not sure his wardings would hold. "Do you know which Aspect of the Lady comes for murderers?" Just beyond his mage sight, he could feel the approach of the Crone, her dark, cold, death embrace awaiting the guilty one. Nervously, the spirit glanced around him, as if he, too, felt the Crone's approach.

"Not the Crone!" he cried out. "By the Dark Lady, I don't want to be eaten, and I don't want to go to the Crone!"

The Crone's imminent approach and the gathering power of the amulet made the hairs on the back of Tris's neck prickle with primal dread. "You don't have much time," Tris said, hoping his voice was steady. "I can save you from the amulet and I can plead your case with the Lady, but I'd need a reason to care."

The ghost's blustering was gone. He threw himself to the floor, just beyond Tris's warding. "I'll tell you everything!" the assassin sputtered. "I got into some trouble in Margolan, and the guards were going to hang me. I've lived a bad life—no one's going to tell you otherwise. Been a thief and a cutthroat and a snitch. No one deserved a noose more'n me, to tell the honest truth." The spirit looked back into the shadows again, and spoke even more rapidly, fearing the Crone's approach.

"I was in the dangler's cell in the jail, where they hold the next men to be hanged. A strange man in a red robe came. The guards were right afeared of him, and they did whatever he said. He called for me, said he had a job, and that if I did it, he would make sure I didn't hang." The ghost's words poured out, his accent blurring them together.

"Well, of course I took the job. And when he said it was a bit of blade work, I wasn't squeamish—done that kind of thing before. He gave me the gold and a horse to get to Principality, told me who it was I should look for." He dared a glance in Tris's direction. "Said I'd have the best chance in the feast crowd at Winterstide. I saw you straight away, with that white hair of yours. Waited for the biter to move away," he said with a disdainful look at Gabriel, "and then I took my chance. Didn't think your friend would be so keen to take the blade for you."

Tris's anger flared, and he struggled to keep his emotions in check. "Did he say anything else, the man who hired you?" Tris pressed. They had very little time. The amulet was gaining power rapidly, and the Crone hovered just beyond sight, as if she, too, listened to the ghost's tale.

Panic was rising in the ghost's voice. "He said that if I couldn't get to you, that I should kill the king, that he deserved to die for taking you in, that anyone who opposed King Jared deserved to die." He glanced around himself in fear as the amulet on the corpse began to glow. "Please, m'lord wizard, don't let them take me!"

"There's something else you haven't told me," Tris said, acting more on hunch than certainty. "You're running out of time."

The ghost shrieked, terrified of the glowing amulet and the nearness of the Crone. "If I could strike and escape, I was to meet a groomsman in the stable, a man named Turas. We were to watch for a time when Princess Kiara went riding, and use a dart to drug her. If I brought the princess to King Jared, the man promised that not only would the king keep me from hanging, but he would make sure I had honor beyond measure." The assassin nearly wept in fear.

Tris wrestled with his feelings at the ghost's casual malice. "He promised you wouldn't hang because he was fairly sure you'd be killed in the attempt. If he promised you honor beyond measure, it's as a sacrifice to the Obsidian King."

Tris could feel the power radiating from the amulet as it searched for the assassin's ghost, and began to draw the spirit into its red glow.

"Please, m'lord! You promised!"

"So I did." Tris was sorely tempted to leave the unrepentant assassin to his fate. Tris stretched out his hand, focusing his power, and sent a blast of energy toward the amulet. A red flare rose in answer. The onlookers gasped and stepped back again, against the outer edges of the wardings.

Tris knew the imprint of Arontala's power. Even at this distance, behind his wardings, he could feel the pull of the Soulcatcher. Tris was braced for the red fire that erupted from the amulet, as it had from the scrying orb at Westmarch and from Alaine's amulet. Only this time, his shields held and the blue fire he sent in answer slowly forced the red fire backward, until the flames consumed the corpse and filled the greatroom with the stench of burning flesh.

"You burned my body!" the ghost cried out. The red flames flared and faded, leaving only a charred corpse.

"You won't be needing it," Tris said, his thoughts elsewhere. That the brigand told the truth about his past and about his mission Tris had no doubt, sensing the spirit's complete lack of remorse. *He deserves everything he was going to get, and more,* Tris thought bitterly, struggling and failing to find neutrality. *I could let him go to the Crone. It would be so easy to just step aside...*

In his mind, he could hear Sister Taru's voice. *Such power is reserved for the Lady alone,* Taru had warned. *The Obsidian King became the judger of souls, and would have made himself a god.*

Swallowing hard, Tris turned his attention to the presence he felt in the shadows, the Aspect of the Crone, come to take Her prize. "Lady most powerful, giver of souls and taker of breath, hear me." It was half prayer, half supplication, and he knew he was on dangerous ground. There was no response, but Tris sensed that the Crone was listening.

"This soul fears his due," Tris said honestly. "And I'm a poor advocate, since he has harmed my friend and would have killed my betrothed. But I gave him my word that I'd ask for mercy if he told his story. And so I keep that word, and know that it is given to the Lady alone to be the judge of souls. If there is a way for him to go to an Aspect other than yourself, m'Lady, hear my prayer."

Tris could feel the presence of the Aspect, though his mortal eyes could not see it. Behind him, he heard Gabriel whisper a blessing, and to the side he saw both Staden and Hant make the sign of the Lady. The guards dropped to their knees.

I hear your plea, Summoner, as I have heard his story. The rasping voice of the Crone sounded in his mind, and his soul shrank within himself. *I'll give him to the Aspect he deserves the most.*

The guards cried out in panic, and Staden cursed in fear. A yawning darkness opened up, like a potent stew of nightmares, revealing visions too terrifying to comprehend. Tris knew, without doubt, that it was the Formless One who came for the cringing assassin. The most terrible of the Aspects, this Face of the Lady was known to the old religion, but disavowed now in the Winter Kingdoms. The

Formless One reached out a shadowy tendril toward the shrieking spirit, and drew him into its maw.

Then as quickly as it came the Aspect was gone, and the ghost's cries abruptly fell silent.

Wearily, Tris released his wardings and slumped forward, caught by Gabriel's strong grasp.

"By the Whore!" Staden cried, looking at Tris with a mixture of fear and admiration. "Never have I seen such a thing!"

"And never again do I want to," added Hant fervently. Tris noted that it was the first time he had seen Hant look rattled. The guards regained their feet, looking at Tris as if he had just transformed into a dragon.

"I didn't call the Lady," Tris said as Gabriel helped him to a seat. "I don't presume to have that kind of power."

"We heard," Gabriel said, pressing a mug of warm, mulled wine into Tris's hand. Tris took a pinch of Carina's headache powder from a pouch at his belt and added it to the wine, swirling it until it dissolved.

Hant turned to the guardsmen. "You heard the assassin. Go find the man Turas. Strip him of all his clothing and any jewelry. Search even his hair. Then give him to me. We'll see if there are more rats to catch." He turned to Staden and bowed. "If there are others, we'll find them, Your Highness."

Staden nodded stiffly and Hant left with several of the guardsmen, leaving two soldiers behind as an escort. The king looked from Tris to Gabriel. "It seems Jared has a longer reach than I imagined," Staden mused. "It's been a generation since anyone's been bold enough to strike at court. We'll make provision." He looked at Tris soberly. "My complacency nearly cost your life. I won't make the same mistake again."

Tris inclined his head in acknowledgement. "We've placed you and your court in great danger."

Staden dismissed his comment with a gesture. "I'm too old to start running from upstarts. You're welcome for so long as it serves your purpose." He paused. "It's late. I suggest you find some rest, if you think you can sleep."

"Thank you, Your Majesty. But we have business with the Blood Council."

"May the Bright Aspects ride with you," Staden said, raising a hand in blessing. With the guards at his back, Staden strode from the greatroom, leaving Tris and Gabriel alone.

"After all this," Tris said, "I hope you're not expecting fireworks and some show of power at the Blood Council. I'll be doing well if my head quits hurting enough for me to ride."

"We have a candlemark before we must leave," Gabriel said. "Mikhail will be joining us. Between us, you'll have nothing to fear from any mortal."

Tris gave him a sideways look and drained the last of his mulled wine. He stretched out on the bench. "It's not the mortals I'm worried about."

CHAPTER THIRTEEN

THE HORSES' HOOVES crunched through the hardened snow as Tris, Gabriel, and Mikhail made their way across the rolling foothills of Principality by moonlight. Even with his heavy cloak, the bitter wind chilled Tris; neither of his companions was affected by the cold. His horse snickered and fidgeted in protest against the wind and the nearness of the *vayash moru*. Ice glinted on the road, forcing them to ride slowly. Tris pulled his cloak closer around himself.

They left the plank road just beyond the city gates. For a time, the road was wide, hard-packed dirt well worn by wagons and travelers to the palace. Gabriel turned from the main road, and the forest seemed to close in around them, blotting out the moonlight and the distant silhouette of the high, sharp mountains. This was an ancient forest. Tris could sense the stirrings of primal magic, old and powerful, in its shadowed depths. Nearby, a wolf howled. Another answered. Tris shivered, though Gabriel and Mikhail were more than a match for any wolf. More likely, he thought, the wolves were known to the *vayash moru*, and announced their coming.

"Who formed the Blood Council? How did it come to exist?" Tris asked Gabriel as they rode, their shadows sharp on the snow in the moonlight. "I meant to ask you earlier, but we got a bit busy."

"Four hundred years ago, there was no Council, and no truce." Tris noticed that his guide's breath did not steam in the bitter cold. "I was newly brought across. I ran from the hunters, the mortals who broke into our day resting places, seeking to destroy us. I saw my kind burned and dismembered. Many mortals used that fear for their own purposes, and not all of the victims were *vayash moru*.

"In time, my kind retaliated, and many mortals were killed. Others of my kind sought to stop the killings by taking control, ruling behind the throne as Arontala seeks to do. It couldn't go on. So the King of Eastmark brought together the rulers of the Winter Kingdoms and made an offer to the *vayash moru*.

"In exchange for an end to the mortals' attacks, we agreed to stop trying to control mortal kingdoms. He gave us Dark Haven, in the disputed lands between Margolan, Eastmark, and Dhasson, as our sanctuary. Principality was not yet a kingdom in its own right. In return, we formed the Blood Council, a ruling body among ourselves, to punish those of our kind who broke the truce, and to enforce the truce with honor.

"Then the unexpected happened. The Dark Lady appeared to the King of Eastmark in a dream. She told him that Dark Haven must have a mortal lord, one She would choose herself, lest we grow to think ourselves as gods. Many of the elders of my kind also dreamed that dream. The Dark Lady is our patroness. So the King of Eastmark named the first Lord of Dark Haven, and Dark Haven has had a mortal lord ever since."

Tris rode in silence for a moment, thinking through the implications of Gabriel's story. "You knew of Jonmarc even before I met you. And now he's the new Lord of Dark Haven. How do you know him?"

"On the eve of the Feast of the Departed, the Dark Lady appeared to me in a dream. She asked me to guide Her chosen. I am Her most humble servant."

"And Jonmarc is the Dark Lady's chosen?" Tris asked. "Does he know this?"

Gabriel chuckled. "My Mistress warned me that Jonmarc could be difficult. He will sleep better if some things are revealed when the time is right." He sobered. "But I fear that I may have failed in my duty. I didn't anticipate what happened this evening."

"Jonmarc is rather difficult to keep safe," Tris observed wryly. "What does the Council require of me?"

"We go to the Council tonight to seek their approval—or at least their neutrality—to strike against Arontala."

"Why do we need their approval? And why should they withhold it? Arontala is killing as many *vayash moru* as he is mortals."

"That's true. Yet there is a strict code of conduct among my kind, and infractions are severely punished. *Vayash moru* are forbidden to wage war against each other."

"Arontala's already declared war on the *vayash moru* of Margolan."

"True again. But there's a difference between having him found guilty by the Council and executed as a traitor to our kind, and permitting *vayash moru* to join with mortals to overthrow both Arontala and a mortal king. Such rules are necessary to keep my kind from meddling overmuch in the affairs of mortals. You can, no doubt, understand the need for that."

"So what does the Council's ruling mean? If they decline, will you change your mind about traveling with me to Margolan?"

Gabriel was silent for a moment. "I've committed myself to seeing you on Margolan's throne, my prince. And for that, I'll pay the necessary price. But we will be more successful if we can gain the Council's approval for *vayash moru* to strike with impunity against Jared's men. They destroy not only our kind, but make Margolan a place of misery for mortals as well."

"Very well. Now what of the Council themselves?"

"There are five on the Council," Gabriel said. "Rafe is even older in the dark gift than I. He comes from a noble family in Eastmark. In his mortal life, he managed his holdings well. Rafe may prove to be an ally. He is swayed only by reason, and he is given to logic.

"Riqua is also of great age in the dark gift, though younger in it than Rafe. She was the wife of a wealthy trader; even now, she drives a hard—but fair—bargain. She also may be an ally. Then there is Astasia." His tone became carefully neutral. "Astasia was the daughter of a wealthy landholder. She was brought across against her will by a poorly chosen lover. Astasia is wild, and she listens to her heart as often as she does to her head. She can be more astute than one might guess, and she can be treacherous. But there are times when she will choose wisely and stand by her choice. She must be handled carefully.

"Finally, there is Uri," said Gabriel. "In life he was a thief and a highwayman, brought across as the penalty for a deal gone wrong. He found the dark gift to be an asset to his pursuits, and his fortunes have been amassed by questionable means. He is dangerous. He alone among the Council is skeptical of the truce. He questions why we, with greater speed and strength, should not rule over mortals, as he believes our gift intends. When the truce is broken, it will be most likely at the hands of one of Uri's brood."

Tris looked at Gabriel. "You said there were five on the Council. You've only named four." Gabriel turned toward Tris, his blue eyes unreadable. "I'm the fifth member of the Council. I seek to preserve the truce."

Tris digested that last piece of information slowly as they rode through the bitter night. How much wealth could one accumulate, over several lifetimes? And when, in the accumulating, would material goods cease to matter? Yet even as he asked the question, Tris could guess the answer. Wealth bought security, not just baubles. Great wealth could assure privacy, buy off authorities, bend problematic rules. Yes, the privileges of wealth might be very attractive to the *vayash moru*, even though they were beyond partaking of many of its indulgences.

He chanced a look at Gabriel. The flaxen-haired *vayash moru* was handsome, appearing to be in his third decade. Only his blue eyes disclosed his true age. Gabriel, who never made any reference to his own lands, position or wealth, who seemed to show up at the most opportune times, and who pledged his personal support to overthrowing Jared. *Just when I get some answers, I find out I wasn't asking the right questions.* He knew he would be thinking about the Blood Council long after this evening was over. Assuming that he lived through the night.

Gabriel and Mikhail turned their horses between the wrought-iron gates of an estate. Dark, bare trees loomed over the long carriage road that led to an elegant stone home. A sense of foreboding nagged at Tris, although the windows of the estate glowed brightly with candlelight. From the shadows, grooms appeared without a sound to take their horses. Tris's mount whinnied nervously. Tris shared the horse's uneasiness.

The three men dismounted and headed up the sweeping, grand stairway. Gabriel led the way. Mikhail followed Tris, who had the strong sense that the group had been watched from the time their horses became visible in the carriage drive. He stretched out his mage sense, searching for signs of danger, but felt only the odd emptiness that signaled the presence of *vayash moru*. That sense of emptiness was more encompassing than he had ever felt it—broken neither by the warm tingle of a living soul, nor the resonance of departed spirits. Tris assumed that meant that the grand chateau teemed with *vayash moru*, and that the few he might meet in the council chamber were not the only undead present.

It took all of Tris's willpower to keep his mortal fear at bay. Although they encountered no one as they walked down the long, dimly-lit hallway, something deep and primal within Tris urged him to flee.

"We have arrived." Gabriel swung open two wide, double doors. Inside, torches lit a formal dining room decorated in the most current style. Rich brocade curtains hung from the tall windows, completely covering the openings. A fireplace the height and length of a tall man sat empty and unlit along one wall. Along the walls, candles glittered in recesses. In the center of the room, a heavy mahogany table with rich, Noorish inlay was circled by velvet-upholstered chairs. The inlay was cunningly designed. For a mage, such complex patterns could serve as the focal point for a working, or a way to calm the mind in order to open oneself to power. It was said that some pieces could take a single master craftsman a lifetime to complete. The oldest and most convoluted of such pieces were prized by powerful mages for their help in producing trance and focusing magic.

"My fellows of the Blood Council," Gabriel said, making a low, formal bow. "I present to you Prince Martris Drayke, son of Bricen of Margolan, Summoner and mage-heir of Bava K'aa."

Tris stepped forward at the introduction and made a ceremonial bow. "Most honored members of the Blood Council, I bid you greetings."

Tris knew the *vayash moru*, with their sharp senses, could hear and smell the blood that pounded in his chest. In the silences of their ride, Tris had searched for the right phrases for this meeting. So many mortal pleasantries would not do. He could hardly wish them continued good health and long life, he thought wryly, and he hoped fervently Gabriel had not lied about the *vayash moru*'s ability to read minds.

"We have been awaiting you, Prince Drayke." The speaker was an angular man with finely-chiseled features and precisely cropped sandy-colored hair. He had a short, perfectly manicured beard and dark eyes that glittered with intelligence. "I am Lord Rafe, speaker of the Council. We bid you enter." Rafe gestured to the young man who stood behind him to close the chamber doors, and Tris stifled a shudder at the sound of the latch.

Gabriel took a seat to the right of Rafe, and Mikhail went to stand behind him. Tris noted that the Council sat on the opposing side of the table. Tellingly, there were no empty seats. It was clear that he had been invited to be seen, interviewed, and possibly heard, but the offering of a seat at the table—both literally and figuratively—was being withheld, at least for now.

I've had mortals trying to kill me for half of the last year, Tris thought, drawing a deep breath and remembering all of his court protocol. *As long as I leave alive, it's a win.* He looked down the table from Rafe, trying to match the Council's members to Gabriel's description. A woman who looked to be in her mid-fifties, with elaborate, upswept dark blonde hair sat to Gabriel's right. *Riqua*, Tris guessed, noting that the woman's gown was one that his mother, Queen Serae, would have found quite acceptable for court. The design of the fabric and the cut of the dress were of the most fashionable style. The rich brocade bodice was daringly low, with a narrow waist and a full skirt that would accentuate the *vayash moru*'s preternatural gliding walk. Dark burgundy satin heightened Riqua's pallor. The effect was beautiful and unsettling.

Behind Riqua stood a younger woman with long blonde hair, dressed in a simple but elegant gown, as if she had stopped by on her way to a court party. Tris noticed that each of the Council members had a second with them, and wondered what service, beyond errands, these attaches provided.

To Rafe's left was a beautiful, dark-haired woman with chestnut-colored hair. She looked to be no older than her mid-twenties, though her eyes told of centuries of experience.

Astasia, Tris guessed. She met his eyes, simultaneously taking his measure. While her figure was provocative and her face was coquettish, her eyes were shrewd and calculating. *She's used to getting what she wants*, Tris thought, unable to completely ignore her plunging décolletage, and the full breasts it barely hid. A handsome young man with red hair stood behind Astasia. While he had a pleasant face and a fit form, he looked barely out of his teens. *Consort?* Tris wondered. *Plaything?* There was a coldness to the young man's eyes when he met Tris's gaze that made him wonder even further about what relationships *vayash moru* formed—or continued—after death.

Next to Astasia sat a man with hair as black as coal, and the dark eyes of a Nargi native. Unlike the others there was no sign of fine breeding in his features. He was good-looking in an unsavory way, and had an air about him of a man who spent too much time in card parlors. His wine-colored doublet accentuated his broad shoulders and stocky build, with an extravagantly cuffed white silk shirt that spilled from beneath its sleeves. Gold glittered in the candlelight, on his fingers, at his throat, and in the lobe of one ear. His dark eyes regarded Tris with unabashed contempt. *Uri*, Tris thought, daring to meet the *vayash moru*'s gaze and not look away.

Behind Uri was a young man whose beauty might even have surpassed Carroway's, marred only by a cruel upturn of his full lips. Sinewy, clad in a form-fitting black velvet coat and brocade pants, with a full frilled white lace collar and foppish, costly lace cuffs, Uri's assistant reminded Tris of a poisonous lizard waiting to strike.

"To what do I attribute the honor of the Council's invitation?" Tris asked, deciding to cut through the pleasantries.

Rafe inclined his head slightly, as if he recognized and appreciated directness. "We have heard much of you, Prince Drayke, both from Lord Gabriel, and from... others. Already, your power as a Summoner is becoming legendary. They say you dispelled the revenants from the Ruune Videya."

"My companions and I had been captured by slavers. It was necessary to survive."

"Living is vastly overrated," Uri commented with affected boredom, eliciting a cold half-smile from the young man behind him and no response at all from the rest of the Council.

"We have also heard of your Court of Spirits," Rafe went on. "And while this Council would question your authority to settle matters between *vayash moru*, it is clear that your power is as formidable as it appears."

"I'm a Summoner, heir to the power of my grandmother, Bava K'aa."

"Several of the Council knew Bava K'aa," Gabriel said. "We remember her battle against the Obsidian King, and the binding of the orb, Soulcatcher, in the foundation of Dark Haven."

"That worked well, didn't it?" Uri remarked.

"We have convened at the request of Lord Gabriel," Rafe continued, ignoring Uri's jibes. "The Blood Council determines what is law among the *vayash moru* of the Winter Kingdoms. And it is we who punish transgressors, even noble ones," he said, with a glance toward Gabriel, whose expression gave no clue as to his thoughts.

"We are aware of the usurpation of the crown of Margolan by Jared the Tyrant," Rafe went on. "We know he and his mage, Arontala, have broken the truce, hunting down *vayash moru*."

"If you know those things," Tris said, "then you understand why Jared must be unseated and Arontala must be stopped."

"For four hundred years," Rafe replied, "we of the Blood Council have stood apart from mortal kingmaking. This was desired by the mortals, who feared we might reign over them, and by the oldest and wisest among our own kind, who knew the danger and the truth of that fear."

"If that is the case," Tris challenged, "then look no further than Arontala. Ten years ago, he tried— and failed—to gain power in Eastmark. Arontala pinned my father, King Bricen, with his magic while Jared stabbed him. It was on Jared's order that my family was murdered. Now, at Arontala's behest, Margolan troops terrorize both *vayash moru* and mortals alike, destroying any who dare to object."

"Yet you don't come here tonight asking us to discipline one of our own, do you, Prince Drayke?" It was Uri, whose mellifluous voice had a knife-edge just below the surface. "You come requesting aid for your revolution, an endeavor that will, in the end, be of greatest benefit to Margolan's mortal residents."

"There is precedent," Gabriel responded with irritation. "Two hundred years ago, when your own people of Nargi tried to drive our kind from cover and kill them all, this Council gave its permission for *vayash moru* to defend themselves and aid their mortal defenders."

"Nargi hardly remains a welcoming place to our kind," Uri rejoined.

"The mass burnings stopped in Nargi and have not resumed," Gabriel replied, leaning forward. "There will always be unfortunate incidents, driven by mortal fear and those who use that fear for their own greed. But what Jared of Margolan is doing goes beyond 'incidents.' I have traveled Margolan, and so has Mikhail. We've seen whole villages burned at the stake, people's heads severed from their bodies, left on a pile with a warning sign that said, 'Thus so to all blood stealers.'"

Out of the corner of his eye, Tris saw in Riqua's expression a shadow of remembered fear.

Tris felt his gorge rise at the description, nauseated at Jared's cruelty, shamed by the stain it brought on the memory of his father and the honor of his family name. Unbidden, the images of the dark sending—and the fate it threatened for Gabriel and Mikhail—rushed to mind and he forced the nightmare vision away.

"What do you seek, Prince Drayke?" Astasia purred, and Tris sensed the danger in her voice. "Do you wish to recruit *vayash moru* as killing machines for your army? Send us by night to make Jared's soldiers vanish in the darkness?" She paused, shifting slightly in her seat, a move Tris was sure was calculated to better display her figure. "What would become of our kind, after you take the throne—assuming that you can? Will you protect us, you—a boy-king and newly minted mage?"

She was being deliberately provocative, both in manner and in words. He struggled with his emotions to avoid giving her the victory she sought. "I'm the only surviving direct heir of King Bricen, other than Jared the traitor," Tris said, keeping his voice carefully neutral. "I realize that I'm young—both in years and in mage training. But my power is strong. Even the Sisterhood couldn't dispel the wraiths of the Ruune Videya. But I did. As for my age—what is the alternative? Should I live in exile for a decade or two while those in Margolan—both living and undead—are slaughtered and oppressed by Jared and his mage?"

He looked at each Council member in turn. "At the Hawthorn Moon, Arontala will awaken the Obsidian King from his exile in Soulcatcher, and free him from his prison. The Sisterhood believes he's powerful enough to do this.

"When that happens, the Obsidian King will possess Arontala's body, infusing him with his power. Think of it. A dark Summoner of immense power, combined with the power of a Fire Clan mage in an immortal's body. Who'll stop him then? Who will dare to stand against him?"

Uri leaned forward, his dark eyes glittering. "Perhaps it's as it should be," he baited, watching Tris closely. "Perhaps the age of mortals is at an end. Perhaps the Obsidian King's rising is an omen, that the age of Those Who Walk the Night is come at last. After all, I've been told that the new Lord of Dark Haven may not even live to see his holdings. Perhaps that's an omen, too."

Tris felt his temper rise, and he thought he saw a glint of anger in Gabriel's eyes as well. Mikhail's posture made his anger clear, though he said nothing.

"You speak rubbish," denounced Riqua sharply, targeting Uri with her ire. "I remember before the truce. We all remember what it was to be hunted, to live off the blood of rats because we dared not venture out to find livestock or human criminals to feed our hunger. I don't want to go back to those days."

"No one wishes to survive such a purge again," replied Rafe carefully. "But we have yet to hear

from Prince Drayke what he proposes." Rafe
turned his attention to Tris. "Forgive my stating the
obvious, but your cause—however noble—seems
unlikely to succeed. What do you offer to offset the
risk of our backing should you fail?"

"If I fail, I'll be in no position to offer anything,
as I'll be food for the Obsidian King," Tris replied,
a morbid smile tugging at the corners of his mouth.
"I know my challenge to Jared's throne—and
Arontala's power—is up against steep odds. But
there's no one else to raise a challenge, no one else
who can legitimately take the throne, no one else
with a Summoner's power to challenge Arontala
and the Obsidian King. I'm the only chance you've
got." Tris hoped he appeared as coolly confident as
Vahanian in this high stakes bluff.

"I don't ask for your help en masse; I ask only
that the Council permit the *vayash moru* of
Margolan—as individuals—to follow their hearts.
Let them act against Jared and his followers without fear of the Council's judgment. Let them protect
themselves and their kin."

"A mortal, asking us to loose the vengeance of
our kind against other mortals?" Rafe asked,
watching Tris closely. "Is that what you really
want? Do you think you can stop that force once
it's turned loose?"

"I don't know. But as it is the truce will shatter
one day. The *vayash moru* will take their vengeance
against all mortals, innocent and guilty, and the
bloodshed won't end at Margolan's borders.
Reprisal will follow reprisal. You'll see your
precious truce dissolve, and all hope of peace with
it. And behind it all will be the Obsidian King,

growing bloated on the blood, increasing his power in an immortal body with no one to challenge him—perhaps for generations."

"I've already made my choice," said Gabriel, rising from his seat. "I am resolved to see Martris Drayke on the throne of Margolan, or be destroyed in the attempt."

Mikhail stepped forward. "And I, likewise," he said, raising his head to meet the gaze of the Council. "I served King Hotten two centuries ago. Now, my kingdom and my people require my service once again. I stand with Lord Gabriel and Prince Drayke."

Rafe looked at the three men in silence for a moment. "You realize that you are in defiance of the Council's truce, for which the penalty is destruction?"

Gabriel returned his stare. "We're within Council chambers, within the borders of my lands, surrounded by my brood. Neither you nor the Council can act against us here. To do so would trigger reprisals, both from my family and from the King of Principality. Either way, the truce ends. Prince Drayke has spoken truly. The only way to preserve our freedom to move safely among mortals is to give our support to Martris Drayke, and trust the Dark Lady that She will give her blessing in our endeavor."

Rafe stood. "The Council will adjourn to deliberate. Lord Gabriel, you will join us," he said. Mikhail moved to stand beside Tris. The Council filed from the room, leaving their seconds behind. Tris was immeasurably glad for Mikhail's company.

"So it's really true what they say, that you can speak with the spirits?" asked the blonde woman who stood behind Riqua. "I'm Elana. She held out out a fine-boned, ice-cold hand in greeting.

"Yes, it's true," Tris said, taken aback at the jarring incongruity between the formality of the Council meeting and this casual small talk.

"I remember Bava K'aa," said Rafe's second. He had the look of a scholar or a priest, with eyes tired from too much reading in dim light. Tris guessed that even in life, the young man had been pale from time spent indoors. "My name is Tamaq. I fought against the Obsidian King in his first rising,"

"Then the Council permitted intervention before?" Tris asked.

Tamaq shook his head. "I was mortal at the time," he said sadly. "I would have died on the battlefield, had not Rafe found me and brought me across."

There's more that's not being said, Tris thought. *The Council maintains its neutrality, but what, then, was Rafe doing harvesting the battlefield on the side opposed to the Obsidian King?*

More to the point, Tris wondered, *does any of this matter once you're no longer afraid of death? When you're able to outlive kings and petty mortal politics, wealthy enough to buy your safety, superior in abilities to outmaneuver all but the luckiest or most concerted efforts against you, why should you care?*

The real question, Tris realized, was not whether he could sway the Council to support his quest for the throne. The true question was why they should care at all.

"I'm more interested in this new Lord of Dark Haven." The speaker was the beautiful young man who stood behind Uri. "Is it really the smuggler Vahanian—the one with the royal death warrant in Eastmark?"

"Leave it alone, Malesh." The warning came from Astasia's second.

Malesh regarded the challenge with a smirk. "Go back to bed, Cailan. Stay out of the discussion, and I won't feel obliged to damage anything your mistress plays with."

"I'll let Jonmarc make his own introductions," Tris said, feeling distaste for Malesh. "My business tonight is with the Council."

Elana smiled at him and licked her lips. A shudder ran down Tris's spine. Elana was quite beautiful, even by mortal standards. "I'm told you announced your betrothal tonight," she said in a coquettish voice that, together with her posture, gave Tris to understand she considered him fair game. "Congratulations, Prince Drayke." She slid a half step closer.

"You're the Lord of the Dead and Undead," she said teasingly. "And while a mortal bride may be necessary for heirs, do consider the alternatives once that obligation has been fulfilled." She gave a look that left nothing to his imagination.

Tris blushed, seeing in Elana's eyes a spark of triumph. Even dead, she was a damnably attractive woman, and while her offer had no appeal to him, it was impossible to completely ignore her sensuality. He made a courteous bow.

"I'm flattered, m'lady, but this betrothal is an affair of the heart. I'm spoken for."

Elana gave him a knowing smile. "In fifty years, or in one hundred, my offer will remain the same, and my gifts to match. Can your mortal lover say the same?"

"That's enough, Elana," Mikhail said firmly.

Tris met Elana's eyes. "I know how transient this mortal body is, and how brightly the spirit glows within. It's true that our bodies fade and die, but a Summoner can extend that union beyond death. On the spirit plain, there is no fading, and no dying. Even *vayash moru* are not eternal."

Something in his words touched a nerve, Tris thought with satisfaction, or perhaps, Elana was unused to being spurned. Pouting, she withdrew to the edge of the group, turning her conversation to Cailan instead.

Malesh took the opening. "It will be most interesting to have a lord once again in Dark Haven," he said, with a dangerously smooth tone. "Though it is said that the Dark Lady Herself chooses, we have had some... turnover... in the lords of late. I hope the hand of the Lady rests on Lord Vahanian." Malesh's voice only thinly veiled his malice. "It sounds like he'll be a breath of fresh air," he added, watching Tris closely.

He knows about the poisoning, Tris thought, forcing down his anger at Malesh's baiting. *And if the knife hadn't been meant for me, I'd wonder if he or his master had a hand in it.*

"I'll pass along your sentiments to Lord Vahanian," Tris replied carefully.

The doors opened and the Council filed back in. Mikhail and the others returned to their places. Tris felt as if he had just run a very dangerous gauntlet.

He looked at Gabriel, but he could read nothing in the *vayash moru*'s face.

"The Council has reached its decision," Rafe said, when the others took their seats. Tris glanced at the Council members. Gabriel appeared as tense as Tris had ever seen him. Riqua looked angry. Uri was positively furious, with a barely controlled rage that roiled behind his dark eyes as he looked away from the others. Astasia seemed annoyed, her beautiful features clouded by a dark mood. Rafe betrayed little, but Tris thought the Council spokesman looked tired.

"After much discussion, it is the will of the Council that we rule in favor of Prince Drayke, permitting the participation by individual *vayash moru* in the matter of the Usurper on the basis of conscience," Rafe declared.

"One more example of why the truce is a flawed, idealistic mirage," muttered Uri.

Rafe ignored Uri's interruption. "Prince Drayke, do not regard this as an endorsement by the Blood Council. We agree that Foor Arontala must be removed, and that your efforts may present the best hope of doing so. But be clear on this point—it is to preserve our freedom that we act, not out of interest in any mortal kingdom."

Tris gave a shallow bow. "I'm grateful to the Council for your ruling. I give you my pledge that should I live to take the throne of Margolan, I will restore the truce and bring to justice those mortals who have broken it in malice."

"*If* you live to take the throne," Uri repeated quietly. The very stillness of his voice chilled Tris. "Right now, Prince Drayke, that is a very large 'if.'"

CHAPTER FOURTEEN

CARINA WATCHED THE notches on the candle burn down as the night wore on. It was well past midnight, and Tris had not yet returned from the Blood Council. That alone worried her. But of more immediate concern was that so far, none of their efforts had made any noticeable difference at all in Vahanian's situation. She was starting to panic.

The partygoers had fled after the assassination attempt. Carina, Kiara, Taru, and Berry kept vigil over Vahanian in the small sitting room off the greatroom. It had been designed for more intimate gatherings than the huge ballroom, with several groupings of settees, tables, and comfortable chairs. Now it resembled a sick room, with basins of water, pots of steaming herbal mixtures, vials and bottles of elixirs, and bags of medicine strewn across every tabletop. Royster and Carroway were still huddled at a table on one side of the fireplace, poring over tomes and scrolls in search of a remedy.

Carina looked over to where Jonmarc lay. Although he was breathing, his body was unnaturally still. He was much paler than usual, and where they had stripped away his shirt and waistcoat, a large bandage covered the wound left by the knife. It took all of Carina's willpower to force back tears. Once again, someone she cared about was going to die, and once again, it would be her fault. Knowing that Jonmarc was in love with her only made it that much worse. This was exactly what she'd feared if she let herself care about someone again. And while she had berated herself for responding to Jonmarc's advances, admitting those feelings to herself scared her even more. *A healer can't do her job if she lets feelings get in the way*, Carina told herself. *I'm no good to anyone if I can't heal. What if Tris can't win back the throne, can't stop Arontala, because I'm not able to heal Jonmarc? The entire fate of the Winter Kingdoms is riding on this, and I'm failing the test.* But as frightening as that thought was, there was another, even more terrifying fear that loomed in the back of her mind, one she refused to allow herself to dwell on.

What if I've returned to Principality City, only to fail miserably—again—at saving someone I care about? Someone who had the bad luck to care about me.

"Maybe you should rest," Kiara said gently, laying a hand on Carina's shoulder.

Carina shook her head stubbornly. "No. Not yet. We don't know how much time we have."

Kiara frowned. "Tris bound Jonmarc's spirit to his body. He set the magic to keep Jonmarc's heart and lungs working. Perhaps by morning the poison will begin to wear off. You said yourself you don't know how long it will last."

Carina brushed back a strand of dark hair and secured it behind her ear. "I don't know if it will wear off at all," she said tiredly. "That's what scares me. Do you remember what I told you about Maynard, the man who led the caravan we traveled with? He used to take a bit of Mussa poison each day to build up a tolerance, so that he would be harder to kill. I healed him once. I could feel the poison in his body, in his muscles. It didn't wear off—it just took a much stronger dose to really hurt him."

"The body is a complex set of humours. Breath and blood are part of it, but not all. I don't know if Tris compensated for everything—if he even could—or if that's in the hand of the Lady herself. The longer this lasts, the more damage there could be."

Sister Taru walked over to join them, checking on Vahanian as she passed. Berry slept sprawled in a chair near the fire, adamantly refusing to leave. Royster sat between two candles, doggedly paging through yellowed texts. Carroway brought with him a plate of food and some watered wine when the last of the palace entertaining was finished. Both food and drink went untouched. Royster set the bard to deciphering some healing rhymes and songs, and Carroway willingly complied.

"He's asleep," Taru said, and took a seat beside Carina. "As far as I can tell, he's in no pain. But you're correct—the magic Tris set won't hold indefinitely. Jonmarc will need nourishment. Even if we could magic a way to sustain him, if we can't heal him, Tris will be obliged to free his spirit. A man like Jonmarc wouldn't want to remain like this forever."

"I haven't had any luck with what I've tried so far. I can't heal around the poison; there's too much of it in his blood. The wormroot has begun to wear off—it doesn't last as long in a non-mage, and all it did was make him throw up. It isn't nearly the problem it is when I'm healing Tris. It's the other poison that worries me."

Carina balled her fist in frustration. "So far, none of the antidotes I've tried have worked. From what Royster could find in his books, it's closest to snake venom, but I don't know from which snake. If I had to bet, it would be one Royster found that is native to Trevath, down on the southern plains. It's a sandsnake, and it kills with one bite. But there's no antidote—there isn't time for one. Sweet Chenne— you saw how quickly it took him."

Carina fiddled nervously with the pendant that hung around her neck. "What I need is a filter," she said. "If there were a way I could isolate the poison and drain it off—"

"Can you do that?" Kiara asked worriedly.

Carina grimaced. "Taru and I tried two candle-marks ago, when you went to see if Tris was back yet. I hoped that if I could pull the poison away from Jonmarc, Taru could purify it in the Flow, a big river of magic energy."

"The Flow is all that and more," said Taru, "but my power isn't sufficient to use the Flow in that way, and we dared not try it with the unknown poison unless we could make it work with the wormroot. We couldn't."

Royster looked up suddenly, as if he only just heard the conversation. "Did you say, 'filter?'" he asked.

Carina nodded. Kiara pressed a mug of tea into her hands, and she drank the warm liquid mechanically, utterly exhausted. *Jonmarc's going to die and it's going to be my failure*, Carina thought. *Just like Ric.*

"A filter," Royster repeated, humming a little ditty to himself. "What do you make a filter from, I wonder?" He mused aloud, reaching from one book to another to flip pages. "Cheesecloth."

"It's not on the outside of his body," Carina protested.

"A fine metal strainer."

"Too big, and we can't get to the poison, it's in his blood," said Kiara.

"Rock."

"Rock?"

Royster nodded without looking up. "Ever been in a cave? Water filters down through rock. So do other things. Not just any rock..." He flipped pages, then glanced up at Carina and smiled.

"Turquoise," he said, eying the large, flat stone in Carina's necklace, "and onyx. Healing stones. Stones to remove impurities from the body. Ward off poison. Filter."

Carina fumbled with the clasp on her necklace, and Kiara reached over to help. "Do you really think it will work?" she asked.

"If it doesn't, you're no worse off than you are now."

They all turned as the door opened behind them, and Tris entered. Carina thought he looked worried and exhausted, but Kiara brightened at his return.

"Looks like Gabriel made good on his promise not to let them eat you," Kiara joked wearily. Tris bent to kiss the top of her head and sat down next to her.

"Your meeting with the Blood Council—was it successful?" Carroway asked. Near the fireplace, Berry awoke, rubbed at her eyes, and padded over to join the group.

Tris shrugged. "Gabriel thought so. We've won their neutrality, and with that group, I guess that's a lot." He looked at Vahanian. "How is Jonmarc?"

Carina peered over Royster's shoulder at a thick, old tome. Her necklace lay on the book and they were both noting passages in the text. Carina looked up. "No better. Royster thinks we might be able to filter out the poisons with the gemstones, but I don't want to risk it alone. Taru can lend me power and help with deep healing, but she can't anchor Jonmarc's spirit. You can. He's fading. I need your help."

"Let's see what you've got."

Carina carried over the gemstones that Royster had pried from their setting. There was a large, flat piece of turquoise and a smaller, black onyx disk. "If Royster is right, I should be able to pull the poison through the stone. If we can do that, then I can heal the other damage. Right now, I can't get through the poison."

"Let's do it," Tris said, moving to sit beside Vahanian. Carina moved a stool to the other side, and nodded to Tris. He gripped Vahanian's arm with his right hand and let himself slip onto the Plains of Spirit.

The soulbond he had set was still in place, but despite his intervention, the blue thread of Vahanian's life was growing dimmer. Tris focused his power on sustaining that glow, something Taru could not do. Carina removed the bandage from the wound on Vahanian's chest. It looked red and sore, proof that the poison blocked Carina's ability to heal.

Carina bit her lip as she slid the turquoise disk over the wound and laid the piece of onyx beside it. Then she placed her fingertips around the edge of the two stones with her palm raised and closed her eyes in concentration.

For a moment, nothing happened. Then Tris felt a stirring in the currents of power, as if distant clouds on the horizon were becoming lighter. He looked at the stones beneath Carina's hand and saw beads of a black, vile-looking ichor beginning to ooze up through the smooth surface of the stones. As the ichor seeped through the stone, a tremor shuddered through Vahanian's body. It grew stronger, until he was shivering so hard that Tris and Kiara had to grab him by the shoulders to keep him still enough for Carina to hold the stones in place.

"It's working!" Kiara cried. "Keep going, Carina. It's working!"

With agonizing slowness, bead after bead of the thick, dark liquid struggled through the stone. Taru rushed to contain the ichor in a small vial from Carina's bag, taking care not to touch it with her bare skin. Finally, when nearly a quarter dram of ichor had been extracted, no more beads rose from the stone. Carina slumped in exhaustion.

Tris retreated to his mage sense and reached for Vahanian on the spirit plain. There was a definite clearing, Tris thought, as if a heavy fog had lifted. He opened his eyes to see Carina, her eyes bright with tears, with a look of triumph. "We did it! The poison is gone. Without it, he should be able to move again. Do we dare see if he can breathe on his own?"

Tris nodded and closed his eyes, following the traces of his magic. With a silent prayer to the Lady, he loosed the spell that kept Vahanian's heartbeat and breathing functioning. Vahanian gasped sharply, and his whole body convulsed. He shuddered, then drew another deep gasp, and his fingers flexed. After a ragged breath, he opened his eyes. Vahanian blinked several times.

"Hooray!" Berry shouted, throwing her arms around Tris and planting a kiss on his cheek.

"Huzzah!" Carroway chimed in from the other side of the room. Kiara and Taru clapped their approval.

Tris laid a hand on Vahanian's uninjured shoulder. "Glad you're back. And thank you," Tris said soberly. "If you hadn't gotten between me and that knife, I'd be dead."

Vahanian gave a tired, lopsided smile. "It's what I do best," he rasped, and Carina brought him a glass of water, helping him sit to drink. He laid back, his struggle clear in his face. "I could hear most of what went on, but I couldn't do a damn thing about it." He looked at Tris. "I don't know how you did it, but thank you."

Vahanian glanced at Carina, who hastily dabbed at the corners of her eyes, and he held out his hand to her. "Thank you, too."

Carina squeezed Vahanian's hand. "The next time I let you escort me to a fancy ball, I'm going to wear red so the blood doesn't show." Vahanian realized she still wore the ruined ball gown from the night before.

"Tris's coronation. You'll look lovely in red," Vahanian murmured, closing his eyes.

Carina blushed. "All right," she said, resuming her best healer's tone. "We've all had a rough night. I'll stay 'til dawn. Whoever is eager for an early morning can take a shift, but let's get some sleep."

Carina watched the others file from the room, and then took the two cloaks Tris and Taru had left near the door. She wrapped one around herself as she dragged a chair near the fire. She slipped the other cloak over Vahanian, who was already asleep.

Carina meant to settle in for her watch, but she found that the nervous energy from the evening wouldn't let her relax. So she paced, with the cloak wrapped around her, as the fire burned down. On one hand, she felt relief. Tris's quest wouldn't fail because of her. Jonmarc was alive. She hadn't let him down the way she'd failed Ric. Despite her best efforts to keep Jonmarc at a distance, he was undeterred in pursuing her. She was as flattered as she was uneasy at his pursuit. In the caravan, she'd been impressed by his ability as a fighter, but even more by his loyalty, although what he did was often at odds with his carefully maintained appearance of not giving a damn about anything. Even that intrigued her. While Jonmarc looked nothing like Ric, that rebelliousness was a characteristic they shared, as was Jonmarc's willingness to break the rules for a good cause, and his foolhardy courage.

She remembered how it felt to dance with Jonmarc at Berry's welcome home feast. She was well aware of how much she had reacted to his touch in their brief encounters since then. The story he'd told her of his own background, when he sat with her after she returned from the citadel, the openness he'd shown her, drew her even closer to him. Close enough that it scared her.

The odds of any of them living through this quest were very slim, she knew, even if they were able to win their goal. Tris and Kiara seemed to have found the courage to acknowledge their feelings for one another despite those odds. Perhaps their love was stronger because it might be wrested away at any moment. Jonmarc already knew what it was to lose a lover to fate, and yet he had decided to act on his feelings. Here she was, too fearful to make the commitment, more afraid of losing him than of never knowing where their story might lead, despairing over either alternative. When they reached Principality, Jonmarc had decided his future, whether to take his reward and go back to the river, or to throw in his lot with Tris and the others. Carina knew that the same moment of decision would come for her in matters of the heart. She hoped that when it did, her courage wouldn't fail her.

CHAPTER FIFTEEN

Despite the assassination attempt on Tris, Staden's court resumed its merrymaking in short course. Festival days were filled with jousts and entertainment, and glittering banquets and feasts kept most of the courtiers awake until dawn. Winter fell much harder on Principality than on the palace cities in either Isencroft or Margolan. Despite themselves, Tris and his friends could not resist the unfamiliar spectacles.

"I thought I knew what winter was in Isencroft, but the cold here is something completely different!" Kiara exclaimed, her breath steaming in the bitterly cold air.

Carina nodded, almost completely buried in a borrowed fur coat that hid everything but her eyes. "I'd forgotten what Principality winters were like. That's one reason the merc troops winter here—the snow is too deep for anyone to attack them, and they're likely to get a decent rest!"

Vahanian shrugged, seemingly unconcerned with the cold. He wore a plain coat of wolf hide, with the leather side out and the fur turned in. What the cloak lacked in opulence, Tris bet it made up for in warmth. "Eastmark's worse. The army has to clear away enough snow to practice. Come spring, the floor of the practice field can be packed snow waist-high above the real ground."

"Mother always said that Isencroft's winter was Eastmark's high summer," Kiara chuckled. "And while she made me bundle up when I was a child, I always marveled that she went about with just a woven wrap most of the time."

Tris laughed. "By comparison, Shekerishet must seem like endless summer. We're further south than any of this, even the Borderlands. Our snows get deep, but not for most of the winter. I don't ever remember it getting quite this cold! Carroway looks like he's frozen solid." He looked toward where the bard played his lute with the other minstrels. Even with short gloves that left their fingers exposed, the musicians looked uncomfortably cold. They stood as close to the fire as they could without damaging their instruments.

"When all this is over, I want to buy one of those sleighs and have it sent to father," Kiara said, with a glance toward the large, graceful troikas that slid across the snow effortlessly behind a team of massive horses. Come winter, Principality nobles traded their carriages for ornately decorated sleighs, and even the merchants replaced the wheels on their wagons with runners. "But for now, let's beg another ride!"

Tris smiled as Kiara left them to find an accommodating driver. All around them, sleighs coursed through the deep snow, and men raced each other with snowshoes over thigh-deep drifts. Daredevils skied down steep slopes, and artists carved complex figures from huge blocks of ice. Groups of soldiers staged mock battles with armaments of snow and ice. The children followed suit; no one was safe from pelting snowballs. Huge bonfires lit the long nights, providing warmth against the bitter cold and making the icy decorations sparkle like the gems for which Principality was famous. All around them, nobles and villagers took comfort in a reminder of light and life during winter's darkest days.

"I don't think I've ever seen so many people dressed in fur," Tris commented. Women snuggled beneath heavy fur coats and blankets in their sleighs; men wore thick fur hats. Carroway confided that it was almost impossible to sing outside for more than a brief chorus or two without his lungs burning and his head pounding from the chill.

"Fur is only one way to stay warm," Vahanian said with a grin. He produced a small flask from a pocket, downing a gulp. Even from a distance, Tris could smell the potent liquor. The chill was a boon to the vendors who hawked wassail, mulled wine, and steaming mugs of warm ale. The crowd, warmed by the alcohol, did not seem to mind the cold.

"Were you watching?" Soterius puffed as he and Harrtuck trudged toward them through the snow. They came from the direction of the mock battle, and their hands and faces were reddened from the cold. "We trounced the other side! A complete rout!"

"Glad to see you've gotten into the festival spirit." Carina laughed, but Tris could see that the joviality did not reach her eyes. As guests of the king, Tris and the others felt obliged to visibly participate in the festivities. But the guards that surrounded them were a constant reminder of the danger. Vahanian in particular chafed at having a bodyguard. Knowing that even here Jared was a threat overshadowed the party spirit. While Tris and his friends could not help enjoying the opulence and beauty of the festival, the companions often withdrew early from the parties, keeping their own company in one of the upstairs rooms, as they had on the road. This night was an exception.

As darkness fell on the longest night of the year, the *vayash moru* joined the festival. They moved through the crowd unconcerned with the bitter cold; they wore no greatcloaks. No breath steamed as the *vayash moru* spoke. They kept their distance from the bonfires, and were indifferent to the carts that sold food and ale. Ghosts milled among the partygoers. They were dressed in fashions ranging over several hundred years. They seemed drawn by the music and the crowd. The spirit of one young man had the power to move objects, and he enjoyed playing pranks on festival goers who had had too much ale, deliberately moving their tankards and pulling out their chairs from beneath them. A few of the ghosts looked on with bittersweet longing from the edges, swaying with the tempo of the minstrels' ballads. One young couple, invisible to all but Tris, lingered just behind Carroway. They held hands, lost in the music. All the spirits, visible or not, bowed as Tris passed them, paying their respects to the Lord of the Dead.

Vahanian nodded toward the other side of the courtyard. "Sahila's back," he said with a glance toward the refugee spokesman, jarring Tris from his thoughts. "I don't think he's here for the sleigh rides."

Tris sobered. "Probably not. Staden and I sent blankets and provisions to the refugee camps, but it's still going to be a miserable winter for them. There's no way to get them enough shelter, even with the old army tents we found. I think Sahila's been making the rounds of the merc troops, using some of the gold I gave him to haggle with them for their worn out tarpaulins and field shelters. Since we've been paying gold to hire the troops' services, it seems the mercs are buying new equipment for the spring march. Sahila's a tough bargainer. He's managed to get wagon loads of castoffs that're better than what his people had before."

Tris received reports now almost nightly from Sahila and the refugees. So many soldiers had deserted from Jared's army that the remaining loyalists had begun capturing men and boys from the villages and conscripting them into service, threatening to destroy their families and villages if they refused. One village had hidden their boys in a secret cellar under a barn, but the soldiers burned the barn in retaliation for the villagers' refusal to give up their sons. The boys had perished, roasted alive in their hiding place. More than one of the mothers had thrown herself on the flaming heap, mad with grief.

It was no longer an isolated incident to hear of Jared's troops harvesting the battlefields, taking away the wounded and dying from both sides of the conflict. The wounded would be used to create more *ashtenerath*, while Arontala would trap the dying men's souls for his Orb to feed the Obsidian King, and his blood magic would grow stronger on their pain and death.

One refugee, a servant Tris remembered from Shekerishet's kitchen staff, recounted the death toll of Jared's lusts. Many of the servants in the palace served as whole families, in positions of honor that were handed down from generation to generation. Bricen had prided himself on his generosity to the servants, who ate nearly as well as the nobles and who received more than adequate clothing and shelter. Bricen's servants were freemen, and the king's openhandedness created bonds of loyalty far stronger than any indenture. Tris knew first-hand that the servants recognized Jared's brutality, and that Jared availed himself of every young girl who came to serve in the castle. Nearly every family had suffered from Jared's vile tempers, his willingness to thrash any servant who displeased him, and his brutality toward the palace animals.

But now, according to the former servant, the girls Jared called for did not return. Their bodies were found in the tunnels beneath the garderobe, or buried behind the barracks. Jared believed himself to be above any law or precedent. The retelling of his atrocities, both from refugees and from ghosts, unsettled even Gabriel and Mikhail. Once again, Tris wondered whether the kingdom would survive Jared, and what it would require of him to put things right should he live through his bid for the throne.

CHAPTER SIXTEEN

A FORTNIGHT AFTER Winterstide, Tris and Carina returned to the citadel of the Sisterhood. Carina did her best to cover her concern, but Tris could tell that she was worried. After his close call during the last training session, he shared her apprehension.

Vahanian recovered from the assassin's attack more slowly than Carina would have liked, a side effect of the poison. Royster could find no other recorded instances of survival from the poison that was used, so he eagerly wrote up the process by which Carina and Tris were able to save Vahanian.

Tris took his leave of Kiara with regret. As a betrothal token and a gift for Kiara's birthday later that same month, Tris had a ring made for her of Margolan gold. It bore his crest as Bricen's second son set with precious stones from his portion of the reward Staden gave them for Berry's safe return.

Kiara worried more about Tris's return to training when he and Carina refused to share details, and so Tris finally told her about Elam's murder and the battle with Alaine, omitting only the dark sendings.

Despite Taru's healing, those images still haunted his dreams. Though they lacked the certainty of the sendings, the nightmares woke him more often than he cared to admit, bathed in sweat, his heart thudding. The memory of those dreams pushed him to master his power. And while Tris saw his growing skills as a way to assure his friends' survival, he told no one that he held very little hope of surviving the confrontation himself.

It was the first month of the new year, and Principality lay under heavy snow. Tris, who thought that he was colder at Winterstide than ever before in his life, discovered that the gray weeks of the Birth Month were colder still. He shivered despite his heavy cloak, mentally calculating just how much further south Shekerishet was, and what the weather there might be at this season. The heavy gray skies and the frigid wind seemed to dampen everyone's mood now that the festivities were over. Even the gathering the night before with Tris and his friends seemed subdued, despite Carroway's bawdy songs and good-natured joking. As the days slipped by, the reality of their quest loomed. There was very little time left for preparation.

At the citadel, even Taru seemed reserved when she met their carriage. She led Tris and Carina back to the same suite of rooms, where a platter of cold meat and cheese awaited them after their journey, and a pot of tea whistled on the hearth.

"How are things with Landis in charge?" Carina asked as she shook the snow from her cloak and hung it near the fire to dry.

"Landis is an able administrator—I've never doubted that. But her focus is on the present, not the future, as Elam's was. She's a manager, not a visionary. I hope practicality will be enough."

Tris realized that Taru's close relationship with Elam would have made the older mage's death a personal loss. "I never had the chance to tell you how sorry I am about Elam's death," Tris said quietly.

Taru smiled. "Thank you. But I understand—you had a few other things on your mind at the time." She paused. "I don't have your power with spirits, but I can sense Elam's presence. She's still here. That's been a comfort. Now that you've returned, perhaps you can tell whether she has a purpose for remaining, or awaits your help to pass over."

"Would you like me to try?" Tris asked as he hung his cloak near Carina's and shook the last of the snow from his boots.

"I'd be grateful if you would."

"Let's do it now—I may not be in such good shape later." He raised his hand and closed his eyes, stretching out along the Plains of Spirit. Elam's ghost came to him quickly, and he accepted her greeting. With a murmured word, Tris made the spirit visible, and opened his eyes. Elam stood before them, her expression sober.

"We miss you," Taru said to the spirit.

Elam inclined her head in acknowledgement. "Thank you. But I'm still here." The spirit looked at Tris. "Your work with the Court of Spirits has helped to ease some of the imbalance in the Flow, but it is still badly damaged. Until the Flow of power can be healed, Arontala's blood magic gains an advantage from the imbalance, and Light magic is not at its full strength. There is no time to fix it, so we shall have to work around it."

Elam's gaze was worried. "Landis didn't fight the Mage War; I did. She understands what's at stake in her mind, but not in her heart. She also didn't know your grandmother as I knew her. Landis is afraid that your loyalty to your friends—and to Kiara—will compromise your judgment." She held up a hand to stay Tris's argument. "Hear me out. Many of the Sisterhood believe that Bava K'aa was weakened by her love for Lemuel and see her refusal to destroy the Obsidian King as proof."

"And what do you believe? You were closer to her than anyone except Grayson."

Elam nodded. "Bava K'aa understood the peril of taking it upon oneself to decide who is expendable, and who is not. In binding the Obsidian King to save Lemuel, Bava K'aa upheld both her duty to the people and to her lover. She didn't want to put herself in the role of the Goddess and determine who should live and who should die."

"How will Landis's opinion of Grandmother affect my training?"

Elam's ghost met his gaze. "I saw the images of the dark sending that Arontala cast though Alaine. Arontala's counting on your loyalty to your friends to constrain your choices. He's ruthless, and he knows that you are not. He'll attack you through those you love."

Tris thought about the assassin at Staden's palace, and his charge to attack Kiara had he survived the attempt on Tris's life. "He already has."

"Landis isn't as scrupulous about such things as I was," Elam said. "She tells herself that because the cause is noble, the means are forgiven. She will design your training with the avatars to test your resolve as much as your battle skills. Landis would like to see evidence that you'll do whatever it takes to destroy the Obsidian King—regardless of the cost."

Tris stiffened. "I'm not afraid to die. But my friends aren't game pieces. They're not expendable. I don't accept that as the only way to win. If I did, how would I be any different from Arontala?"

"I agree," the ghost replied. "But Landis thinks differently. Your trials may resemble the sendings more than you care to think. Prepare yourself."

Tris swallowed hard. "I understand," he said, avoiding Carina's gaze as the healer looked at him questioningly. "Would you go to your rest?"

Elam shook her head. "Not yet. When your grandmother was dying, she sent for me. She made me promise that if you ever came to me in need, that I'd do everything within my power, for her sake. At the time, I thought it an odd request, since I had no reason to think you were a mage, and princes do not often seek the help of the Sisterhood. But I made a vow. I intend to honor that promise."

"Thank you," Tris said. He let the spirit fade, knowing that Elam remained nearby even though the ghost was no longer visible to the others.

Taru sighed. "I'm afraid I agree with Elam's opinion of Landis. She has a tendency to interpret what is 'light' and what is 'dark' by what profits her own viewpoint. And she wants the destruction of the Obsidian King, no matter what."

"How can you send Tris into training knowing that?" Carina demanded.

"Because without the training, I won't be strong enough to find that other alternative," Tris said quietly. "The stronger I am, the more choices I'll have, and the more chance there'll be for everyone else."

Taru nodded. "I agree." She managed a smile. "Enough of this talk. Eat something, and get some rest. Tomorrow morning, we start your new lessons. You'll have over a week to train—and recover. Late next week you'll face another trial. This one will use avatars. And it will be warded."

Tris hoped his nervousness did not show in his eyes. "I'll be ready."

TRIS'S NEW BATTLE trainer Laisren, a *vayash moru* hand-picked by Gabriel for unquestionable loyalty, pushed Tris's fighting skills and reaction time to their limits. It was unsettling to fight an opponent that could regenerate from everything except all-consuming fire, decapitation, and a clean strike through the heart; Tris found that his nightmares now had a whole new quality of realism. The worst of the wounds from their skirmishes were healed, but the scars remained to keep the lessons fresh in his mind.

Sometimes, Laisren wore a null magic charm, forcing Tris to hold his own with fighting skills alone. The null amulet dampened his magic, pushing it out of reach. Fortunately, the charm's influence was limited and its power dropped off completely outside of the immediate presence of its wearer.

When Tris wasn't skirmishing with his undead opponent, Taru's lessons in defensive magic pushed him to exhaustion. Tris learned to counter the pain spells that Theron used against him, and to sense and deflect spells like the one that stopped Elam's heart. Tris guessed that Taru went well beyond the usual boundaries of acceptable gray magic to test him against an array of magical attacks. Tris was grudgingly proud of the fact that he managed to survive, and to send back counter spells that appeared to strain even Taru's defenses.

A week and a half after his return to the citadel, Tris stood before Landis, ready to go into the catacombs for his trial.

"What is the task?" Tris asked, hoping his voice was steady.

"The task is always the same," replied Landis. "Overcome the traps. Best the avatars. Defeat a mage and wrest the Orb from his possession. And, if possible, live through it."

"Your penchant for self-sacrifice is noble, but impractical. You must be willing to pay whatever price success demands. You may find that your own death is not the dearest coin." Landis flicked her wrist, and the door opened behind him to the catacombs.

"Now go. And may the Lady in all Her Faces look with favor on your battle."

Tris descended the stone stairs carefully, and felt the death warding snap into place behind him. Although he had expected it, the tingle of its magic was unsettling. Tris listened in the shadows with both hearing and mage sense. He knew that he was not alone.

Deep in the catacombs beneath the citadel, Tris stepped warily from the shadows. The dark, damp stones carried the imprint of old and powerful magic. At intervals, mage-fire torches lit the corridor, but between them stretched dangerous shadows. The tunnels formed a convoluted maze, with hidden rooms and real peril.

A rush of air was the only warning.

Tris pivoted, Mageslayer ready in his grip. Immortally strong hands seized him from behind. Tris could feel the chill of the *vayash moru*'s grip even through his tunic. "What now, Lord of the Dead?" Laisren's voice taunted near his ear, close enough to the blood pulsing through his neck that Tris fought the urge to shiver. While the other opponents he would encounter would be avatars, the *vayash moru*, exempt from the death warding, was very real.

"*Lethyrashem*!" Tris spoke the word of power, and the *vayash moru* dropped his grip as if burned. Tris turned, placing Mageslayer between them. The ensorcelled sword's faint glow lit the shadows. He had barely raised his sword when the *vayash moru* vanished from sight.

Tris swung with Mageslayer and felt the blade connect; his opponent withdrew to the shadows with a hiss. Mageslayer, possessing its own version of sentience, "understood" to blunt its magic against the *vayash moru* trainer. Laisren, in turn, agreed not to use his superior speed and strength to kill Tris. And while Tris believed that his Summoner's magic would make it unlikely for him to be brought across against his will, he did not want to find out how much blood he could lose before those magical protections set in.

Moving faster than mortal sight, the *vayash moru* pinned Tris from behind, and threw him sideways into the damp stone wall. Before Tris could find his feet, the vice-like hands tossed him into the air again. He landed hard enough to feel his collar bone snap and ribs crack, felt blood start along his side and face as he scraped along the rough wall.

Laisren struck again, avoiding Tris's swing with Mageslayer. Flung backward against the chamber's wall, Tris's head swam. He gasped for breath as impossibly strong arms lifted him and pinned him.

"Hurry, Lord of the Dead," the *vayash moru* whispered. The *vayash moru*'s breath was cold against his neck, and Tris felt mortal fear fill him as teeth sank against his skin. Dizziness washed over him.

Tris fought panic and closed his eyes. He felt himself weakening, struggling to find the center of his power. On the Plains of Spirit, he could see the *vayash moru* clearly, though darkness blocked his mortal sight. Tris summoned his power, and with the magic came a rush of spirits, called like moths to flame. The magic bore him up as his mortal body weakened. In his mind's eye, he saw his power fill him, saw it glow and burn through his skin and eyes, white-hot.

Laisren hissed sharply, lifting his teeth from Tris's neck and loosening his grip. Reeling, Tris relied on mage sight to swing Mageslayer, running his attacker through the belly. Tris staggered as the *vayash moru*'s weight fell against the sword. Laisren's face came into focus, an ironic smile on his lips.

"Next time I shall make it more difficult," he said, falling still as Tris withdrew his sword.

Alone again in the darkness Tris gasped for breath, feeling his injuries fully. Left collar bone cracked or broken, at least one rib on the same side likewise. Blood trickled from the punctures in his neck, evidence that he had truly surprised his attacker, who had the means to leave a bloodless bite. Tris looked at the *vayash moru*'s still form, and wondered whether his attacker would feel any worse for the wear after he regenerated.

Tris started forward again as soon as his heart slowed and the vertigo passed, alert for traps both magical and mundane. His Summoner's power meant that many traps that often protected magical places and items would not deter him. In winning Mageslayer, he had proved his ability to wrestle with hostile spirits, quell reanimated fighters, and dispel a demi-demon. But magic, he knew, posed only one threat. Even powerful mages were constrained by the limits of their bodies. Traps to ensnare mortals could just as easily kill an unwary mage. Tris moved forward cautiously into the darkness.

Tris's mage sense prickled a warning, and he tested the steps ahead of him with his power. At his touch a section of the floor gave way, yawning into blackness. Tris tested the other side of the chasm carefully. He used his newly-honed climbing skills to find toe holds in the rough stone wall and cross the gap. As he reached the other side, Tris heard wind roar up from the pit. Mageslayer brightened at the danger. Tris stepped backward against a solid rock wall. Trapped.

Rising from the chasm, a vortex of wind swirled with storm power, buffeting him against the wall. From the depths of the darkness it brought with it shards of stone and bone, blinding dust, and stinging grit. Tris flung up shielding, and struggled to hold it against the force of the storm.

His skin burned with the grit that swirled in the air around him as his shields snapped into place. The wind was powerful, and the close quarters seemed to double its force. Such a storm could rage for days, far longer than he could hold his shields. Around him the wind howled, full of debris that could strip skin from bone. Despite Mageslayer's glow, it was almost impossible to see.

The winds were not sentient, so his spirit magic was of no help. The storm surged, threatening to break through his shields; Tris knew he could not hold out forever. *Even if the wind storm doesn't kill me, it can make enough of a mess of me that it will take forever for Carina to put back the pieces,* he thought.

The winds howled louder. Tris seized on a slim hope.

He threw his cowl over his head and took a deep breath, tightening a two-handed grip on Mageslayer. He let his shields fall.

As the storm howled toward him, Tris focused on Mageslayer, willing his energy and power to become one with the blade. *Fire*! he willed, letting his magic thrum along the blade until the metal glowed hotter than forged steel. The winds reached him and the grit and shards began to tear at his clothing and exposed skin. The force of the storm threatened to sweep him off his feet into the pit, but

Tris closed his eyes, willing his power through the blade.

With a roar, fire erupted from Mageslayer's blade, so hot that Tris felt his breath leave him. A blast of concentrated flame struck at the heart of the winds. Long ago, the palace smithy told him that fire burnt air; a fire in a closed place will take the air until there is none left to breathe. As the heat rose, Tris held firm to Mageslayer's grip, though the metal burned his hands and the buffeting of the storm strained his outstretched arms. The air filled with the smell of scorched rock, but Tris felt the wind weaken, dropping its lethal cargo of grit and shards. Arms aching, Tris held on to the sword. A reaction headache was beginning to pound in his temples. Then with a rush, the winds died.

Sweat-soaked, bleeding from tiny cuts, and heaving for breath in the thin air, Tris dropped to his knees. Mageslayer gradually dimmed to a faint blue light.

I'm alive! Tris thought, lightheaded from the scorched air. Just as quickly, he remembered that he was trapped against a sheer stone wall, with the pit between him at the cool, sweet air of the passage.

Aching in every muscle, Tris reached for a flask at his belt and took a drink. Carina swore that the herbed water would sustain him from minor injuries and fatigue. While it did nothing for the pain in his ribs, Tris felt the pounding of his headache recede. The sting of his cuts and burns faded. Still dizzy from the loss of blood and the thin air, Tris searched a pouch at his belt for a wad of pummeled rope vine, about as thick as the tip of his thumb. He pushed the wad between his back teeth, and bit down hard, hoping it would help to clear his head. After a few moments he felt strong enough to stand, Mageslayer held warily against any surprise from the pit.

When nothing stirred from the blackness, Tris turned his attention to the rock wall at the back of the passage. He felt his way toward the magic that tingled in the rocks. As Tris slid his free hand across the rough stone, he also let his mage sense play across the wall until both touch and magic located a loose stone. With Mageslayer gripped in his right hand Tris carefully felt the edges of the stone with his left, finding that it would neither pull nor push, but could be rotated with effort.

The stone clicked into place and the wall gave way, sliding very slowly backward. But before Tris could withdraw his hand, a whirring noise buzzed from within the hole and a sharp pain in his palm made him jerk back his hand.

A tiny dart was embedded in his palm. Tris pulled it free, but already the wormroot burned through his veins. He staggered into the newly opened corridor, falling against the cold stone wall.

He clenched his fist around Mageslayer, drawing from its power to fight the poison. Tris chewed harder on the rope vine, letting its bitter juice course down his throat.

Sweet Chenne, Tris thought, willing himself not to be sick. *I'm barely in one piece, and I've yet to face the avatars!*

With the help of Mageslayer and the rope vine, Tris clung to his power. He was flushed with fever and the headache pounded, but he willed himself forward. Although his palm burned from the poison, he reached for a dirk from his belt. The corridor turned and he saw pale red light glowing from an open doorway.

The Soulcatcher! Tris thought, remembering the deadly orb in Arontala's study, the prison of the Obsidian King. It took conscious effort for Tris to keep his power within his grasp as he made his way carefully down the corridor, Mageslayer gripped white-knuckled in his hand.

Tris reached the doorway. Inside the stone room, Soulcatcher lit the vaulted ceilings of the chamber, glowing like a captured sun on a pedestal in the center of the floor. A cowled, red-robed figure stood, arms upraised over the orb, his back to the door. Tris heard Arontala's cold chuckle from an avatar that looked to be a perfect replica. But unlike in his confrontation with Alaine, neither the orb nor the avatar radiated the imprint of Arontala's power.

"Come to join your sister?" Arontala baited with a smile that showed his long eye teeth.

Tris loosed a burst of power toward Arontala and the Fire Clan mage brushed aside the assault without raising his shields. His counterstrike nearly tore Mageslayer from Tris's grip.

"Come now. You'll have to do better than that."

The mage's next strike almost broke through Tris's shields. Tris could feel the poison in his veins growing stronger, eroding his control, making his magic a wild and unpredictable force.

Tris clasped Mageslayer tighter, drawing from the spelled blade against the poison, and he ground his teeth on the rope vine. His ribs throbbed and his head pounded, making it difficult to focus his vision.

"I have the offering," a familiar voice said. Tris's blood ran cold. Straight from his nightmares, Jared stepped into the room from a side door, dragging with him a battered and bound Kiara.

They're just avatars, Tris struggled against the anger and instinct that boiled up in him. *It's not really him, not really her. Not real. Can't be real.*

"We have a visitor," Arontala purred, inclining his head.

Jared's familiar leer twisted his handsome features. "Hello, Tris." He intentionally pulled on the ropes that bound Kiara's wrists, eliciting a groan. Her eyes were closed, one cheek bruised, and her tunic was smudged and bloody. The gash on Jared's sleeve and his torn shirt told of the fight that victory had required. "My mage assures me that once we feed her soul to the orb, what remains will be sufficient for my... needs."

A cold, rational corner of Tris's mind calculated his odds. The battle with the *vayash moru*, his injuries from the storm, and the wormroot had already taken a toll, pushed further by the exchange with Arontala. He would have one chance, if his magic would obey his will at all. Although he stood equally close to Arontala's avatar as to Jared's, a move toward either would bring a counter from the other. And there was Kiara. Avatar or not, he would not accept her sacrifice.

"Bring her," Arontala ordered. Jared dragged the Kiara-double forward, forcing her to kneel beside the glowing orb.

In the back of Tris's mind, one possibility presented itself.

Tris plunged onto the spirit plains and found the glow that was Mageslayer's power. His magic was waning as the poison worked its way through his blood. Drawing on Mageslayer for support, Tris hurled the dirk in his left hand, catching Jared in the chest.

With Mageslayer as an athame, Tris sent a blast of power toward Arontala, using the orb as a lens to magnify the effect. Spent to the point of exhaustion, Tris sent the last of his power toward Kiara, covering her with a fragile shield. The explosion at Westmarch when Tris forced power back through the scrying ball did not compare to the firestorm that erupted from Soulcatcher, incinerating Arontala and blistering Tris's skin. Everything in his sight turned to black, and Tris collapsed.

FIRST CAME PAIN, then consciousness. In the darkness Tris heard voices, but whether the lightless space was in a room or inside his own mind he did not know.

"He failed," snapped one voice.

"Tsk, Tsk," chided another. "Define failure. He made it through the traps, past the wormroot. And his solution worked—after a fashion."

"He has his grandmother's weakness," said a third. "He might have survived the explosion if he had been willing to let her go. If he dies in the attempt, we are no better served. Jared's bastard will become the rightful king."

"If you're so worried about the girl, keep her from accompanying him," said the first voice.

"Have you forgotten? It was the will of the Oracle," argued the second. "She may be in greater danger of being taken—or turned—if she is alone, or if they wed and she stays behind to bear his child. This is the will of the Lady."

"I've found," noted the third voice dryly, "that the will of the Lady is always clearer in retrospect. He did what we required—destroyed the orb, Jared, and Arontala. Landis seemed intent that he be willing to sacrifice someone. He sacrificed himself. We did not actually say he must survive the encounter."

"It was implied," sniffed the second. "Bava K'aa's foolish sentiment endangered us all, and now, his weakness will do so again."

"Perhaps he'll learn from his recovery," noted the first voice, growing faint in the darkness. "It won't be pleasant."

The voices might have said more, but the darkness and fever took him. He did not remember anything else.

WHEN HE FOUND the strength to open his eyes, Tris could make out only shadows in the dim light. *I'm a Summoner, so I should know if I were dead*, he thought. *It doesn't look like the spirit plains. But maybe they look different from the other side.*

"Don't even think about moving," a familiar voice instructed. The shadow came closer in the twilight, bringing a cool rag for his forehead and a cup of water. "Slowly," she cautioned, lifting the water to his parched lips as she helped him rise from his pillow. The water tasted of herbs and medicines. Even the slightest movement hurt, and he realized he was wet with sweat.

"Where—"

The shadow gently laid him back and wiped his face with the rag. "You're still in the citadel," the voice said. Tris realized the shadow was Carina, though he could not see her face in the darkness.

"Why so dark?" He was barely able to form the words. Excruciating pain radiated from behind his eyes. His whole body seemed on fire.

"Shh," Carina hushed gently. "It's been three days. They weren't expecting what you did back there. They barely shielded you in time. Sister Taru has been helping me. It was too close, Tris. It was just an avatar, dammit! You shielded her instead of yourself, and it wasn't even a real person!"

"It was the right thing to do," Tris managed, finding his throat sore and his lips cracked.

"There was so much wormroot in your system it took a day before we could even begin to heal," Carina said. "I saw everything you did," she reached out to take his hand. "You were amazing."

"Not good enough," Tris murmured.

"You were amazing," Carina repeated. "But we need you to live through the real thing, do you understand? It's not complete unless you live to take the crown."

Tris wanted to respond, but her potion drew him back into the respite of the darkness.

CHAPTER SEVENTEEN

A LITTLE MORE than a week later, Tris and Carina returned to Staden's palace in time to see Soterius and Mikhail off on their journey back into Margolan.

"Now that Ban's an outlaw hero, he'll probably have twice the number of ladies vying for him," Carroway teased. He set his lyre down. The group was still chuckling at the off-color ballad he'd dedicated to the high points of Soterius's upcoming ride into Margolan to inspire dissent. Even Staden dabbed a tear from his eye as the laughter subsided.

"I figure you advised him on the high-born ruffian look," Tris rejoined, grinning. "The hair and the beard, the leather cloak; I just assumed it was all for the benefit of the village girls!"

"Mikhail's done the same, so it must be in fashion," Kiara added. She gave a sly grin in Tris's direction. "We're waiting for you and Jonmarc to pick up on the trend."

Soterius rolled his eyes, taking the ribbing good naturedly as the small group laughed. "I doubt we'll have much time for trysting," he observed. "Although I'm hoping that we won't be completely without good ale."

The friends were assembled in Staden's private dining room. Servants cleared away the dishes from a sumptuous farewell dinner in honor of Soterius and Mikhail. Only the companions from the road, plus Royster, Staden, and Berry attended, and everyone seemed committed to keeping the conversation light.

"Keep your ale—I'm hoping the forests haven't been hunted clean of deer." Mikhail said.

"Actually, I thought Carroway might volunteer to go with us," Soterius returned the teasing. "I suspect we'll raise enough of a ruckus to make a few good stories."

Carroway gave him a skeptical look. "And I imagine you think sneaking Tris back to the palace won't be exciting enough?" Tris watched the others as the servants brought the dessert course. Soterius professed full confidence in his mission, but Tris knew his friend well enough to see his worry. Tris didn't blame Soterius for being nervous. While the idea itself was brilliant, it was another thing altogether to slip into a land at war, recruit its army against its king and live to tell the tale. Even Mikhail seemed preoccupied.

Staden cleared his throat. "I can't help you with the ladies—not that either of you seem to need assistance," he said with a raised eyebrow. "But you'll find two excellent horses ready for you in the stable, and all of the provisions you'll need. I've instructed my groom to leave the horses unkempt so that they don't look like they've come from my stable."

"We're in your debt, Your Majesty," Soterius said.

"And there's Isencroft tack for both of you," Kiara added.

Mikhail looked at her. "How did you manage to come by that out here? Isencroft tack doesn't usually stay long on the shelf."

"Berry helped me make a few connections," Kiara said and Berry giggled. "We made sure it's seasoned, so it doesn't look new. But if you need to fight and ride, there's nothing better to help you keep your seat."

Tris reached into his pocket and pulled out a small pouch, which he slid across the table to Soterius. "There'll be gold for your journey in your packs," Tris promised. "But this will either convince doubters that you really are on my side—or it'll get you hanged faster if you're caught. I suggest you keep it well hidden."

Soterius emptied the pouch into his hand. A golden ring tumbled out, a replica of Tris's own signet with the crest of Bricen's second son. Soterius weighed it in his hand for a moment, then slipped it back into the pouch and nodded.

"Wouldn't be surprised if that tack Kiara's talking about doesn't have a few secret compartments for something just like this."

Gabriel reached into the breast pocket of his doublet and withdrew a similar pouch, which he handed to Mikhail. "It may not be an original gift," he said with a dry smile, "but it might help if you encounter some of our kind who have not heard the Blood Council's ruling." Mikhail withdrew a signet like the one Gabriel wore on his left hand, with a crest Tris now recognized as the mark of the Blood Council.

"If we're handing out gifts," Carroway said, "then I've got something for both of you." He reached into a small pack under the table and withdrew two bundles. The larger bundle he handed to Soterius, and the smaller one to Mikhail. "Well—open them!"

"We ought to take on harebrained stunts like this more often if it comes with dinner and gifts!" Mikhail joked. He was first to open his bundle. Inside was a small set of pipes. Mikhail lifted them to his lips and played a few bars of a popular tavern ditty.

"You've already memorized all the songs I've written to stir up trouble," Carroway added. "And I've heard you play when you didn't think anyone was listening. Not bad... for someone who's not a bard, that is."

Soterius tore the paper from around his bundle. A bandolier of stawar leather tumbled out, complete with a set of throwing knives. Soterius raised the leather belt appreciatively. "Now *that* is beautiful."

Carroway grinned. "You can thank Jonmarc for the leatherwork. Berry and I supplied the knives. Pity you can't throw as well as we do, but maybe you'll improve with practice."

Soterius gave him a sour look that sent the rest laughing. Harrtuck reached behind him for his pack, and emptied it out unceremoniously onto the table. Out fell a collection of small weapons—daggers, shivs, darts, and metal knuckle guards. Few of the items were considered legal; they were the equipment of a mercenary or a brawler rather than a regulation soldier.

"I'd rather not explain my sources," Harrtuck said with a sideways glance at Staden, who laughed. "But I took up a collection from the boys in the company. They decided that if you're going to act like mercs you should be outfitted like them."

When the group finally stopped laughing, Carina reached under the table for her gift. "This may not be as much help for Mikhail, since he doesn't need my services," she said as Soterius unpacked the cloth bag. "But it's got enough herbs and powders to patch you up a few times at least. Try not to need more."

"I'll make it up to Mikhail with this," Royster said, and withdrew a leather-bound book from beneath his chair. "It's by King Argus's court scribe; it has a full recounting of the king's best military battles. Rather engrossing, if you ask me. Perhaps there's something in the strategies you can use."

Mikhail smiled as he weighed the book in his hands. "Argus was a friend of mine. And although I couldn't join him in his ale, he was a man with an appetite for good times."

Tris shuddered, remembering the crypt beneath the Library at Westmarch. "Since I met him after he was already dead, I wouldn't know. He was determined at the time to take me with him."

Mikhail chuckled. "Argus had a temper. And he could hold a grudge. But he was one of your grandmother's most loyal supporters. Like everyone else, I suspect he had a bit of a crush on her. For a sorceress, she had more than her share of admirers."

When the dessert was finished and the plates were cleared, an awkward silence fell over the group. Staden cleared his throat and stood.

"I suspect that you'll be getting your nights and days turned around if you intend to ride together," Staden said with a glance between Soterius and Mikhail. "But since I'm guessing that we're into the early bells of the morning, perhaps we'd best let you get some rest before you set out." He bid them rise, and stood in front of Soterius and Mikhail.

"'Tis not an easy thing you set off to do," the king said gravely. "But from what I've seen, there's no one more likely to make it happen. May the Goddess ride with you." He clapped a large hand on each man's shoulder with a force that might have felled a frail person. Tris and the others crowded around them.

Kiara whispered a blessing and kissed Soterius on the cheek in parting as Jae hopped from foot to foot on her shoulder. Carroway shook Soterius's hand and made his exit quickly after leaving them with a bawdy rhyme. Vahanian slapped Soterius soundly on the back and wished him well. Harrtuck embraced him until Soterius cried out for release, and then parted with a ribald prayer for the Lady's favor. Berry pressed a small cockade into Soterius's hand, a sign of her favor, and hugged him. Even Carina stretched up on tiptoe to kiss Soterius on the cheek in blessing and wish him well. The group also made their goodbyes to Mikhail, though a bit more formally, as seemed fitting. Then everyone was gone, save Tris, Mikhail, and Soterius.

"I'll get the horses ready," Mikhail said, bowing slightly to Tris. "If the Lady's hand is on us, we'll see you again at Shekerishet. May the Dark Lady favor you." He made the sign of the Lady. Tris and Soterius were silent until after Mikhail closed the door behind him.

"If there's something formal I'm supposed to say," Tris said, "I don't know what it is."

"The only reasonable thing would be to try to talk me out of it, but we both know it's too late for that."

"I know."

"Hey, quit acting like it's my funeral. We're going to drink about this at your coronation, where you can amply reward me with some high-flying title."

"You, on the Council of Nobles. I shudder to think."

"We'll shake them up a little," Soterius promised. "Show them how to have a good time." He fell silent. Tris could see the stress in his friend's face.

"Ban, if you're having second thoughts—"

"Not on your life," Soterius answered a bit too quickly. "I mean, hey, we've all got a part to play in this, right? After all, I helped get us into this. If we hadn't been snooping around Arontala's window like houseflies—"

"We'd be dead."

Soterius grimaced. "Well, yes, I guess so." He rested one foot on the bench of the table and leaned forward, picking the last traces from the meat platter. "You know, Tris, Carroway is right. They'll be singing about this in the taverns for generations.

Martris Drayke, the Summoner King of Margolan."
He shot a sly look in Tris's direction, "And his
noble queen, Kiara of Isencroft."

"That's enough of that," Tris said, rolling his
eyes. They were silent again for a few moments.

"Well," said Soterius awkwardly. "I guess I'd better be going."

"I guess so. I'll see you back at Shekerishet,
right?"

"I might even beat you there," Soterius said, managing a grin. "I'll be watching your back, just like
always."

"Be careful, Ban," Tris said, clasping his friend in
a tight farewell embrace.

Soterius stepped back. "You too. I think the Lady
really does have Her hand on you, Tris, but be careful anyway."

Tris murmured a blessing and then turned away,
steeling himself against looking back, and closed
the heavy door behind him. But it took him many
candlemarks that night to fall asleep, and dreams,
when they came, left him restless.

TRIS FOUND THAT nearly as many petitioners waited for him after his return from the citadel as were
there before Winterstide. He balanced his duties as
a Summoner against the growing list of decisions
that demanded his attention as the time for their
return to Margolan grew closer. Even the training
with Vahanian took on new urgency, and Tris ached
from the candlemarks spent trying to perfect the
difficult Eastmark fighting style that required both
agility and full concentration. He despaired of ever
matching Vahanian's skill, although he secretly

took pride in the complicated moves he had mastered. And after the salle came more study with Royster, until Tris's eyes blurred. He had fallen asleep at his desk more nights than he wished to remember, adding a stiff neck to his list of injuries.

Tris held his Court of Spirits in the evening, so that he could also serve the petitions of *vayash moru*. Gabriel and Vahanian took turns guarding him at all times. Tris accepted the protection ruefully, though he declined Staden's offer of more guards, fearing that soldiers might scare away too many petitioners.

It was early in the second month, the Hunger Moon, when Tris found himself more homesick than usual. Outside snow fell heavily, covering the Principality hills in drifts higher than a horse's hocks.

"Didn't anyone tell you?" Tris joked with Vahanian as the fighter pulled his cloak closer around himself. "We hold the Court of Spirits inside. You're dressed for a ride through the snows."

Vahanian grimaced. "Every time one of those spooks shows up, the temperature in here drops another notch. Can't draw a sword if I can't feel my fingers."

Tris chuckled. "If you mind the cold, make sure you mention it to Gabriel before you head to Dark Haven. It's in the foothills, and given that the caretakers are all... *unconcerned*... about the cold, it may take a bit to ready the fireplaces for a mortal resident."

"You make it sound absolutely charming," Vahanian muttered.

A group of petitioners ventured forward. Tris looked up. It was unusual for a group to come all at once.

One man stepped forward. "Hail, Prince Martris," he said, bowing low. He spoke Margolense with a midlands accent, from the area near Shekerishet. His blond hair was dirty, and he had the raw-boned look of a farmer. Though he appeared to be only a decade older than Tris, his hands were already broadened from hard labor.

"If it please Your Highness, hear my petition."

"Tell me what you seek."

"My name is Nascha. We've come to ask for your help," said the man. "We are the families of the *scirranish*, the vanished ones." The word he used, "*scirranish*," was from the old tales, where it meant "taken by monsters." Tris saw that Vahanian was paying close attention.

People crowded behind Nascha, a group of at least twenty ragged men and women, their expressions etched with sadness. From their soiled and torn clothing, Tris guessed that they were refugees. Most were badly underdressed for the frigid weather, their faces and hands reddened with the cold.

"We're camped three days' ride from here, just over the Principality border from Margolan," said Nascha. "We come from every corner of Margolan, but our stories are the same. King Jared's soldiers came to our villages and dragged us from our beds. Some, they burned as *vayash moru*, even though they were mortal. Some of the men they executed as spies, for the crime of possessing a sword. Our boys they took for their army, our young women for their lust, and our winter crops for their bellies.

They left the rest of us to starve." Beside Tris, Vahanian muttered a potent curse.

"How can I help you?" asked Tris, struggling with the anger that rose inside him against Jared.

"You're a Summoner," said Nascha. "We don't know what happened to the *Scirranish*. We don't know whether to mourn their passing and make their gifts to the Lady, or whether they still live, and might, through some miracle, return to us. We beg you, Prince Martris, show us their fate, so that we can make our peace."

Every face in the group watched him with desperate hope. Tris rose, and walked out among the refugees. Vahanian fell into step behind him, and the crowd parted. "I will show you what I can," Tris said.

Tris breathed a prayer to the Lady as he raised his wardings and opened himself to the Plains of Spirit. He let his thoughts focus on each petitioner's face by turn. As he did so, he called out to the lost and wandering spirits. Each of the supplicants whispered the names of their missing ones. Gradually at the edge of his mage sight, like clouds heavy with impending snow, Tris could feel the spirits heed his call. He struggled with his own feelings as the ghosts presented themselves: men bearing the wounds of war and torture, boys barely old enough to lift a sword marked by battle, girls not old enough to wed whose wraiths showed the evidence of their disgrace and death.

"Crone take Jared's soul," Vahanian swore as Tris focused his power, making the spirits visible. Around him there were shouts, cries, and the high-pitched keening of mourners as the living claimed their dead. Tris pushed aside his feelings so that he could focus his power more clearly. The spirits' images became more solid, and Tris lent them the power to speak aloud so that he did not have to bear tidings for each one.

In groups of twos and threes the refugees welcomed their dead, tearful over the violence of their passing and the certainty of their death, and relieved at the finality of the knowledge. The emotions of the living Tris could shield from his consciousness, but the strong feelings of the dead washed over him like pounding waves. Gradually, the room grew quiet. Tris looked to the refugees and their dead.

"Would you go to the Lady now?"

"By your leave, Lord of the Dead," answered one spirit, a burly man whose throat bore the marks of a noose. "We are agreed. We're not ready to rest until Jared and his mage be destroyed."

"What would you have me do?"

The ghosts moved forward, leaving their mortal loved ones behind, and formed a solemn row in front of Tris. "Is if true that you mean to challenge King Jared?" asked the burly ghost.

"It is."

"Then we wish to fight," said the ghost. "Lord of the Dead, grant us this request. Let us return to the places were we're buried. Give our spirits the power to show ourselves to the living and to be heard. Our bodies lie along the roads and in the ditches. When Jared's soldiers pass, our spirits will rise up and take our vengeance."

"Seems to me we met a whole forest like that once," Vahanian murmured under his breath.

"What word do you give that only the guilty will be punished?" Tris asked. "My friends and I were nearly killed by the spirits of the Ruune Videya. Those ghosts were also slaughtered by an unjust king. They came to hate every living soul."

The burly ghost knelt in fealty, and the other spirits silently followed suit. "You're the Lord of the Dead, and the rightful king of Margolan," said the ghost. "We are yours to command. We want to make Jared's soldiers pay for what they stole from us. May my soul go to the Formless One if I punish the innocent," he pledged, and the other spirits murmured their assent. Tris felt a chill go down his spine, remembering the approach of that dark and fearful Aspect.

They might forget their vow and harm the innocent, thought Tris, weighing the choices. *But so might any living soldier, and I've sent Soterius and Mikhail out to raise an army of malcontents and outlaws. They could also harm the living.* He remembered the anger, the longing, and the loss he had sensed in the spirits of the Ruune Videya, long denied their vengeance, unable to take their revenge upon those who had unjustly ended their lives. Finally Tris nodded solemnly, and stretched out his hands in blessing and commission over the kneeling spirits.

"Go then, to the places where you rest, with the power to make your spirits visible to the living. Take your vengeance, but stay your hand against the innocent, even if he wears the colors of the crown. Do you swear?" Tris asked. Power filled him as he raised his hands in benediction.

"We swear it, Lord of the Dead," said the ghosts, in voices that sounded like the winds of a distant storm.

"Rise then, and fight. When this war is over, return to me, and I will give you passage to the Lady."

"So it shall be." The spirits turned to their loved ones with a final parting gesture, their images growing less solid until they disappeared, leaving only the weeping of the refugees.

"Thank you, my prince," said Nascha, and the refugees surged forward, thanking Tris through their tears.

"There are others who await your help," Nascha said, "more families of the *Scirranish*. Perhaps, Prince Drayke, we'll have our answers, and you'll find your army." He bowed low once more, and the group made their way toward the door. Tris retreated to his seat, emotionally spent. Vahanian's face made his feelings plain.

"If the rest of the people in that outer room are here for the same reason," Vahanian said, "it's going to be a very long night." He looked at Tris. "I should probably worry that watching you do this kind of thing doesn't seem strange any more. But ghosts, attacking soldiers—are you sure about that?"

Tris shrugged. "No more than I'm sure about any of the plans. Mercenaries, ready to invade Margolan if I give the signal. *Vayash moru*, freed to protect themselves outside the truce. Ban and Mikhail, rallying deserters and turning them against the army. Those ghosts are of Margolan blood, just as surely as the deserters and the *vayash moru*. It seems to me that we're going to need all the help we can get." He paused. "Since the meeting with the Blood Council, Gabriel's carried word of the ruling to the *vayash moru* houses in Margolan. He says many of them will fight against Jared."

"We have to ride back through Margolan to get to Shekerishet," Vahanian said. "Let's just make sure that everyone's clear about whose side we're on."

TRUE TO NASCHA'S word, the petitioners who filled the outer room were the families of *Scirranish*, some from Margolan's plains and some from the Borderlands, some from the southern lands near Trevath and some from the mountains, but all came with the same story and the same plea. After the ninth bell, Gabriel came to replace Vahanian.

As the night wore on, group after group told of atrocities that shook Tris to his core. One of the men who came to Tris's court told of searching for his missing daughter and finding a heap of bodies dumped with Shekerishet's refuse, bodies of those Arontala had captured and tortured to discover the Sisterhood's weaknesses. The man's voice broke as he described the mangled bodies, each bearing the torturer's mark. Some with crushed feet or limbs dipped in boiling oil, from which the flesh peeled and shredded. Others burned by molten lead, or blinded with hot pokers. A few, he said, had been crushed by heavy rocks, with the weight gradually increased as the victim refused to give up his secrets, until the boulders snapped through bones and suffocated the unfortunate beneath.

One method seemed to have particularly caught Arontala's fancy, the man reported, so shaken by his own tale that even a glass of brandy did not steady his voice. For Arontala's special victims, those whom he suspected had important information, Arontala did not need his magic; all he required was a couple of starving rats, a solid bucket, and a shovel of hot coals. With the victim immobilized, Arontala placed the rats in the bucket and upended the bucket over the victim's belly, placing the hot coals atop it. As the temperature within the bucket became unbearable, the rats sought their only escape route—by gnawing through the body of the victim. He wept as he described how he had found the body of his daughter, a minor mage with the Sisterhood, eviscerated, her skull crushed. Tris felt tears hot on his own cheeks as he called forth the dead girl's spirit. The young mage corroborated her father's story, and gave details of Arontala's tortures that Tris knew would haunt his dreams.

Sweet Chenne, Tris thought, as the enormity of Jared's crimes became clear, *I knew Jared was a monster, but I thought even he had limits. What would he do, if Arontala gains the powers of the Obsidian King?* But deep inside, Tris knew the answer to his question. Jared would seek to extend his power over the Winter Kingdoms, beginning a war that would embroil all seven kingdoms in a disastrous conflict. The Obsidian King in Arontala's body would feed on the souls and blood of that conflict, obliging the surviving mages to band together against him, opening up the cataclysm of magicked war. *I never wanted to be king, let alone have the fate of the Winter Kingdoms rest on my actions. But there isn't anybody else to do this—and there may never be.*

When the midnight bells tolled Tris motioned for the guards to shut the doors, although the outer room was still filled with petitioners. Carroway and

Royster, who had faithfully scribed the stories of the dead, wiped at their eyes as they packed up their parchments and pens and slipped from the room. That left only Tris and Gabriel.

Tris became aware of a ghostly presence, and turned toward the fireplace.

"Show yourself," Tris commanded. In the shadows near the hearth, the spirit of a dark-haired young man appeared. He was dressed in the uniform of an independent soldier—a merc—and a dark stain marked the death wound in his side. But it was the young man's eyes that looked familiar, and Tris searched his memories. *A little older, harder, yes, that's it.* The ghost resembled General Gregor, the soldier who had captured them when they crossed Gibbet Bridge. He remembered Carina's story about her lost lover, Gregor's brother, and knew who the spirit was.

"Ric?" Tris asked, bidding the spirit come closer. He was a handsome young man, with the confidence of an accomplished swordsman and the bearing of a professional man of war.

"Lord of the Dead, a word with you, if I might," Ric said, bowing low.

"Why have you come?" Tris watched the young man closely. He remembered Carina's tearful confrontation with Gregor when she pled their cause, seeking their release. *Two of a kind?* Gregor had taunted Carina in their cell, when Vahanian had come to her defense. Though Ric and Vahanian looked little alike, Tris could see a certain resemblance in their manner. *Carina's lost one lover to the sword. No wonder she's skittish around Jonmarc.*

"My lord," said Ric. "Seven years ago this night, I died in the arms of my betrothed. I couldn't sever the bond between us, and it almost killed Carina. Since your return to Principality, I've watched over her, but I can't show myself in my own strength."

"What would you have me do?"

"I never wished to see her grieve for me. Perhaps, my lord, if you can let her see me, I might convince her to let me rest, and she could live without guilt."

"I'll warn you," said Tris. "I'm rather protective of Carina. She's kinswoman to my own betrothed, and soon kin to me. She's been though a lot, and she's worn ragged by the training we've been doing. If you can give her peace by making yourself known, then do it. But if you'll only bring her grief, leave her to those among the living who love her."

Ric looked pained. "I would never wish to bring her grief. I swear it by the Lady on my soul. Carina blames herself for my death, when I know it was in the hands of the Lady. I want to free her to move on, and take my rest."

Tris looked at Ric in silence for another moment. Then he turned to Gabriel. "Send for Carina."

Though it was late, Carina arrived quickly, giving Tris to guess that she had still been up studying the old healing tomes. "Are you ill? Is there a problem?" Carina rushed to where Tris stood. Then she froze, sensing a presence in the room. Before she could turn, Tris took Carina gently by the shoulders.

"There's someone who wants to talk with you," Tris said carefully, seeing a mixture of fear and pain in Carina's eyes. "He swears he wishes you well. If you don't want to see him, I'll send him away."

"No." Her voice was tight. "It's all right."

Squaring her shoulders, Carina turned slowly toward the shadows near the fireplace. From their depths, Ric stepped forward. Tris lent him the power to make himself visible without his death wound, hoping to spare Carina.

"I didn't think you would ever come back," Ric said.

Carina did not try to brush away the tears that slid down her cheeks. "I didn't want to. Gregor was right. It was my fault you died. I didn't have the right to live when I couldn't save you."

Ric moved closer. "Gregor's an ass. I tried to push you clear, when my spirit left my body, but... it's all a little strange. I couldn't get you untangled, and I didn't want to pull you with me. I stayed with you, at the citadel, but you couldn't see me. Then Cam came and took you, and I didn't know what became of you until I felt you cross into the city."

"I'm so sorry—"

Ric reached out to touch her cheek. "Enough of that now, love. I've watched over you since you crossed Gibbet Bridge. You can't let me become an excuse to stop living, Carina. You've mourned long enough."

"I wanted to be faithful to you."

Ric smiled sadly. "And you have been. Long enough, my love. Your guilt binds me to this place, and I want to rest. You have to let me go."

"How can I let you go, when I love you?"

"Keep my memory," Ric said, touching her hair. "But you're too young to pine for the dead. Especially when there is another worthy brother-at-arms who loves you."

Carina blushed. "I don't—I mean, we haven't—"

Ric chuckled, and took her hands. "You owe me neither apologies nor explanations, love. I came back to give you my blessing, because I fear that without it, from my own lips, you'll continue to punish yourself. Follow your heart, Carina. Whatever you decide, do it because of what you feel, not out of imagined duty to me."

Carina squeezed her eyes closed against the tears. Though insubstantial, Ric reached out for her, folding his arms around her. "Had I been a little faster with my sword, we might have had the future we dreamed about," Ric said. "But that's closed to us. Will you give me your promise that you'll let me go?" He smiled sadly as Carina wiped away her tears. "Even in the arms of the Lady, I'll see, and I'll know."

"If that's what you want."

"I want it because I love you still," said Ric. "I don't want you to be lonely. So tonight, perhaps, we are both set free?"

"I'm never going to stop loving you, you know that."

"I know. But there is room in your heart for more than one love."

Tris stretched out toward Ric's spirit and felt a sense of completion, of peaceful resignation, settle over the ghost.

One more small task, m'lord, before you send me to my rest, the spirit asked as Tris began the passing over ritual. *Give me the power, I ask of you, to make myself visible to one more person.*

Tris paused on the Plains of Spirit, and understood. *I'll help you*, Tris promised. *When you're ready, return to me, and I'll give you rest.*

Carina stood in silence, still staring at the spot where Ric's ghost had vanished.

Tris put his arms around her and let her sob against his shoulder. "Why don't you let us walk you back to your room? I'll get Kiara to stay with you."

"Thank you," she murmured, and looked up at ·Tris. "Thank you from both of us."

IT HAD BEEN a very long day. Vahanian threw his cloak across a chair in his room and poured himself a glass of brandy. Between the Court of Spirits and the bitter wind that howled outside, he did not think he would ever feel warm again. Sipping the brandy, Vahanian edged closer to the fire.

The air in the room took on a sudden chill, and Vahanian recognized the prickle at the back of his neck. He had felt it all evening, when he stood guard over Tris in the Court of Spirits.

"Who's there?" Vahanian challenged, his hand falling from habit to his sword.

Just beyond the edge of the fire's glow, a ghost began to grow solid, until the image of a young man dressed in the uniform of an Eastmark merc stood before him. It was the same ghost he had glimpsed in the crowd at Winterstide. Vahanian took in the man's uniform, the stain of his death wound, and the uncanny resemblance to Gregor. He felt a mix of apprehension and jealousy.

"You know who I am?" The spirit lifted his hands, palms up and open in a gesture of truce.

"Yes."

"Take good care of Carina. Watch over her, and keep her from harm." The ghost raised a hand in farewell and, to Vahanian's astonishment, faded without another word.

Gradually the fire warmed the room, removing the only evidence of the ghost's presence. But Vahanian sat staring at the embers, brandy untouched, long into the night.

CHAPTER EIGHTEEN

AT THE PALACE, preparations continued for the beginning of the assault on Margolan. Tris, Vahanian, and Kiara met more frequently with the mercenaries and Staden's military advisors. Carina and Carroway found a lull in their own schedules. Tris's practice at the Sisterhood still consumed part of his time. But as his skills in magic and defense sharpened, Carina's talents were needed less intensively, which gave her an opportunity to recover from the strain. With the end to the Winterstide festivities, Carroway found respite from the holiday parties and the constant demand for entertainment.

Carroway and Carina kept each other company in the sitting room near the dining hall, where Carina prepared her potions and powders. Carroway took advantage of the lull to work on new songs, intending to create several haunting ballads and stirring tunes that would help to inspire his listeners to action. Royster often joined them, working with Carroway on both song and history. Some evenings Berry dropped in for a game of tarle, but she had turned in early this night, leaving Carina and Carroway alone.

For several candlemarks, Carina worked on her powders, grinding up freshly dried leaves and roots with a mortar and pestle and heating them in the fire. Carroway's tunes were lively, and made the candlemarks pass quickly. Later, his songs grew pensive. One, a haunting tune, told of a beautiful musician with her silver flute, who played so perfectly that the spirits took her. Carina found herself drawn into Carroway's newest ballad, a sad tune about a spirited young girl killed by brigands. Only at the end did she realize that it was an ode to Tris's sister, Kait.

Ready for a break from her work and stretching to relieve her aching back, Carina drew up a chair and watched Carroway as he tinkered with the fingering on the lute. He tried one chord and then another, with different embellishments, until he found the perfect match. Not for the first time, Carina was deeply impressed with the bard's talents as a musician.

She clapped when he finished, and Carroway grinned sheepishly. "You're very kind." Carroway tilted back in his chair. "But the songs are still too rough for a real performance."

Carina leaned forward against the table and rested her chin on her folded arms. "You know, I realized as you were playing that you and Ban are still the mysterious ones."

Carroway chuckled. "Mysterious? My, that sounds quite romantic."

Carina smiled. "I mean it. I've learned a lot about Tris and Jonmarc, but you and Ban have said very little, except about your escape the night of the coup." She looked from the lute to Carroway's eyes. "I'm not surprised that a bard of your talent would be at court. And Ban is a good soldier and a loyal captain at arms. But you're both closer to Tris than your roles would suggest. So tell me, what's your story?"

Carroway set his lute aside and took a sip from a glass of port, silent for so long that Carina wondered if she said something amiss. "My story isn't very important," Carroway said finally. "Ban likely feels the same."

He ran a hand back through his long, blue-black hair. Carina wondered why the handsome young man seemed so completely unattached, when the ladies of the court vied for his attention. On the road, disheveled and dirty, Carroway had charmed uncounted serving wenches out of dinner and ale and bartered his music for shelter for the group and food for their horses. Carroway stood as tall as Tris but he was thin by comparison, though Carina knew the bard was much stronger than he looked. Fine-boned and long-fingered, he cut a handsome figure in the opulent court clothes that he so obviously enjoyed wearing. Light blue eyes under long lashes were as pretty as any maiden's, and his classic, even features reminded Carina of the sculptures of the Lady's companions of legend. Yet for all his talent and beauty, Carina sensed a vulnerability in Carroway that intrigued her.

"Ban's father was a general under King Bricen. He was injured and left the army to go to his manor house up in the high country. Not quite as far north as the Borderlands, where Jonmarc is from, but well into the northern mountains. Bricen and Lord Soterius were famous for their hunts together. I don't know that Ban ever had much thought of a career other than the guard.

"Ban was fostered out to Bricen's court as soon as he was old enough to squire. Tris knew him from the hunts—Bricen had a hunting lodge a candle-mark's ride north of Shekerishet, and both Ban and Lord Soterius used to join the king there." Carroway smiled sadly. "Tris and Kait spent as much time at the lodge as they could. Tris kept his dogs there away from Jared; truth be told, he and Kait preferred the lodge because it kept them away from Jared, too. Jared never had the patience for the hunt, although he relished the kill."

Carroway sighed, remembering a life now gone forever. "My father's lands were in between Bricen's lodge and Lord Soterius's holdings. I was the eldest of six. My father realized early on that my gifts lay with music. So he fostered me to court early, asking Bricen for an apprenticeship with the court minstrels. I was only ten when I went to live at court, and I was quite lonely. Bit of a lost soul, really."

He looked toward the fire, and sipped his port. "Tris and I hit it off immediately. Looking back, I guess Tris needed a friend as much as I did. Jared was an awful bully, and Tris and Kait often took a thrashing from him. Tris was always trying to protect Kait; he got between her and Jared and took her beating more times than I care to remember. All except for the last time."

Carina touched his hand, trying to draw him away from the dark memories of the coup. "Tell me more about what it was like when you came to court."

"Bricen always seemed larger than life, hale and in good spirits most of the time. Queen Serae was so beautiful, so elegant. I think she felt sorry for me, because she 'adopted' me from the start. Tris and Kait and I were inseparable, and whenever Ban could be free of his squire's duties, he joined us, too."

"Tris said that Bava K'aa trusted you to help with his training," Carina supplied.

Carroway nodded. "I liked Tris's grandmother, even though there were kings and armies that feared her. She was always kind to me, and she doted on Tris. So when she offered to let us help her, we jumped at the chance. Funny thing," Carroway said, rubbing his forehead, "is that I don't clearly remember very much of what we did, other than that I liked being there." He chuckled. "Maybe Tris is right, that Bava K'aa hid those memories—for both Tris and me."

Carroway paused, longer this time, and Carina saw his eyes darken with sadness. "I'd go home during the summer, because many of the nobles who frequented the court during the winter months left to see to their own holdings, and there was less call for minstrels. Although my parents and my brothers and sisters visited Shekerishet often, it was wonderful to be back home with them.

"The summer of my twelfth birthday I hadn't heard from my parents in a long time. They had always sent for me at the end of the spring feasts, but this year there was no word at all. Then one day, Queen Serae came to find me. She told me that a plague had broken out at father's manor, a plague so terrible that no one survived. A servant was on his way to Shekerishet with a letter to me, but the soldiers wouldn't let him pass. They were afraid that he carried the plague, and he did. He died in a cave by the road; they burned his body and the letter with it. And so my family was gone." Carroway looked down.

"I'm sorry," Carina said, touching his sleeve.

"Bricen and Serae did their best by me. They took me in. I've always been grateful for that. Oh, I inherited father's title, and the lands, but lands have no value with no one to work them and a title means nothing when the wealth to go with it molders in a plague-ridden manor. So in truth, I had no means and no family. Without Bricen's kindness, I'd have been a beggar. The court whispered at first, but I was determined to earn my way. By the time Tris went for his fostering to Dhasson, I was in demand as a musician.

"I did especially well with the older ladies, who enjoyed the attention of a pretty young boy," Carroway said with a self-deprecating smile. "Lady Eadoin, especially, was a great patron. Gradually, I found that the noble houses were willing to pay handsomely to have me entertain when I was free of obligations at court."

"And did you leave someone behind when you left Margolan so suddenly?"

Carroway blushed. "Yes and no. Tris and I seemed to spend more time outrunning the girls at court than wooing them, if you want to know the

Lady's truth. We were Margolan's most eligible bachelors. Tris and I were so good at eluding their clutches that one rumor had Tris taking vows as an acolyte to the Lady. Other rumors suggested that perhaps we'd pledged to each other." Carroway chuckled. "Either way, the rumors deterred the more persistent and ambitious of the nobles' daughters, so we weren't inclined to set the record straight.

"But to your question—not exactly. Soterius stood up a date the night of the coup, but he never stayed long with any girl. Me, I fancied a pretty flute player named Macaria. Her talent, Lady bless her, is truly magic, and not earned with bleeding fingers like my own." Carroway sighed, and Carina thought it was only partly exaggerated.

"What's she like?" Carina asked with a smile.

Carroway rested his chin on his hand and looked off into space. "Hair like midnight. Dark eyes that flash with flecks of gold. She's got Trevath blood, and the skin to go with it—like *kerif* with cream. And a figure that would stop traffic in the middle of the town square on the busiest market day." He sighed once more.

"And with all that, talent and magic besides. Oh, I can do a little magic myself—less than a hedge witch, even—but it makes for dramatic effects when I tell my stories. Nothing of use to anyone but a storyteller—the ability to make smoke into figures and shapes." He paused. "Macaria, on the other hand, has magic in her music. Not like Tris, not a sorcerer. But the very best entertainers—whether they're musicians or bards or acrobats—have magic in their talent. My music was earned the old fashioned way—with lessons and practice. Hers, on the other hand, is from the Goddess. When she plays her flute, even the ghosts come to listen.

"But what's a bard without unrequited love?" he asked. "Alas, m'lady never gave me a glance or showed the slightest interest in anything other than my music."

Carroway sobered. "Perhaps it's just as well. I've heard from the musicians we've met along the way that Jared took revenge on the palace entertainers after we escaped. We changed into their costumes, although they knew nothing of it, but I'm sure Jared would never believe that. So in saving ourselves, we unknowingly placed them in peril. I'm told that many of the entertainers disappeared, either to protect themselves, or at Jared's hand.

"I fear what I'll find, when we reach the palace. Hearing the tales of the families of the Vanished Ones who've come to Tris's Court of Spirits made me worry. I know nothing can ever be as it was, but I hope to find a few familiar faces. I'd like to go on believing that Macaria found safety, and that maybe, once Tris is secure in his throne, I'll have another chance to court her.

"I haven't had the courage to ask Tris to call for her among the dead. I need to believe that she lives. I don't think I could handle it right now, if she…" He paused, swallowed. "And so I tell myself that she's clever enough to have found a way to get by, and that things will be different when I return. Maybe if I'm a hero as well as a bard, she might notice me.

"Of course," he went on, "planning the entertainment for both a coronation and a royal wedding might also get her attention." Carroway gave Carina a sly glance. "For a small retainer, I'm willing to travel. To Dark Haven, perhaps, to plan a handfasting?"

Carina, to her chagrin, flushed scarlet. "You have quite an imagination!" Carina knew Carroway meant no offense, but hearing the possibility said aloud filled her with a strange mixture of feelings.

"Really?" Carroway laughed. "The castle gossips have had you and Jonmarc paired off for months now."

"I thought Kiara and Berry were the only ones matchmaking around here!" Carina exclaimed. She felt flattered and pressured, exposed and oddly pleased all at once, in a heady mixture that was new.

"I'll give you a special rate."

"I just hope there is an 'after,'" she said with a sigh. "The closer we get to the trip into Margolan, the more unlikely this whole thing seems. I never really expected to get caught up in a revolution, you know. Cam and I went looking for a cure for Donelan's illness."

"I know the feeling. Tris and Ban and I were just celebrating Haunts, and by midnight we were wanted men. It may sound romantic in the ballads, but it didn't seem that way when we were outrunning the guards."

"I'm glad that Cam was able to take back an elixir from the Sisterhood to help Kiara's father bear up under the wasting spell. But King Donelan won't be cured until we destroy Arontala. He's the mage who caused the sickness. Cam and I had only been apart once before. I miss him terribly." She managed to grin. "Although without me around, he's probably taking the opportunity to woo the ladies. He always said he intended to marry the daughter of a tavern keeper, so that he would never lack for fresh ale and good food!"

Carroway chuckled. "Funny, that's Harrtuck's idea of an ideal girl, too. Now if we found an innkeeper with two daughters, they'd be set!"

"Well," Carina said finally, rising from her seat. "I'd better get back to making some powders for us to take with us on the road. It won't be too much longer before we head for Margolan. Gabriel might not need the potions and remedies, but I'll sleep better knowing that the rest of us have them handy."

Carroway went back to his lute and soon he was strumming softly and singing to himself, working on a difficult bit of fingering. Carina returned to her potions, but she found her thoughts straying back to Isencroft and to Cam until the midnight bells tolled and she finally headed for bed.

THAT EVENING, TRIS walked Kiara back to her rooms after a grueling session in the war room. For a time they walked in silence, holding hands, content with each other's company, deep in thought over the conversations of the day. Tris could feel a looming pressure as the winter days passed and the time for their departure into Margolan grew closer. Fear, excitement, dread, and purpose all rolled together in anticipation.

"Skrivven for your thoughts," Kiara teased as they walked along the palazzo. They had taken the long route back to her rooms, content for a few moments to be alone. The guards who were their new constant companions hung back, permitting them some privacy.

"I was thinking about my dogs, to tell you the truth," he admitted. "Two wolfhounds and a bull mastiff. I didn't dare keep them at the palace—Jared had a way of making animals disappear. Father owned a hunting lodge, up near Soterius's father's lands. Kait and I spent as much time up there as mother would allow, escaping from Jared, and court. I kept the dogs at the lodge.

"You wouldn't believe how many times I've thought about them since we left Shekerishet," Tris said. "Father's retainers lived at the country house and kept it up, but with Jared on the throne, who knows what happened to them? Kait's falcons were in the mews at Shekerishet; they were something even Jared wouldn't touch. They seemed to know what Jared was like, and they'd peck and swoop any time they saw him. I'd love to know that they've survived—it would be like having a little bit of Kait left." His voice drifted off, and Kiara squeezed his hand.

"The lodge sounds nice," she said. "Maybe we can keep it as a sanctuary, just you, me, the dogs—and Jae!" she added as the little gyregon flew in a circle around them and came back to land on her shoulder. "Back in Isencroft, he always joined on the hunts with the falcons. They seemed to have some kind of arrangement—it was as if they could understand each other. The falcons and Jae would work as a team. The falcons harried the prey—they were faster—and Jae usually made the kill, since he was larger and a bit heavier. Quite a spectacle!"

Tris turned to her, and took her other hand so that she faced him. "These past few months, I've been the closest I'll ever be to knowing what life would be like without the crown. One of the reasons I never wanted to be king was that I wanted the freedom to make my own decisions.

"I've always thought that the king was less free than anyone in the kingdom," Tris said quietly. "Council, pressuring for one decision or another, always driven by the self-interest of the nobles. Gossip and intrigue at court. Retainers, crowding for favors. So many people who want to be your friend, so long as you give them what they want."

Tris smiled sadly. "I always counted myself fortunate to be the second son. I wasn't required to be at Council, and no one cared about my comings and goings. I was just a spare, in case something happened to the heir." He paused again, longer this time.

Tris sighed. "I used to dream that when I married—if I ever found someone—we could go off to the lodge, out of sight of the court and the gossips and Jared." He met Kiara's eyes. "More than anything, I don't want the court and the crown to taint what we have, Kiara. I want to find some little corner where we can still be the way we were on the road, two nobodies from nowhere, without the crown and the throne looming over us."

Kiara stepped forward and reached up to kiss him. Tris folded her into his arms. "Mother nearly died bearing me, so there were no other children," Kiara said quietly. "I always knew the scrutiny of being the heir. And as Abelard told you, my parents' romance was something of a scandal, but there was more than that."

"If Eastmark was unhappy about losing its princess to a foreign kingdom, there were many in Isencroft who were even less happy to have a foreign queen," Kiara said wistfully. "Over the centuries, Isencroft was overrun by every nation on its borders—and even by some on the far side of the Northern Sea. So we're fiercely independent. Mother could never rid herself of her Eastmark accent, though she spoke Croft fluently. And she never gave up her devotion to the Lover, while Isencroft worshipped Chenne."

"While she and father were very much in love, that love wasn't shared by many in the kingdom. The ladies at the court were merciless. Nothing father did seemed to help. So mother made sure that there was nothing they could say about her daughter." Kiara laughed bitterly. "I had to be more thoroughly Isencroft than anyone. I had to excel with the sword, because that was the Isencroft way. I had to make public devotion to Chenne, so that no one could say I was a heretic. Mother fought teaching me Markian, because she wanted me to speak Croft without any accent.

"The betrothal contract with Margolan was always in the back of her mind," Kiara went on, leaning against Tris's shoulder. "I learned to speak Margolense as a child, from Margolan tutors, so that I'd have no accent. I made devotion to Chenne in public, and to the Lover in private, with mother. My tutors taught me the ways of the Mother and the Childe, so that when the time came I'd make a proper queen for Margolan." Kiara smiled sadly. "Mother didn't want anyone to be able to say a word about my suitability. I'm afraid she kept me quite protected. And it ruled out suitors, being betrothed from birth."

"So I was your rebellious fling on the road?"

"Even a princess can dream," Kiara said. "But father might have sent the guards after me if I'd taken off with a tent rigger from a caravan."

"Do you think your mother would approve—of your tent rigger?"

Kiara smoothed back a lock of his white hair. "She'd approve that I followed my heart. That was one thing she always did. And if we can add horses to the menagerie at the hunting lodge, I know she'd approve. Mother loved horses. That's how she died—out riding."

"She's proud of you, you know," Tris said. Kiara looked at him oddly for a moment, and then understood. "She's with you, just out of sight. Even on the road I could sense a presence near you, a guardian spirit."

"I've seen her on Haunts. She loved me fiercely, and I knew she would be near. So you've met her?"

"Not formally," Tris said. "I try not to intrude on other people's ghosts without permission."

"Even with all of the intrigue at court, she and father never stopped being in love." Kiara touched his cheek. "Perhaps we can carve out something of the same for us."

"We will." Tris promised, bending to kiss her. "I promise."

In his mage sense, Tris felt the strong presence of a spirit, and saw the ghost of the beautiful Isencroft queen. Viata's ghost extended her hands in blessing. Tris drew back from his kiss with Kiara, feeling oddly embarrassed, as if someone had walked in on their embrace. He had the strong sense that Viata wished to be seen.

"About that introduction—"

"She's here, isn't she?"

"I think she'd like to speak with you."

"I'd like that, too."

Tris stepped back. He let himself stretch out onto the Plain of Spirits and lent his power to Viata's ghost until the queen stood before them. Tris saw an immediate resemblance between Viata and Kiara. Kiara took a half step forward, and the ghost moved to embrace her.

"You're as pretty and clever as I knew you would be," Viata smiled.

"Father says I take after you."

"I was afraid Donelan would be joining me before his time," Viata replied, growing more serious. "But at least for now, the wasting spell is halted. While I want our spirits to be together eventually, there is no hurry."

Viata looked past Kiara to Tris, who felt himself suddenly color. "And this is your young man?"

Kiara wiped away her tears and reached out to take Tris's hand. "I'd like you to meet Tris—Martris Drayke of Margolan, Bricen's second son. My betrothed."

Viata nodded solemnly. "I was grateful that Bricen intervened with the marriage pact because I didn't want war. But I worried as I came to know more about what kind of man Jared Drayke had become. I'm pleased that you've found a more desirable solution."

Viata's ghost met Tris's eyes. "I've seen your training, and I'm most impressed. You have my blessing to wed Kiara, and my prayers to the Lady that your quest will be successful."

Tris gave a courteous bow. "I'm honored, m'lady."

"Kiara," Viata said, and Kiara turned toward her mother's ghost. "Even when you can't see me, never doubt that I'm watching over you. I've resolved not to go to the Lady until Donelan can join me and you are safely established. Death doesn't end love."

"Thank you," Kiara whispered. "I love you, too."

Tris bade Viata's ghost farewell and the spirit faded from view. Kiara leaned against him, letting him hold her in silence, until the bells sounded midnight.

CHAPTER NINETEEN

"How do you like my garden?" Jared of Margolan asked the middle-aged noble at his side. It was early in the second month. The day was cold but clear. A light snow no deeper than a horse's fetlock covered the ground. Jared and the noble stood outside Shekerishet, next to the pattern of long, sharpened stakes that from above made the crest of the House of Margolan.

Thirty stakes, and on each of them, a body.

Some were impaled through the back, others face down through the gut. *Vayash moru* were staked facing east, so that Jared might see whether they burst into flames at dawn. Others, around the perimeter, were either coated alive in wax or soaked in oil, making human torches that burned as night fell.

Jared's favorite punishment, however, he reserved for those from whom he truly wished to exact the greatest revenge. A sturdy, sharpened pole impaled the victim between the legs, on a stake just tall enough that the victim could remain on his toes for several candlemarks, until his strength failed, and he finally sank low enough for the stake to pierce vital organs. Jared found the death dance mesmerizing. Today the moans of his dying victims sounded like a distant wind.

Lord Curane's expression was neutral. "Your parties are always memorable, Your Highness."

"It's been a good day," Jared said amicably, taking another deep draught from his flask. He had been drinking Tordassian brandy since early in the day, even before the show trials of a dozen deserters, tracked down by faithful officers and brought back in chains. The deserters had been hanged at noon in the castle square and their bodies still dangled from the nooses, a cautionary tale to any who might have contemplated similar treason.

The real event, however, was the trial and execution of General Lothe. Jared felt his mood darken just thinking about Lothe, who claimed to be loyal to Margolan, and apolitical when it came to kings. Whether Lothe was a convincing liar who remained loyal to Bricen or whether he had a change of heart, Jared neither knew nor cared. What mattered was that Lothe had tried—and failed—to poison him, and for that, Lothe had paid dearly.

Broken on the rack, his skin seeping with fresh burns from the torturer's irons, what was left of Lothe was poisoned with the same tincture that Lothe had tried to use on Jared. Jared found it particularly satisfying to watch Lothe writhe in pain as the slow poison worked, and then, finally, to have Lothe's body burned in the public square.

The executions were well attended, and a party mood filled the air as the sun set. Musicians played lively tunes, but remained circumspect in their choice of ballads and songs, taking caution from the disappearance of a few of their fellows who had the poor judgment to sing of Bricen and his victories in battle. The smell of roasting sausages mingled with the odor of burning flesh from the human torches, and ale flowed freely. Jared knew that one maiden already awaited his pleasures inside the castle, a girl he had chosen from the crowd and pointed out to his guards. Yes, he thought, it was a good day, a very good day indeed.

"A fine party, Your Majesty," Curane agreed, snapping Jared out of his thoughts. "But I wonder, my king, if I might have a word with you."

"Speak." Jared took another long draught of his brandy.

"I bear tidings from my wife's uncle, Lord Monteith," said Curane. His voice dropped. "As you may recall, my king, the Monteith family is one of the oldest noble houses in Trevath, and quite well-regarded by their king. They have significant influence on the opinions of the Trevath crown."

"And?" Jared interrupted. Curane was useful, and was one of Jared's staunchest supporters. Curane did not even flinch when Jared had demanded a dalliance with his granddaughter, though she was barely of marriageable age. Curane willingly supplied the girl, drugged and pliable, for Jared's pleasures, and just as willingly made her disappear when Jared tired of her. What became of her,

Jared neither knew nor cared. Now, Jared imagined, Curane was going to expect some reward.

"I understand from Lord Monteith that the King of Trevath is most impressed with Your Majesty's resolve in securing the throne. Most impressed. It's also known in Trevath that you have made alliance with Nargi, a frequent trading partner with Trevath."

"Get to the point," Jared snarled. The brandy was taking much too long to reach his head, and he felt far too sober.

"As you wish, my king. Lord Monteith believes that the King of Trevath might be approachable for a similar alliance. Such an arrangement could be quite profitable, and might serve to deter some of the other kingdoms, which may not have yet seen the advantage in allying with your power."

"Not seen the advantage?" Jared · roared. "Isencroft, Principality and Dhasson have recognized my traitor brother. I consider that a declaration of war. Only Eastmark has 'not seen the advantage.' But their silence to our approaches is an answer in itself." Now Jared could feel the brandy rising in his blood, filling him with a boldness which, of late, seemed more and more elusive.

"A thousand pardons, my king," Curane said, bowing low. "I hoped to bring you good tidings from Trevath. They are a wealthy and powerful nation, with an esteemed army. Such an alliance might show the others the error of their ways."

And it certainly wouldn't hurt your standing with their king, either, Jared thought cynically. "All of this is speculation," he snarled. "When their king is ready to sign a treaty, then he'll have my interest."

"Of course, my king," Curane said. His obsequiousness both pleased and annoyed Jared, and the king only barely restrained his temper, reminding himself of Curane's usefulness.

"And while you're in Trevath," Jared said, his words slurring as he finished the last of his flask. "Tell them to send better brandy. This year's batch was pig slop!" He hurled his empty flask into the fire.

"Of course, my king, as you wish," Curane said, with the same imperturbable smile he always wore. He backed away, bowing low, and made his exit. Alone, except for the guards that now always accompanied him, Jared watched the partygoers with detachment, feeling an odd mixture of disdain and jealousy. Disdain, for the trivial intrigues and the self-absorbed interests of the courtiers, and jealousy, because they bore none of the weight of the crown, nor the dangers of kingship.

Both disdain and jealousy were doubled when it came to Tris. Just the thought of his half-brother made Jared want another brandy. Tris, whose life had been as charmed from birth as Jared's had been cursed. Queen Serae could do no wrong in the eyes of the court, while even after Eldra's death, dark rumors persisted about Bricen's first wife. Jared had taken care of that. He'd noted since childhood who among the noblewomen had been uncharitable toward his mother's memory. They had been the first to die when he gained the power to make things right.

Eldra had been avenged, but it didn't bring her back. But a Summoner could, a Summoner who wasn't chained by weak concepts of rules and ethics. When the Obsidian King returned, adding his power as a Summoner to Arontala's magic, Arontala promised Jared that Eldra would return to take her rightful place beside him. Together, they would rule Margolan.

That was something Tris could never understand. Jared grabbed a tankard of ale from a passing vendor who bowed low and scurried away. He downed the ale in one long swallow, wishing it would go to his head. No, Tris never got passed from one servant to another, servants who barely noticed a small boy's existence. Tris had both mother and father; Bricen had doted on his second family the way he had never had time to do with his first. But Serae and Kait would both pay. Arontala had locked them away in the Orb. They would experience the torment they deserved.

Now Tris was the darling of the Winter Kingdoms. Jared spat to one side. He pushed his way through the crowd, and the partygoers scattered to clear a path for him as he strode through the throng. Staden had received Tris like a real king, instead of a boy with delusions of grandeur. Word had it that King Harrol of Dhasson and King Donelan of Isencroft had also recognized Tris as Margolan's rightful king—a travesty, considering that Jared was the first born and heir.

Tris had even inherited magic. Bava K'aa had always kept a watchful eye on Jared, and Jared had hated the old crone witch for it. He'd assumed it was because Serae was Bava K'aa's daughter and Tris her grandson. He'd stayed out of her way, hating how uncomfortable he felt around her, as if she could read his mind. That Bava K'aa let Tris and

Carroway help in her study never bothered Jared at the time. He'd assumed the old witch was just using the two for free labor. Now, he understood. All those years, Bava K'aa had been training Tris, right under Jared's nose. Training him to seize the throne, to acquire immense power, to push Jared aside as Jared had always been pushed aside. Even then, they'd been plotting.

And then there was Kiara. Jared's fists clenched. She was his by right, by covenant. Kiara had been promised to him twenty years ago, when she was born. But Bricen had stalled, refusing Jared's demands to claim his bride when she turned sixteen, easily of marriageable age. Bricen had invented one reason after another to keep Jared from visiting Isencroft, keep Kiara from coming to Margolan, although by the betrothal contract, they were as good as wed already. Bricen had kept Kiara out of reach the same way he had always dangled the crown. Jared came to realize that something had changed in his father, that Bricen did not intend for his first-born son to take the throne. That was when Jared had decided to seize his own destiny.

Kiara and Tris added another humiliation, announcing their betrothal in defiance of the covenant. By ancient law, Jared now had the right— the duty—to have both of them put to death for treason and adultery. *You got the childhood I never had. You got a mother—and father's attention. But I'll be damned if you think you'll steal what belongs to me!*

"Careful that you don't take a chill, my king," a familiar voice said from behind him. Arontala's approach, as always, was completely silent.

"What do you want?" Jared snapped as Arontala fell into step beside him. Arontala's presence parted the crowd around them. Even the guards kept their distance. In the midst of the throng, they were utterly alone.

"I bring news, my king, from Principality."

"And?"

"Our assassin did not find his mark," Arontala reported. "He nearly killed one of the ruffians who accompany your brother, a smuggler who is not unknown to me. Sadly, the encounter was not fatal."

Jared wheeled on the mage, staggering from the brandy. "You promised results."

"And results we have, my king," Arontala replied. "Your brother—and King Staden—now realize that they are not safe from our reach."

"Not enough."

"There is more," Arontala remarked, almost off-handedly. "I understand, through a very reliable source, that the Blood Council convened in Principality for the purpose of determining whether *vayash moru* would be granted permission to fight against you. The majority of the Council gave their assent." Arontala held up a hand, staving off Jared's irate response. "This is in our favor."

"How?" Jared roared. Nearby partygoers shuddered, though none dared to look toward the angry king.

"Because, my king, it legitimizes what we have told the people about the *vayash moru*. When the people see *vayash moru* attacking mortals, we will not need to urge them to take their revenge. Yes,"

Arontala said with an unsettling smile. "This is a very good thing."

"The only good thing will be when my brother dangles from that noose." Jared pointed at the gibbet.

"Patience, my king. We're closer than ever to the Hawthorn Moon. Whatever grandiose dreams your brother may have, there is no time for him to move against us. In just a few months the Hawthorn Moon will be upon us, and we'll seize power that will last for generations to come."

"Unless you fail—again," Jared sneered. "One of my platoons disappeared, near the Principality border. They brought the lone survivor to me, a raving madman who swore that vengeful ghosts had ripped his comrades to shreds before his very eyes."

Jared leaned toward Arontala. The brandy made it possible to ignore the smell of stale blood. "Such a thing could be done by a Summoner." Jared made the word a curse. "But of course, my mage has assured me that my brother could never gain such power so quickly."

"When the Obsidian King is freed, you will have your own Summoner, my king. The greatest Summoner who ever lived, hosted in my body and combined with my power as a Fire Clan mage. Your brother stands no chance against that power." Arontala smiled, his sharp teeth prominent.

"When I took the Orb from its hiding place in the foundation of Dark Haven, it did more than damage the great house and kill the lord. Bava K'aa meant to use the power of the Flow, one of the great rivers of energy, to contain the Obsidian King. But in wresting the Orb from its mooring, I altered the balance of the Flow. The imbalance in the Flow changed the timbre of magic in the Winter Kingdoms. It makes me stronger, and it makes the Light mages weaker." He licked his lips. "That power is increased by blood magic. And once the Obsidian King is free to combine his spirit magic with my fire magic, the altered energies of the Flow will give us even more power."

"Power? Your blood magic couldn't even produce useful fighters from the wretches they captured for you. They turned on our own troops so often that the captains don't want them. And the troops that did use them had to kill them when they were done because they wouldn't go back in their damn wagon!"

"The troops lack patience," Arontala replied dismissively. "Powerful magic takes time."

"Spare me your talk of magic," Jared said. "I want results!"

"You'll have your revenge," Arontala promised. "When I'm a Summoner, I can help you question your brother. I can bind his soul to his body, so that you can enjoy his questioning for as long as you want. Think of it. I can keep him from dying. How many times do you want to kill him? How far past mortal endurance do you want to push him? Force the Isencroft bitch to watch, so that she appreciates your power. Is that sweet enough for you?"

"It's only sweet if it happens," Jared said, his eyes narrowing. "You've made a lot of promises. I'm expecting to see them come to pass."

"Very soon, my king, very soon. You'll have everything you desire, and more, at the Hawthorn Moon."

CHAPTER TWENTY

"What's on your mind, Ban?" Mikhail asked as they rode. The early spring weather was unseasonably cold, and the steady rain pelted their cloaks and soaked their horses. The rain made the night seem even darker. The roads were deep in mud that splattered with each step their mounts took. Soterius wanted nothing so much as a warm fire and a dry bed.

Soterius shrugged. "I just can't shake the feeling that we should be further along, I guess."

Mikhail chuckled. "Impatience does get easier with immorality," he said. "Let's see. We've trained sixty fighters in the refugee camp, and sent out six teams to seal off the roads around the border to Principality and the Dhasson Pass. Andras's village gave us twenty fighters, and promised to hold the roads and tributaries south to Ghorbal. Pell got us thirty fighters and three new leaders. With Tabb's

337

help and the thirty fighters his village supplied, we'll have cut off all the main northern roads through the Borderlands to the Northern Sea." He dusted off his hands. "Not a bad job for two month's work—considering that we've added at least thirty *vayash moru* to that number," he said with a grin.

"I know. Anybody else would probably think we'd made a great start. But we've still seen too many soldiers on the roads for my taste. There's little reason for soldiers to be patrolling this far out in peacetime—except to steal from the farmers and the townspeople."

"It would be nice if they would do something about the brigands and cutpurses while they're out here," Mikhail added. They had passed at least a dozen Margolan soldiers in pairs and small groups over the last few days, backtracking to go around a contingent of fifty soldiers camped by the side of the road the night before. Despite the soldiers' presence, nothing seemed to deter the highwaymen that lurked along even the best-traveled roads.

"I used to travel this way often in the old days," Soterius said. "Even alone, I had nothing to fear of thieves while Bricen ruled."

"We made short work of the two who wanted our horses," Mikhail chuckled.

"And the three before that, who wanted our money," Soterius said. "If the rest of Margolan is like this, I hope Tris has a kingdom left when he gets here."

"We'll reach the citadel none to early for my liking," Mikhail said, shaking his shoulders to get some of the rain off his cloak.

"I didn't think you minded the cold and the rain. Isn't that one of the advantages of being dead?"

Mikhail snorted. "Shows what you know. Cold is one thing—soaked to the skin is another. Just because I'm not alive doesn't mean I like being uncomfortable."

"At least we haven't gone hungry. I think I've actually had my fill of deer meat since I've traveled with you. Remind me to invite you to the next King's Hunt!"

"I used to love the hunt, before I was brought across. Now, I'm afraid my senses are too sharp. I can find the deer on smell alone. There's no challenge anymore. But it does keep both of us well fed—you with meat and me with drink."

They fell silent for a while. Reading a *vayash moru*'s body language was not easy, but Soterius had the distinct feeling Mikhail was worried about something he had not put into words. "There's something you're not saying."

"Just a feeling. We've passed too many soldiers headed in the same direction. It could mean word has reached Jared that some of our first groups have cut off main roads. Or they could be planning something else. That's what worries me."

"You're sure the citadel we're headed for will take us in? I'd hate to find out we're not welcome."

"I've known Sister Fallon for many years. We'll be welcome—and safe."

They reached their destination just before dawn. The citadel of the Sisterhood was a walled enclave atop a hill with a village clustered at the foot of its high, ancient stone walls. Sister Fallon greeted them at the gate.

"Welcome," Fallon said with a perfunctory bow that Soterius and Mikhail returned. "You're lucky to have arrived when you did. Soldiers are on their way, and it's nearly daylight."

"Why?" Soterius asked.

"They've been sent by King Jared to hunt down and destroy the Sisterhood."

Soterius let out a low whistle. "Jared is taking on the Sisterhood? Can he harm you?"

"Strong as we are, we do bleed and die," she said ruefully.

"Can you hold them off?"

"Oh yes, at least, long enough. The villagers worry me the most. Once, before we realized what was happening, a group of soldiers destroyed a whole village on the rumor that one of our Sisters was among them." She gestured at the citadel's walls. "I've sent Sisters to gather the villagers into the citadel. Most of them are already here. We'll try to keep them safe, until the soldiers can be turned away."

"I don't understand," Soterius pressed. "How can the soldiers hope to win? After all, they're only regular men, against mages!"

Soterius thought he glimpsed sadness in her eyes. "King Jared, I fear, knows our weakness, that the Sisterhood abhors the taking of life if it can be avoided. Arontala knows we will try to turn the soldiers back, not destroy them outright. He's gambling that in the process, the troops will overcome the odds."

Mikhail scratched his stubbled chin. "But why?" he asked. "Why does Jared even want to fight the Sisterhood, let alone destroy it?"

"Because of Bava K'aa."

"Bava K'aa is dead."

"A mage of her power does not simply cease to exist," she said. "After all, any soul with a purpose can remain among us. That's even truer for a spirit mage.

"King Jared fears the spirit of Bava K'aa will take revenge for what he's done. Even more, he fears that she might transfer her power to another mage who would rise up against him. Arontala cast a spell over Shekerishet to banish the spirits that guard the king. Only then was he able to kill Bricen." She paused, worry clear in her eyes. "Jared may fear that his brother is a greater threat than he expected."

"But why is Jared attacking the Sisterhood if none of you can stop Arontala?" Mikhail pressed.

Fallon folded her hands in frustration. "Because he believes that Bava K'aa's body is buried in one of our citadels," she replied. "He thinks that if he finds it, and destroys it, that he will end her power and influence."

"Can he? I mean, would it?" Soterius asked.

"Who can say?" she replied. "Bava K'aa was the greatest mage of her generation, save the Obsidian King himself. I don't know whether a mage of that power is governed by the rules that limit lesser mages. There are ways to desecrate the body that also bind the spirit."

"If the Sisterhood knows what's happening in Margolan, then why in the name of the Crone don't they do something to help?"

"The Sisterhood never quite recovered from the Mage Wars. We feared that Bava K'aa was the last of the great mages. The mages that survived the war—and the ones born since then—have not equaled the power of the mages who fought that war. We haven't seen another mage of her power— until now. Until Martris Drayke."

"So while my Sisters have many fine words to talk all around the issue, the Sisterhood does not get involved because many of the Sisters are afraid. They don't think they have the power to stand up to Arontala, or to the Obsidian King. The Sisterhood has always walked a fine line between intervention and meddling—not everyone would agree on the difference. Now, I'm afraid their fear has turned them inward. Those of us who are willing to put ourselves at risk— like myself and Sister Taru—are distinctly in the minority. You understand that you will not be able to leave this citadel until the soldiers are defeated."

"I don't claim to understand magic or mages," Soterius said, "but I understand the oath I swore to Tris. And I'm doing a poor job of it locked up in a tower!"

"I understand. But a large force is headed this way, with siege machines. We can't permit you to leave until the confrontation is over—else, I fear, you will find yourselves captured by Margolan troops."

"We can't just sit here," Mikhail objected. "We have a job to do."

Fallon looked quietly at the two men, as if she were making up her mind. "Yes, you do," she agreed. "And perhaps, for that reason, the Lady has brought you to us."

"So we just wait? I don't like this." Soterius began to pace. "A siege could take months! We don't have that kind of time."

"Perhaps," Fallon interrupted gently, "events will take their own course. But today, and for a while to come I fear, this will be your home. Rest. You look like you've traveled all night. One of our Sisters will show you to your rooms and bring you food. Your rooms are in the levels below ground where no daylight will intrude."

She turned. "Before you came, I was headed for a Council meeting. We must get ready for the attack."

"We're grateful for the shelter," Soterius said, with a glance at Mikhail. "But we're both soldiers, and we have no love for Margolan troops. Give us a way to help."

She seemed to consider his offer. "Yes, you may indeed be here for a purpose." Fallon signaled for a Sister to take Soterius and Mikhail to their rooms.

Soterius and Mikhail found themselves in two adjacent sparse rooms, with a small sitting area between them. Another Sister arrived with a platter of salt pork and a bowl of boiled eggs for Soterius, and a carafe of fresh goat's blood for Mikhail. In the weeks since they had left Principality, Soterius found that the *vayash moru*'s choice of nourishment no longer bothered him. He did not watch the dark red liquid being poured, or think too hard about its source.

"I don't think I like the way she said that, about being here for a purpose," Soterius grumbled.

"I've always believed," Mikhail said, "that the Lady keeps her hand on those who do for themselves. So if we do what we can here, where the Lady has led us, perhaps we can change the course of what happens later."

"Maybe," Soterius said thoughtfully. "Who here would know Margolan tactics better than you and I? If anyone can find the troops' weakness, we should be able to do it."

"You have a point there."

"We've got to get into the Sisterhood's strategy meetings. We don't even know how this citadel is situated, or where it's vulnerable. I'd rather fight than sit around waiting on the Sisters to save us."

FALLON NEEDED NO convincing. As the evening bells began to toll, Soterius and Mikhail found themselves on their way through the windowless twisting corridors to join a war council of the Sisterhood. Soterius felt the heady, fear-edged antic- ipation that always surged through him on the eve of battle. Mikhail, usually imperturbable, looked nervous as a cat.

Fallon led them through the corridors with a ball of blue mage light carried in her hand, and stopped before a great wooden door. Iron-bound and ancient, it swung open to reveal a large, circular room, lit by brilliant torches and a fire that roared in a massive hearth. Along the stone walls, tapes- tries recounted battles whose names were lost to time. In the center sat a great table, a massive scry- ing orb fitted at one place. At the table sat eight brown-robed Sisters.

"Come in," a Sister gestured for them to enter. Her face was lost in the shadow of her cowl, and her voice sounded ancient. Fallon stepped back for them to pass, and closed the door behind them. "We have heard your tale from Sister Fallon," the cowled Sister continued. "And we know that you are swordsmen." She pointed a gnarled finger at Soterius and Mikhail. "You have both served the armies of Margolan. Within a day, those troops will be at our door. Where does your allegiance lie?"

Soterius stepped forward and made an awkward bow. "My lady," he began, "we are the liegemen of King Bricen. At his death, we swore our vows to his son, Prince Martris. We will not serve the traitor Jared. His armies are our enemies."

"You have spoken well, swordsman," she said. "Come closer." It was eerie, Soterius thought, to hear the rasping voice from beneath the brown cowl, but see no face. On the far side of the table were two empty chairs. "Please sit down." The other Sisters watched them in silence, giving Soterius cold shivers down his back.

"Fallon tells us that you have volunteered to serve the Sisterhood in this matter. Is that true?"

Soterius hoped he looked confident. "I was King Bricen's captain at arms."

"And in my mortal lifetime, I was liegeman to King Hotten," Mikhail said.

"I trained Margolan troops and I know their tactics," said Soterius. "If you can tell us more about this citadel, and the terrain around it, perhaps we can find a way to turn their attack."

"This citadel stands on the Plains of Marccam, built by King Lwelyn more than five hundred years ago. It can support several hundred troops for many months with its own water supply and a more than ample stockpile of food. We can protect our villagers, but not indefinitely." She paused. "The tower rises as high as five buildings atop each other, and has withstood fire, battering rams and siege."

"What of the troops from Margolan?" Soterius said, frowning.

"Jared may send several hundred soldiers. It is not, however, the number that I find of concern," the cowled woman said, "it is their tactics. Arontala has prepared each group with specific knowledge about our strongholds. Some his mages burned, setting so many fires and speeding them with pitch that we had no choice but to abandon the structure. Even mages have their limits. We were unprepared. At another, his mages diverted a river, sweeping the building away.

"In each case, the mages could have saved themselves. But Arontala knew we would protect the villagers, and in doing so, be unable to fully protect ourselves. We lost many villagers and Sisters, and abandoned several of our strongholds. We have also lost libraries, artifacts, and magical items which can't be replaced." She spread her gnarled hands, palms up, in a gesture of frustration. "Each attack grows stronger. In the last two, Jared sent dark mages with the troops. Disarming their magic kept the Sisters busy while the siege troops did even greater damage."

"How can we help?" Mikhail asked.

The Sister inclined her head. "This citadel has many defenses of its own, and we have trained our villagers. But dark mages can play havoc with simple things. In one tower, the defenders were prepared to pour down boiling oil on the attackers, only to have the pot wrested from their hands by magic and poured upon their own people. We know his mages will find ways to challenge our protections. The battle must not be our villagers against the troops while the Sisters fight the mages. We have to find a way to stop his mages, and then rout his troops."

"I'm all for that," Soterius agreed.

There was a dry chuckle from beneath the cowl. "Good. Then you can help us plan."

CHAPTER TWENTY-ONE

A HEAVY FOG lay over the land the next evening. Soterius and Mikhail watched from the citadel's highest point while the Margolan troops took their places. Soterius wrapped his own cloak tighter around himself against the cold winds. As Fallon had predicted, several hundred soldiers were encamped against the citadel.

"I don't like this." Soterius looked down at the ring of soldiers. He had made that comment more times in the last few candlemarks than he could remember.

"They've got to be relying on their mage," he added, surveying the soldiers. "It's as if they're waiting for us to come out."

"They have a plan."

Within a candlemark, one of the Sisters had returned with news that the citadel's water was tainted. "We protected the ground around the tower," she explained, "but the water springs from a river beneath the ground. A water mage could easily have caused it to be fouled before it ever reached our protections."

"That cuts down our time," Soterius said soberly.

The Sister shook her head. "It's bad, but not hopeless. We've stored some water, wine and ale. Two of our water mage sisters are trying to purify water from the pump. They can't extend their powers far enough to cleanse the spring where it has been fouled. It will be a hardship, because they can only purify a few barrels at a time. And it diverts their powers from other uses."

Just then, another Sister joined them. Her robes were stained with mud and smelled of the stables; dirt streaked her face and hands. "There is madness among the animals," she reported. "None have seen its like. It is, I fear, mage sent. Two villagers were killed before we realized what was wrong. Sittra is there now to see what can be done. We can barely contain the beasts, and we don't dare slaughter any for food."

"They've made the first strike," Soterius grumbled.

"Our land mage has been busy himself. Do you hear that?" Fallon asked, leading Soterius over to the thick wall.

He concentrated, straining to hear beyond the citadel's heavy fortifications. Then he heard it, a constant, steady cawing of crows. "Crows?" he asked, frowning. "How many crows does it take to make that much racket?"

Fallon smiled. "The ground is black with crows. They are clever birds; they elude the soldiers' arrows. They will foul the tents with their droppings, and their noise will be a constant annoyance."

"Why don't you just call down wolves and be done with them?" Soterius asked disparagingly.

"We won't call the wolves to their slaughter. Although I believe you'll hear them, beyond archers' range. And come dusk, our guests may see a cloud of bats like never before."

"Your mage talks... to bats?" Soterius said dubiously.

"A land mage can 'speak' to all things living, and persuade them to aid his cause."

"Persuade?" Soterius questioned. "He gives the bats a choice?"

"That's the difference between a mage that serves the light, and one that serves darkness. A Light mage doesn't force any living thing to act against its will, or take from the land and seas what can't be given back."

"When you're done asking the bugs for permission," Soterius replied, "We'll be down teaching the villagers to fight."

Soterius and Mikhail found the villagers in the enclosed courtyard milling about nervously, several dozen in all, their few belongings tied up in sacks. The villagers greeted them heartily. Every able-bodied person who was not needed to suckle a child or tend an elder heeded the call to arms. For several candlemarks, Soterius and Mikhail trained them in the basics of castle defense. They separated those who could serve best as lookouts from those strong enough to help defend the gates. Together they worked with the villagers until the late evening bells tolled.

As the sound of the bells faded, Soterius paused. At first, he took the distant humming for the constant noise of the birds. But within a few seconds the hum became a roar, a force battering against the double wooden doors of the courtyard. "There's something out there trying to get in!" one of the villagers cried.

Once again, the wind roared and something hammered again at the doors. "Quiet everybody!" Soterius shouted above the din. "Quiet!"

"We're going to move for higher ground," Soterius explained in his calmest voice. "Let's start to move quickly to the stairs—"

The doors gave way.

A rush of freezing air swept through the courtyard, nearly taking men off their feet. As screaming villagers scrambled over each other to reach the stairs, the air began to swirl, growing colder and colder. "I don't know what it is, but I'm not staying to find out!" Soterius shouted above the din as Mikhail struggled to herd the last of the villagers into the main citadel building. Soterius signaled frantically to a few stragglers who were attempting to lug their packs with them.

The swirling wind caught up the debris in the courtyard like the tornados that sometimes laid waste to the Margolan plains. Bits of straw, splinters of wood, and shards of broken glass were hurtling through the air, embedding in the wooden posts.

"Come on!" Soterius urged, hanging onto the door. The two stragglers, realizing their folly, began to run, their path blocked by the swirling wind that kept even Mikhail from intervening.

Soterius's eyes grew wide as the icy spiral seemed to anticipate the stragglers' lunge for freedom. He threw up an arm to protect himself as the vortex enveloped the stragglers. Their screams filled the air; blood spattered the courtyard walls as the violent wind cut them to ribbons. Soterius threw his weight into closing the massive inner door, praying to the Goddess that it might withstand the onslaught. Mikhail joined him, adding his supernatural strength. Together, they managed to seal the door and throw the bolts just as the wind slammed into it.

"What was that?" Soterius asked breathlessly. Beyond the door, the vortex howled. In the hallway, babies screamed and children shrieked in terror, while the villagers, still clinging to their weapons, flattened themselves against the opposite wall, their faces pale with fright.

"An Elemental." They turned to find Fallon behind them.

"A what?" Soterius breathed, still feeling his heart thud.

"An Elemental," Fallon repeated. "Called by a mage." She sighed. "Perhaps we can be thankful that it's not a fire Elemental."

"Will the door hold?" Mikhail asked, still braced against the force.

"It's spelled to resist magic from the outside. We didn't spell the common gate because there had never been a need." She looked pained. "An oversight."

"Then we're trapped," Mikhail said, looking levelly at Fallon. "Water fouled, our escape cut off, our source of food limited. Unless there's a way to stop that thing."

"There's a way, but it isn't easy. An Elemental, once called, can only be destroyed by the one who called it, or by breaking the concentration of the mage that cast it. I imagine," she said, her dark eyes weary, "that the mage is out there, among the soldiers. And our only way out, with the stable blocked, is through the archers' slits, too narrow for any man or child, or from the roof of the tower itself."

Soterius's eyes lit with inspiration. "If someone could get down there, how could the warding be broken?"

"A mage could do it with a word. Or a mage might put the spell on a small chit, a piece of pottery that bears her wizard's mark, to send it with someone else." She frowned. "But no one here can fly. And if we send a mage closer or try to move the chit by magic, their mage will surely detect it."

Soterius exchanged glances with Mikhail. "Either of us, by our own means, can get to the ground. I come from the high country, where climbing up and down cliffs is as natural as breathing. I've climbed the walls at Shekerishet many times. Give me cover, hand me the chit, and find me some rope and the leather to make a climbing harness. I'll get it there." He looked thoughtful. "And a few other ingredients our friend Carroway used for distractions might be useful, too."

"Absolutely not," Mikhail said. "I'll go." He held up a hand to stay Soterius's argument. "I'm faster. I'm stronger. I have more natural defenses," he said. "And I'm already dead."

Fallon shook her head. "We've already tried. The Margolan mage placed a warding that drove the *vayash moru* back. They were unable to cross."

"Then send me," Soterius argued. "Anything's better than waiting here to be cut to ribbons or starve to death."

Fallon was silent for a moment, then nodded reluctantly. "They sensed our mages as quickly as they sensed the *vayash moru*. We have no other experienced soldiers. There is no other choice."

"If I can't go, then let me get Ban safely to the ground," Mikhail cut in. "I *can* fly. I can have him at the tower base in a fraction of the time it would take to climb, and without the exposure."

Soterius remembered Gabriel's demonstration back in the salle in Principality City. "I'm willing."

Fallon folded her arms. "Then it's settled. In the meantime, rest. We'll provision you." It took Soterius much of the next morning to mix, by trial and error, smoke and light pellets like the ones that Carroway had used to highlight his songs and tales. He rested for the afternoon, rising at the supper bells to get ready for the night's work. As he finished, Fallon appeared with a thin, angular woman. "This is our land mage, Latt," Fallon said. "She'll raise a fog at moonrise and call the creatures of the wood to give you cover."

"I'm ready." Soterius looked at Latt. "You can talk to the bats about that cover."

Fallon smiled at the characterization. "Our mages have been doing a great deal more than conversing with bats and wolves," she said as they climbed the twisting stairs to the top of the citadel. "Our fire mage attempted to strike, but there's a powerful warding which let a direct hit bounce away harmlessly. Our water mages have called on the springs to bog down the ground, making it a sea of mud, which should hamper their use of war machines. Latt's spell to spoil their food may have worked, in which case, you may find them... indisposed."

"I used to think a mage would just look at someone the wrong way and 'poof,' they'd be gone, or burned to a cinder," Soterius said. Mikhail joined them at the third landing, climbing with them in silence. "After hanging around with Tris, I get the idea that it might not be quite that easy."

"It's taking a considerable amount of our mages' energy to avoid going 'poof' when *their* mage sends something our way." Fallon replied. "Which I'm sure is why Arontala added the mages."

They reached the top of the tower. The moon was full and bright. Soterius frowned, wishing for clouds to dim its light. "I wish you well," Fallon said. "Wait until the twelfth bell. Then listen for the bats. They will be your cue."

"I was kidding about the bats," Soterius said with an anxious glance. "Never really liked bats," he added beneath his breath.

"Latt also called a fog, which should help to hide your movements," Fallon added. She handed him a folded cloak. "This cloak has been spelled to be magic-neutral. It will hide the spelled chit from detection, and may protect you from magic directed at you."

"May?"

"We don't know the skills of the mage Arontala has sent. The cloak should shield you, but it can't protect you from everything. Use caution."

"Thanks a lot."

"Don't forget this," Fallon said. She stretched out her palm, and her opened hand revealed a plain-looking piece of buff pottery, stamped with an intricate design that seemed to blur and move. "It's a wizard's mark. This chit has been spelled to break the mage's warding and destroy his Elemental. You must be within an arm's length of him for it to work, and it must touch his body."

"What if he has some sort of, I don't know, protections or something?"

"You'll have to improvise."

"Great. Anything else I should know?"

"The cloak will let you pass among our mage's traps without harm," Fallon told him. "You need fear nothing from the wolves, or the bats. But beware of the Elemental."

Soterius raised an eyebrow at her tone. "The way you say that makes me worry."

Fallon frowned. "Elementals are unpredictable. They're a temporary creation, wholly created from the will and power of the maker. I can't predict what will happen when you break the wizard's warding."

"Meaning what?"

"Meaning that the Elemental may dissipate or—"

"Or what?"

"Or it may return to its maker before its energy is spent."

"And I have to be within reach of its maker."

"I've not seen many Elementals," Fallon said. "Because of the danger they pose to the maker, wizards of the Light rarely call such things. I have no way to know how spent its fury may be if it returns to its source. It could destroy the wizard alone—or the entire camp. Even the cloak can't protect you completely from the energy of an Elemental," she cautioned. "I suggest you escape quickly."

"I'll keep that in mind," Soterius retorted. Beneath him, the bells tolled eleven times. "I'd like to study the lay of the land from here," he said. It wasn't the first time that day Soterius had climbed to the tower's top to survey the enemy. But in moonlight, the terrain took on a different look. He wanted to prepare, knowing there would be no time once he reached the ground.

"Goddess go with you," Fallon said, making the sign of the Lady. "I'll leave you now."

"Thanks," Soterius said, as she moved to the door. "Keep a watch out. I'll need someone to let me back in."

CHAPTER TWENTY-TWO

THE CANDLEMARKS SLIPPED away, and soon the bells tolled midnight. Soterius drew a deep breath, ready for the night's work. He wore the mage's cloak and the spelled chit hung beneath his tunic in a pouch on a strap around his neck. His sword hung ready and his dagger belt crossed shoulder to hip.

Just then, Soterius heard the velvet rustle of a thousand bat wings.

Soterius stepped up to the edge of the wall. He tried to quiet a primal panic as the *vayash moru* stepped up behind him, encircling his chest with inhumanly strong arms. In one smooth motion, Soterius felt his feet leave the ground. Then they were aloft, over the top of the crenellations and descending so quickly it made Soterius's stomach flip.

They touched down lightly, and Mikhail released his hold, seeming to vanish in the next heartbeat.

The night air was cold enough to frost Soterius's breath, and he was grateful for his heavy cloak. He looked up. *Just as long as I don't have to climb back in*, he thought, adding a short, fervent prayer to the Goddess.

The cool mist of a thick ground fog greeted him, and Soterius dropped to a crouch. He lifted the spelled cowl over his head. He made his way through the mud, silently cursing the effectiveness of that particular spell. The cloak shielded him from the worst of the chill. Ahead, the fires of the camp burned brightly, their light diffused by the fog. From the woods beyond the camp, Soterius heard the howl of a wolf, and the answering cries of the pack. A shiver ran down his spine, despite Fallon's assurances that the wolves had been warned of his approach. He had met up with wolves on campaign more times than he liked to remember, and the flash of their teeth and hunger of their snarls were clear in his memory.

Heart thudding, Soterius approached the camp, careful to skirt the rim of firelight, staying well into the shadows. *How do I tell which one is the mage?* The troops wore the livery of Margolan, he noted bitterly. Close enough to see their faces, he watched the soldiers move about their camp, looking for anyone he recognized, surprised at how cold he felt inside at the thought of making war on men he once trained. The officers' tents were close to the center of the camp, while the enlisted men's tents circled the periphery. Soterius could spot the cook tent and the latrine, and a small wooden enclosure that served as a temporary stockade. There were more than enough soldiers to keep the citadel imprisoned for quite some time. To his relief, the siege engines and catapults appeared to be mired in deep mud. It was obvious that the commanders were prepared to play a waiting game.

Soterius had made nearly a full circle before he spotted the mage, a solitary figure near the center of the camp. His shadow was outlined by the light inside his tent, his arms raised, a scrying ball silhouetted beside him. Soterius smiled coldly, his target in view. This part of the job he understood completely.

It was joyous to do the work of a soldier once more, and he rose to the challenge. With a practiced eye Soterius set a course for himself, making use of what little concealment the camp provided. He took a deep breath, steeling himself to walk purposefully across the camp as if he belonged there.

Behind him the wolves howled louder. The bats, nearly wingtip to wingtip in the dark sky, squealed and fluttered overhead, diving at the soldiers, too fast and small to fear the swords. The bats took most of the idle soldiers' attention, enabling Soterius to slip past the guard.

Soterius closed the distance to the tent, moving silently, Carroway's pellets in one hand and the spelled chit in the other. He reached the shadows at the back of the tent and knelt. He was ready to slip beneath the back edge of the tent when he heard a crunch on the ground behind him, and the sound of a crossbow being drawn.

"Throw down your weapon and stand up."

Soterius stiffened, and held out his sword hand as if to surrender the blade. His wrist jerked and the pellets went flying, blinding the guard with red and green fire as they struck the ground and giving Soterius enough cover to throw a small shiv that sank hilt-deep into the guard's chest. Knowing he was about to lose his chance completely, Soterius dove beneath the tent and flung the chit at the startled mage, grazing his leg.

There was a clap like thunder, and then the howl of a distant storm. As the camp erupted into chaos, Soterius ran for his life toward a trench along the perimeter. He huddled in the bottom of the ditch, flattening himself against the ground with the cloak pulled over his head. In the distance he heard terrified screams as the hum of the Elemental grew louder. The winds battered him, pulling at his cloak with such force that he thought they might lift him from the trench and hurl him into the air. Soterius tried to make himself as small as possible, curling into a tight ball.

Above the shriek of the wind, Soterius heard screams in the darkness. He felt the power of the storm sweep over him. Even on the edge of the camp, as far away as he could get from the mage's tent, the wind beat against his magicked cloak. He held on to its fabric until his hands cramped and his fingers bled. Debris pelted him, and from that the cloak gave no reprieve. Soterius stifled a cry as wood and rock slammed against him; he prayed to the Lady that none of the debris would rend his cloak. Soterius closed his eyes, prepared to die.

The wind stopped, and the camp fell silent.

His heart pounding in his throat, Soterius rose slowly. Tents, set afire by scattered coals from the camp's fires, blazed out of control. The Elemental had carved a path through the heart of the camp.

Where the mage's tent had been, the ground was bare and burned.

Soterius ran for his life. His breath steamed in the cold air. He zigzagged his way back along the lines, using the wreckage as cover to elude the remaining soldiers who tried to round up their panicked comrades. As Soterius hid behind a ruined wagon, waiting for two soldiers to pass, a streak of color in the mud caught his attention. Tattered by the Elemental and sullied by the campaign, the banner he pulled from the mud was still recognizable. It brought a lump to his throat and stung his eyes. Soterius held the banner of Margolan clenched in his fists.

He did not have to worry about having to scale the citadel tower to regain entry; Mikhail waited at the base of the watchtower to welcome him back. Joyous peasants spilled into the bailey. Soterius passed among them, oblivious to their glee, managing a smile only when they pressed around him and hoisted him onto their shoulders, carrying him in victory.

He left as soon as the opportunity presented itself. Mikhail followed him when he made his way back up to the tower roof.

"You're the hero," Mikhail said. "Your party is downstairs."

Soterius struggled with his memories. "You didn't hear the soldiers die, when the Elemental came."

"You've been to battle before, Ban. You know it for what it is."

"They never had a chance."

"Did the villagers in the outer bailey?" Mikhail replied. "The mage who called the Elemental didn't mind starving us out, or driving the villagers mad with thirst."

"It was slaughter," Soterius said quietly. Overhead, the winter constellations burned brightly. He pulled the shreds of flag out of his cloak pocket, and looked out over the plain once more, the ruined soldiers' camp just a silhouette of tumbled tents and nearly spent fires.

"You saved those villagers down there, and the Sisters, and their citadel. That's something to be proud of," Mikhail said. "They're from Margolan, too."

"I feel as proud as if I'd knifed those soldiers in their sleep. They were Margolan troops, Mikhail." He shook his head. "Fallon told me that the Elemental could return to the camp. She warned me it would be dangerous. But being there, hearing it… It's hard to be proud of winning if it isn't a fair fight."

"The soldiers made their choice when they swore allegiance to a murdering pretender. They obeyed Jared's orders to kill their own people. Jared's not worthy of that flag. And the troops that do his bidding aren't worthy of your pity."

"I want to drive the bastard out," Soterius said. "I want to go home."

"So do I. But not until a king I trust sits on the throne. We have to put Tris there, Ban."

Soterius looked across the plain at the burning camp. "I know. I know."

"Come on. Give the villagers a hero to celebrate. Lady knows they've had little enough cause for happiness lately. And afterwards, Fallon's got a bottle of Cartelesian brandy waiting for you in your room. Seems our good Sisters partake," he said with a grin. "Then to bed with you. We've got a ride ahead of us tomorrow night."

Soterius took a deep breath, knowing Mikhail was right; the villagers needed a symbol and a hero more than he needed the luxury of quiet grief. The men wound their way down the stairs toward the bailey, where the sound of revelry and music echoed throughout the ancient fortress.

Soterius attempted his best show of lighthearted gaiety, obliging the village girls who waited for a dance with the evening's hero, embarrassedly accepting the heaping trenchers of food brought to him by village matrons, and washing them down with tankards of ale that the farmers and townsmen kept filled. It was well past mid-morning before the celebration began to wind down, and the sun hung in the afternoon sky before Soterius was free to find his bed. The morrow would come too quickly, Soterius knew. And while it would not be the first time he rode with a throbbing head; it was just as well that he would have something to take his mind off his memory of the night's work, and what it truly meant to raise steel against his own flag.

CHAPTER TWENTY-THREE

THE LAST OF the spring rains ended late in the fourth month, the Lover's Moon. When the roads were dry enough to ride without bogging down, Tris and his companions prepared for the final campaign into Margolan.

Their departure was unheralded, with only Staden, Taru, Berry, and Royster on hand to bid them farewell. Staden made sure they were provisioned with excellent horses and supplies. Berry, as close to tears as Tris had ever seen the feisty young princess, hugged them all and promised prayers to the Lady for their success. Royster mentioned vague plans to return to the Library at Westmarch, although Tris privately wondered if the librarian would give up his newfound freedom easily. Gabriel had left the night before their departure to meet with his "family" in Margolan and arrange for safe houses and *vayash moru* escorts along their way.

He had promised to meet up with Tris and the others once they reached Margolan.

The group would make the best time on the journey south traveling the river Nu, whose deep, swift course would save them a dangerous overland passage. Staden sent them with a letter to his friend Sakwi, the land mage who had helped Kiara on her journey north. The letter asked for Sakwi's assistance and his help in securing a boat for both them and their horses. That letter waited safe in the breast pocket of Tris's tunic.

Though both Staden and Kiara attested to Sakwi's trustworthiness, Tris was worried about the river journey itself. The river was the best way to avoid a dangerous passage through Margolan's northern mountains, but it would be wild and swift from the melted snows. The only other land route ran through Dhasson, but Tris had no reason to believe that Arontala's spell to call the magicked beasts had lost its potency. They would stay close to the Margolan banks when they passed along the Dhasson stretch. The river would let them bypass the mountains to reach the southern plains and Shekerishet more quickly. Once they left the banks of Principality, they would be back in hostile territory, and closer than ever to Jared and Arontala.

"I hope the weather holds," Kiara said. She lifted her face to the wind, and let it rustle back through her thick hair. She looked up, scanning the clouds. "It can change without warning on the river."

"Here's hoping the Lady's with us all the way," Tris said. "I was thinking the same thing."

* * *

THEY REACHED THE village where Staden had said they would find Sakwi near dusk. It smelled of fish and wood smoke. It was just far enough from the banks of the river that the yearly floods would not sweep it away. The village housed only a handful of families. Nets were hung from the trees to dry and skiffs were pulled up on the banks. The streets were deserted as Tris and his friends rode up, but once they passed the first small house, Tris could feel that they were being watched.

"We seem to be leading a parade," Carroway said from behind them, as their horses splashed down the muddy road. Tris glimpsed a silent congregation of ill-clad villagers slip from their homes to keep a watchful eye on the strangers.

When they reached the center of the small town, Vahanian stopped, and turned in his saddle to look back at the villagers who followed them. "We're looking for a traveling mage," he called to the group. "A land mage named Sakwi."

A bearded man stepped forward. "What do you want?"

"We were told this mage could help us navigate the river on our journey south," Vahanian replied. "We have a letter of introduction from a friend."

"I'm Sakwi." They turned to see a thin, slightly stooped mage whose racking cough silenced him for a moment after he spoke.

"Sakwi!" Kiara called in greeting. She slid from her horse and ran to the mage.

"Please, come inside," Sakwi said, gesturing for them to tether their horses and follow him into a small house. "If I'm to be of help, I must understand your journey. You'll be safe here," he said, with a nod to the villager who first intercepted them. The fisherman nodded in return. In the dim light, Tris caught the glint of a dagger in the man's hand. Tris looked around at the group of villagers, noting that each was well-armed by common standards. This might be the last safe haven they would have for quite some time, he thought. He would enjoy it while it lasted.

"Sakwi gave me the key to Westmarch, and introduced me to Grayfoot the fox," Kiara explained once the door was closed. Briefly, she told Sakwi of her trek northward, and of the magicked beast she encountered and Grayfoot's sacrifice.

"I believe Grayfoot had some idea of what might befall him," Sakwi said. "He was a bit of a mystic."

"The fox?" Vahanian asked incredulously. Kiara glared at him.

"I'm not sure what he was, but he wasn't your average fox," Kiara reproved.

"Actually," Sakwi said, "he was quite average. The fox are very intelligent... for those who know how to speak with them." Sakwi turned his attention to Tris. "I doubt you've come to reminisce. How can I help you?"

Tris pulled Staden's note from his pocket, and waited as Sakwi read it over.

"We need safe passage for ourselves and our horses down the river. I'm Martris Drayke, son of Bricen of Margolan. My friends and I go to unseat Jared the Usurper and his mage." He paused. "And we would like to travel as quietly as possible."

Sakwi looked from Tris to Kiara and back again. "King Staden is a good friend. I'll do as he requests. I've seen what is going on in Margolan, and I've tried to bring some relief to the refugees. Speaking of which, there is someone I'd like you to meet," Sakwi said. He leaned outside the door and spoke a word to a boy waiting there. After a while, a bent, haggard man appeared.

"Come in, my friend," Sakwi greeted him, ushering him toward a seat. The newcomer regarded Tris and the others suspiciously. "These travelers will have a great interest in your story," Sakwi said, "I know it's difficult for you to speak of it, but I ask you to tell your tale once more."

The stooped man wrung his gnarled hands for a moment; the lines that etched his face seemed to deepen in the firelight. "I canna sleep," he admitted, staring down at his hands. "I might as well tell the story since it won't leave me 'til the day I die." Tris heard the thick accent of the Margolan farm country in the man's rough voice.

"I worked the land my father worked, and his father before him," the farmer said, looking not at Tris but at the wall over Tris's shoulder. "And until the last harvest, I cared nothing of what happened in the city, or ought what the palace folk did. Then the riders came."

"Riders?" Tris prompted gently, leaning forward.

"Aye, the guardsmen of the king," the farmer replied, still looking at the wall, as if he were replaying the scene in his mind. "At first, they wanted gold. Then, when there was no more gold to give, grain and pigs. When those were gone, they took our daughters." His eyes were hopeless and haunted. "Like the grain and the gold, we never saw them again."

Beside him, Tris felt Kiara stiffen. "What happened then?"

"The village in the next shire refused to give up their women. We found the menfolk hanging in the forest, cut open like deer, their hands and tongues cut off.

"We had nothing left to lose," he went on, his voice flat. "They came for our women and stayed to take our boys in chains to train for soldiers. It was too much." He turned his haunted gaze on Tris. "Dark Lady take my soul, I know 'tis treason to raise a sword against the king's men. But it was too much to bear. We rose against them with whatever we had at hand, our poor hoes and axes against their swords.

"We should have known that more would come when the first never returned." As he spoke, a lad of a half-dozen summers slipped into the room and sidled up beside him. Tris felt his throat tighten as of the firelight revealed the boy's face. A scar ran from the boy's collarbone to his severed ear, leaving the side of his face puckered and discolored. Carina reached out reflexively for the boy, who shrank back into the shadows.

"When they came back, they brought demons with them. Out of a box wagon, they came. Like dead men walking they were, blind with rage, striking everything in sight. We didn't know what to make of them, and they killed so many. They left my boy for dead," the farmer went on. "Burned the village, and took our women and boys anyway. Of one hundred souls, only my boy and I escaped. We wandered the woods like *vayash moru* until Sakwi found us and brought us here." He looked back at the hands he twisted in his lap, hands stained from a lifetime of working the soil and broadened by the plow.

"Thank you," Sakwi said quietly. He pressed a chunk of meat and a loaf of bread into the man's hand, and enticed the boy from the shadows with a wedge of cheese so that Carina could heal his wounds. She worked for over a candlemark to restore the boy's hearing, relieve the pain of the badly healed wound, and lessen the scarring that marred his face. When she was finished, after profuse thanks, the farmer led the boy to the door, then turned and looked back to Tris and the others.

"Stay clear of Margolan," he warned. "'Tis the demon's own now, mark my words."

Tris was silent after the farmer and his boy disappeared into the night. Vahanian muttered a potent curse. The mix of anger and grief that welled up inside Tris was too strong to put into words. His loathing for Jared deepened, and the pain he felt for his homeland, for all the deaths and destruction, swayed him dangerously toward overwhelming anger. Kiara laid a hand on his arm, sensing his struggle. Tris could hear the Sisterhood's warnings in his mind, but every attempt to dispel the hatred he felt fell short. It was several moments before he could even trust himself to speak, before his eyes cleared and he could let the desire to destroy Jared drain from his body.

"The story is unfortunately a common one," Sakwi said, pausing while a coughing fit took his breath. "This winter was harsh, and the soldiers left little for the people to eat. They will starve come summer, before the next crops are in."

"What did he mean, 'dead men walking?'" Vahanian asked.

"Probably the same *ashtenerath* fighters Ban ran into," Tris replied. "Arontala can't do spirit magic, so he can't reanimate corpses. But his blood magic and torture could bend a man to his will."

"There are plants and mixtures that will produce visions—or nightmares," Carina added. "Absinthe, for one. Certain mushrooms, and strange plants from the southland deserts. The priestesses use them in rituals to see the Lady. Without the proper precautions, they can drive a man mad."

"Yeah, well if they're the same madmen Ban fought, then they die off quickly. That's one good thing." Vahanian replied.

"Esme showed me the body of the fighter they brought back from the border. I could sense the blood magic," Tris said. "But Arontala can't make too many of them without depleting himself. They require a good bit of power to control. And Esme says that because of how badly they're broken before Arontala can make fighters of them, they're already dying—the pain is part of the madness." Tris balled his fists as he struggled to control his anger and re-channel its force. "By Chenne, I'll bring Jared down—and Arontala with him."

Sakwi regarded him silently. "I hope so." He rose to stir a pot on the fire. "There's much to do if we're to head downriver. But first, we eat."

Sakwi boiled water for tea and readied a meal of hard cheese, bread and meat. Vahanian, Carina, and Carroway warmed themselves by the fire, their sodden cloaks raising a fine mist in the warmth.

Tris answered Sakwi's questions about his training and their preparations for the journey. On the hearth, Jae picked at a wedge of cheese. Sakwi reached out a hand to the little gyregon, who hopped toward him without reservation. Jae fluttered his wings and hopped up to perch on the land mage's shoulder. Absently, Sakwi reached up to scratch the little gyregon under its chin. The land mage made a murmuring noise, and Jae answered with a similar gurgle.

"I think I've seen everything now," Vahanian muttered. "You're talking to that gyregon?"

Sakwi looked up. "Of course. It's the polite thing to do. He's a bit put out that we have no chickens to spare." The gyregon preened and headed back toward the warmth of the fire.

"I haven't seen such a pretty gyregon in a long time," Sakwi said to Kiara. "They're native to Eastmark, you know. The royal family there doesn't like to let them out of the country. He's quite a prize."

"He was a gift from my uncle," Kiara murmured, reaching out to stroke the small hunting dragon. Jae, seeming to sense he was momentarily the center of attention, made a trilling sound and rolled onto his back, inviting a belly rub.

Sakwi pulled a large leather traveling pack from a cupboard and began to fill it with necessities for the trip. "The stories of monsters along the Dhasson border are not the inventions of men with too much ale," Sakwi said as he packed, and paused, taken by a coughing fit that shook his thin form. Carina started forward, but Kiara shook her head, warning her not to intercede.

Tris saw that for as frail as Sakwi might be in some ways, the rest of his slight body was well muscled and whipcord strong. "I've heard the witness of the foxes and the wolves, who have seen the monsters," Sakwi went on when the fit passed. "I've also heard that 'things' infest the river, and even the northern sea. We'll need to travel carefully."

Sakwi paused, as if pondering a question to himself. "The horses make it a little more challenging," he said finally. "I assume you wouldn't be comfortable if I just instructed the horses to meet us and sent them on their way?"

"Did I just hear him right?" Vahanian said in amazement. "He wants to *talk* to the horses?"

Sakwi raised an eyebrow, but did not turn toward the fighter. "Horses are quite reasonable creatures. And amazingly forgiving, which is why they put up with people the way they do. They're very good with directions, and they can make much better time when they're not hauling us around on their backs."

Tris smiled at Vahanian's obvious vexation, and Kiara barely hid a chuckle. "I think we'd rather keep the horses with us if we can," Tris said diplomatically. "Just in case we can't take the river the whole way to Margolan."

"Suit yourself. I think I know of a boat that can take us all, and a pilot, but it will take me a while to find him and obtain provisions." Sakwi stood. "Make yourselves comfortable. It should take me about two candlemarks to make arrangements."

"I'll be glad to come with you," Vahanian offered.

"Very well. Come if you like." Sakwi took down a moss-colored cloak from a peg near the door. Vahanian followed him with a glance to the others that made it clear that his intention was to keep an eye on the mage.

"I can't say I much fancy a river ride in this weather," Carroway said, pulling up a chair beside Carina, close to the fire.

"Can we trust Sakwi?" Carina asked, looking to Kiara.

"He had no reason to hide me from the guards at the camp, but he did, and the refugees trusted him. Staden trusts him. And I don't see much choice, if we're going down the river."

"I don't like the sightings of 'monsters' in the river and the Northern Sea," Tris said as they finished the tea Sakwi had made for them. "If those things spread, travel and trade in the Winter Kingdoms will be impossible."

Jae gratefully accepted a bit of the dried meat from Kiara, and left the hearth for Carina's lap near the fire. The little gyregon picked at his tidbit for a moment, lifted his head to gobble it down, and then stretched, circling once before settling in a contented ball.

Carroway found a small lyre in the corner of Sakwi's room, and absently began to strum it, humming to himself. Other than the bard's quiet singing the group waited in nervous silence, their weapons close at hand, waiting for Sakwi to return.

"I FOUND THE pilot," Sakwi announced a few candlemarks later, shaking the rain from his cloak. "He's getting the boat ready now. It'll be tight with all of us and your gear and the horses, but it's a sturdy ship. It'll do."

Vahanian entered a step behind Sakwi and stamped the mud from his boots. "It's as good as we're going to get."

Sakwi moved to the hearth and put out the fire. "It's a day's trip downriver to the next village. We'll need to provision there for the next several days. We won't be able to stop again before Margolan."

Kiara frowned. "Surely there are villages between there and Margolan?"

"Nargi villages," the land mage replied.

"I'd really rather not stop there, if it's all the same to you," Vahanian said.

Sakwi looked at Vahanian. "You sound as if you've met our Nargi neighbors."

"On several occasions. Did a great business, but the priests weren't real impressed. I only heard part of what they were shouting when I left, but they got rather descriptive, and most of the details had to do with *after* they killed me."

"We'll do our best to avoid them," Sakwi said. "I doubt Tris and I would fare better. Nargi priests are rather jealous of their power."

"Lovely," Carroway grumbled. "Monsters in the river, now Nargi priests. And the only thing Nargi priests like *less* than mages are bards."

"I hate to say it," Kiara said, "but we could end up with a Margolan honor guard if we don't get going soon."

"You're right." Sakwi took two leather pouches from the cupboard, and tucked them safely beneath his tunic. "For my cough," he said apologetically.

"Perhaps I—" Carina started, but Sakwi shook his head.

"I'm sure you are a fine healer, my lady," Sakwi said, "but there is nothing that can be done. It can no more be changed than the color of my eyes. I believe the Lady left me with it to keep me humble."

Carina looked askance at him, but said nothing more. Jae fluttered to join them, rising from Carina's lap. The gyregon gave a squawk of protest before alighting on Kiara's shoulder.

"Let's get moving," Vahanian said.

The rain made the trail to the riverbank slick with mud. Their cloaks were soon heavy and damp in the steady drizzle. Whinnying disapproval, the horses protested as Tris and the others led them down the pathway. "There it is," Sakwi said as they reached the edge of the dark, swift water.

A boat lay at anchor just off shore, with a sturdy gangplank ready for them. They could hear the rush of the river and the lapping of the water against the boat, but in the darkness, the other shore could not be seen. Vahanian led the way, coaxing his restless horse toward the walkway.

"Come on, be reasonable," he urged the frightened animal, to no avail. The stallion stopped at the edge of the gangplank and planted its hooves firmly. "Come on," Vahanian muttered between gritted teeth. "We haven't got all night."

"Let me," Carina said, slipping in front of him.

"Be my guest."

The healer stood in front of the stallion, reaching up to gently stroke its face. At her touch, the horse relaxed visibly. Its ears pricked up at her words, murmured so softly that none of the others could hear. The horse whinnied once more. It took a step forward, onto the planking, and then another and another until, backing up the gangplank in front of the horse, Carina led him safely onto the ship and turned his reins over to Vahanian.

"How did you do that?"

"Finesse. It's the opposite of brute force."

"Funny," Vahanian muttered. "Very funny."

On shore, Sakwi repeated Carina's effort with Tris's mount, while Carina turned her attention to Kiara's. Before long, all the horses were safely secured in a small corral in the center of the ship.

"This is our pilot," Sakwi said, as a burly, dark-haired man stepped up. The pilot's eyes were nearly hidden beneath his broad-brimmed hat, and he wore a voluminous cloak that made his immense proportions seem even larger.

"I'm Nyall." The man's voice was loud enough to carry over the water's roar. "Take these." He thrust two long poles toward them. "We need to get out into the channel."

Once they were away from the bank, the swift current caught them quickly. Nyall ordered Tris and Vahanian to use the long poles to push clear debris and keep them out of shallows. The drizzle continued, making visibility almost impossible and soaking them through. Jae chattered his disapproval from his perch on Kiara's shoulder where the other three huddled near the horses. Sakwi seemed unaffected by the journey's discomforts, his face raised to the storm as if he were listening to a song. Carroway huddled in his cloak, saying nothing but obviously unhappy with the circumstances of their trip. Carina clung to Kiara, looking ill.

"Don't tell me you're going to be sick," Vahanian said with concern.

In response, the healer dodged to the railing at the edge of the ship and threw up. Kiara stood beside her, holding her shoulders and steadying her against the rise and fall of the waves.

"I never really expected her to do that," Vahanian said abashed.

"I don't like boats," Carina retorted, still keeping a white-knuckled grip on the rail. "I've never liked boats. Boats move too much."

Sakwi stirred from his thoughts to join them, reaching into one of his many pouches for a rubbery leaf. "Chew this." He pressed the leaf into Carina's palm. "It will help."

Carina nodded her gratitude, and Sakwi returned to his position in the center of the ship.

"What's your friend doing, listening to the frogs?" Vahanian asked Kiara.

Kiara glanced back at Sakwi and shrugged. "No idea. Maybe he's feeling the storm."

"I'm feeling the storm myself," Vahanian muttered, shoving a tree limb away from the boat with a poke of his pole. "It's going to be a long trip if this keeps up."

"What you said about the Nargi, you were serious back there?"

"Dead serious, pardon the expression."

"What in the name of the Lady were you smuggling?"

"Silks and brandy," Vahanian said, pushing more debris away from the hull. "Ask Tris. He met some of the priests back in Ghorbal. They're a friendly bunch."

"They wanted to flay him alive," Tris confirmed. "We barely outran them."

"Barely?" Vahanian shouted back. "Barely? We were way ahead of them. What do you know? You were buried in a pile of silk. They were way behind us."

"They seemed a lot closer to the back of the wagon," Tris said.

"Is that how you learned to speak Nargi?" Kiara asked. Carina, ashen, leaned back over the railing and was sick once more.

"Nope," Vahanian replied. "I learned that the hard way. Got captured by some raiders. After a couple of years, you pick it up."

Kiara frowned. "No one lives that long as a Nargi captive."

Vahanian leaned on his pole. "I took down three of them when I was captured. When the bastards finally got me, their captain made me a deal. Fight in their betting games, or die right away." He shrugged. "Didn't look like I had much of a choice."

"I've heard about those betting games," Kiara shuddered. "Loser dies."

"Uh huh," Vahanian said, turning away to push loose more debris from the swiftly flowing water.

"And you survived, for how long?"

"Two years," he said. "Long enough."

"How did you get away?" Carina's voice barely carried above the wind. Tris glanced over to see the healer, looking pale and nauseous, hanging onto the railing.

"The captain who owned me made a few enemies. He got called to the palace one day, and didn't
expect to come back. He let me escape, then blamed
a rather nasty lieutenant who had it coming. I got
away, the flunky got the blame, and the captain
managed to do his double-crossing little second-in-
command out of the hottest betting game champion
in Nargi."

"Owned?" Carina asked quietly.

Vahanian's dark eyes lost their bantering glint.
"Yeah. Owned. I told you, I don't like Nargi."

"Hard to port!" Nyall shouted, and the ship
lurched, knocking Kiara off her feet and making
Carina and Vahanian cling to the railing for support. Tris stumbled backward into Carroway, who
grabbed at his cloak with one hand and held onto
the corral rail with the other. Sakwi barely moved,
his concentration unbroken, and it was then that
Tris guessed the land mage's purpose. The horses in
the corral, while restless, displayed none of the
panic Tris expected. He looked from the quiet horses to the mage and back again in awe.

"What was that?" Vahanian shouted above the
wind.

"Rocks," Nyall clipped. "Hard to see. Less talk
and more work with the poles if you don't want to
swim."

"Look!" Kiara shouted, pointing toward the
churning waters. Vahanian followed her gesture,
then cursed, jumping aside as a sodden mass
washed onto the deck.

"What is it?" Tris called over the storm.

"Looks like a piece of one of those 'magic monsters' Sakwi was talking about," Vahanian said,

poking at the fleshy pile with his pole. Kiara drew her sword and Carina stepped back. Even from the other side of the boat, Tris could tell that the tentacle belonged to no creature he had ever seen.

"If that's a finger, I don't want to see the rest of it," Vahanian muttered, probing at the thing with his pole. Jae squawked from where he crouched on Kiara's shoulder, partially shielded from the storm by her cloak.

Sakwi left the horses with a warding gesture and moved closer. When he stood next to the tentacle, he closed his eyes and stretched out his hand, palm down, just above it. Sakwi recoiled, his eyes opening wide. "Fascinating."

"What?" Carina asked.

"I can't explain entirely," Sakwi replied, "but it doesn't *feel* natural. It's tainted with blood magic."

"Great. Can you tell if it has teeth?" Vahanian snapped as he pushed the boat away from a rock.

"Such things are made to kill," Sakwi said, pushing the severed tentacle back into the swift waters. "Keep a sharp eye out. Whatever lost that might still be alive—or have friends."

Tris and Vahanian kept their posts on either side of the boat for the rest of the night. At daybreak, Carroway and Kiara relieved them, and Tris and Vahanian lashed themselves to the side of the corral for what troubled sleep they could find. Carina, ashen and miserable, clung to the corral, trying to help Sakwi keep the animals quieted when she was not making dry heaves over the boat's rail. Jae found a perch on Kiara's horse and settled, his wings folded and his head down.

The rain lasted all day, with a cloud cover that made noon as dark as twilight. Even their heavy cloaks were no match for the constant rain. By midday, Tris found it impossible to stay warm, resigning himself to numbed hands and a constant shiver. By the looks of them, Kiara, Carroway, and Vahanian were equally miserable. Carina looked truly wretched, her face drawn from lack of sleep, unable even to watch the others eat. Although Carina bore it stoically, Tris had no doubt that she longed for dry land.

"You know, I haven't seen a fish this whole trip," Vahanian mused as they headed through a quiet stretch of water.

"Neither have I," Tris agreed.

"Maybe it's not a good fishing area," Carina said.

"Or maybe something's eating them all. I saw a few deer carcasses on the shore that didn't look like they'd been eaten by any wolf I've ever seen. I don't like it," Vahanian muttered. "The sooner we're on dry land, the better."

They docked at dusk against a rickety platform in a floating city. On both sides of the river, a fleet of houseboats bobbed and swayed. Some were hardly more than tents on rafts. Others looked to be true ships, moored and used as dwellings until their captains decided to raise sail once more. Some were solid floating cabins, hard used and smelling of fish.

Tris had heard talk of these floating cities, temporary boat-villages that came and went with the seasons and the fish—and sometimes, the interest of local authorities. At the core were a half-dozen larger boats. Those were permanently moored—traders' ships that served as a provisioning stop for river travelers.

Swinging bridges linked these trading ships to dozens of other boats down the Margolan side of the river. Fishermen might leave their village for the season and tie up with such a floating city, bringing each day's catch to a broader market. Provisioners of all types tied up for the duration—food sellers, tavern-keepers, hard-bitten men and women selling clothing and tools, fishing gear, and baubles.

Across the water Tris could hear music, and bet that more than one of the garishly decorated boats served as brothels. On the decks of the boats men drank and gambled. Dirty-faced children scampered sure-footedly from boat to boat, and worn-looking women rested babies on their hips and talked in clusters. Metal stove boxes set on slabs of slate provided for both cooking and warmth. A month from now, all but the provisioners' ships might be gone, moved to better fishing areas. The floating cities were as lawless as they were temporary, and were reputed to be a haven to many whose reputations made them less welcome in the caravans and towns.

Nyall waved for them to follow him ashore. Carina held Vahanian's arm as they disembarked, looking miserable.

"This way," the river pilot said. Nyall walked so quickly that they had to run to keep up. They worked their way down the maze of intersecting docks while dodging the ropes and jugs, fish bones and nets that littered the rickety structures.

The denizens of the floating city called out their greetings to the river captain in a thick patois that made it difficult for Tris to catch their comments. Vahanian appeared perfectly at home, countering some of the comments with rejoinders in the same thick accent.

"I get the feeling Jonmarc's been this way before," Carroway commented.

"He said something about having traded on the river," Tris said, ducking under a clothesline. The docks were a hazardous gathering place, jumbled with small cook stoves and drying nets. Ragged children ran between the nets and grizzled old women sat atop the pylons, smoking their pipes. Jae fluttered and squawked as Kiara bent low beneath the ropes that criss-crossed the narrow walkway. She jumped as a cat squealed and dove in front of her. Tris kept his hand near his sword, and he noted that Kiara and Vahanian did the same. Carina leaned heavily on her staff, looking as if she longed for nothing so much as dry clothes and a solid footing. Unfortunately, the docks themselves floated on thick logs, so that the whole city undulated with the currents of the river.

"In here," Nyall said. He stood aside for them to walk up the short gangplank of a large, dusky yellow houseboat. Its smoky interior hung heavy with the smell of burned lard and onions. "A good tavern. They'll have something to fix you up," he said, nodding to Carina, "and Mama will take good care of you while I get us provisioned for the next leg of the trip."

Mama was a gargantuan woman. She grinned at them toothlessly. "Welcome," she said in the thick river accent. "You're friends of Nyall's and Jonmarc's. Sit. I'll get you something."

Tris and the others exchanged uneasy glances and sat down. Vahanian stood near the bar, leaning with feigned casualness where he could watch the door. Mama looked back at them from the small table where she was chopping vegetables and dropping them into a well-used pot.

"Miserable day, wasn't it?" Mama asked, not expecting an answer, and went back to her work humming tunelessly. She squeezed her bulk through the doorway and bustled down the gangplank with a pronounced limp. She re-emerged after a few minutes, dusting her hands against her stained apron. Mama frowned, looking at Carina, and dug in a bin beneath the table, rising with a handful of hard crackers.

"Here, dearie, eat these," she said. "You look like you've lost your supper all the way down the river." Mama's tone was matter-of-fact. "Make you some tea, too. There's a window back there if it won't stay down."

Pale and cold, Carina accepted the gift gratefully and began to nibble on the cracker. Mama gathered their sodden cloaks and hustled them away, replacing them with threadbare but dry blankets or shawls. Tris watched through the porthole as Mama loaded the soaked garments over her arm and headed for a large wood stove that burned on a piece of metal in the center of the docks. A makeshift tarpaulin fluttered over it, giving some shelter. Mama carefully arranged the cloaks as best she could around the stove to dry them. She surveyed her work critically, and then with a nod, walked determinedly back to her charges, stopping to check the stew and pour tea into a chipped mug.

"Feeling better, dearie?" she asked Carina. "Owner of the place should be back soon. He'll be glad to see some customers for once, paying or not." Mama headed back to her work, laughing heartily at her own joke.

From his spot near the doorway, Vahanian asked a question in the unpronounceable patois. Mama threw back her head in laughter, then shot back a rapid-fire answer which seemed to suffice.

"What's going on?" Tris asked, hoping that he would soon stop shivering. The tavern boat was warmer than the raft, but its sole heat was a small metal firebox on a flat stone in the middle of the table. Its thin walls and shuttered portholes offered little true protection against the storm.

"Just getting an idea of how much traffic has been by here recently," Vahanian replied. "It's a good way to tell whether the Nargi are feeling obnoxious."

Mama went behind the bar and took down a large flagon from which she began to pour liberal draughts, offering the first to Vahanian, who tossed it back effortlessly. Tris was chilled through enough to gratefully accept the libation, as did they all except Carina. Tris took a small mouthful, struggling to keep from spewing it out as his tongue and lips caught fire. Kiara and Carroway were having the same difficulty, which sent Mama into a seizure of laughter. She poured Vahanian another draught.

"My friends are from the city," Vahanian said in the Common tongue, with a sidelong glance to let the others know he had intentionally let them understand his jibe. Mama laughed even harder, until her sizable form shook, and she clapped Sakwi on the back so hard the mage inadvertently swallowed his mouthful, resulting in another extensive coughing fit. Mama looked alarmed, but Sakwi managed to hold up his hand to stave off her ministrations.

"No, really, I'm all right," he gasped, clutching the back of a chair. "Just a little cough."

Mama looked at him with the skepticism of her vast experience. "Harrumph," she said, narrowing her eyes. But she did not press the matter, and busied herself fixing dinner. Tris found that, once he persuaded his throat to accept the potent liquor, it warmed him rapidly. He would not have cared for a second helping. Vahanian did not appear to be affected by the liquor, although Tris noted that the next time Vahanian spoke to Mama, his river accent more closely matched hers.

From outside, the sounds of a commotion reached them. Through the tavern boat's slatted windows, Tris glimpsed a stout man bustling through the chaos on the docks.

"By the Whore!" a man shouted heavily climbing the gangplank, "do I have to do everything myself?"

The man strode into the room and ripped his cloak over his head, stopping dumbfounded in amazement. "Jonmarc?" Maynard Linton, owner of the ill-fated caravan that sheltered Tris and his friends on their flight from Shekerishet, looked at Tris and the others as if he were seeing ghosts.

"Maynard!" Carina cried, starting from her seat. Tris, Carroway, and Vahanian slapped the sturdy trader on the back and crowded around him.

"What happened?" Tris asked as Linton made his way to the bar and poured himself a draught of Mama's liquor. "The slavers told us you were dead."

Linton tossed back two shots of the strong whiskey before he thumped his chest and cleared his throat. "Nearly was," he said in a raw voice. He shook his head to clear the last of the drink from his throat. "Miscalculated the dose and slept for three days."

"Mussa poison," Vahanian said.

"But I've sworn off it now, by the Whore," Linton said with a grin. "Stuff gave me the damnedest headache when it finally wore off."

"You're just lucky the bastards didn't slit your throat to make sure you were dead," Vahanian said.

"Calculated risk, m'boy," Linton said. "When I woke up, there was no one left. So I salvaged anything that might be of use and took off for the river. I had a few coins hidden about. Enough to set me up with this," he added with an expansive sweep of his arm to indicate the tavern, "and here I've been."

Carroway told the story of their escape from the slavers, with more than one poetic flourish that made Tris wince and caused Vahanian to roll his eyes. Linton listened intently. At Carroway's suspenseful retelling of the battle at the Ruune Videya, the caravan master glanced from Tris to Vahanian and back again to assure himself of the truth of the fantastic tale. Mama hunched over the bar, spellbound. By the time Carroway had recounted their journey to the Library, their reunion with Soterius and Harrtuck in Principality, and the word from Isencroft of Cam's safe arrival, Linton grinned and slapped his thigh.

"Goddess True, that's a tale for the bards!" he exclaimed, motioning for Mama to bring another round of drinks. Tris and Carroway waved away anything but ale, while Vahanian joined Linton in another of the throat-numbing whiskey.

"So you're the ones who put up with his mangy hide before he came here," Mama sniped good-naturedly as she brought the drinks. "Well if you be a mage, then magic away those monsters what swim in the river before they eat up every last fish. Fishermen can't make a decent living no more, with those *things* in there. Every so often they eat up a sailor what falls in, too." She waddled back out of earshot and busied herself at the bar.

"That's only a slight exaggeration, m'boy," Linton said seriously. "It's been edgy on the river since the thaw. There are *things* in the river that aren't born of nature, and there's more than one old hand has seen them. There've been Nargi on the move, too, but we don't know why." Linton glanced toward Vahanian on the last comment. Vahanian frowned but said nothing.

Kiara and Carina joined them at the table. Mama hustled back up the gangplank with a steaming stewpot and distributed enough chipped, mismatched bowls for each of them. She ladled out a generous amount of fish stew, pungent with onions and garlic. Coarse, crisp flatbread accompanied it, together with ample portions of salty butter.

"Someone was through here not long ago that might interest you, though she didn't tell the full tale of where she'd been, I see. Alyzza turned up, looking a little worse for the wear, two moons ago," Linton reported. "Cagey as hell when I'd asked where she'd been or what had happened with the slavers. Now I know why. Said she was bound for Margolan," he added. "Something about old business to finish at the Hawthorn Moon."

"You're sure she said the Hawthorn Moon?" Carina asked.

Linton nodded. "Certain. Didn't think much of it, an old hedge witch wanting to be somewhere for a witches' moon. Why?"

Tersely, Tris recounted what they knew of Arontala's plans, and of Alyzza's past with the Sisterhood. "Damn my soul," Linton swore when Tris was through. "I never thought to see the likes of that." He looked at Vahanian. "Picked a hell of a guide's job on this one, didn't you?"

"You know me, Maynard. Never a dull moment."

"Watch your step, Tris," Linton cautioned. "There've been more than a few guardsmen through these parts with as heavy a Margolan accent as you'll ever hear. They might be a little more interested in your travels than you'd like."

THEY TALKED UNTIL mid-afternoon, much of it Linton and Vahanian catching up on river news. Tris cradled the steaming bowl of stew in his hands for a while before he ate, appreciating its heat. The others did the same, to Mama's amusement. She called out something to Vahanian, punctuated by a sharp laugh, and he turned to them with a grin.

"She said to tell you that she hopes you aren't trying to pass for river folk," he translated. "River folk have ice for blood."

"They must," Carroway said, earnestly eating his stew. "I'm never going to be warm again."

When she could force no more stew or bread on her guests, Mama plied them with hot tea and some small, caramelized nuts. Then she withdrew the flask again and offered more of its contents, but this time, even Vahanian declined to join her. She fixed him with a scornful look and muttered a pointed remark that elicited a shrug in return.

"I think she just called you something," Kiara jibed.

"She did," Vahanian said, with a wink at their hostess. "But out of respect to the healer here, I can't repeat it."

Mama pushed past them to dig through a box of jumbled belongings. From it, she withdrew a half-moon pendant of carved bone on a leather strap, which she brought on an outstretched hand to Carina. "Please, m'lady, if you would," Mama said earnestly in the Common tongue, "a blessing for an old woman."

Carina took Mama's stained hand in hers. "I don't think I'm qualified to bless anything," she said. Mama looked crestfallen. "But perhaps I can help that limp if you like," she added quickly.

Mama brightened and tucked the pendant into a pocket of her ample apron. "A healing is twice as good as a blessing. What do you think I wanted it blessed for?" She laughed raucously. The others made room for Carina to examine the woman, trying not to watch as Carina let her hands move slowly over Mama's hips and legs. Finally, Carina stood, brightening for the first time since they left Principality.

"I can fix that," Carina said confidently. "Just sit down while I work." For the next half candlemark,

Carina worked as Carroway kept Mama diverted with stories. It seemed to lift the minstrel's dark mood, and had Mama clapping in delight. Sakwi looked on with interested approval.

"Try standing," Carina urged Mama.

The river woman struggled to her feet, then cautiously took a step. Slowly, her bulk settled onto her forward foot. She relaxed with a look of wonder, taking another step and then a third, until she made a hop of joy that rocked the houseboat

"Oh, dearie!" she exclaimed, running to clasp Carina in a bear hug. "That leg has hurt me for more years than I can count. The Lady was good to me today," Mama said. "You're welcome here any time."

"Nyall's coming," Vahanian called from the doorway. Mama bustled to meet him.

"Nyall," she shrilled. "Nyall. Come look what your healer's done. She fixed my leg, good as a little baby's!" Mama exclaimed joyfully. She made a giddy pirouette for the river pilot, who smiled indulgently.

"I told you they were good folks," the pilot man said. He sobered as he turned back to Tris and the others. "Boat's ready. Like as not, you'll want to get going. Got a break in the storm, but no telling what'll come next. Wind's blowing like more rain."

"Wonderful," Carroway muttered as he reached for the dry cloak Mama proffered.

"Here, take these with you," Mama said, rummaging around the small houseboat in a frenzy as her guests prepared to leave. She tossed items into a bag. "Some crackers, dearie, for your stomach," she said with a nod to Carina, "and some of those sugar nuts for that cough," she said to Sakwi. "A little tea for all of you tonight—Nyall never remembers to take enough tea. A little dried fish to keep up your strength and this," she said, withdrawing a second small flask and lifting it in salute to Vahanian, who grinned. "To warm you up."

"Now off with you," Linton said with mock gruffness, "before she gives away my profits for the month." He paused, and laid a hand on Tris's shoulder. "Goddess go with you. Good luck."

"Off with you!" Mama protested, waving them away. "And Goddess be with you." She reached into her pocket to finger her pendant, watching them from the gangplank. Nyall led them into the maze of docks once more, and the houseboat disappeared from view.

CHAPTER TWENTY-FOUR

THE RAIN HELD off until late afternoon, when the clouds rolled in once more and began a steady downpour. Vahanian's mood became decidedly worse once the floating city was behind them and they headed downriver, into Nargi territory. His banter disappeared, and his replies, if he spoke, were terse. He was clearly alert for trouble, and his jumpiness made a noticeable difference in all of their moods.

Despite Mama's crackers Carina once more looked sick. Kiara was troubled, foregoing her rest breaks and joining Carroway in watching the riverbank for danger. Nyall, too, wore an expression that made it clear that the pilot looked forward to completing the passage. His unruly black beard and brows were like storm clouds, and his piercing black eyes harbored an unspoken worry. Even the horses seemed affected, and it took all of Sakwi's and Carina's skills to quiet them.

"I never thought I'd feel safer in Margolan," Carroway grumbled as Tris leaned past him to clear debris from their path with his pole. "But the sooner we're off this river, the better. Something feels wrong."

"I've had a bad feeling since we left Mama's," Tris agreed, looking along the gray forests of the riverbanks and seeing nothing but shadows. "I don't like it either." He had sensed the spirits of the river ghosts after they left the houseboat village. The ghosts kept their distance, watching them in silence. Tris had a distinct feeling of uneasiness from them, and sensed a foreboding that made him wish for shore.

"What's that?" Kiara called. Tris and Carroway came at a run. Jae took to the air and flew ahead of the boat, circling and squawking.

"What's what?" Carroway asked, scanning the river.

Kiara shook her head. "It's gone." She squinted for a better look. "Something in the water, something big."

"Maybe a log," Tris suggested hopefully, scanning and seeing nothing.

Kiara shook her head. "Logs don't move like that."

"Look there." Vahanian pointed, and they swiveled starboard just as something dark and large dipped below the river's surface. "That was no log. I don't like the look of it." He turned to Nyall. "Can this thing go any faster?"

The river pilot gave him a withering look. "This isn't a little smuggling skiff," he replied. "We put up a sail in this wind and we'll be capsized in a moment. You ever see horses drown?"

"You've made your point," Vahanian said. "But I—"

His words were lost as something crashed hard into the bottom of the boat.

"Hang on!" Nyall shouted, throwing his bulk into turning the rudder. Everyone but Sakwi and Carina rushed to the rails, poles in hand, watching the turbulent, dark waters. The horses squealed and reared in panic. Sakwi and Carina struggled to restore calm, but the frightened animals shied, lifting their heads as if they smelled danger on the wind.

"There's something out there!" Sakwi shouted.

"No kidding," Vahanian shot back, anxiously scanning the waters.

"I can feel it," the land mage returned. "Something big."

"Tell it to go away," Vahanian said.

Sakwi's eyes squeezed closed in concentration, then opened wide in alarm. "It's not listening," the thin mage reported, as Carina turned to him worriedly. "Something's very wrong. Whatever's out there... shouldn't be. It's not a living thing."

Kiara and Tris exchanged worried glances. "Magemonster," they said at once. The river erupted around them, hitting them with a wall of water. The deck of the ship suddenly pitched, sending them all into the black water of the raging Nu.

An unnatural shriek pierced the night and a huge, scale-covered tail thrashed out of the water, shattering the ship and sending beams and boards flying amid the terrified horses that flailed for their lives in the swift current. Tris felt something brush his leg and he lashed out an arm to grab for Kiara, who was struggling toward shore.

"Hold onto this!" he shouted, thrusting a bit of decking toward her He felt something grab onto his leg, dragging him under.

Mud churned in the cold water, making sight impossible. Tris knew he had only moments to break free before he was doomed by either the chill or the current. He grabbed for the knife on his belt and slashed at the thing which held his leg. His blade, sharp enough to slice a thin leaf to ribbons, bounced off harmlessly. Tris was growing lightheaded, his chilled body barely responding as he pulled at the heavily muscled tentacle.

Something streaked past him in the water. Tris felt pressure, then a sudden release. The tentacle jerked free, releasing a cloud of ichor that burned his skin. A strong hand grabbed at the front of his tunic and pulled upwards.

Around them, the water churned and more tentacles reached for them. Tris jabbed and slashed with his blade as he and his rescuer struggled to evade the slippery river creature. Tris knew they were both fading fast. His lungs ached for air; pinpricks of bright lights danced in the darkness before his eyes. As he began to lose consciousness, Tris stretched out with his power in one urgent cry for help. His rescuer stopped struggling, and the dark form began to sink. His hand closed around a thin, strong wrist. *Kiara*, he thought, making one last, futile push toward the surface.

The waters stirred. Expecting to feel the monster's grip, Tris instead was borne up on hands strong but insubstantial. As he slipped toward unconsciousness, he could sense the spirits rallying around him, driving back the creature in response to his summons before he blacked out.

TRIS SPUTTERED, AND spat river muck out of his mouth. "If I hadn't seen it with my own eyes, I'd have never believed it," Nyall was saying over and over again, pounding Tris on the back to clear the water from his aching lungs. "Never in all my life. Dark Lady save me. I've known there are ghosts on a river's bed, poor souls, but never in my life have I seen the dead bear up the living and deliver them nice as that onto the bank." He stopped his pounding when Tris could finally wave his arms in protest.

"Kiara," Tris managed, still spitting grit from his mouth.

"Over here," she called in a weak voice. Tris turned, his ears ringing painfully, and saw his bedraggled companion a few paces down the riverbank. Jae strutted on the wet bank next to Kiara, hissing his concern. "Whatever that was," she said shakily, "I don't want to meet another one."

"How did you..." Tris began, and Kiara produced a small dagger with a golden hilt from her belt.

"The Sisters gave me it when I began my Journey. They told me it would turn the undead, and in the hands of a mage, destroy their soul. I wasn't sure it would work on a magemonster, but I thought it was worth a try."

"Lady be," Nyall swore. "What are ye, that you've got mage-made daggers and talk of the Sisterhood?" The river pilot made the sign of the Lady in warding.

"Well, whatever it was," Tris said, sidestepping the captain's question, "it worked. Thank you."

"Don't mention it." Kiara managed a grin. Jae perched on her shoulder and nuzzled her ear. "Be pointless if we get to Margolan without you, now wouldn't it?"

"That's all the horses," Vahanian said, striding up. Tris looked downriver to see Sakwi secure one of the panicked beasts to a tree, stroking the animal's neck to soothe it. "Glad to see you're breathing," he said curtly to Tris and Kiara. "Looks like you had a few friends down below. You know, after traveling with you, I'm starting to think there's a body under every rock. Nice work, Spook," he said to Tris. Abruptly, Vahanian stopped and looked worriedly at Nyall. Where are the others?"

"I thought they were with you," Nyall replied.

"What's wrong?" Kiara asked, still wiping grit from her face. Jae hopped from foot to foot on the riverbank, hissing and squawking. Sakwi sat nearby on a fallen log, shivering and coughing.

"Carroway and Carina," Vahanian replied, starting out at a brisk pace down the riverbank. Nyall followed him. Tris and Kiara, still lightheaded from their near drowning, waited nervously for the two men to return.

A candlemark's search turned up nothing. Vahanian planted his hands on his hips and surveyed the dark, swift water. "They're not here."

"I never saw them after we went over," Nyall said. "Maybe they floated further downriver. The current's swift."

Vahanian shook his head. "Not alive, they didn't. Water's too cold. We were lucky to get out. There wasn't time to go further."

"Can you call for them?" Kiara asked Tris, struggling to keep her voice steady. Tris felt a lump in his throat, understanding the assumption implicit in her request.

"I'll try," he said. Ignoring Nyall's open-mouthed astonishment, he closed his eyes and slipped into a trance. He could sense the river spirits, to whom he sent warm thoughts of gratitude. Up and down the river, he felt the flickers of restless ghosts. But to his great relief, neither Carina nor Carroway answered his call.

"They're not dead," Tris said, opening his eyes.

Kiara exhaled in relief. "Thank the Lady."

"You're a Summoner," Nyall said in an awed voice. "By the Dark Wench, you're a spirit mage, aren't you?"

Tris nodded.

"We've got to get some shelter," Sakwi said. The land mage's lips were blue.

Vahanian stared down river at a distant building cantilevered over the water. He turned to Nyall. "Wait a minute. I know where we are. That's Jolie's Place down there, isn't it?"

"Yes, but—" Nyall began.

Vahanian gestured impatiently. "Come on. We've got a place to stay." He headed through the brush. Tris refused help, although his lungs ached from the water that he had coughed up. Sakwi leaned heavily on a makeshift staff he had made from a fallen branch. Tris slipped an arm around Kiara's waist, steadying her when she looked as if she might fall.

"I really don't think—" Nyall started, then shook his head and gave up, following them through the tangle of branches as they made their way down-river.

The sounds of raucous music reached them above the rush of the river, along with the scent of spicy roasted fish. They could hear laughter and a jumble of voices as they climbed the twisting wooden steps toward the door, Vahanian leading the way. A burly man blocked their path.

"You're not welcome here," he said roughly, taking in their bedraggled appearance. "Off with you."

"I have a message for Jolie," Vahanian said in the Common tongue, then repeated it for emphasis in the river patois.

"What message is that?"

"Tell her Jonmarc is here. Tell her now."

The guard gave him a skeptical glare, but shuffled off toward the doorway. He called aside a passing man whom he dispatched with the message. They waited in silence, chilled and shivering in the wind, for what seemed like forever. Then, from inside, came quick footsteps.

"What are you using for brains, river sludge?" a strident woman's voice sounded. "You kept them outside, in this weather? Move, move, I'm in a hurry." With a flash of crimson, Jolie burst through the door. "Jonmarc!" she exclaimed, embracing the smuggler. "Come in, come in," she welcomed them, with a glare to the burly guard, who shrugged his innocence.

One of Jolie's servants brought an armful of blankets, which Tris and the others gratefully accepted. Jolie and Vahanian dropped into a barrage of the river talk, punctuated by Jolie's flamboyant gestures. Walking a step behind the pair, Tris sized up their new host. Jolie was in her middle years, with the figure of a young woman and wild, flame-red hair that cascaded to her shoulders. Her gown, Tris noted, was in fashion several years ago at court, its fabric expensive and opulent. Gold glittered at her throat, on her fingers, and stacked in bracelets up her thin arms. Heavy gems danced in her earrings. A dusky perfume clung to her, like incense for the Dark Lady, permeating the room.

"Where are we?" Kiara asked under her breath. Gaming tables packed the room filled with foppishly dressed men and revealingly clad young women. Minstrels played raucous tunes, with an impromptu chorus from several of the guests who were well into their ale. In the back of the room, a tavern master did a brisk business, slipping patron's drinks around the shapely young woman perched on the bar who sang along with a minstrel.

"Someplace Jonmarc thinks is safe," Tris replied. "Question is, safe from what?"

"Your friend must have connections," Nyall said from behind him. "Jolie doesn't let just anyone in."

They followed Vahanian and Jolie through the bustle of the gamers, toward the back of the crowded room. Jolie talked continuously to Vahanian or to the players and their ladies who jostled together in the crowd. Finally they reached a small door in the rear of the noisy gaming area, which Jolie opened with a key she withdrew from her bodice. They filed inside and she shut the door behind them. Jolie locked it and replaced the key with a pat.

"Now, Jonmarc, tell me what brings you here looking like a river rat."

"I was taking a group down the river to Margolan when something tossed us into the water. We made it to shore with our horses, but we're missing two of our party."

Jolie eyed him for a moment. "Water's ice cold. They're dead by now."

"They're not dead," Kiara said.

"Swordswomen aren't common on the river," Jolie drawled in heavily accented Common. "And that one," she said pointing to Sakwi, "is a mage, or I'm a virgin. That was a nice start to the story, Jonmarc," she said, her accent softening the consonants into a deceptively lazy blur. "Now the rest, *cheche*, if you please."

"It's not my story," Vahanian said ill-humouredly. "Ask them if you want it." Tris glanced at Vahanian for a signal. You can trust Jolie," Vahanian said and their hostess glowed. "If she couldn't keep a secret, she'd have been dead a long time ago."

"Secrets are my business, *cheche*," Jolie said in a throaty voice that spoke of strong liquor. "People leave them with me, and I keep them safe. Now what could you possibly have offered Jonmarc to bring you through Nargi territory?"

"Jonmarc is guiding us back to Margolan," Tris replied evenly. "I'm Martris Drayke, Bricen's son."

"You're going to challenge the king?" Jolie asked skeptically.

"And his mage."

"A mage called Arontala?" Her accent made the sorcerer's name a purr.

"Yes."

"Bold words for one so young." Jolie looked at Vahanian. "But Jonmarc, I thought you swore off hopeless causes years ago."

"He's a Summoner, ma'am," Nyall spoke up, wide-eyed. "Saw it myself I did. Called spirits from the river to save himself and the lady here."

Jolie returned her scrutiny to Tris. "A true Summoner?" Tris nodded, and her light-brown eyes regarded him from beneath heavy lids. "And you?" Jolie said, looking now to Kiara and appraising her carefully. "You've said little, swordlady. What is your role?"

Kiara drew herself up tall. "I'm Kiara Sharsequin of Isencroft," she answered. "Jared Drayke and his mage have threatened my lands. I go with Tris to set things right."

"Um hmm," Jolie looked back to Vahanian, who was clearly impatient with her questioning. "You've got your own little revolution brewing here, Jonmarc. That's not like you."

"There are two people out there we can't find," Vahanian snapped. "Damn the reason we're here. We've got to find them. If they're alive, and they're not on our side of the river—"

"Then they're as good as dead already," Jolie retorted coldly. "They're in Nargi hands. Give them up."

"No!" Kiara said. "We can't!"

"Jolie, I need your help," Vahanian entreated.

"To commit suicide? No, *cheche*," she said, shaking her head. "I won't do that."

"We need a safe place to stay until the horses are ready to ride," Vahanian continued, undaunted. "Dry clothes. Provisions for the ride."

"You're not thinking of going after them, are you?"

"I have to."

"Have you forgotten everything?" She turned to Tris and Kiara. "Jonmarc came to us eight seasons ago, running from the Nargi. He managed my gaming tables, tended my bar, and was the best 'peacekeeper' I ever had. I will not support you if you want to kill yourself, *cheche*. No. Not Jolie."

Her tirade had no effect on Vahanian. "It's a healer and a bard," he said tersely. "A woman healer."

Tris saw a flicker of something in Jolie's eyes. "So? They're in the Lady's hands. Leave them to Her."

Vahanian's jaw clenched, making the cords on his neck stand out in anger. "Damn you! You know the Nargi. You know what happens to prisoners."

"You seem to have forgotten," Jolie said. "You're not talking about a smuggling run, Jonmarc, in and gone. They haven't forgotten you. You won't come back if you go marching into one of their camps."

"Let me worry about that," he retorted, only a hand's breadth from Jolie's face. "Will you give sanctuary?"

Jolie's eyes narrowed. "What is this woman, that you would die for her?"

Vahanian looked away. "They're friends."

"And for these 'friends' you would sacrifice yourself?"

"She saved my life. What would you have me do?"

"I taught you to survive," Jolie snapped. "I took you in when you ran from shadows, taught you to smuggle, gave you the contacts you needed to live on this river."

"And what did you expect for that? Or did you think *you* owned me, too?"

"No," she said in a deep, bitter rasp. "Nobody is owned here. Not in my house. Not while I live." The rage drained out of her. "Go then, if you must. Your friends will be safe here. When Arontala is done hunting mages and *vayash moru*, he'll come for my kind. They always do."

"Thank you," Vahanian said raggedly.

"Sometime, the fledgling flies, hmm, *cheche*?"

Vahanian gave her a peck on the cheek. "You're first class, Jolie."

"Damn right," she rejoined, and turned her attention back to Tris and Kiara. "Don't mind the little family spat. Jonmarc is used to my temper. Come. There are rooms upstairs where you can sleep safely." She eyed Kiara. "Unless you've got objections to an upstairs room at my house."

"I've marched with an army and camped with mercs," the Isencroft princess replied, settling her hand on the pommel of her sword. "I doubt your house will rival that."

Jolie threw back her head in throaty laughter. "At last! Someone else with a proper attitude!" She slipped an arm around Kiara. "I think we're going to get along just fine. Come with me."

CHAPTER TWENTY-FIVE

DAYBREAK FOUND JOLIE's place altogether different. The gaming tables stood silent in the morning sun. Where the musicians had played two servants slept in chairs, while a third gathered debris into a basket. Jolie's girls, so elegantly dressed and festive the night before, came to the long breakfast table dark-eyed and yawning, dressed in simple shifts with their hair in plain braids.

Nyall and Kiara sat with the girls, already eating breakfast. Jae perched on the table beside Kiara, much to the girls' delight, eagerly accepting bits of food from any hand that would offer. Even without her armor Kiara could never be mistaken as one of them, Tris thought as he joined them, the smell of breakfast luring him from his sleep. Tanned and lean, Kiara's stance and walk revealed her training even before her sword came into view.

He noted that her sword hung at her belt this morning, a reminder that she felt only somewhat at ease here. Tris guessed that worry had kept her from getting much sleep. She looked haggard and preoccupied. Beside her, Jae nudged a roll toward Kiara's hand as if entreating her to eat, but she ignored the gyregon.

"You don't look like you got much sleep," Tris said as he sat down.

"Hardly any. Not with Carina out there," she said, looking toward the river.

"We'll figure out something. Jonmarc won't have to go after her alone."

"I'd already decided to go with him. Thank you."

"That's out of the question." They turned to see Vahanian.

"We're in this together. We're going," Tris replied.

"No you're not," Vahanian repeated, as Jolie forced a plate into his hands. "For one thing, the only mages in Nargi are priests. They'd spot you and Sakwi before we even crossed the river. And princess, don't take this too hard, but women don't carry swords in Nargi." He swung one leg over a chair and sat. "They've got too many brats clinging to their skirts."

"What about the *vayash moru*?" Kiara asked. "Can they help?"

"Nargi hate *vayash moru* almost as much as they hate mages. Got magical protections set up all around their camps to keep them away. We wouldn't get within spitting distance of the camp without bringing the Nargi down on us."

"You can't go alone," Tris protested.

"I'm safer that way. You don't speak Nargi. You don't know the Nargi. You couldn't pass for one even if the only Nargi you met was deaf and blind. Trust me. I can get in, find them, and be out before you know it. No problem."

Jolie's angry glare made her opinion clear. At the end of the table her girls said nothing, intent on their food. Nyall, too, gave no opinion, looking so determined to stay out of the discussion that he might have built a wall around himself.

"If we can't go with you," Tris said, "then I guess we'll just keep watch to make sure you don't get any unexpected company. We'll help Nyall get the horses and packs ready."

"We'll be on our way in the morning," Vahanian promised, though his voice showed more confidence than his eyes. "Just watch."

By sunset, Jolie's place was crowded once more. Jolie's girls, like finely plumed birds, flitted through the room welcoming the guests. Gaming masters called out numbers, while a bard told bawdy stories to an appreciative audience near the tavern master's table. In the back room, Tris and Kiara watched Vahanian make his final preparations to cross the river.

"I think that's it," Vahanian said, checking his weapons for the fifth time. He wore the uniform of a Nargi soldier, thanks to Jolie, who mentioned something about it having been left behind in haste by its previous owner. Hidden over his body was an assortment of daggers, and his sword hung in its scabbard. He wrapped the dark uniform headpiece expertly, finishing with a trailing piece that covered his face.

"You're lucky the Nargi are in their winter uniforms," Jolie observed from where she leaned against the fireplace. "That scarf hides your face. Good thing. You look as much like a Nargi as I do the Goddess."

"Any other useful comments?" Vahanian asked.

"Jonmarc, take this." In Kiara's open palm lay a pottery chit on a leather strap, stamped with an intricate, strange rune.

Vahanian regarded it suspiciously. "What is it?"

"The Sisters gave it to me, when I left on my Journey. They said that I could use it if I ever needed to escape and there was no other way out. Snap it in half; it can transport a short distance. Concentrate on getting back to Tris. But you must be together, actually touching."

"The Sisters gave you this?" Vahanian said with a hint of skepticism. "Those witch-biddies? Can they do magic like that?" For a moment he turned the chit in his fingers as if debating whether to accept the gift, then finally slipped the strap around his neck.

Sakwi appeared at the back door, slipping off his cloak. "Thank the Goddess you haven't left yet."

"What were you doing, talking to the owls?"

Sakwi accepted the remark without offense. "In a way, yes. When you go, I'll call to the animals of the forest to protect your path. If they can help you, they will. They'll regard you as one of their pack. You need fear nothing but men."

"That's usually enough," Vahanian replied. "Thank you."

"This type of magic is very draining," Sakwi warned. "It will take me a while to recover."

"So if you can't do more, and Tris shouldn't for fear of calling Arontala to our doorstep, you're telling me I'm really on my own," Vahanian summed up, dropping the chit down his tunic.

"Jonmarc," Kiara said. "Thank you. May the hand of the Lady be on you." She made the sign of the Goddess.

"Be careful," Tris added, fixing Vahanian's gaze. "You've got a score to settle."

"More than one."

Jolie unlocked the back door to a path leading down to the river. She followed him outside, closing the door behind them. "You know what I think about this."

"I can guess."

"This healer—you love her?"

Vahanian stopped and drew a deep breath. He did not turn. "Yes."

"And she cares for you?"

"Doesn't matter. She saved my life. I can't let them die."

"I laid out Jalbet cards last night, to see what the fates said about this. The omens were dark."

"The omens are dark without the cards. I know what I'm doing."

"I hope so."

"Don't wait up for me."

A CHILL WIND swept down the river's course as Vahanian paddled silently across, making him glad Nargi troops dressed adequately for the weather. He had much less confidence about the prospects for success than he had admitted to Tris and Kiara. Carina and Carroway had already spent one night in Nargi hands. Unless they had been deemed useful, their chances of surviving many more were slim.

Worse might be the use found for them. Carina's healing gifts would be dismissed because she was a woman, making her useless for healing men. While she might assist in childbirth, the Nargi's penchant for multiple wives made surviving that ordeal less urgent. He closed his eyes, trying to forget what he had seen happen to other women captives.

Carroway's lot was hardly better than Carina's in Nargi hands. Bards were outlawed, as were the taverns and gaming rooms where they tended to work. Bards also carried news, something the Nargi priests liked to control themselves. Artists, unless dedicated to the Crone cult, were viewed with suspicion.

· Going after Carina and Carroway would be the easy part, Vahanian thought, dragging his small raft up on the bank and hiding it in the bushes. Getting back out was the challenge.

Vahanian made one quick pass up and down the bank, looking for signs of his companions. Upstream, almost across the river from where he and the others had come ashore, he found a sodden leather pouch like the ones Carina carried on her belt. There were boot prints on the muddy shore. The river plants bore signs of a recent struggle, with broken and trampled branches lying along a freshly made path.

Vahanian had the sudden feeling that something was watching him, and he glanced up sharply, sword already in hand. On the path ahead of him stood a large gray wolf, a mature male, well-fed and strong. Vahanian froze as the creature's blue eyes fixed him with a knowing stare. To his surprise the animal made no sign of aggression, neither baring its teeth nor advancing. Instead it sat down, dog-like, and wagged its tail. Then it jumped to its feet, trotted down the path, and returned, tilting its head at a curious angle as if to ask a question.

Sakwi, Vahanian thought. *Dark Lady take my soul. No wolf alive acts like that, unless it's been sent. Damnedest thing I've ever seen.* He took a hesitant step forward. The wolf seemed to approve, bounding ahead and then returning, signaling him to follow.

"I don't know where you're taking me, but I'm hoping it's to the camp." He stopped and shook his head. "Wolves. I'm talking to wolves. Too damn much time around Spook." The wolf waited impatiently for him and he followed, closely watching the woods around them for danger.

Twice, the wolf laid its ears back and growled a warning, in time for Vahanian to hide himself in the thicket as Nargi soldiers passed by. Overhead the owls hooted an "all clear" when the danger passed. His guide kept its speed and choice of pathways to those Vahanian could follow with relative ease. *If wolves are this smart*, Vahanian thought, *no wonder they're so damn hard to shake once they're hungry for you.*

He sheathed his sword in favor of a small crossbow, which worked better than a sword in tight spaces. Vahanian and the wolf traveled for at least half a candlemark, and Vahanian noted that the wolf was leading him to high ground, taking a wide circle around a center point. Finally, after scrambling up a hillside muddy from recent downpours, the wolf led him to a protected spot on an outcropping with a view of the land below. It waited, as if inviting Vahanian to come and look.

Below them was the Nargi camp. It was only a small camp, but home to at least two or three dozen Nargi soldiers. From the permanence of its structures, the round, canvas-covered baled straw constructs the Nargi favored, Vahanian surmised that the camp was a river garrison. *Probably making sure none of the "faithful" cross over to Jolie's place.*

The wolf sprang to its feet and its ears pricked, listening intently. It moved a few paces to its right, indicating a path, then dashed back, urging Vahanian to move. Vahanian needed no additional prompting. He crouched and followed the wolf as quickly as he could without noise. A heartbeat later, two Nargi soldiers came into view, patrolling the perimeter. Vahanian waited in the shadows, watching as one of the soldiers noted his tracks on the wet ground. But before the soldier could take a step, Vahanian heard a wolf howl, and realized that his guide was no longer behind him.

The Nargi stopped abruptly, glancing around nervously. The wolf howled once more and was answered by another, summoning the pack. The lead Nargi made a brusque command and motioned the other to follow him, beating a quick retreat. Vahanian breathed a sigh of relief and looked up to see his guide wolf padding back toward him. *That's the most satisfied looking wolf I've ever seen.* He resisted the urge to laugh.

"Thank you," he said in a hushed voice. The wolf cocked its head once more and then padded off, making no invitation for Vahanian to follow. Vahanian watched his guide leave, and then turned his attention to the camp below once more, memorizing the layout and guessing at the purpose of each circular structure.

The horses were tethered together at one side of the encampment, while a trench at the other side marked the latrine. A cluster of structures were barracks; a larger, separate one was the captain's quarters. A cook fire in front of another building indicated a kitchen. In the center was the practice ground with its quintain, hard used from many practices. Vahanian caught his breath. Next to the practice ground, just beyond the barracks, was a sturdy cage made of hewn logs. Even from this distance, he could make out the two figures imprisoned inside.

Still, Vahanian thought, *not impossible*, as he surveyed the layout. If the horses didn't scare, he might be able to approach from that side, along the barracks' walls, shielded partially from view. But the cage was out in the open. Any approach would require a dive across an open area, and exposure for as long as it took to open it. Not good. Resolute, he started a cautious descent.

Fog began to roll in half way down the slope. He watched it rise from nowhere, slipping toward the camp, thicker and thicker until the fires twinkled in its haze. *Sakwi*, he thought. *Has to be. Nothing natural brews up a fog like that so fast. A little more assistance like this and I might just get to like spooks after all.*

Vahanian waited more than a candlemark until the camp's priest rang the bells for late prayer, and the guards made their devotion to the Crone. By then, Vahanian had crept close enough to hear the prayers. He took a place at the very back of the assemblage, his face hidden by the uniform's scarf. The words of the prayer came back with eerie ease, something he had heard every night of his long captivity. His stomach knotted as he mouthed them with the others. Finally, the devotion made, the soldiers broke formation. Vahanian slipped away, getting as close to the cage as he dared before the last of the fires were banked and the lamps in the barracks went dark.

From here, he had a clear view of the stockade. Inside it, Carina and Carroway huddled together against the cold, still in the muddied clothing they wore when they went into the river. Vahanian could glimpse no blanket or shelter to give any comfort to the captives. His anger, already white hot, grew stronger still. His finger twitched on the trigger of his crossbow.

"You there," said a voice behind him. "Why are you out of barracks?"

Vahanian moved the hand with the small bow down and into the folds of his cloak before he turned. "Going to the latrine, sir," he replied in perfect Nargi.

"I gave no such permission."

"My abject pardon," Vahanian replied, giving the deep bow Nargi custom required.

"What is that in your hand?" the Nargi lieutenant asked, stepping closer. His eyes widened. "That's not a standard bow." Vahanian stepped into his path, raising the bow against the lieutenant's chest. The arrow discharged soundlessly, and the astonished lieutenant sagged against him.

"Useful for hunting vermin," Vahanian said against his ear, supporting the dying man. He steeled himself not to turn as footsteps approached.

"Explain."

Vahanian looked into the piercing stare of a thickset sergeant. "He's sick, sir. I'm helping him to the latrine."

The sergeant nodded. "Very well. Straight back when you're through."

"Yes, sir." Vahanian moved off in the direction of the trench until no one was in sight, and then dragged the lieutenant behind the cookhouse. He stashed the body behind the garbage bins. That wasn't going to fool anyone for long, Vahanian thought, his heart racing. But the fog held, and with each moment he escaped detection, the camp became quieter.

Two guards usually kept patrol on a Nargi camp this size. Crouching, Vahanian lay in wait behind the cookhouse. Before long, his quarry came into view. A young recruit shivered against the cold. Vahanian did not wait to be intercepted. Springing from the shadows, he leapt into a perfect Eastmark kick, the heel of his boot connecting solidly with the man's chest, knocking the wind from him and driving him to the ground. In a flash, Vahanian was astride the guard, drawing his knife across the man's throat with one seamless movement. Vahanian dragged the body to lie beside the lieutenant, returning to scuff away the blood.

The second guard came around the corner. With cold precision, Vahanian notched an arrow into his bow and sent the shaft flying. Caught in the throat, the guard fell with only a gurgle. Vahanian sprinted toward the stockade, making no effort to hide the last body.

"Wake up!" Vahanian hissed urgently. He tried his knife on the lock without success, then turned his blade on the ropes binding the stockade together. Carroway startled, and laid a hand over Carina's mouth as the healer struggled awake.

"Lady bless!" Carroway swore under his breath.

"Can you walk?" Vahanian questioned.

"We're all right," Carroway replied, although Vahanian doubted it was completely true. He had only the barest glimpse of their faces, but it looked to him as if both the healer and the bard had been roughed up. Their captors had not wasted effort on gentle handling, Vahanian thought angrily, hacking at the ropes.

"Where are the others?" Carina whispered, as she and Carroway crawled toward him.

"Back across the river," Vahanian said as one of the ropes gave way beneath his knife. He passed knives to Carroway and Carina, who began sawing away at the ropes in earnest.

"Jonmarc, behind you!" Carroway cried. Vahanian heard the boot steps and spun, kicking high.

"Intruders!" the guard shouted as he fell. Vahanian drew his sword and slashed downward, silencing the Nargi guard.

"Here." Vahanian wrested Kiara's chit from around his neck and thrust it through the bars of the stockade to Carina. "Grab Carroway's hand and keep hold of my cloak. Break the chit in two. Concentrate on reaching Tris. It's our way out of here." He turned to face the soldiers that were coming at them at a dead run. He felt Carina clutch his cloak and heard the snap of the clay chit, sensing a tingle as a blue light came from nowhere.

Several of the soldiers dropped back at the mage light. But one ran onward, sword raised, fearless of the otherworldly glow. Vahanian stepped forward to parry the falling blade and felt his cloak pull free of Carina's grip. Light flared behind him and disappeared in a heartbeat. The cage was empty.

Vahanian turned to face the Nargi.

"WE SHOULDN'T HAVE let him go alone," Kiara said, pacing in the back room at Jolie's place. Jae fluttered from the tabletop to land on Kiara's shoulder. Jolie watched from her seat on the edge of a table. Across the room, Tris paced. Sakwi knelt by the fire, deep in trance, holding the fog that gave cover for the escape and maintaining his link with the wolves and bats to provide distraction.

"Jonmarc has always done as he pleases," said Jolie.

"What's to keep the Nargi from barging in here after us?" Kiara asked. "It's hardly a fortress."

"Astir," Jolie called. The dark-haired man who stood guard outside the doorway appeared immediately.

"Yes, m'lady?"

"Our guest raised a concern about our security. Can you reassure her?"

There was a sound of rushing air. Without appearing to have moved, Astir stood next to Jolie. "What did you want to know?" Fast as thought he was again at the doorway. Jolie tossed a poker from the fireplace at the guard. He caught the iron implement and twisted it off-handedly, dropping it aside like crumpled parchment.

Jolie turned back to Kiara. "Astir only works at night. He has many friends here. They're always welcome in my home." Astir made a little bow and ducked outside the door once more. "Their reputation makes this a very civil house."

"How many?"

"They come and go. The heat of so many people together at night draws them. Why do you think I slaughter so many goats? We've never had an incident with a guest that wasn't deserved. We're all predators," Jolie added, "of one sort or another. Or else we're prey. Personally, I prefer the first choice. Why don't you go out front and forget about it for a little while?"

Kiara glanced over to Tris, standing against the wall, and at Sakwi, who sat in silent concentration. "No thanks."

"You ought to know a thing before you judge it."

"I'll pass."

"You think this is just another type of jailhouse, don't you, *cheche*?"

"That's exactly what I was thinking. I don't understand how you can do it to those girls."

"Who's safer? The people outside the jail, or the one in the cell?" Jolie walked around Kiara appraisingly. "A jail can be a haven, if you've just escaped from hell."

"Do you know the choices a woman has out here, away from the palace, Lady Princess? Not many. Marry whoever is chosen for you, and die birthing one brat after another, if your husband doesn't beat you dead first. Go to the Lady and serve an oracle, never leaving the temple. Not much better than death, but they might teach you to read. You might be able to apprentice for a trade, if they'll take a woman and if you have the money to buy your way into the guild. Or you come to a house like this, where you earn a living with the only skill they've let you learn."

She held up a hand. "Hear me out. My house is different from the others. No one stays here against her will. No one may be harmed in any way. My guards make very sure of that. And once my girls have learned to read and write, made a purse full of coins and found another skill, they leave. There are no guarantees they will succeed. But most of them would rather die trying than take their other choices."

"I hadn't thought of it that way," Kiara said, not quite ready to concede. Tris was sure Kiara was thinking about the arranged marriage she had fled, and what desperate lengths she might go to in order to avoid such a union.

Sakwi stiffened and gave a strangled cry, his eyes snapping wide open. A haze twinkled in the center of the room, glowing brighter and brighter until it flared too brilliantly to watch. Jae fluttered and hissed, beating his leathery wings. When Tris dropped his arm from across his eyes, Carina and Carroway stood in the middle of the room, dazed and shaken.

Tris dashed to help Sakwi as the land mage slumped. Kiara rushed forward to greet Carroway and Carina, but Carina resisted her embrace. "Where's Jonmarc?" the healer cried, looking around them in panic. "He was with us an instant ago."

Tris eased Sakwi onto a low bench. "I'll be all right," Sakwi said in an exhausted voice. "Something went wrong. Only two," he said as a cough stole his breath. "Only two." Tris helped him free one of the herb pouches from his belt for a remedy, watching as Carina collapsed sobbing against Kiara. Jolie met his eyes with an accusing glare, not needing to put her venom into words. His friends were safe, almost certainly at the cost of Vahanian's life.

Sakwi waved him away. Tris stepped over to Carroway, who stood silently beside Carina, watching as she sobbed on Kiara's shoulder. "What happened?" Tris asked, bringing them cloaks from a peg on the wall and guiding Carroway to a chair. Some of Carroway's ordeal showed in the bruises on his face and in the bloodied tunic that hung in tatters.

"I had a hold of Jonmarc's cloak," Carina said brokenly, "but my hands were so numb, I could barely make my fingers move. Just as Carroway broke the disk and the light began to glow, the soldier came. Jonmarc stepped forward and I lost my grip." She covered her face with her hands, and Kiara pulled her close.

"We barely made it out of the water last night," Carroway said tonelessly, looking at his hands. "We weren't there long before the guards came. They found us and dragged us off before we had a chance to think about finding the rest of you.

"I don't speak Nargi, so I have no idea what they said, but they aren't very gentle. There was no question as to who had the upper hand. The one time Carina tried to speak, one of the guards cuffed her so hard I thought she'd passed out.

"They took us to a tribunal, maybe a priest. He sentenced us, and they put us in the stockade. All day, the soldiers stopped by. It didn't take a translator to get the gist of some of the ideas."

"They'll kill Jonmarc," Jolie said in a cold voice. "He's struck at their pride, taking captives out from under their noses. And he used magic to do it." It was clear from Jolie's eyes that she did not consider the two prisoners' safe return worth the cost. "It won't be a quick death. And if any recognize him for what he was, it will be worse." She walked defiantly to face Tris. "Prove to me you're what you claim," she challenged. "Save him."

"Sweet Chenne!" Carroway exclaimed. "Do you want Arontala and the Margolan army on your doorstep? We're close enough that Arontala will know if Tris uses magic."

"Only the Dark Lady Herself could get him out of there," Carina murmured. "They'll be on high alert for the next year."

"If only the Dark Lady can save him," Tris mused, "then let's send the Dark Lady."

"You're mad," Jolie told him. "Even you can't summon the Goddess."

"Maybe I won't have to," he said, with a meaningful look at Carroway. The bard looked puzzled for a moment, and then brightened.

"What are you talking about?" Carina asked. Her eyes were red-rimmed from crying and showed the strain of her ordeal. "There's no way to get back in there." She looked from Tris to Carroway. "Is there?" She dragged a torn sleeve across her face. "Whatever you're thinking, count me in."

"And me," Kiara added, standing and laying a hand on Tris's shoulder.

"And me," Sakwi murmured from where he lay. "If I have strength to help, I'll do whatever you ask."

Jolie gave Tris a long, measuring glare. "If there's a chance, I'll help," she said finally. "And so will any of my people." She crossed to a shaded window and looked out onto the river. "Do it soon, or it's a corpse you'll bring home."

CHAPTER TWENTY-SIX

VAHANIAN BARELY PARRIED the Nargi's blow as his attacker launched a frenzied onslaught. But the flare behind him told him all he needed to know. The magic had taken the others to safety. He was alone, and in Nargi hands.

Instinct drove him on against the odds. Before the first attacker hit the ground, two more rushed to take his place. By then, the whole camp was roused so that no escape was possible. The Nargi commander barked an order and a soldier with a crossbow stepped up, training the cocked weapon at Vahanian's chest.

"Drop your sword," the captain snapped.

Trapped, Vahanian had no choice but to comply.

"Kneel, and place your hands on your head," the captain ordered. Two soldiers rushed up as Vahanian obeyed, binding his wrists with leather straps. The captain stepped closer, and the soldier kept the crossbow leveled at Vahanian. The captain reached out and tore the headgear away, exposing Vahanian's face.

"What are you, outlander?" the captain asked. "You dress like a Nargi and fight like a Nargi."

"Go screw the Goddess," Vahanian retorted in Nargi. The captain cuffed him so hard it nearly knocked him over.

"I wonder," the captain said, grabbing a handful of hair and yanking Vahanian's face up. "I heard stories, once, of an outlander who could fight like that. Many years ago. But he'd be too clever to come back, wouldn't you think?"

"You're the one with all the answers. You tell me."

"Interesting," the captain said thoughtfully. He turned to a soldier behind him. "Fetch the commander. Tell him we have a captive I think he'll find most interesting."

The soldier acknowledged the order with a low bow and ran off to the horses, setting off at a gallop. Just then, another soldier ran up from the direction of the cookhouse.

"Captain," the soldier shouted. "We found three bodies behind the cookhouse, and a guard dead along the perimeter. We lost Lucan, Cashel, Piaras, and Newry."

The captain regarded the soldier dispassionately. "Burn the bodies," he ordered. He returned his attention to Vahanian. "You'll die for what you've done."

"I figured that out already."

This time the captain's blow sent Vahanian sprawling, his ears ringing.

"Quick death is an honor," the captain said. "You'll have time to reflect on your mistakes." He turned. "Take him away. Go over the stockade pole by pole to see what he's done to it, and post two guards at all times. If the prisoner escapes, those guarding him will share his death."

"Yes, sir," the second-in-command replied. Two soldiers yanked Vahanian to his feet and shoved him toward the stockade. He staggered into the cell. The other soldiers filed back to their barracks, except for the one who began earnestly inspecting and mending the stockade, and the two sharp-eyed soldiers who stood guard.

Vahanian rested his head in his bound hands. *You sure picked a bad time to lose your luck*, he thought. *What in the world possessed you to try a stunt like this?* But he knew. The others were more important to the effort to destroy Arontala and unseat Jared Drayke. They would go on. The quest could continue without him. If they succeeded, he would finally have his vengeance against the dark mage. More than that, Carina was safe. And while he might never have been able to earn her love, he could at least repay the many times she had saved his life. *Maybe it's time. You always knew it was going to happen, sooner or later.*

The approach of a swift horse woke him from an uneasy sleep. Vahanian rose warily to his feet as the captain ran to meet the rider. The two men spoke for a moment, silhouetted in the moonlight, then strode toward the stockade. By the walk and carriage of one silhouette, Vahanian could identify the rider even before the man's face became clear in the dim light. What little hope he held vanished.

"Well done, captain. Bring him to your quarters. I'll question him myself."

"Hello, Dorran." The guards opened the door and roughly maneuvered Vahanian out of the cage. "I figured you for buzzard food long ago."

"Just as I remembered," Dorran said, a cold smile touching his thin lips. "We have some catching up to do. Bring him inside."

Forced to kneel while one guard kept a crossbow trained on him, Vahanian watched the thin commander lay aside his cloak. "Amazing. You caused me no end of trouble with your... *escape*. When the general let you go free, he thought it would discredit me." Dorran circled Vahanian as he spoke.

He stopped and reached out, a dagger in his hand, to tilt Vahanian's face up until their eyes met. "I would have been a general myself by now, without your little ruse. I've thought a long time on just how you might make that up to me."

"What about his companions?" the Nargi captain asked.

Dorran shrugged. "Riffraff. There's no time to chase petty smugglers down the river. Ready your men for Margolan."

"Expanding your horizons?" Vahanian baited.

Dorran regarded him coolly. "I've spent almost a decade rebuilding the career you damaged. This will reclaim my honor. We've made an alliance with the new king of Margolan to remind some insurrectionists about the power of a king."

"I thought Margolan had an army for that kind of thing." Vahanian tried to keep his interest from seeming too apparent.

"His army is soft. They lack the will of their king. We'll teach them. And for that, I'll be handsomely rewarded."

Vahanian said nothing more; the point of the dagger pricked into his throat. Dorran twitched the blade, tracing the thin pair of parallel scars that showed where a slave collar had left its mark years ago.

"This time, no one will arrange your escape," Dorran said, returning his knife to his belt and beginning to turn up the sleeves of his uniform. "I intend to enjoy myself quite thoroughly." Without warning, Dorran wheeled, landing a kick on the side of Vahanian's head that sent the smuggler sprawling. "Get ready to see the Lady. Your luck has just run out."

The beating continued until Dorran, panting and winded, could do no more. His uniform was spattered with Vahanian's blood. Vahanian lay sprawled on the floor of the Nargi captain's barracks, unable to drag himself to his feet, his wrists still bound in front of him. Blood trickled from the corner of his mouth, and one eye was swollen shut. He could taste more blood in his mouth, and the pain in his chest assured him that several ribs were broken.

"Take him to the healer," Dorran commanded, wiping his hands on a towel. He looked down at Vahanian. "You know the ways of Nargi healers. They're quite efficient. If I've done any real damage, they can set it right."

"Why bother?" Vahanian asked thickly.

"I haven't finished my sport yet. Tomorrow, I'm going to let the garrison have a private audience with the general's great champion fighter. Only this time, it won't matter if you win or lose. Either way, you'll still die. I've been looking forward to this for a long time, Vahanian." Dorran stepped over the fallen fighter and strode into the night. The guards dragged Vahanian to his feet and pushed him, staggering, toward the priests' quarters.

Back in the stockade, Vahanian watched the dawn come with a leaden feeling in his stomach. True to Dorran's word, the Nargi priests had reversed the worst damage. Vahanian spat blood and nursed his split lip. The priests, ascetics as they were, did not bother with any wounds which might not threaten his life or his ability to fight. Vahanian awoke from a restless sleep with the feeling that he had been ridden over by a wagon team. He replayed Dorran's boasts in his mind. *Nargi, ready to march into Margolan.* Tris would be cut off from behind, and the influx of expert fighters might be all Jared needed to turn the game.

Vahanian strained against his bonds. There was no way to reach Tris with the crucial information. His sacrifice to save the others would mean nothing. All the wishing in the world wouldn't get him out of here; Tris would walk right into Jared's trap. With the Nargi on the march into Margolan, Tris's quest was doomed.

It took all of his will to rise impassively when his captors came for him. The practice ground was full of Nargi soldiers and Vahanian was led into their midst. A soldier cut the strap that bound his wrists. Vahanian rubbed his numb hands. Dorran watched from a chair on the side.

"I've highlighted your accomplishments as the general's champion for those who don't remember,"

Dorran said. "I told them what a privilege it is to fight you. As you can imagine, there have been many volunteers."

"And if I refuse to fight?" Vahanian asked.

Dorran' eyes narrowed. "Fight, and you'll die a warrior's death. Refuse, and I'll have you burned alive with the bodies of the men you killed. Any other questions?" At Vahanian's silence, Dorran clapped twice to call the troops to order. "Let the first contestant come forward."

Vahanian faced a Nargi soldier almost twice his size. The two began to slowly circle, each looking for an opening. As in the days of the betting games, neither carried a weapon. That, Vahanian remembered grimly, was part of the sport the Nargi so enjoyed. Barehanded combat. Winner lives. The big man lurched, surprisingly fast for his bulk, and swung at Vahanian with fists the size of melons. Vahanian dodged, ducking and coming up beside the man, then executed a flying pivot and landed a kick that sent the big man reeling. The crowd cheered as Vahanian's attacker roared in rage and lumbered back at a dead run, murder in his eyes. Vahanian narrowly evaded the man again and scored another kick, but the attacker wheeled and caught his leg, bringing them both to the ground.

The big man jerked Vahanian's arm behind him sharply enough to pull it from its socket. Bucking desperately, Vahanian threw the man off balance and scrambled out of the big man's hold, swinging wide with his free hand and connecting his knuckles with the giant's nose, driving the power of his blow up and in. The soldier staggered, dropping his grip on Vahanian. He gave a deep rattle then slumped and lay still. Vahanian staggered to his feet. The soldiers who ringed the practice area cursed him and called for his blood.

"Very good, Jonmarc. Nicely done," Dorran praised cynically. "You're doing us a tremendous service, showing us which of our soldiers are inferior. You may now test the training of another soldier." He made an abrupt gesture, and a second soldier entered the ring. Setting his jaw, Vahanian moved to meet his opponent.

He bested three of Dorran's men before he could no longer fight. The contest became a free-for-all, and might have ended there if Dorran hadn't shouted for order and sent guards into the fray to pull Vahanian from the angry mob. They dragged him back to the priests for healing. This time, it took longer for the priests to repair the worst of the damage.

When the priests were finished, Vahanian was led to a post in the middle of the practice ground. A guard tore away what remained of Vahanian's shirt, and lashed his wrists around the post. Vahanian's heart thudded as he saw Dorran approaching with the quartermaster, who held a knotted whip in his hands. He had seen Nargi martial discipline meted out during his captivity. Forty lashes could leave a strong fighter incapacitated. More than forty at one time were likely to kill. He hoped his expression was impassive as Dorran and the quartermaster stopped in front of him. A Nargi priest stepped up beside the quartermaster.

"Offenses in a military camp are subject to military law," Dorran announced as the camp began to assemble in a circle around the post. "For the crimes of murder, theft, trespass, impersonation, and blasphemy, I sentence Jonmarc Vahanian to death."

The crowd roared its approval. Vahanian watched balefully as Dorran basked in the spectacle, then held up a hand for silence. "I'll mete out the final punishment myself," Dorran added, to the cheers of the group. "But first, it is only fitting that he pay fully for his crime."

Dorran looked at Vahanian. "I could have you flogged to death. You've seen it done."

Dorran turned back to the crowd. "Forty lashes," he pronounced, and the crowd cheered for more. Dorran looked to the priest. "Keep him alive. I don't want to be cheated out of the satisfaction of killing him myself."

Vahanian closed his eyes, bracing himself. He clenched his jaw as the whip snapped, and the first lash fell.

NIGHT HAD FALLEN when the guards returned Vahanian to his cell, throwing him in to land face down on the hard-packed dirt.

"When I call for you the next time, I'll kill you." Dorran said from outside the stockade. "You can't know how much I enjoyed this afternoon. You truly are the best fighter I've ever seen. Pity. I've had the healers patch you up to keep it from being too easy. I do enjoy a challenge. Sleep well, Jonmarc. Perhaps tomorrow, if you beg, I might cut my pleasure short."

"Go to the demon," Vahanian managed, tasting dirt in his mouth.

"Not this time. You'll see Her first."

The only way out of this one is in the arms of the Dark Lady, Vahanian thought. Thanks to the healers his mind was clear, although his body barely moved at his command. By their work, the priests denied him the respite only shock and unconsciousness could bring.

The camp was silent when Vahanian heard the call. It roused him from a distressed sleep, barely audible over the snoring of his guards. A child's voice, calling his name. Sure he was hallucinating from the pain, Vahanian raised his head. The camp lay in a heavy shroud of fog, so thick that he could not see the banked fires across the practice area. As he watched, the door to his prison swung open. In the doorway stood the transparent image of a young girl, beckoning him to come.

"Come, Jonmarc," the apparition said. "It is time."

Vahanian had passed the point of fear. Already resigned to death, the vision made him catch his breath. "Are you the Childe?" he rasped, his swollen lips barely able to form the question.

"Come," the vision repeated impatiently. "It is time."

Vahanian crawled toward the open door, stopping part way to glance back, expecting to see his own crumpled form behind him. "It's time to go," the ghostly child urged, standing with an outstretched hand just beyond the stockade. In the distance, Vahanian could hear the thunder of a horse riding at full gallop, and heard the guards rouse. But he dragged himself to stand, clinging for support to the posts of the stockade. He was unprepared for the sight that burst through the fog. A cloaked rider on a white horse, riding at demon speed. Beneath the heavy cowl, eyes burned like fire.

"The Dark Lady!" Vahanian whispered, sure now that he was dead.

The Nargi soldiers pointed at the specter in terror. Half of the them fell to their knees, prostrating themselves before the rider with a babble of desperate prayer as the priests begged the apparition for mercy. The other soldiers, frightened but dubious, held their ground, freeing a hail of arrows at the rider that bounced harmlessly off its cloak. With strangled cries, the archers dropped their weapons and fled.

Heedless of the confusion, rider and horse bore down directly on Vahanian, never breaking speed. The cloaked figure reached down, grasping Vahanian's arm and tossing him like a broken doll across its lap.

Borne into the fog, Vahanian lost consciousness.

WHEN THE REAR door opened at Jolie's place, the room erupted into chaos. Nyall took the body of the unconscious fighter from the arms of the cloaked figure and carried him to a cot. Sakwi looked up from stirring a cauldron of healing herbs. Carroway and Carina rushed forward to help Nyall.

The cloaked figure shrugged back the cowl to reveal Tris's face. The illusion of the Dark Lady blinked out of sight, leaving only the theater make-up Carroway had improvised. Kiara handed Tris a moist towel to wipe away the last vestiges of the night's work.

"You found him," she exulted, helping Tris out of the heavy cloak, exposing a breastplate of leather and ring mail.

"Thank you for insisting on the armor. Nargi are quick archers." Tris released the buckles on the armor, and set it aside. "And thank you for the cloak." He handed her the magic-shielding cloak from the Sisterhood. "I felt a little less like a beacon for Arontala, even though it didn't require much actual magic."

"The river ghost, did she come?"

Tris chuckled. "She thought it was a great game. I hate to imagine what Jonmarc made of it."

"When he finds out he's still alive, he may forgive you." Kiara planted a quick kiss on his cheek. She took his hand and they approached the cot where Carina worked.

"Sweet Chenne," Carina swore under her breath, surveying the damage. Vahanian's face was purpled and swollen almost past recognition, and the gashes and deep bruises on his chest and arms bore mute witness to his ordeal. "Let's see what we're dealing with on the back," Carina replied, her growing anger clear in her clipped instructions. Carroway complied, gentling Vahanian onto his side.

Carina blanched. Welts criss-crossed Vahanian's back, evidence of a thorough lashing. Red and angry, they already bore signs of infection. Reflexively, Carina laid her hands over them. Some of the marks immediately began to fade, losing their color and puffiness. She signaled Carroway to ease Vahanian back down.

"How bad is it?" Tris asked. Jolie stood behind him, her expression making it clear that she would have no difficulty taking the lives of those responsible for Vahanian's injuries.

"He's been healed several times—deep healing. Damn them!"

"I don't understand," Kiara said.

"They didn't heal to end the pain, they healed to prolong it. They fixed just enough so that he didn't die too quickly and spoil their game."

"Can you help him?" Jolie asked.

Carina nodded. "Whoever healed him before knew what they were doing. What's here is bad, but not life-threatening. Some broken bones, a lot of deep bruises, some torn muscles and tendons, deep cuts—his back is a mess," she listed dispassionately, attempting to distance herself enough to work her gift. "They must have been striking to maim, not kill, because they obviously had the opportunity to do otherwise."

Tris moved to stand beside her. "Draw energy from me, if it will help."

"Can you do that without alerting Arontala?"

Tris shrugged. "I've never sensed him when I've helped you heal—I'm not sure it's enough power for him to read. And you've pulled from both Cam and Carroway for energy, and they aren't mages. It's a chance I'm willing to take."

Sakwi appeared at Carina's side with the cauldron of steaming herbs and a fresh cloth. For the next two candlemarks Carina worked in silence, easing her way down Vahanian's body, first healing as best her strength would allow, and then applying Sakwi's poultices and binding the wounds that remained. Any materials the healer required needed only Jolie's terse word to the guards outside the door, who returned with the desired articles in minutes.

Nyall hunched near the fire, clearly overwhelmed by the company in which he found himself. The others stood ready to respond to Carina's increasingly ill-humored commands, as the fatigue of healing coupled with her anger. Jolie stood silent sentry near the foot of the cot, her hard eyes unreadable. Carina worked for more than three candlemarks, until she was pale with the exertion and both she and Tris wavered from the strain.

Finally, Sakwi intervened, taking Carina's shaking hands in his own. "You're exhausted. There's nothing more you can do tonight."

Carina shrugged free with a glare. "There's always more to do."

"I'm still too spent from the spells I wove to help you." Sakwi laid a hand on her arm. "But I can feel what you've done. He's in no danger now, and he rests as comfortably as is possible. Now, you must rest."

Unwillingly, Carina let herself be led away from the cot. Kiara gave Tris's shoulder a squeeze in farewell, and sprang up to slip an arm around her cousin. "I'll take her back to our room," Kiara said, frowning at Carina when the other began a faint protest. Carroway, too, looked ready to drop from his ordeal, and made his way to a chair by the fire.

"Astir," Jolie summoned the *vayash moru* from where he stood silently by the door. "Take Jonmarc to the room I've readied for him upstairs. Anjela will show you. He can rest undisturbed there."

"Someone should sit with him," Carina said. "He shouldn't be alone."

"Nyall can spend the night in a chair," Jolie decided, and the river pilot made no protest. "The rest of you look worse than when you dragged yourselves out of the river. Off with you, to bed. Wake when you will. There'll be food enough for you whenever you rise." The others fell tiredly into line for the journey upstairs. The gaming house was silent, its patrons and its ladies asleep, and the barkeeper was just finishing up his sweeping. With all the night's excitement, Tris doubted that he would quickly find sleep, but his exhausted body decided otherwise as he stretched out on his bed, and sleep overtook him.

KIARA GUIDED HER cousin into their room like an overtired child. "Let me help you dress for bed," she said solicitously, but Carina shook her head.

"Not yet. I need to clear my head from the working." Her voice was ragged. She hadn't bothered to heal her own bruised cheek. The purple of the wound made the dark circles beneath her eyes more pronounced.

Kiara stooped beside the fireplace to pour a cup of hot tea from the boiling kettle Jolie's people had readied. She pushed the warm cup into Carina's hands, and the healer paced over to the window, looking out across the moonlit river, toward the darkness on the banks of the other side.

"Jonmarc had to know what would happen if they caught him," Carina said after a long silence.

"He knew."

"Then why did he come after us?" Carina turned from the window. Her hands trembled as she raised the steaming cup to her lips, and sipped the hot liquid like elixir.

Kiara kicked away from the wall and ambled slowly over, resting against the back of a chair. "He told Jolie it was because you saved his life, because you were his friends. Jolie tried to talk him out of it. I thought they might come to blows."

"I might have liked to see that. I'd put my money on Jolie."

"Not on this one. The Lady herself couldn't have stopped him."

Carina looked down, as if she sought the answers to her questions on the surface of her tea. "I wasn't frightened when we went into the water. It was so cold. I knew that if we didn't reach shore, it would be over quickly, like falling asleep. Carroway's a strong swimmer. He pulled me out."

"I guessed where we were when the soldiers came. But I don't think I was frightened until the next day, after the tribunal, when the soldiers kept stopping at the stockade. I knew what they thought should be done with us, just by their gestures." She shivered. "Some things don't need words."

"Carroway was frightened, but he tried to take care of me. I think we'd both given up hope. And then, when Jonmarc came..." She shook her head. "It's my fault they captured him. If I'd kept a proper hold on him, he would have come through with us."

"It was an accident," Kiara protested. "You can't blame yourself."

Carina shook her head. "I tried to hold on, but we had been outside all night, still wet from the river, and my hands were too numb. Mother and Childe, Kiara, how did we ever get mixed up in this?"

Kiara laid a strong arm around her shoulders, hugging Carina tightly. "Blame the Lady. I know you'd give anything to be getting ready for the Hawthorn Moon back in Isencroft."

"But that's not possible, is it? If Tris doesn't succeed, we'll never be able to celebrate like that again. I never wanted to make history, Kiara. I just wanted to heal my patients and not worry about the rest."

"I don't think any of us bargained for this," Kiara said reassuringly. "No one but the Goddess could have put together such a group of misfits. Look at the bright side. The healings you've worked on Jonmarc alone should qualify you to open the best healer's school in the Winter Kingdoms."

Carina smiled. "You may be right. But wouldn't I have to have him stuffed and mounted to display?" Tired as she was, the absurdity of that image made her chuckle.

"I'll remember to tell him you've finally found a use for him, once he wakes up."

Carina looked away. "What's wrong?" Kiara asked.

"I'm so afraid, Kiara. After what happened with Ric, I've been afraid to let Jonmarc get too close. But all day yesterday, not knowing whether we could get to him in time, I can't pretend anymore. Goddess help me, Kiara, I love him," she said, tears streaming down her face. "I can't help loving him, but I'm so afraid I'll lose him, too."

Kiara wrapped her arms around her cousin. "Have you noticed how often Tris starts a sentence, 'If I live to take the throne?' Every time he says that, I think my heart will break. But he's right, of course. We both know the odds. This whole thing is an awful gamble—and I'm not sure I'd place bets on us."

"Jonmarc has lost so much. I don't know how he has the courage to try again."

"Jonmarc is a soldier. Soldiers know better than anyone that you can't take tomorrow for granted. All you have is today. I guess that's all we ever have, but most of the time, we're not aware of it. It's not too late. Stop running away, and let him catch you."

"Maybe I should let him recover a little, so the shock doesn't do him in." Carina gave Kiara a hug. She slipped out of her healer's robes, pulled her chemise close around her against the chill, and crawled tiredly into bed. "If I don't get some sleep, I'll be done in. There's more to do before Jonmarc's going to be able to go anywhere."

"I'll sit up for a while, in case you need me," Kiara offered.

"Thank you." Carina yawned, but she was asleep before Kiara could reply.

CHAPTER TWENTY-SEVEN

CARINA WOKE AT dawn. She shook her head, trying to separate the reality of the night before from the dreams that had made her sleep sparse and fitful. Her bare feet had hardly touched the cold floorboards before she tore her shift over her head and slipped her robes in place. Her stomach growled but she ignored it, intent on checking her patient.

Nyall sprawled snoring in a chair near the fire in Vahanian's room, rousing as she entered. She motioned for him to be quiet and indicated with a jerk of her head that he was free to join the others for breakfast. Gratefully, the river pilot abandoned his post.

Carina approached Vahanian hesitantly. She and Tris had worked until exhaustion on the healing, but there had been much left undone. She drew a chair up beside the cot and looked silently at

Vahanian, afraid to discover whether he slept or had not yet regained consciousness. Carina closed her eyes and stretched out her hand, running it lightly just above his face and chest to ensure that she had overlooked nothing vital. A hand locked around her wrist with an iron grip, and her eyes snapped open to find Vahanian looking at her.

"Are you dead, too?"

"I'm not dead," she said gently. "Neither are you. You're at Jolie's place. You're safe."

Vahanian dropped his hand, and closed his eyes. "How?" he managed with a dry mouth.

Carina fetched a glass of water from a pitcher on the nightstand and helped him sit enough to take a drink.

"Tris bent a few rules to go after you," she said, settling him again.

"Arontala—"

"Tris managed to do it without much magic. With some help from Sakwi and Carroway."

"The Goddess," Vahanian murmured. "I saw—"

"You saw one of the river ghosts," Carina explained, wetting a cloth and laying it across his forehead. She checked his bandages as she spoke, then nudged him onto his side to assure herself that the welts on his back were healing nicely. "The rider was Tris. Sakwi managed the fog, and Carroway handled the disguise. I wouldn't be surprised if Sakwi sleeps for a week, after what we've put him through."

"I didn't think... anyone would come."

Carina bit her lip as tears filled her eyes unbidden. "Did you really think we'd leave you there?"

"It was too much of a risk."

"And what you did wasn't a risk?"

"Now we're even," he replied weakly. "Truce?"

"Truce." She broke the awkward pause by standing. "Well," she said professionally, "you need to sleep. I'll just go downstairs—"

Vahanian held out a hand to her. "Stay with me. Please."

She moved a step closer and reached out to take his hand. He said nothing, but his whole form relaxed. Within moments, the regular pattern of his breathing told her that he was asleep. She looked down at his hand, cut and bruised from his ordeal, and beneath those wounds, older scars. *Maybe we're not quite so different after all*, she thought, placing her other hand gently atop his. She settled down in the chair, resting his hand in her lap, and dozed in the warmth of the fire.

Vahanian woke with a start some candlemarks later, and Carina laid a reassuring hand on his shoulder. She glimpsed fear in his eyes, enough to tell her that his sleep had been uneasy, his dreams haunted. "You're safe. No one can harm you here."

"Get Tris," he said urgently. He tried to sit up, discovered his folly, and lay back again. "I have to tell him something important."

"You need to rest."

"This is important. Nargi... in Margolan..."

"All right. I'll get him—if you promise not to move."

"Promise," Vahanian replied, his voice lacking its usual timbre. "You have my word."

Carina found the others in the back room, readying gear for the rest of the march south. Kiara and Tris were mending some leather armor that Jolie had "found" for them. Carroway had just returned from tending the horses. Nyall made himself useful reprovisioning their packs with dried meats, fruits, and cheese, together with the other necessities they would need for the ride. Sakwi dozed in a chair near the fire, his sleep interrupted by deep coughs.

"How's Jonmarc?" Tris asked. Kiara rose to ladle out a bowlful of warm porridge from a pot on the fire and bring it to her cousin.

"He's awake. And I think he's out of danger. He'll be sore for a while. and it will probably be a few days before he's ready to ride, but he'll be all right after I do some more healing today." Carroway poured a cup of steaming *kerif* from a kettle on the hearth for himself and brought a cup to Carina, which she accepted eagerly. "He says he has to see you, Tris. Something about Nargi in Margolan."

Tris and Kiara exchanged worried glances. "Will it hurt anything if I go up to see him now?" Tris asked.

Carina shook her head. "Please go. I'm afraid he'll try to drag himself down here if you don't."

Sakwi stirred in his chair. "I would like to hear what he has to say," the land mage said, looking only slightly recovered. "Perhaps I can help." Kiara gave the thin mage a hand up from his chair, but he waved off further assistance. Carina followed Tris up the stairs.

Vahanian had managed to prop himself up. In daylight, the bruises and cuts that marred his face looked as prominent as they had the night before. Only Carina's memory of how swollen and painful they had truly been made her able to meet his eyes without wincing.

"Rough night?" Vahanian greeted them.

Tris grinned and drew up a chair next to Vahanian's bed. "Leave it to you to give us a real challenge."

"Thanks for getting me out of there. I didn't think I was going to beat that one." Vahanian managed a wry grin. "You put on one hell of a show."

Tris chuckled. "Too much time around Carroway. Now, what did you want to tell me so you can go back to sleep?"

"Ran into that lieutenant I told you about from the betting games. Only he's a commander now. Might not have been in for quite such a bad time of it if he hadn't recognized me," Vahanian said, wincing. "Name's Dorran. A real son of the Demon.

"Dorran figured on killing me, so he did some bragging. Told me he was going to salvage his military career, which my 'escape' back then derailed, by doing a job for the Margolan king. Something about taking troops into Margolan to put down a rebellion." Vahanian gave a mirthless smile. "Sorry. I didn't catch more details, but he had just walloped me on the head."

"That's quite enough." Tris glanced at Kiara.

"Doesn't do much for our odds, does it?" she said grimly.

"Sounds like even Jared might have pushed too far, if the army can't keep the peace."

"Maybe the army is the problem," Kiara observed, putting one boot up on the foot of Vahanian's bed and leaning forward onto her knee. "Maybe Ban found a good audience."

"Nargi, marching into Margolan," Tris repeated. "There'll be nothing left."

"There may be a way to stop them," Sakwi said thoughtfully, and they turned to look at him. "I'm from Eastmark, and my travels have taken me to the palace there many times. My king has no love for the Nargi. It would be of great interest to him to know that they stood ready to invade Margolan. It's my duty to tell him. If he were to launch an offensive, it would force the Nargi to withdraw their southern troops to guard their flank."

"I'll help," Kiara added. "King Kalcen was my mother's younger brother. They were quite close, I'm told. Let me send a letter with you, explaining the situation. He may decide he has a personal stake in not seeing me married off to Jared."

"And how do you propose to get to Eastmark?" Vahanian asked Sakwi skeptically.

Sakwi smiled. "The forest will find a way. I'll be ready to go by afternoon."

No amount of argument would dissuade the mage. Carina saw little choice if Tris's gambit were to succeed. Sakwi took his leave of them to get ready.

"I think we'll let you get some rest, too," Tris said, standing. "Now that you're awake, Jolie will have food sent up. You've still got a real beauty of a lip there. I'll tell her to make sure whatever she sends is soft."

"Better phrase that carefully in a place like this," Vahanian replied with a wink. "You might not get what you thought you asked for."

Tris glanced at Carina. "He'll live. Sounds like he's back to his old self."

Carina watched the door shut behind Tris and Kiara. "Now, that's quite enough," she said in her healer's tone. She crossed to Vahanian's bed and gently slipped the extra pillow from behind him so that he could lay flat. That he permitted it gave her some indication of how he was feeling, but he caught her sleeve as she turned to go.

"I never got the chance to ask," Vahanian said, meeting her eyes. "Did they hurt you?" He raised a finger gently to the still-visible outline of the bruise on her cheek.

"I'm all right," Carina said, but she could tell from his eyes that he knew she was lying.

"Never bluff someone who's made a living gambling," Vahanian said. "You don't always have to be the one with the answers, you know. The healer can need healing, too."

His acknowledgment of her ordeal, coupled with the strain of the past days finally overwhelmed what remained of her reserve. She turned away as tears began to streak down her face, finding that her will was no longer sufficient to hold them at bay.

"I'll be all right," she said again, swallowing hard. "It's just going to take a little time." And then, her resolve crumbling, the tears came in earnest, for the near drowning, the Nargi, as cold and enveloping as the swift waters of the river. She covered her face with her hands, her shoulders shaking as deep, racking sobs shook her.

How he managed to stand she never knew, but Vahanian stepped up behind her, turning her gently and folding her against him. He let her sob like a child, wordlessly stroking her hair. She dragged a sleeve across her eyes, aware of what a spectacle she had made of herself.

"I'm sorry," she managed, her voice cracking.

"No one's invincible. Trust me, I know."

"There isn't time for this. There's a job to be done…"

"Let someone else do it for a while." He pulled her with him to sit on the edge of the bed, his strength fading. He slipped his arm around her shoulder, drawing her close to him, and she did not shrug away "You've carried your share. Stop running for a while."

"What makes you think I'm running?"

"We have that in common," Vahanian replied.

"We're not that much alike."

"No? Let me see. Stubborn, willful, driven, self-sufficient, arrogant, and damn good at what we do." His lip twisted wryly. "You're right. Nothing in common."

"Was that supposed to make me feel better?"

Vahanian shook his head, wincing at the effort. "No. *That* takes time. But as you're so fond of telling me, you have to let the healer close enough to heal."

"Sakwi isn't up to any more than he's done already."

"I wasn't thinking of Sakwi," Vahanian murmured, close enough now that she could feel his breath. "There was something I promised myself in the Nargi camp, if I lived through it."

"What was that?" Carina murmured.

"This," he said, lowering his mouth to hers. For an instant she hesitated. Then she leaned into him, surprised at herself even as she returned the kiss with gentle fervor. A moment later he drew back, and she thought he looked both pleased and a little astonished.

"I love you, Carina," Vahanian said, tilting her chin up to look her in the eyes. "Last night, in the camp, I didn't want to go to the Lady, leaving it unsaid."

Carina felt tears start down her cheeks, but she did not look away. "I love you, too," she whispered, her voice choked. "I've wasted so much time, being afraid—"

He kissed her again, cutting off her words, reluctant to draw away until he began to sway as his strength failed.

"I really ought to be going back downstairs," she stammered, completely at a loss.

Vahanian made no attempt to hold her back, but his eyes searched hers. Carina had the uncomfortable feeling that he could see right past her defenses. She helped him lay back down.

"Come back soon. Don't be afraid," he murmured, looking as if he were about to pass out. "Your virtue is quite safe."

Carina blushed. "Considering where we are, that's saying something. Now get some sleep, before I have to re do what I did last night. When I come back up, I'll see what I can do about the damage that's left."

Vahanian took her hand and pressed the back of it against his lips. "As you wish, m'lady," he said, his eyes closed. She sat with him until he fell asleep again, and while her heart was still thudding, she found that the sense of relief at the confession seemed to push her fears far away, at least for today.

CHAPTER TWENTY-EIGHT

Everyone but Vahanian and Carina gathered in the back room late that afternoon to bid the Goddess's blessing to Sakwi. Outfitted for a long ride, the thin mage accepted their well-wishing graciously, politely disagreeing with Tris about resting longer before striking out on the dangerous trek to Eastmark.

Tris watched the mage with mixed emotions. He was grateful for the possibility that Sakwi might be able to persuade the Eastmark king to ally against Jared. Yet he knew with Sakwi's departure, the burden of the success of the journey fell even more heavily on his own shoulders. *I'm not ready. There's so much left to learn.*

Sakwi stepped to the edge of the brush along the river. In the dimming sun, Tris saw a large stag among the bushes, a powerful animal with antlers that spoke of a long and cunning life. Sakwi murmured something that Tris did not quite hear and the stag moved closer, awaiting the mage's needs. With a wave of farewell, Sakwi hoisted himself onto the stag's back. Making the sign of the Goddess, he leaned forward and clung tightly to the beast as it bounded off.

"You know," Kiara said to Tris, "every time I think I've seen it all, I get another surprise. There's never a dull moment."

"Stick around. The fun's just starting." He looked around them. "Has anyone seen Carina?"

"Jolie brought a note down from Carina asking that someone sit with Jonmarc tonight." Kiara shrugged. "I imagine Carina's finally getting some sleep. Goddess bless, she deserves it."

"It'll be a few more days until Jonmarc can even think about sitting a horse. I guess we might as well make ourselves comfortable."

Kiara's expression made it clear that she did not consider the delay unacceptable. "We could all use the rest. Especially you. Although I know what you're thinking. Every day that goes by makes it closer to the Hawthorn Moon."

They followed the others back into Jolie's place. The back room had become a place for Tris and his companions to make their plans and preparations in private, avoiding the curiosity of the gamers and guests in the front rooms. That they had not already been carried away in chains bound for Shekerishet gave Tris confidence in Jolie's repeated reassurance of her discretion. He still found it impossible to relax.

Nyall, too, seemed uneasy with the delay. Tris imagined that the river pilot's anxiousness lay in his wish for his part in the adventure to be at an end. Nyall spent his days testing and improving the new boat Jolie had helped him secure, building a corral for the horses and checking the boat's maneuverability in the swift river. He went to bed early, looking for any excuse to flee from the back room after dark. Now that the river ghosts' early reticence was gone, they sought Tris's intercession on a nightly basis. Even Jolie seemed taken aback at the spirits that came to Tris for his help in resolving old business or making the passage to the Lady.

Although the Sisterhood had assured Tris that his mediation would not draw Arontala's attention and would help to ease the imbalance in the currents of magic, Tris still felt vulnerable. He woke each morning surprised and grateful to find no Margolan troops waiting outside their door.

"If Sakwi isn't here, I guess we're on our own to pick a safe path across Margolan," Kiara nibbled on some fruit and bread.

"Looks that way," Tris agreed. He rested a boot on the bench across from her and leaned forward to take a wedge of cheese from the bowl Jolie kept well-filled. "Here's hoping Ban can recruit some deserters, and that Harrtuck can bring a little pressure on the northern border. I'll feel better thinking that Jared's attention is on something other than me."

Kiara chewed thoughtfully. "Do you think Jared expects you to challenge him?"

"He went to a lot of trouble hiring assassins. Having me dead would give him one less reason to watch his back."

"You've certainly got Arontala's attention."

"That's more than enough to worry me. Now the question is—can we drop out of sight long enough for them to get careless?"

"It's a risky thing to count on."

Tris grimaced. "It's all risky."

A DAY LATER, Vahanian made his way down the stairs to join them. It was more bravado, Tris thought, than an indication that the fighter was truly ready for action. Two days later, against Carina's strident protests, Vahanian proclaimed himself ready to ride if not to fight. He would hear no more of going back to bed to recuperate.

Although Tris chafed at the delay, he had to admit that the rest had made a visible difference in Carroway, who looked to be himself again. Something had also changed between Carina and Vahanian in the wake of Vahanian's close call. The two were now clearly a couple. Tris was glad for them. While the road afforded no real privacy and few enough opportunities for conversation, he knew how much it meant to him to have Kiara.

By the Dark Lady, Tris thought tiredly, *I guess the journey is getting to all of us. Only a complete fool would be unafraid.*

At sundown on the day they were to leave, an insistent rapping sounded at the door to the back room. "There's a visitor for you," Jolie called, and stood aside to reveal a thin, flaxen-haired man in a dark cloak.

"I'm glad I reached you before you left," Gabriel said as he swept past Tris, foregoing any kind of greeting. "I received the message Sakwi sent with the wolf only yesterday. It was a considerable distance to cover in such a short time."

From his seat at the table, Vahanian shook his head. "Sure, no problem," he murmured. "A land mage rides out of here on a stag and sends a wolf to fetch a *vayash moru*. What's so strange about that?"

"Stop that," Carina chided.

"So glad to see you survived your encounter with the forces across the river," Gabriel said. "You had merely a taste of what my kind have experienced for centuries at their hands."

"You and I almost had being dead in common," Vahanian quipped darkly.

"The Lady guards her servants well." He returned his attention to Tris. "I intended to meet you downriver to help you cross Margolan. I've been successful in securing a promise of safe passage through the holdings of my fellows on the Blood Council. Many *vayash moru* are sympathetic to your quest. They're joining up with Soterius's fighters. Some have offered to escort us on the road. We've lost a great deal to Arontala's forces. With or without the approval of the Blood Council, they were ready to take up your cause."

"Jonmarc found out that Jared made an alliance with the Nargi," Tris told Gabriel. "He intends to use Nargi troops to make up for the desertions in the Margolan army."

"How interesting," the *vayash moru* mused. "My people hate the Nargi even more than they despise Jared. It might be most helpful to have *vayash moru* patrol this side of the Nu River. It should pose an effective deterrent to having Nargi cross over into

Margolan. Not all of their charms and wardings work as... consistently... as the Nargi like to think."

"I've been hearing the tales from the river ghosts for days now. The ones that didn't drown by accident died fleeing the Nargi, or were dumped into the river after the Nargi killed them. Many of the ghosts have asked for a way to help with the coming battle. If the ghosts were to help the *vayash moru* hold the river border, we might be doubly protected." Tris paused. "I'll speak to the spirits that didn't want to go to their rest."

"And I'll make arrangements immediately with the *vayash moru*," Gabriel said in agreement. He looked around at the preparations for the road. "It appears you're ready to leave. I'll join you."

Nyall's eyes were big as saucers. "Don't worry, Nyall," Vahanian cracked. "Gabriel finds his own provisions on the trail."

"Dark Lady take my soul," the river pilot swore.

Gabriel fixed the uneasy boat master with a stare. "Pray that she does not." He turned back to Tris. "We have little time, and a great distance to cover. Let's go."

Jolie waited for them at the river. She had already gifted them with fresh cloaks and clothing, and seen to it that Nyall had all the provisions he required. Now she huddled in her woolen wrap on the bank, watching their preparations as if her attentiveness might ensure their success. She bid each of them farewell as they boarded Nyall's boat, kissing Vahanian on both cheeks and admonishing him to take care, although her voice and expression made it plain she did not expect to be obeyed. Jolie also gave Carina a peck on the cheek and said something the others did not hear, something that made the healer flush scarlet. Jolie looked toward Vahanian with a motherly smirk.

Tris, the last to board, stopped and took Jolie's hand in both of his. "Thank you for everything," he said gratefully. "It was a risk for you, taking us in."

"The day I start worrying about risk is the day I should get out of the business. The Lady's hand be upon you."

The unlikeliness of that luck lay unspoken between them. "Get going," Jolie urged, breaking the silence. "I'll be looking for news of you. I'll hear. Jolie hears everything."

Nyall pushed the gangplank away. Tris and the others took their places, long poles in hand, as the river pilot guided them out into the swift waters. The lights of Jolie's place remained visible for quite a distance, until the river changed its course, whisking them along in its current, deeper into Margolan.

CHAPTER TWENTY-NINE

NEAR DUSK ON the first day they glimpsed a dozen soldiers riding together not far from the river. The well-armed men lacked both flag and livery, raising Tris's suspicions. Tris and Vahanian poled their raft toward the shallows and waited in the thin cover of dead reeds and overhanging branches until the guardsmen were gone. They traveled the rest of the night in silence, scanning the riverbanks. Though they saw no more guards, the camps of ragged sojourners dotted the forest's edge, more refugees fleeing Margolan for whatever the road might offer. By night Gabriel traveled with them, his enhanced sight aiding Nyall through the shallows and rocks of the swift river. By day Gabriel disappeared, leaving them to their wits to navigate the difficult river.

The deeper they traveled into Margolan, the more Tris felt the ghosts of his homeland tugging at his senses. Their restlessness became mirrored in his own. The rivers' ghosts drifted near the raft, substantial enough that the others glimpsed them through the spring fog. Fearing the dreams that plagued him nightly, Tris slept little, pushing himself until Carina chided him and exhaustion gave him no choice. But he could not evade the dreams, the sound of Kait's plaintive call in his mind, the memory of the desperate look in her eyes. Worse, the images of the dark sending haunted him most nights. He finally let Carina use her healing magic to put him into a deep sleep while Gabriel stood watch. It was the first dreamless rest he could remember in a fortnight.

THEY BEACHED THE raft on the banks of a deserted fishing village in the waning light of the moon. A feeling of dread settled over Tris as he helped Carroway wrestle the heavy boat far enough onto the beach that the horses could be unloaded safely. Without Sakwi, Carina had been preoccupied for the journey keeping the horses calm on the raft. Now she led the animals one by one down the gangplank and onto dry land, working in relay with Vahanian until the horses were safely ashore.

The wind changed, and a foul smell drifted down toward the river. Nyall waited nervously near the raft, making it clear by his stance that he would go no further. Tris dug into the pouch he carried beneath his tunic for gold, and added half again to what was promised to the river pilot.

"Thank you for your trouble," Tris said, pressing the coins into the boatman's hand. With a mumbled word of blessing and a nervous glance in Gabriel's direction, the river pilot sprinted across the gangplank, pulled the boards up behind him, and poled back into the current.

"He certainly didn't waste any time," Kiara said.

Tris shrugged. "Why should he? He already got a lot more than he bargained for."

"You could say that," Carroway observed.

"What happened to this place?" Carina said, heading toward the ruins of the village.

"Smells like someone left all of last year's catch out in the sun," said Vahanian. The others held their scarves over their noses as the foul smell returned, stronger now. What remained of the small cabins and stone houses was gutted by fire, so that only portions of the walls still stood, open to the sky. Abandoned nets hung from the trees and bushes where they had been stretched to dry, swaying in the wind like ghostly moss.

Even without consciously stretching out his senses, Tris could feel the restless dead. Their anger washed over him like a cold wave, and he struggled for control against the unseen presences that buffeted him. Without warning an image of the slaughter came to him, then another and another, the testament of eyewitnesses sent with a fury that battered his control.

Soldiers, in the livery of the King of Margolan, wielded swords and battle axes against villagers armed with hoes and sickles. No quarter given, even as women and children begged for their lives. Terror, as the soldiers took their pleasure of the village's young girls before casually slaughtering them. On the Plains of Spirit, the ghosts' emotions washed over him, as hungry for vengeance as the spirits in the Ruune Videya. Tris staggered and clutched his head, closing his eyes. He dropped to his knees, overcome, reinforcing his wardings. The brutal images continued, and the ghosts cried out for justice.

"Tris!" Kiara cried. Tris opened his eyes to see Kiara and Vahanian with swords drawn, ready for a cautious advance.

"I can feel what happened here," he said, struggling for composure.

"Look there." Carroway pointed. In the twilight, a man's ghost stood ahead of them.

Tris, Kiara, and Vahanian stepped forward to follow the beckoning ghost, swords unsheathed and ready. Tris saw the glint of a dagger in Carroway's hand, and noted that Carina gripped her walking staff a bit more tightly. Jae flew on ahead, his leathery wings making the only sound as the ghost led them toward the large common barn. Gabriel took the rear.

"Wait for us!" Kiara hissed at Jae as the ghost vanished. With the others just a pace behind, Tris swung open the barn door and recoiled. The smell was overpowering. Inside, barely visible in the dim light, hung what remained of dozens of villagers, their corpses suspended by nooses from the barn rafters.

Tris called hand fire to his palm and used it to light their way as he and Vahanian pushed forward, swallowing hard against the stench. A sword thrust up from the barn floor and from it hung a bit of cloth: the royal standard of House Margolan.

"Nice touch," Vahanian said acidly. "Just in case someone didn't get the message."

"Such messages have become common in recent days," Gabriel said from behind Carina. The *vayash moru* seemed unaffected by the carnage, though he had unsheathed his sword. "Arontala has grown bolder, and the list of crimes that prompts such vengeance grows by the candlemark. Come. We must find sanctuary."

"Not yet," Tris said. "Not until I've given them their peace."

"Do it fast," Vahanian muttered. "I don't want to meet up with those guards on their return trip, if it's all the same to you."

It took two candlemarks to cut down the corpses and carry them to a nearby cave. When the bodies were laid out and covered with makeshift shrouds, Tris lifted his hands in farewell as the ghosts once more made themselves visible.

"I can't give you your lives," Tris said, "but I bid you rest. I am oath-bound to the Lady to destroy the one who caused your deaths."

A bearded man who bore himself with the dignity of a village elder stepped forward from the silent line of specters. "We don't want to rest yet," the elder said. "We want to fight. Give us the power, Lord Summoner, and let us hold this ground and this river crossing so that none of the usurper's soldiers can pass."

Tris nodded, and stretched out his hands in blessing. "By the crown of my father, King Bricen, I honor your service. Take your vengeance on Jared's troops, but let no harm come to innocent travelers who pass this way."

The elder bowed in acceptance. "Your word is a bond upon us, m'lord. We'll do as you command."

Gabriel and Vahanian moved a large boulder into place to block the entrance, burying the unfortunate villagers in a rough cairn.

"Can we *go* now?" Vahanian asked. Carina opened her mouth as if to chastise Vahanian, but at the look on his face, she said nothing. Tris guessed that it was the memory of Vahanian's own village, destroyed by the magicked beasts, which loomed in the fighter's mind.

No one spoke as they retraced their steps to where the horses were tethered. Tris looked over to Vahanian, trying to appraise his companion's condition. While Vahanian had made a valiant effort aboard the raft to keep up, it was apparent that he had not yet fully recovered from his injuries.

"Ready to ride?" Tris asked.

"Never felt better," Vahanian lied blatantly. To prove his point, he swung up into his saddle. Tris saw him wince as pain flickered across his face. So did Carina, who made sure that she rode where she could keep an eye on him.

"Welcome back to Margolan," Carroway said as they rode. They kept a brisk pace, alert for any signs of patrols.

"This way," Gabriel directed. "We must hurry."

Tris rode in silence in the darkness. The story they heard from the old man in Sakwi's village, the murdered villagers in the fishing town, and the desolation they saw along the road wore heavy on him. Margolan, so prosperous and peaceful under Bricen, had been reduced to starvation in less than a year. Tris's anger against Jared warred with Alyzza's warning about power used in hatred, and as they rode, Tris bowed his head, letting his cowl hide the tears that streaked down his face for his homeland and his people.

Kiara rode up beside him, and he was grateful that she did not try to talk. She seemed resolved to comfort him just by her silent presence. He doubted she could guess just how much that gesture meant. His heart was long past breaking for his land, his people, his lost family. He knew that he must quiet his anger, master his hatred, or risk being turned by the Obsidian King. Tris focused on the pathworkings that Alyzza had taught him, the small magicks for bringing calm and clearing the mind. Gradually, he felt some of the tension ease, although the fresh grief he felt still ached.

They finally slowed to a stop; silhouetted in the moonlight were the ruins of a temple. Tris felt a tingle of old sorcery as they approached. One look at Kiara confirmed that she, too, sensed that ancient and powerful magic had been worked here long ago, the traces of it dimmed by years.

"Want to put in a few prayers for luck?" Vahanian jibed, and Carina gave him a withering glare.

Gabriel secured their horses in the shelter of a ruined stable, out of sight of casual passers-by. "This way," the *vayash moru* beckoned, leading them amid the ruins. In the gray just before the dawn, it was almost possible to imagine those broken arches soaring toward the sun, buttressing high stone walls, awash in the brilliance of stained and beveled glass. Nothing remained of that former splendor, save some of the marble flooring and broken walls.

At the very front of the ruins, Gabriel pushed aside a heavy stone altar. Underneath, steps descended into darkness. "Here," he indicated, standing aside.

Kiara gave him a skeptical look and Jae squawked in agreement. "You want us to just... go down there?"

"You'll be safe. Hurry. The sun is about to rise." Vahanian moved to lead the way, drawing his sword.

"That won't do you any good," Gabriel said.

Vahanian glanced over his shoulder. "For luck," he said, stepping carefully into the darkness.

Tris, Carina, and Carroway followed, then Kiara, with Gabriel behind them to pull the heavy stone back into place. Tris conjured hand fire, which lit the tight corridor with a blue glow. The darkness smelled of mold and rotting cloth, and the metallic-sweet tang of fresh blood. Even without a conscious effort, Tris could sense other beings near them, not living but not dead, restless spirits neither mortal nor at peace. He raised wardings around the group, unsure what he would do should Gabriel's estimation of their hosts prove incorrect.

Tris felt a rush of wind, heard the scuff of leather on stone. Carina gasped and Vahanian cried out as something lunged for them in the darkness. Gabriel moved faster than sight, blocking the creature that grabbed for Tris. Tris sent fire to flare in the torches on the walls around them. A door at the end of the corridor opened, and more torchlight flooded into the corridor. Framed in the doorway stood Riqua, and behind her, dozens of *vayash moru*.

"Hail, Riqua," Gabriel said, making a low, courteous bow. "I have brought you the Lord of the

Dead and the new Lord of Dark Haven. We seek sanctuary for the night."

Reluctantly, Tris and the others followed Gabriel into the next room, a large vault with a catafalque in one corner. Although the crypt was freezing cold, it was otherwise appointed like a fine salon, with comfortable chairs, rich tapestries, and fine furnishings in the most current fashion. Riqua returned Gabriel's bow, and held out her hand in greeting to Tris. Without hesitation, he took it and kissed the back of her ice cold hand, making a courtly bow.

"Our deepest gratitude, Lady Riqua, for your welcome and sanctuary," Tris said. The deference seemed to please Riqua.

"Hail, Lord of the Dead," she said in a tone that walked an indistinguishable line between true respect and sarcasm. "And which of you, might I inquire, is the Lord of Dark Haven?"

"I am," Vahanian answered, stepping up behind Tris, his hand still near his sword. The move seemed more for Tris's defense than as an indication of comfort with his new title.

"Well, well," said Riqua as she circled Vahanian, taking his measure. "A long way from Chauvrenne and Nargi, aren't you, Lord Vahanian?"

"It's been an interesting road."

Riqua exchanged glances with Gabriel. "So it is always with the will of the Lady."

She looked at the others, who stood in silence, alert and still braced for an attack. Riqua paused for a moment in front of Kiara, staring intently at the Isencroft princess. Even Jae seemed to shrink at the inspection. "I knew your mother in the court of Eastmark," Riqua said, watching for Kiara's reaction. "Her spirit was as wild as the stallions she rode. Welcome, Viata's daughter. You'll be safe here."

Whatever Kiara's misgivings, her court training served her well. She made a gracious courtesy. "Your hospitality is most appreciated, m'lady Riqua." Kiara's hand never strayed far from the pommel of her sword.

Riqua's attention moved to Carroway. "I've seen you in Bricen's court," Riqua said with a faint smile. "You're far from home, Bard Carroway."

"Thank Jared," Carroway replied. "Until Tris takes back the throne, I'm where I should be—at his side."

Riqua looked at Carroway a few seconds more in silence, and Tris wondered again whether Gabriel had told him the whole truth about *vayash moru*'s ability to read mortal minds. While he suspected that his own power as Summoner afforded him unique protections and Vahanian seemed to have unusually good shielding for a non-mage, Tris wondered if the same was true for the others.

"When this is over, Bard Carroway, look again to Glynnmoor, and your lands. The plague that took your family is gone. My brood has watched over the manor house, as a favor to your father these ten years past. It is free to be claimed again by mortals."

Carroway tried and failed to cover his astonishment at Riqua's knowledge of his past, something Tris himself had not heard Carroway speak of in years. But before he could say anything, Riqua's attention turned to Carina.

"And who are you, lady healer?" Riqua asked.

"Carina Jesthrata," Carina replied.

Riqua's eyes narrowed as she struggled to place her. "King Donelan's court healer, yes? I heard some time ago that you went to the Sisterhood to find a cure for Donelan's sickness. Yet here you are."

Carina gave Riqua a defiant look. "Foor Arontala is the cause of the king's illness. Until Arontala is destroyed, Donelan won't fully recover. This is my proper place."

"Well, well, well," Riqua said, directing her comment this time to Gabriel. "You've certainly assembled the players. I can say we've not seen the like here, at least, not alive. You are most welcome here. These are my lands. In better days, I would have received you in the manor house, but it burned. So here we are."

"Is it true, that you are a spirit mage?" a young man barely out of his teens asked Tris. When Tris met the eyes of the *vayash moru*, he saw centuries, not decades, in the dark gaze.

"A Summoner," Gabriel replied. "The Blood Council itself promised him sanctuary among our kind."

"All but Uri." Tris turned to see Elana, the blond *vayash moru* who had been with Riqua at the Council meeting.

A faint glimmer of annoyance crossed Gabriel's face. "As usual, our esteemed colleague takes a somewhat different view of circumstances. But the Council has ruled." Together, they walked into the midst of the other *vayash moru*, who watched Tris and the others with barely concealed hunger.

"You may rest here until nightfall," promised Riqua. "I give my word you'll be safe."

Although none of his companions spoke, Tris knew that they shared the same skepticism. Riqua's offer looked good only compared to the certain dangers outside.

"Thank you," Tris replied with a slight bow. "We're grateful."

A cold smile touched her lips. "If you can stop Arontala, it is we who will be in your debt, son of Bricen." Riqua turned abruptly. "Kolin," she said to the young man behind her, "bring extra cloaks to warm them. Fetch wine from the casks. Make them comfortable." She turned back to Tris, clearly acknowledging him as the group's leader. "We have no need of your food here," she said, her sharp, white teeth clear in her smile. "But there is old wine in the cellar you might find acceptable."

Tris nodded. "We brought provisions with us."

"Elana," Riqua called.

"At your service, m'lady." The blonde *vayash moru* might have appeared demure had it not been for the complete lack of innocence in her blue eyes.

"Show our guests to the inner chambers. They've traveled far. We must make them as comfortable as we can."

"Of course," Elana answered. "Follow me."

She led them down a narrow corridor, from which branched dozens of rooms filled with shrouded and mummified dead. The corridors of the necropolis reeked of decay. Carina put a hand to her face, covering her nose and mouth with part of her shawl.

"These look like the tunnels underneath Isencroft's palace," Kiara said.

"You've been there?" Elana inquired.

Kiara and Carina exchanged glances. "Yes, many times."

Elana glanced back at Kiara over her shoulder. "I've taken refuge there more times than I can count. It is a well-known sanctuary."

"I never knew," Kiara murmured.

"There's much your kind does know about us." Elana opened the doors to two empty crypts that branched off the corridor. Carved into the stone, they were furnished as comfortable bedrooms, with stone slabs where beds might have been. "Here are your rooms."

"For the ladies." Elana gestured to the smaller crypt off the main hall. "It was built for two," she said with an unsettling smile. She turned to the men, "And you may sleep here." She pointed to the larger crypt across and down the corridor. "We have no other rooms that are not... occupied."

Her gaze lingered a moment longer than necessary on Tris. "Kolin will bring anything you need. You won't be disturbed. We too, will rest until nightfall. Then, we go hunting." And with that the *vayash moru* left them, no longer troubling to move at mortal speed, disappearing in the blink of an eye.

"If we ever travel together again," Carroway mumbled, "I'm choosing where we stay." He moved to the doorway of the second crypt, and shuddered. "Forgive me for not being grateful, but this wasn't what I had in mind when I thought of a safe place to sleep."

"Where's Gabriel?" Kiara asked, looking for their guide.

"He stayed behind with Riqua," Vahanian replied, positioning himself so that he could look down the corridor. "I'm not crazy about being split up like this."

"Neither am I," Carina agreed. "I'd feel better if we could stay together."

"So would I," Tris agreed, "but the rooms are too small for all of us, and I don't have the feeling we've been given permission to wander around."

"You're the Lord of the Dead," Vahanian tossed back. "Aren't they supposed to listen to you?"

"Royster was a bit obscure on that point. As far as the *vayash moru* go, I have the distinct feeling it's an honorary title," Tris replied.

"They're bound by the Blood Council's ruling, aren't they?" Kiara asked, pulling her cloak more tightly around her.

"So I'm told. Let's hope Gabriel is reading his people correctly."

They gathered in the larger crypt, which was barely big enough for them all to find a seat. Tris lit the torches. Here beneath the ground, it was cold enough that Carina began to shiver, gratefully accepting Vahanian's offer to share both his seat and his cloak. Kiara also drew close to Tris. After a while, body heat together with the torch fire helped to warm the small room.

Carroway distributed food for them out of the packs from their horses. Kolin delivered extra cloaks and wineskins filled with an old, sweet vintage, then left them to their meal. Jae was quiet, picking at the bits of meat and cheese Kiara put out for him. The group ate in silence, each deep in thought. Or perhaps, Tris mused, the uncertainty of how close their hosts might be lingering and how well the undead could hear. He was sure that each of them was putting off sleep just as long as their exhausted bodies could remain awake.

He knew his own opportunity to rest would have to wait. Here among the bones of the dead, the restless spirits clustered around him, so thickly that he was amazed his companions could not see them. He couldn't resist their pleas for intercession and release, and so he worked until his head throbbed and he could no longer fend off sleep.

Tris's companions waited until finally fatigue won out over fear. Carroway took the first watch.

"Sleep with one eye open, all right?" Kiara joked nervously.

"I don't think you need to worry about that," Tris assured her, seeing the uneasiness in her eyes as he kissed her forehead. From the moment they had approached the ruined temple, the whispers of the dead brushed his mind, like a hushed conversation just beyond hearing. The presence of the ghostly watchers was likely to keep him from getting any restful sleep, even if he could banish the memories of the murdered villagers from his thoughts.

Kiara and Carina disappeared into their crypt, and Carroway took up his post at its door. Just then, Riqua appeared from the shadows of the corridor. "I see you haven't yet gone to your rest," she said to Tris.

"Forgive me, but that sounds a bit ominous, given where we are," Tris said with a thin smile.

"Come with me, Prince Drayke. I have something for you, a gift from Bava K'aa."

Tris exchanged a glance with Vahanian. "Get some sleep, Jonmarc. You need it more than any of us."

"I don't sleep well in crypts," Vahanian said. "And I'm sworn to keep your royal hide in one piece. So if it's all the same to you, wherever you're going—I'm going."

"As you wish," replied Riqua. She led them down a maze of corridors. Tris called hand fire to light their way, and Vahanian carried a torch from their crypt, pushing back some of the tomb's darkness. They followed Riqua to an older part of the necropolis where dust and the smell of death permeated the air.

Riqua stopped at a mausoleum wall, where the dead were laid to their rest in stone drawers behind intricately carved slabs that depicted their likeness and the dates of their life. Vahanian hung back, keeping watch on the entrance to the corridor. Riqua moved to one of the plainer slabs and effortlessly opened a heavy drawer that might have taken three strong men to close. She reached inside, undeterred by the old corpse that lay shrouded inside. From beneath the body, she drew a small, thin book.

Tris felt his heart begin to pound as he recognized the binding.

"Do you know what this is, Lord Summoner?" Riqua asked, handing him the slim volume bookmarked with a yellowed, thick envelope.

"The missing diary of the Obsidian King."

Riqua gave a short, harsh laugh. "Missing? Is that what the Sisterhood told you? It's never been missing. Bava K'aa gave it to me, years ago, for safekeeping. Do you know why? Why she chose to keep its location secret, even from the Sisterhood?"

"Because it contains something so powerful, with such a great potential for misuse, that she couldn't trust it to anyone else."

"Because it holds a secret of life and death," Riqua said. "It's time for you to hear the whole story about your grandmother, and why her love nearly cost the Winter Kingdoms their freedom. But first, pay heed to that envelope, and the page it marks. You hold in your hands something beyond the wealth of kings, beyond the greatest spoils of war. Tell me what's written on the page—mind that you do not speak the words aloud."

Tris read over the yellowed handwriting. His hands began to shake as he realized the meaning of what he saw. He looked at Riqua, ashen. "It's a spell to separate the soul from the body," he said quietly. "Gray magic, if it belongs at all to the light."

Riqua took the fragile envelope from his trembling hands, and withdrew a sturdy vial on a strong leather strap. Riqua slipped the strap over Tris's head, so that the vial hung around his neck. "What could equal the importance of the spell?" Tris asked.

"Before her death, Bava K'aa made one final potion. Doing so weakened her, and hastened her passing. What you hold in your hand was created at the peril of Bava K'aa's very soul, because its working is indeed gray magic. It's a potion capable of curing a mortal wound. Such a potion requires the power of a very great sorcerer, and drains the maker of such power that those few powerful enough to create it can only do so once in their lifetime. Think, Prince Drayke. How much would a dying man pay for such an elixir? How many people would a desperate man kill?"

"I don't understand," Tris said, staring at the vial as if it might burn him. "What does the combination mean?"

"There's one more item you have not seen," Riqua said. Tris realized that there was a sealed note slipped into the back of the book. He was shaken to see his own name written on the envelope, in the unmistakable hand of his grandmother.

"Read it."

Within the envelope was a small sheet, and on it, one sentence: "You must do what I could not, because you have what I did not," he read in a voice just above a whisper.

"Before his fall, the mage who became the Obsidian King was in love with your grandmother." Riqua said. "His name was Lemuel, and he was one of the most gifted Summoners of his age. Like your grandmother, he rose on his gifts alone, without a noble name or a wealthy family. And like your grandmother, he became the advisor to kings and almost without peer in mortal influence."

"And that power corrupted him. He presumed to the rights of the Goddess."

"That's what the Sisterhood told you, and it's true—in part. Lemuel pushed the boundaries of knowledge within that gift farther than anyone—even Bava K'aa—had ever gone. But something went wrong when Lemuel attempted a very old working. Bava K'aa, who was with him when it happened, believed that an ancient, evil spirit took possession of Lemuel. She blamed herself for not being able to intervene. That spirit called himself the Obsidian King, although the Sisterhood believes that he has been known by many names throughout the ages, taking and abandoning human hosts as it suits him."

"Possessed by the Obsidian King, Lemuel took Bava K'aa prisoner," Riqua continued, "and the Obsidian King used him to inflict great suffering, trying to get Bava K'aa to give up the secret of this elixir. Lord Grayson, a great warrior who was friend to both Lemuel and Bava K'aa, risked everything to free her from the prison of the Obsidian King. Bava K'aa never spoke of those dark days, and neither did Grayson nor the Sisters who took Bava K'aa in and healed her. Grayson, who had secretly loved Bava K'aa but stood aside because of his friendship with Lemuel, wed Bava K'aa in private during her recovery. Before long, her only daughter—your mother—was born.

"Even after all the pain that the Obsidian King—in Lemuel's body—inflicted on her, Bava K'aa couldn't destroy him," Riqua said, remembering. "She believed to the end that Lemuel's spirit remained a prisoner within his own body, tortured by the evil the Obsidian King forced his body to perform."

"That was why she imprisoned him in Soulcatcher," Tris murmured, thinking of the deadly red orb. "Because she believed that somewhere Lemuel might still exist. There was no way to kill the Obsidian King without also destroying Lemuel."

"After the binding, Bava K'aa discovered this journal. She knew it must be hidden. Maybe she anticipated that the Obsidian King would rise once more, and that you, her mage heir, would fight anew the battle. Make no mistake, son of Bricen— the first war very nearly killed your grandmother. Some say it was the Lady herself who spared Bava K'aa. I've found it... unwise... to count on divine intervention."

"If the Obsidian King existed before he possessed Lemuel, then who was he?"

Riqua shook her head. "Even the Sisterhood isn't sure. Bava K'aa knew more than anyone, having been his prisoner. She said the Obsidian King was a spirit willful enough to defy death itself, a mage who wanted immortality and unchallenged power."

"Thank you," Tris said.

"Guard the vial well. There's no mage strong enough to make it again, and the way of its making went to the grave with your grandmother."

In the distance, they heard a scream.

CHAPTER THIRTY

KIARA AWOKE WITH a start to find a cold palm pressed across her nose and mouth and a firm grip pinning her to her bed. The reed torch had burned down to embers, just enough for Kiara to make out the silhouette of a woman poised above her.

"You can hear me?" Elana whispered close to her ear. Silently, Kiara nodded. "Good. Someone has been looking for you, Kiara of Isencroft."

Kiara struggled against the seduction of that voice, like a warm blanket of honey enveloping her, draining her will. Instinctively, she glanced toward the other bed, where Carina slept soundly, her back to them.

"Your friend can't help you. My kind have certain... talents... to make sure we're undisturbed." As if in answer to Kiara's unspoken question, a bundle of cloth tumbled and squirmed on the floor.

"Your pet will be no help," Elana added conde-scendingly. "Lord Gabriel and the others are resting. They won't hear."

Elana smiled coldly. "Don't blame Riqua. Her welcome was sincere. But she's not my maker," the blonde *vayash moru* said with a hint of bitterness. "I have no choice." Her eyes glinted with old pain. "Come."

Elana drew Kiara to her feet and Kiara stood, panicked that her body seemed incapable of obey-ing her will, captivated by Elana's voice. She took one step, and then two toward the hallway. Once into the corridor, she would be lost. She had no doubt who Elana's master was. Arontala had sum-moned his creations, and once delivered to the dark mage, Kiara had no illusions about her fate.

As she moved toward the door, she brushed against her sword belt where it lay on the foot of the slab, sending it and her dagger clattering to the floor.

Elana gave a hiss of anger and wheeled, grabbing Kiara by the throat with a hand strong enough to crush her neck. The pressure on Kiara's throat made her gasp.

"Kiara?" Carina called. Seeing the silhouette of Elana with her hand gripping Kiara's throat, Carina screamed. Elana whirled as Carina dove for the fall-en sword.

With a desperate cry Carina lunged, plunging the blade through Elana's belly. Elana struck back, toss-ing Carina against the stone like a rag doll. The distraction was all Kiara needed as Elana loosened her grip. Kiara twisted, using her legs to knock her attacker to the floor. A cold hand closed on her leg as Kiara struggled to get away. Boot steps pounded in the distance.

Carina struggled to her feet and dove at the attacker with her full might. Elana hurled Carina away and released her prisoner as a cold wind swept through the room. Kiara, pushed backward against the wall, had the barest glimpse of her own dagger glinting in the dying light of the torch. She heard the sickening thud of dagger's blade meeting flesh.

Carroway burst into the room, sword drawn, a torch aloft in his grip. An instant later, Tris and Vahanian joined him. They stopped in utter astonishment. Riqua stood over Elana's motionless form. In Elana's chest, buried hilt deep, was Kiara's spelled dagger and, protruding from both sides of Elana's body, Kiara's sword. Carina, thrown hard enough against the crypt wall to have the breath knocked out of her, was struggling to her feet, her expression a mix of determination and terror.

"What the hell happened?" Vahanian demanded.

Kiara shook her head, trying to clear the last of the *vayash moru*'s influence. "She was going to take me to her master," Kiara said. "I... I couldn't resist her."

"I gravely miscalculated," Riqua said coldly, looking down at Elana's body. "I believed that I knew who had made Elana. It appears that I did not. What did she tell you?"

"That she had no choice, that she had been told to bring me to him. She didn't have to say his name."

"Arontala," Tris supplied.

"Great. Just great," Vahanian snapped, with an accusing glare at Riqua. "Are the rest of your brood coming after us now, too?"

"You have nothing to fear from them. They are my creations. This one," she said, with a disdainful look at Elana's remains, "came to us a few months ago. Perhaps Arontala has planted his own among all the families, watching for you."

"Does he know we're here?" Tris asked.

"Doubtful. Elana wasn't strong enough to alert him. More likely, she'd been given orders to watch for you, in case you showed up."

"The dagger," Kiara said, looking down at the hilt in Elana's corpse. "It can turn the undead or destroy the soul." She reached down and withdrew the blades, cleaning them on the hem of Elana's dress before resheathing them.

Carina sat down on the slab, visibly shaken. "I didn't even realize that I grabbed a sword," the healer murmured. "I just knew someone was taking Kiara away."

"You picked a good time to get over using a blade," Vahanian said.

"Elana was sure the rest of you couldn't interfere," Kiara said.

Vahanian glared at Carroway. "You were supposed to be on guard duty."

"I was. I didn't see anything," Carroway said, appalled. "I swear by the Lady."

"You couldn't have prevented what happened," Riqua said. "We're skilled at passing unnoticed."

Gabriel joined them, and Tris thought he saw uneasiness in the *vayash moru*'s face. Riqua looked at Gabriel. "I thought you were sleeping."

"I've learned to sleep lightly."

Kolin and Keir joined them and, at Riqua's word, pushed their way in to gather up Elana's body. "Place it outside, where it will catch the sun. She doesn't deserve burial."

When they were gone, Riqua turned to Gabriel. "If Arontala has his fledglings planted among our houses," she said, "you can't be safe among any of our kind you didn't make yourself."

"I'll revise my plans," Gabriel said.

"Do we get a vote on that?" Carroway muttered.

"We can't lose more time," Tris said. "The Hawthorn Moon is only a few weeks away."

"You'll reach Shekerishet by the Moon," Gabriel vowed. "You have my word."

"Cross your heart and hope to die?" Vahanian asked.

"Now, despite this… misfortune," Gabriel said, "you need to rest, and so do I."

"I don't feel very tired right now," Kiara replied, rubbing her neck where Elana had gripped her.

"I think we should stay together," Carina added.

"I'll watch over you personally," Riqua said. "I have eternity to rest and, unlike Gabriel, I don't have to save my strength for the journey. I assure you, none of mine will harm you while I'm your protector."

Vahanian looked as if he were about to make another comment, then saw the ice in the *vayash moru*'s eyes and thought better of it. "Let's get to it, then," he said.

What Vahanian lacked in diplomacy, Kiara thought as they filed out, he made up for in voicing the sentiments of them all. She fastened her sword belt and walked to the door, where Tris waited to follow her.

Riqua led them to her own quarters, a sumptuous tomb obviously intended for one of noble birth. It had been transformed to a well-appointed boudoir, with one significant difference. In the center stood an ornate catafalque, and atop it an alabaster image of Riqua. Exhausted, Kiara and the others made impromptu beds of couches and pillows, choosing to stay close enough together that no one could pass among them without waking the others.

Kiara gave Carina's hand a grateful squeeze. "Have I ever told you how happy I am that you're a light sleeper?"

"I'm glad I was able to stop her. But I can't believe I used a blade."

"What exactly do your healer rules say?" Vahanian asked from where he had stretched out, blocking the doorway with his body. He closed his eyes, trying to relax.

"The taking of life or the shedding of blood in anger with a knife or blade is forbidden."

"Then you're clear."

"What?"

Vahanian opened one eye. "Elana was already dead. Undead. You didn't take her life. And whatever that stuff was on the floor, it wasn't *her* blood."

Kiara chuckled. "He's got a point, Carina. I like his logic. And admit it—it wouldn't be the first time healers have split hairs on some obscure rule."

"I'll have to think about it tomorrow," Carina said, settling in next to Vahanian and sharing his cloak. "That just might make sense in the morning."

Kiara smiled, finding a spot beside Tris, glad for the arm he slipped around her shoulders and the warmth of his heavy cloak.

When the others were quiet, Tris turned toward Kiara. "I have something I want you to carry for me."

"Not another magic dagger, I hope?"

Tris carefully withdrew the precious vial of Bava K'aa's elixir from where it hung on the strap around his neck. He slipped it over Kiara's head. "Wear this for me, please."

"What is it?" She looked at the vial, which glowed a faint violet through the thick glass.

"It's a potion. Grandmother left it for me with Riqua. Quite literally worth a king's ransom." He reached out to touch her cheek, and kissed her. "It will cure a mortal wound." She gasped, looking at the vial with renewed respect. "Keep it safe, please? If it's needed—and I hope it isn't—you're more likely to be able to do something with it than I will."

"I don't like it when you say things like that," she said, suppressing a shiver as she carefully slipped the vial down the throat of her tunic.

Tris put his arm around her. "I have every reason to want to live through this," he said, tangling his fingers in her hair, glad for her nearness. "You know that."

"I know. But it doesn't make me worry less."

Tris kissed her gently, and she leaned back against his shoulder. "I've thought a lot about what you said, back in Principality, about being the 'hound of the Goddess.' Coming when the Lady calls and doing as She bids. I only wish I were a fox hound, and not turned out after a beast."

"But look at your pack," she said. "A good pack can bring down a very large bear."

"Have I mentioned, recently, how much I love you?"

She nestled closer. "Yes, but tell me again." Tris let his kiss answer her, and then folded her close. They shared the warmth of his cloak in the crowded room, content for the company as they fell asleep in what might be the last safe night before the Hawthorn Moon.

CHAPTER THIRTY-ONE

Ban Soterius shivered and gathered his cloak tightly around him in the harsh winds of northern Margolan. It was the fourth month, the Lover's Moon, but the winds had turned unseasonably cold, even for the unpredictable weather of the north. Rain fell, mixed with sleet, in a last winter storm. Soterius had ridden a candlemark since leaving the shelter of the village where he raised his most recent cluster of fighters, and had yet another candlemark to ride before reaching his destination. Although it was not yet dusk, the heavy gray clouds made it seem much later. Soterius found himself wishing for sundown, when Mikhail promised to join him.

The trek across northern Margolan had been successful so far. He had gathered thousands of volunteers and deserters into the ranks of his militia, seeding small groups of rebels to harry Jared's troops.

It had started with the refugees and the three deserters from the Margolan army in the Principality camp. Soterius knew there was plenty of bottled up rage against Jared, but he had no idea just how deep the feelings went, or how broadly they were shared. Once his purpose became known, the number of volunteers swelled. He and Mikhail were moved from village to village, protected by ties of kin and marriage, hidden in barns and wagons, caves and sheds.

Many a tavern keeper welcomed them by the back door, tired of Jared's troops busting up their inns and taking liberties with the women. Soterius and Mikhail slept in crypts and barrows, watched over by ghosts and the undead. Out in the villages one's kin included the living, dead, and undead. Those ties of kinship were as binding as any blood oaths; Soterius found that many of the families were linked from village to village all along the Borderlands. When multiplied by many generations with the inclusion of kin who were *vayash moru* or ghosts, Soterius came to see the villages as a tightly woven net of families, similar to the nobility at court.

Opportunities to test the skills of their trainees were readily available. Both Soterius and Mikhail led skirmishes against Jared's troops that heightened their renown and drew volunteers to their cause. As the successful strikes grew more numerous, Soterius amassed a better store of uniforms and weapons, wagons and horses. These he hid in the caves that pock-marked the foothills, until the time was right to march an army of his own toward the palace.

The villagers who volunteered were men old enough that Jared's troops had not conscripted them and women who had been subjected to the lusts of Jared's soldiers, or who had lost daughters and sons to Margolan's army. Those who could leave their villages Soterius and Mikhail trained to fight, helping them understand how to turn the land itself into a weapon. Those who could not leave became spies, passing along information as valuable as ammunition. Willing tavern masters became important gatekeepers in the resistance, noting the movement of troops and the number of soldiers passing through an area. Mikhail, a reasonably skilled musician, made sure to teach Carroway's defiant songs to the minstrels he met. He added stories of Tris's prowess as a Summoner to the bards' tales. Thanks to Mikhail, Soterius did not doubt that Carroway would find all the minstrels and bards he needed to create chaos in the palace city on the night of the Hawthorn Moon.

The courage of the rebels increased with every victory against Jared's army. After a few months, Soterius noted that the army did not venture north without large numbers. By then, the rebels were well-trained enough to harry the intruders, decimating their numbers and keeping them off balance and in constant fear. Soterius showed the village militias how to appear more numerous than they were. Mikhail taught them how to move silently and hide themselves.

From the villagers' web of family ties came another unexpected boon. Soterius knew that Tris had given his blessing to the ghosts of the *Scirranish* to avenge themselves and their families. Tris had also lent his power to make those ghosts visible. As the spirits of the *scirranish* returned to the places of their slaughter they called to the ghosts of their ancestors, until the forests and passes of the northlands were too dangerous for even the most intrepid of Jared's troops. Soterius heard tales of the encounters between the spirits and the Margolan army. If they resembled even a fraction of the truth, the murdered villagers had fully avenged themselves. Even without Tris's magic, Soterius was more aware of spirits around him than ever before, especially since he almost always rode by night to accompany Mikhail and avoid detection.

Vayash moru were more numerous than Soterius expected among the volunteers, until he heard the stories of how relentlessly Jared's troops had persecuted the undead, hunting them to their day crypts and burning them in the sun while they were vulnerable. Those *vayash moru* were kin to the villagers, and had remained part of the lives of their families and villages even after they had been brought across into the Dark Gift. And so the fear that Jared hoped to instill of the *vayash moru* became loathing for the usurper king who severed bonds of family and marriage that even death had not sundered.

Feeling the barely suppressed rage of the villagers, the anger of the spirits, and the cold resolve of the *vayash moru*, Soterius felt like he was watching storm clouds brewing on the horizon. The storm's center would be Shekerishet, and its fury would fall on the night of the Hawthorn Moon. Until then, he and Mikhail had a kingdom to lead into revolution.

Although Gabriel had given Soterius the names of Margolan nobles likely to aid the rebellion, those holdings were further south. So it was the villagers and farmers who offered shelter and hiding places, as well as provisions and safe passage. But now, just a few candlemarks from his father's lands, Soterius felt the need to go home and see how his own family fared.

Soterius passed an inn but did not stop. It was unlikely that anyone would recognize him, Soterius thought wryly, dressed as he was in a worn leather riding cloak with a full beard and his hair grown long. He was more likely to be taken for a brigand than the captain of Bricen's guard, but there was still no sense in tempting fate. He rode on, though a mug of ale and a few moments by the fireside would have warmed him.

Once he passed the inn, the road grew quiet. Soterius rode on high alert, wondering if he had been wrong about insisting on riding alone. But these were the roads he knew from his childhood, and he had never before felt in danger here. Now, in Jared's Margolan, Soterius wondered if he had been reckless. Again he wished for dusk to come, so that he would have Mikhail's company. Something felt wrong, very wrong. Soterius thought about going back to the inn, but decided that it would take longer to go back than to go forward. Besides, he argued with himself, Mikhail would be looking to meet him at Huntwood, the Soterius family manor. Chilled to the bone, Soterius decided to continue forward.

The sleet fell harder, glazing the wet ground and covering the bare branches of the trees so that they looked spun from glass. Soterius came to a rise in the road and saw Huntwood in the distance, a dark shape against the horizon. Only then did he realize the source of his sense of foreboding. The road to the manor, usually well-traveled, lay covered with an unbroken skin of ice, marked neither by hoof prints nor wagon tracks. The fields to either side of the road, usually home to cattle, goats, and sheep, were empty. No lights flickered from the manor house windows, and no smoke rose from its chimney.

Soterius urged his horse on, as fast as he dared to go on the icy roads. Within a few moments, the turn to the manor house came into view, as dark and undisturbed as the road itself. Feeling a rising panic, Soterius galloped up the long approach, hearing his horse's hoof beats pounding in the silence. He reached the great entrance and stopped, feeling his heart rise to his throat.

Huntwood was a ruined shell. The dim light of evening was visible through the upper floor window casings, where the roof had been burned away. The manor's windows had been shattered, their casings blackened by fire. The front door was splintered. From the overgrowth of the bare shrubbery, it appeared as if no one had tended the gardens for many months.

Soterius lightly tethered his horse to a hitching post and drew his sword, advancing toward the steps warily. In the distance an owl hooted, but there were no other sounds of life. Heart pounding, Soterius realized he was holding his breath as he approached the doorway, stepping over the broken pieces of what had been massive oaken doors.

The smell of smoke and charred wood still lingered. Little remained of the manor's furnishings. What had not been destroyed by fire appeared to have been slashed or hacked to bits. Icy rain fell from the gaping hole in the ceiling. Leaves swirled around Soterius's boots in the ravaged front hallway.

Numbly, he made his way through the ruin of the familiar manor, but found neither life nor any sign of recent habitation. He slipped from the back entrance into the terraced yards of which his mother had once been so proud. The gardens with their carefully tended hedge mazes and roses had been ridden down, and parts of them had burned.

Soterius found it difficult to breathe. He looked down over the sloping yard, toward the barns that were now charred timbers, and toward the fields that appeared to have been torched instead of harvested. *Gone, all of it gone*, he thought in shock. *All gone—*

He heard a crunch of ice behind him, and then a cry. Soterius could not see his attacker, but the man had to be at least double his bulk and a good bit taller; he easily crushed Soterius to the ice-covered ground and pinned him with his knee. He grabbed for Soterius's sword hand and slammed Soterius's knuckles against the ground until he could pry the sword away and throw it well out of reach.

"There's nothing left to take, thief," a man's voice rasped near Soterius's ear. "Your kind has taken it all. Give me one reason I shouldn't slit your whore-spawned throat!"

Soterius felt the blade of a knife press against his skin. He struggled in his shock to place the voice.

"I'm not a thief!" Soterius said. "I'm Lord Soterius's son."

He heard a rush of air and a strangled cry from his attacker, who was suddenly lifted from off his back. Soterius scrambled to turn over and saw Mikhail, holding a burly man aloft with one hand so that the man's feet dangled a few inches off the ground.

"You!" the man gasped. "I *should* slit your throat! It's because of you they're dead—they're all dead!"

Shaken, Soterius regained his feet. Mikhail returned the attacker to the ground but did not remove his hand from the assailant's neck. Although the man was unkempt and an unruly growth of beard altered his appearance, Soterius recognized his brother-in-law, Danne. Danne's words gave him no doubt as to the fate of his sister, Tae.

"Danne, what happened?"

"Soldiers came just after the Haunts. When your father met them at the door, they ran him through. Your mother, your brothers, the children, Tae—the soldiers chased them down, through the house, into the fields and killed them. Even the servants. All but Anyon, who hid in the well. I was gone to market with Coalan. When we came back, the fires were still smoking. Everything was gone."

Soterius staggered, and fell more than sat on the remnant of the garden wall.

"Anyon said that as your father lay dying, the soldiers told him that you were a traitor, that you had helped to kill King Bricen and then fled like a coward."

Soterius closed his eyes for a moment, unable to speak. It was Mikhail who broke the silence. "Is that what you still believe?" the *vayash moru* asked. He released Danne's throat, but stood between Danne and Soterius, blocking the big man's way.

Danne glared at Soterius; his shoulders sagged as the fight left him. "At first, we knew nothing else. But it made no sense, none at all. Ban had no reason to kill the king, and no profit from it." Danne's pain was clear in his eyes.

"I've known Ban since we were boys. I feared he might die for the king, but betray him—never." He took a heaving breath that shook his large form. "Since then, since Jared took the throne, we heard rumors... that Prince Martris survived, that he was spirited out of the palace, that his friends had gotten him to safety. I wanted to believe that. I wanted to believe you saved the prince, and that he might return. But seeing you, here, alive—you didn't see how they died, Ban. You didn't have to bury them. You didn't have to bury them." He covered his face with his hands.

"Tris and I saw Jared stab Bricen," Soterius said tonelessly. "We had climbed down the outside wall, trying to break into Arontala's workshop. We saw the king die. We found Serae—and Kait—dead by the sword. It was all Carroway and I could do to get Tris out of there alive. Harrtuck joined us, and we headed east." The full moon cast blue shadows across the ice-covered landscape. He was so chilled by the cold and so numb from grief that the words seemed to belong to someone else. "That's why I'm here. To help Tris take back the throne. To bring Jared to account. To destroy Arontala."

"Can he do it?" Danne asked. "He's no older than you are."

"He's a Summoner, Danne. Bava K'aa's mage heir. He's got the backing of three kings and the Blood Council. He'll take the throne—or die trying." He stopped, feeling his throat close again. "I wish father could have known the truth."

"Perhaps he does," Danne said. "They say the dead are watching." He looked toward the old kitchen house, and Soterius saw a thin wisp of smoke rising from its chimney. "Come on. Anyon and Coalan have a fire started. I'm sorry what I said—about slitting your throat. I swear to you on Tae's grave, I'll cause you no harm."

"Accepted. But first," Soterius said, "first, show me where they're buried. Please."

Danne hesitated, and then nodded. "All right. Follow me."

Soterius and Mikhail followed Danne down through the ruins of the garden, toward a stand of tall trees near the broken fence line. Under the massive oak trees was a large cairn. Soterius gave a strangled cry and fell to his knees, weeping.

"We did the best we could, the three of us," Danne recounted quietly. "Those that didn't die in the fire we bathed and shrouded and brought out here. We wrapped the others, what we found of them, and then we raised a cairn because the ground was too cold to dig. There was no one but ourselves to send them to the Lady, but we gave them our blessing." In the moonlight, Danne looked tired and old, though he was only a few years Soterius's senior. "By the Whore, no man should have to do that. Many's the night I wish I'd gone with them."

"I'm so sorry," Soterius said.

"I don't mind the cold, but perhaps we should take shelter or you may have your wish," Mikhail said gently. Soterius struggled to his feet, following silently as Danne led the way back to the kitchen house.

Inside were a man in his third decade and a boy who looked about five years younger than Soterius. They looked up as Danne entered. Soterius recognized the man as Anyon, his father's grounds keeper, and Danne's son, Coalan. Anyon moved with a limp that was new, and Soterius saw a deep scar slashed across his cheek. Coalan's light brown hair and hazel eyes looked so like his mother that it almost made Soterius weep for his lost sister. Coalan regarded the two newcomers with suspicion, his eyes glinting with loss and fear.

This time, it was Danne who told Anyon and Coalan of Soterius's tale. Soterius saw questions in the eyes of the two men, but to his great relief, neither seemed inclined to doubt the story.

The kitchen house was filled with the remnants of what could be salvaged from the manor, bits of charred furniture, cookware, a few books that still smelled of smoke, and lanterns. Pieces of heavy tapestries covered the windows, keeping any passers-by from seeing the light within.

"We've made do off the land," Anyon said, setting a piece of roasted venison and some leeks in front of Soterius, along with a wineskin. Mikhail raised a hand to forestall a similar offer. "Deer and game from the forest, some fish from the stream, and what was left in the fields that didn't burn. Some of the stores in the cellars weren't ruined, so we've had wine and dried fruit and cheese. Enough to get by."

"What will you do, now that it's almost planting season?" Soterius asked.

Danne met his eyes. "I guess that's up to the lord of the manor." Soterius's eyes widened as he took Danne's meaning. With his father and older brothers dead, the title and lands now fell to him. It was a windfall as undesired as it was unexpected.

"There isn't a future, until Martris Drayke holds the throne," Soterius said. "Maybe after that, I can think about it. But I'm oath-bound to raise rebellion against Jared. That has to come before anything else."

Danne stroked his beard thoughtfully, listening as Soterius told them of the rebels he and Mikhail had trained and the deserters they recruited. "You can't house your soldiers here," Danne said when Soterius finished. "Margolan troops come by every so often—maybe to see if you've returned."

"I have a suggestion of a place that might be ideal for a base camp, if you dare," Mikhail said. He gratefully accepted a tankard of deer's blood, which Anyon had drained from the carcass hanging at the back of the kitchen. "The Carroway manor house, Glynnmoor, is barely a candlemark's ride from here. It's near the main roads south, which we will need to secure as we head toward Shekerishet."

"The plague house? Are you mad?" Coalan exclaimed.

Mikhail held up a hand. "The ill humours that caused the plague have long since gone. Mortal squatters and vagrants have taken refuge there over the years with no ill effects. Some of my kind, out of friendship with Lord Carroway, chased off the squatters and cleaned out the manor, burning the bodies and their intimate goods that might have carried plague. While it's not as it once was, it's habitable and in much better shape than Huntwood. And as you say, even those living near-by stay clear. So we may be spared the interest of passing soldiers."

Soterius struggled to focus on Mikhail's words, using all of his battle training to center on the task at hand, and step back from the grief that threatened to overwhelm him. "If we can survive there without taking sick, it might be perfect," Soterius agreed. He looked to Danne and the others. "If you'll shelter us tonight, we'll leave tomorrow. I don't want to add to your pain, and we have a job to do."

Danne looked to Anyon and Coalan, who met his eyes, and nodded in silent agreement. "If you'll have us, we're of a mind to go with you," the big man said. "There's nothing for us here but to starve. We're none of us soldiers, but after what happened here I'll have no problem killing Jared's troops."

"Nor I," swore Anyon, straightening. "There's vengeance due."

"Count me in," said Coalan. Soterius started to object that his nephew, only fifteen summers old, was too young for battle. But the look in Coalan's eyes, the anger and pain and loss that Soterius saw there, silenced his objections.

"We would welcome you," Soterius said. "I'd be honored."

When the others had gone to bed Soterius was still awake, staring into the small fire. He stood and

506 The Blood King

walked to the door, letting himself out into the cold moonlit night. After a time, he felt Mikhail's presence, though the *vayash moru*'s approach was silent.

"Ban, I'm sorry about your family."

Soterius looked up at the full moon. "I was thinking about Tris, the night we left Shekerishet. How he seemed to move in a fog. We were running for our lives, and he didn't seem to share the same urgency the rest of us felt. I was so impatient with him that night. I needed him to make decisions, to tell us what to do. I didn't know what to do with his grief. And I was so proud of how battle-calm I was, so unruffled. Such a perfect soldier."

Soterius kicked at the ice, and looked out at the shadow of the ruined manor house. "I feel like that deer in there—like I've been gutted and left to bleed dry. I guess that's how Tris felt, too. Only I was too busy playing soldier to understand. And when we met Jonmarc, I was so sure he couldn't be trusted, that anyone who sold his sword would be a turncoat."

He looked up at the moon, and the silent tears tracked down his cheeks. "But Jonmarc understood. I didn't realize then, but I know now what he went through, what he lost. I've been such an ass. Playing the hero while the people I loved were dying because of it. Danne was right. They died because of me. And while—Goddess help me!—I couldn't have done anything differently, Father died, thinking me a traitor. I wish I could make that right."

For the first time in their acquaintance, Soterius glimpsed old pain in the *vayash moru*'s eyes. "Even if you hadn't saved Tris that night, Jared would have sent his troops. Your father was one of Bricen's closest friends. The same has befallen any who didn't have the good luck to hear of the coup and go into hiding before the soldiers could come. Without your sacrifice, there would be no hope of unseating Jared, no one to defeat Arontala."

"I know that," Soterius said.

"Maybe when all is settled, Tris would come to Huntwood, and let you make your peace," Mikhail suggested. "He's done so for strangers—would he do less for you?"

Soterius swallowed hard, and shook his head. "You're right, of course. It's just that tonight, it seems so far out of reach."

Mikhail gave a sad smile. "One of the things I miss most about being mortal is the ability to get drunk. I've seen much that I wish I could forget, even for a little while. But perhaps, my friend, you can take some solace in wine and find your rest. You need fear nothing—I'll stand watch."

Soterius nodded, but paused as he turned to go back into the kitchen house. "Does it get better—with time?"

He saw the centuries in Mikhail's eyes. "All things fade in time," the *vayash moru* replied. "But even faded, there are those things that death itself cannot erase."

CHAPTER THIRTY-TWO

"W HY SO GLUM, Carroway?" Carina nudged her horse onward through the unseasonably cold rain.

The bard gave her a sour look. "Because it's nearly dusk, and every nightfall seems to bring us to a place to stay that's even more dreadful than the last." Their horses splashed through the water-filled ruts as they trudged down the muddy roads. "Crypts. Basements. Abandoned buildings. What I wouldn't give for an inn with a fireplace!"

Kiara chuckled. "I understand completely. Last night, I think I saw the biggest rat in Margolan in that basement!" Jae, snuggled for warmth in Kiara's lap, gave a gurgle of agreement.

"All I know is that the next time I go somewhere with Tris, I'm going to be in charge of where we stay," Carroway said. "I may never be warm again!"

Vahanian, who was riding point, stopped to let the others catch up. "Can't say I disagree," he said, flexing his cold hands, nearly numb from holding his reins. We're still a good ways from Shekerishet. Perhaps a warm place to stay and a hot meal would do us all good."

"Do you remember the inn we stayed at on our way to Ghorbal?" Tris asked the bard. "The one with the young man's ghost?"

"Is that the way you remember all the places you've stayed—by what haunts them?" Vahanian turned his horse to avoid the worst of the rain that ran down his leather cloak and dripped from its hem.

"Lately, yes."

Carroway stood in his stirrups to get his bearings. "We should be close. Why?"

Tris looked out over the horizon. "It would be a safe place for us—I'm sure of it."

Carroway nodded. "The innkeeper was willing to hide us—even before you sent away the ghost. He's unlikely to turn us in now."

"Whatever we're doing, can we decide before I freeze?" Carina put in.

Tris and Carroway conferred on the roads, and the group headed out with considerably lighter spirits at the prospect of a night in a real inn. A steady flow of traffic passed them, bound for the palace city and the upcoming festival. Still, Tris noticed that the travelers seemed shabbier than in years past, and the carts of provisions less full than before. It was a marvel that the people of Margolan had the will to celebrate at all under Jared's yoke.

When they reached the Sparrow's Roost Inn, Tris and Carroway exchanged glances. "Looks like getting rid of the ghost was good for business," the bard remarked. The inn, which had been in need of repair and nearly empty on their flight from Shekerishet now had a freshly painted sign, a tidy exterior, and a stable filled to capacity with guests' horses.

"Apparently so," Tris said. "Let's go around back."

Tris gave his reins to Carroway and bade the others stay back a few paces as he approached the kitchen door. He gave a few sharp knocks, and the stout innkeeper's wife came to the door. "Go 'round to the front if you need something," she said. "But mind that we've got no rooms left tonight." She started to close the door and Tris caught it, letting his hood fall back in the rain. The woman caught her breath and brightened, throwing her arms around Tris in a hug that nearly took him off his feet.

"Bless the Lady—you're back!" she cried. "Lars, Toby, come quickly!"

The innkeeper and his son came to the door, and puzzled looks quickly changed to broad grins of welcome. "Come in, come in," the innkeeper said, looking beyond Tris to where his friends waited. "But tell me, sir mage, why do you come to the back door like a beggar?"

Tris extended his mage sense, feeling no threat in the presence of the innkeeper and his family. While he was glad of their welcome, he did not wish to put them in danger. He thought it best to tell a limited version of their story. "We'd still prefer to stay clear of the king's troops," Tris said honestly. The others secured their horses in a copse of trees a little way from the crowded barn and joined him in the kitchen. "Not everyone is as glad as yourself to see a mage these days."

Lars, better fed and less harried than he had been, nodded. "Aye, there's many in the land today have a reason to stay clear of the king's troops, that's for sure. Have no love for them myself, as you know. Bust up the place, and then charge a fee if I want to keep them from busting it up again.

"But since you sent that young man to his rest, folks will stay the night again—and I don't lose so much ale spilled for no reason. We're in your debt, m'lord mage. Thought we would starve to death until you came along." Lars welcomed the others into the crowded kitchen, which smelled of roasting venison, cooked leeks, and the dark, rich ale for which Margolan's southern plains were famed.

"Come in, come in. I'll give you my best table, and all the food and ale you want," Lars said.

Tris smiled, knowing the welcome was genuine. "We're grateful for your kindness, but we'd like to keep a low profile. We'll be happy to eat in the kitchen."

Carroway lifted his head, listening. "Do I hear a bard in the common room?"

Lars nodded. "Had more than a few musicians traveling through with the festival. You're welcome to go join them—don't think we've ever had the like of you since you left."

Carroway grinned at the compliment. "My fingers are too frozen to play, at least right now," he said, flexing his hands. "But there's something familiar in that voice. I'd like to see who's out there."

"Keep your head down," Vahanian cautioned.

"You know me," Carroway tossed back with a grin. "I blend into the crowd."

Carina and Kiara chuckled. Even in drab riding clothes, with his long black hair pulled back and soaked, Carroway cut a handsome figure. The bard disappeared through the kitchen doors and the innkeeper's daughter motioned the group to a work table in the back of the kitchen. She and Toby began to bring out the first hot food the group had enjoyed in several days.

"Perhaps I risk my neck by saying this," Lars began with a nervous glance at the doors, "but since you've got no love of the king's troops, I'll wager I'm safe. Since King Bricen died—the Lady rest his soul—this year has been the demon's own. Got plenty of guests tonight, but people aren't traveling the way they used to—scared of the highwaymen, and the guards, too. And what's to travel for anymore, I ask you? Half the farmers ran away—can't blame them, being burned out by the guardsmen. The others can't eke out enough to feed their own families, what with the looters and all, let alone take more to trade in the city. Don't see so many merchants either. And there hasn't been a caravan through here since slavers got one group up near the pass last Fall.

"We've fixed the inn up since you took care of the ghost, and it's been good for business. But many's the night there's no one at all on the road to stay anywhere. And it wouldn't do to look like we turn much of a profit—would just invite the guardsmen to double what they charge me to keep them from busting up the place."

Lars shook his head. "Never was like this under King Bricen. How he had such a rotter for a son, I don't know, but King Jared"—he paused to spit on the floor at the name—"belongs to the Crone herself. Guess those are hanging words, and I ought to be more careful. But it's gotten bad, m'lord mage. I don't go nowhere, but I hear everyone who does."

He leaned forward. "It's worse in the city. King's got his guardsmen, and they make anyone who dares speak against the king disappear. Leave the bodies in the street the next day, as a warning. I imagine they'll be watching the festival this year, to keep things from getting out of hand. Now that's the demon's own, ain't it?"

Vahanian cursed, and Kiara laid a hand on Tris's arm. Tris had gone pale at the innkeeper's story, and it was only with great effort that he held back his anger and sorrow. "Perhaps the Lady will show pity," Tris said. "Maybe She will give favor to a champion."

Lars glanced nervously over his shoulder. "She didn't favor that general who tried to poison King Jared, that's for sure. Drawn and quartered he was."

Lars leaned closer. "But I've heard that to the north, the spirits are restless. I've heard that some of the king's troops were set on by the ghosts of the poor bastards they've killed, and that none but the horses survived. They say that there's bands of deserters stalking the king's troops on the main roads. Got so the army won't even go to the highlands no more, because they don't come back. Just last week, heard tell that on the plank road, the one that leads north of Ghorbal, a whole unit of guardsmen just disappeared." Lars snapped his fingers with a malicious smile.

"Maybe your spirits can tell you true," Lars added with a glance at Tris. "But that's what I hear, anyhow."

Carroway returned to eat with them, and then went back to the greatroom with a promise to be their eyes and ears. Carina noticed a burn on Lars' daughter Lara's arm. She smiled gratefully as Carina healed it to a faint, pink scar. Tabethe, the innkeeper's wife, prevailed on Carina for help with a bad back. In return, she brought the group food and ale until they could eat no more.

"Picked a good night to be inside—it's still raining out there," Vahanian observed from his post near the door. Tris sat toward the corner, out of the way of the busy kitchen staff. Jae lazed near the hearth, much to Lara's amusement, who dropped bits of venison near the little gyregon until it finally fell asleep, completely sated. "What's got you so deep in thought?"

Tris looked up from the diary of the Obsidian King. "Just looking for anything I can in the diary. I was hoping we could get an early start," he said with a glance toward Tabethe, who was bustling near the fire, "but our business has to start and end on the main night."

Beside him, Kiara dozed in a chair until it was her turn on watch. Carina slipped into the greatroom with Carroway. Tris immersed himself in the small, tight handwriting that crowded the precious diary.

What he found troubled him. Tris hoped to find a way to approach Arontala before the Hawthorn Moon, destroying the orb and the dark mage before Arontala could even begin his working to free the Obsidian King's spirit. But as Tris studied the journal, it became clear that the only way magic worked on a witches' moon could be dispelled was on that same eve of power. An advance strike was doomed to fail. Only on the night of the working could he intervene and destroy both the orb and the one who sought to escape it. Their opportunity for victory was much smaller than he had hoped.

"Do you think Riqua was right about Lemuel?" Vahanian asked. He kept a wary eye on the rear window and leaned against the wall near the door, his hand close to his sword.

Tris put the book down and blinked to ease his tired eyes. "That he got trapped and taken along for the ride, so to speak?" he asked, being deliberately vague because of the innkeepers' family within earshot. "Yes. It makes sense with what I heard from... 'my sisters,'" he added, thinking it unwise to refer to the Sisterhood by name.

Vahanian caught the evasion and chuckled. "I like that. Your sisters." He sobered. "Poor guy, if that's what happened to him. So he's been a prisoner—all these years—in that big ball you talk about?"

Tris cast a glance toward Tabethe and Lara, but they seemed wholly unconcerned with the conversation, bustling about the front of the kitchen to serve their festival-bound guests. "Grandmother apparently thought so. Who knows if he even exists anymore? I know that's where Kait is—and possibly mother, too. When this is over, if their spirits survived, I hope I can send them to their rest."

Just then, there was a tap at the door. Kiara roused from her nap and straightened. Vahanian moved quickly, his hand on his sword as the door opened. Gabriel stepped in, shaking the rain from his cloak. "So this is where you are," the *vayash moru* said. "Tired of my accommodations?" Tris feared the innkeeper's wife might run screaming from the room, but Tabethe merely afforded Gabriel a nod.

"Good evenin', m'lord," she said, as Lara went for a mug. "Deer's fresh today, if you want a nip."

Gabriel smiled and gave a shallow bow in greeting. "I would be grateful, dear lady. Many thanks."

Tabethe refused Gabriel's gold when she realized he was with Tris and the others. With all that Jared had done to foster fear of the *vayash moru* among the people, Tris gave Tabethe credit for her matter-of-fact greeting; a sign, he thought, that at least some in Margolan saw through Jared's fear-mongering.

When the last of the greatroom patrons had departed, Carroway and Carina came through the door from the outer room, followed by three musicians whom Tris immediately recognized as Carroway's inner circle at court. First through the door was a man just a little older than Carroway, with touseled, short blond hair framing a youthful face with mischievous blue eyes. Next was a slip of a girl who looked barely more than sixteen summers old, carrying a flute. She had lank, dark hair, and cynical brown eyes. Beside Carroway was a tall young woman with short dark hair and violet eyes. She had a lyre over her shoulder.

"Look who we found!" Carroway grinned, and the musicians looked from the bard to Tris as if they had seen a ghost. "You remember Helki, Paiva and Macaria—from back home?"

"By the Lady, can it be?" asked Helki with a gasp. "My prince!" he exclaimed. Carroway made hushing gestures. To Tris's chagrin, the three minstrels bowed low.

Lars came through the door just then, with a small bag of coins for the minstrels. "I have your pay, unless you're of a mind to leave without it," the innkeeper said, stooping to pick up a coin that fell. He froze, looking at Jared's image on the gold piece, and then rose slowly, looking from the coin to Tris and back again as if the coin might burn him.

"M'lord mage," the innkeeper croaked. "I mean no disrespect, but 'tis the Lady's truth that there is a powerful resemblance between you and the king."

"The minstrel called him 'my prince,' just now," Tabethe said, nervously edging toward Lars.

Resigned, Tris stood and spread his hands. "I didn't mean to deceive you," he said to the innkeeper, who looked pale with fear. Vahanian and Gabriel moved closer to him, and Kiara stood, her hand near her sword. "I wanted to spare you the burden of dangerous knowledge. You're correct. I'm Martris Drayke."

The innkeeper gasped and then elbowed his wife, who stood with her mouth open. "Curtsey, you fool," Lars whispered as he made an awkward bow. Tabethe, after a moment, found the presence of mind to attempt an equally unpracticed curtsey, and nearly lost her footing. Lara and Toby stared wide-eyed from near the wall.

"The rumors are true then!" Lars exclaimed, finding his voice. "By the Goddess! Prince Martris lives! Oh me, and what I've said, please, my prince, take no offense—"

Tris smiled at the innkeeper's flustered apology. "None taken. We're grateful for your shelter, both before, when we fled for our lives, and now, when we're still in danger. I don't wish to put your family at risk. If you'll keep the secret of our passing, we'll leave."

"On a night like this?" the innkeeper cried. "My prince, we're honored to have you under our roof. Oh my, what am I thinking? There's royalty in the inn, and we've got them in the kitchen!"

Tris burst out laughing. "Good sir," Tris said, "believe me when I tell you that yours are the best accommodations we've had in many a fortnight."

Lars brightened, blushing with pride. "Truly? We're honored, Your Highness. You're welcome to sleep in our own rooms, humble as they are, rather than here in the kitchen."

"We're quite comfortable here, near the fire, with some bedding if there's any to spare," Tris said. He was grateful for the man's offer, but preferred the quick exit of the back door. "But I beg of you, for your own sakes, tell no one that you've seen us."

Lars looked shrewdly at Tris and the others. For the first time, the innkeeper took in their swords and the manner of both Kiara and Vahanian, which clearly spoke of battle training. "I take your meaning. There can be but one reason you've returned, my prince. And if there's aught that we can do to help you, just ask. All we have is at your service." With that pledge, Lars knelt, and his family also.

"Please, rise," Tris said. "Tonight we're happier than you can know with a warm meal and a roaring fire. But now you know why I welcome your news and your rumors from the city—and why I'm anxious to hear what these minstrels have to tell us."

"We'll leave you to your business," said Lars, motioning to his family. "If you need aught, just call. No one will bother you in here. I'll stay in the greatroom myself, to make sure."

"Thank you," Tris said. "We're in your debt."

"The prince himself, in my inn!" Lars murmured as he turned toward the door. He was still talking to himself in amazement as he left the kitchen. Tris sat, bidding the others to do the same. Vahanian took up a post at the greatroom door, while Gabriel moved closer to the outer door.

"Can we trust him?" Kiara asked. She sat next to Tris as he motioned for the minstrels to gather round.

Tris looked toward the door through which Lars had gone. "We have no reason not to, and every reason to believe him. He's right—where would we go, in this weather, that would be safer?"

"You can trust Lars, my prince," said Helki. "If you want to know the truth of it, he's run something of a resistance out of this inn. It hasn't been safe for us to stay near the palace. Lars took us in— glad for the entertainment, no doubt, but watchful that when guards came, we could make ourselves scarce. Many times, Lars and his family have hidden people fleeing King Jared. Some of the palace staff, and not a few deserters from the army, have passed this way. They spread the word among themselves as to which are the safe houses, and they are spirited away, as if on a ghost carriage."

Helki looked at his companions, whose expressions still reflected their utter amazement at seeing Tris and the others. "By the Mother and Childe! It's good to see you well, my prince."

"What can you tell us about Shekerishet since we left?" Tris pressed.

"Nothing good, Your Highness." It was Macaria who spoke up. Tris suppressed a smile, knowing that the dark-haired musician caught Carroway's eye. She seemed to be completely unaware of Carroway's attention, even now, when the minstrel watched her with unabashed joy. "I don't know how far news travels, or what you've heard, but it's been terrible."

"Some of the bards have gone missing altogether," Macaria said. "Though whether dead or in hiding, I don't know. I've heard that Lady Eadoin is hiding some of the court musicians, the ones Jared particularly disliked. Eadoin's brother's family was killed for harboring fugitives. We managed to keep out of Jared's sights, but I've heard tell of minstrels who have been hanged for singing tales about King Bricen, or telling a story that raised Jared's ire. In the city, the king's guards are always prowling around, looking for someone to make an example of. They've beaten men in the street for telling jokes about the king, and dragged others out in the middle of the night for one 'crime' or another. No one ever sees the poor blokes again."

"How is it you're here?" Carroway asked, and Tris noted that Carroway never took his eyes off Macaria as he spoke. She didn't seem to notice.

"We left the city during the winter," Paiva said. "One step ahead of the guards. Since then, we've made what living we could singing for our keep in taverns, playing for our supper at the baker's and butcher's, and begging, if you want to know the truth of it." She sighed. "But there's been talk all Spring that something would be afoot at the Hawthorn Moon, and so we thought that with the crowds and all, we'd chance going back." Paiva grinned, and elbowed Carroway good-naturedly. "Looks like our pretty bird here has landed himself smack in the middle of a revolution!"

"You don't know the half of it!" Carroway said. "But if you're game, and you're tired of Jared on the throne, there's a part you could play."

"We're in," Helki said. "Anything to be rid of that bloody tyrant!"

The group huddled around the table. "While Tris and the others do what they need to do," Carroway said, "I thought that perhaps Carina and I—with your help—could stir up a little riot or two in the city. There's another friend of ours, a hedge witch named Alyzza, who's headed this way as well. What do you think—can we work up a mob?"

Macaria grinned wickedly. "Like that's a hard thing, with all the ale that'll be flowing?" The other bards laughed. "'Tis the Lady's truth—the only ones getting rich from Jared's rule are the barley growers and the rum smugglers, since any that haven't left the country drink to drown their sorrows."

"Out here in the country, the songs I get the most requests for are the ones they'll hang you for in the city—the stories of King Bricen's battles, and of

King Hotten's victory, and about the sorceress Bava K'aa," said Helki. "I dare say that might get a crowd going."

Paiva snorted. "I can do you one better than that. Remember the songs we heard up in Ghorbal, the ballads about the maidens taken by the king's men, and the empty village with its ghosts? Had the biggest men in the room dabbing their eyes as they swilled their ale. I wager we could write a few more like that, to remind them what's been stolen from them and get them in an ugly mood." The girl's lip curled into a devious smile. "I'll get to work on it."

Helki looked at Tris. "My prince, you've got to be careful. King Jared's sorcerer is a demon. He's grown strong on blood these many months, like a big red spider. Even if you can take Shekerishet, how will you stop Arontala?"

"He's a Summoner, he is," said Toby. Tris and the others looked up to see the innkeeper's son, who had been watching wide-eyed from near the fireplace. "Saw it myself, I did. Talked to the ghost that was busting up the place, and made him plain for all to see. Had a conversation with him, he did. Got robbed, poor bloke, and so I took word to his family the next day, to help him to his rest. He's a Summoner, by the Lady, he is!"

"Really?" Macaria asked.

"Do you remember the ballad we used to sing, about the ghosts of the Ruune Videya?" Carroway asked.

Macaria gasped. "There were wild stories that the forest is no longer haunted. You mean they're true? How?"

"You wouldn't really want to know," Vahanian said from his post near the door. "Trust me on that."

"Tris did it—we were there. And that was before Tris trained with the Sisterhood," Carroway added. "He can handle Arontala."

"My prince," Helki said. "We're honored to help with your return. We'll do as Carroway bids, and help you raise your diversion. I'd rather die fighting than spend the rest of my life running away."

Macaria and Paiva murmured their agreement.

"You may help to win the night," Tris said with a tired smile. "Carroway taught me a long time ago never to underestimate a bard!"

"I don't mean to spoil the reunion," Kiara said, nudging Tris, "but it'll be daylight soon, and I think we might ride better with a little rest."

"By your leave, my prince, we'll keep watch in the outer room," Helki offered. With Tris's nod, the minstrels took their leave.

"I'll go with them," Carroway said, standing. "We have a lot of catching up to do."

Tris looked at the others after the bards were gone. "Every time I hear us say aloud what we intend to do, it sounds too far-fetched to be possible. The damndest thing is, I haven't come up with a better idea."

"That's what makes it brilliant," Kiara said. She found a chair with a back and drew it up near the fireplace, where the banked embers made a warm red heap in the center. "No one else will think we're crazy enough to pull off a stunt like that."

"I really wish you wouldn't put it quite that way," Vahanian objected. He gladly gave up his post for

Gabriel to stand watch, and stretched out on one of the empty tables with his cloak over him. Carina and Tris found tables or benches of their own, and drew up close to the hearth.

"I've found that the Lady blesses the most unlikely of heroes," Gabriel observed from near the door. "Let's hope that Her blessing is on equally unlikely tactics."

Tris echoed that hope as he drifted off to sleep, resolutely determined to enjoy a last night of warmth and safety before they reached the outskirts of the palace city.

CHAPTER THIRTY-THREE

BY MID-MORNING, Tris and his friends left the Sparrow's Roost, with the innkeeper's pledge of secrecy and saddlebags full of wine and provisions. Helki and the minstrels promised to meet up with Carroway and Carina by the fourth bell on the night of the Hawthorn Moon in the Bristle Boar Inn, a favorite with local musicians. They set out, blending with the festival crowd, heading for Shekerishet. The rain was over, and the early summer days warmed considerably as the skies cleared.

To avoid being conspicuous, Tris and the others split up the party as they rode. Tris and Carroway rode together ahead of the others. Kiara and Carina rode behind. Kiara bound up her long hair and secured it beneath a cap. She wore a man's tunic and pants that hid her figure well and made it unremarkable for her to carry a sword. Vahanian rode rear guard, on alert for trouble. They stuck to the back roads as much as they could. There were more travelers on the road than they had seen in other parts of Margolan, but not the crush of people Tris had expected so near the city just before a major festival.

Trouble found them a day's ride outside the palace city. "Look there," Carroway noted under his breath as they rode, and Tris froze in his saddle. Six Margolan guardsmen rode toward them in the livery of the king, boisterously taking up more than their half of the road and crowding other travelers into the ditch. Tris struggled to relax as the guardsmen rode closer, dropping his head and turning his face to the side as the soldiers passed without a second glance.

"What have we here?" one of the guards said as they rode toward Carina and Kiara. Without turning, Tris and Carroway slowed their mounts to narrow the gap between them and the women. When neither of Tris's companions replied the guard captain drew closer, matching the women's pace.

"A pretty lady," another soldier said, side-stepping his horse to block Carina's path.

Tris steeled himself not to turn. He let his mount slow further so that he could catch every word. Out of the corner of his eye he could see that Carroway gripped his reins white-knuckled, anticipating a fight.

"I'm a healer," Carina returned haughtily. "I've been summoned by a merchant in the city and I must not delay. Please move aside."

"You've strange tastes in escorts, if you pick a beardless one like that," the third soldier said, still blocking the road.

"We've been on duty for a long time," the captain said, moving closer to Carina. "The company of a lovely lady would be *very* much appreciated."

"Move aside," Carina repeated, but the guards now blocked their way completely.

"That's no soldier with her," one said suspiciously. "They're both wenches."

The captain chuckled. "There's a clearing over there. Let's go." He drew his sword.

Kiara's draw was lightning quick, blocking the captain's sword. Jae, on his way back from hunting, descended with a shriek, raking his talons across the soldier's face. At the sound of drawn steel, Tris and Carroway wheeled their horses. Vahanian galloped in from the rear, standing in his stirrups, sword aloft.

"Ambush!" the captain cried, turning to deflect Tris's advance. Kiara battled the first soldier, and Vahanian drove at another hard enough to topple him from his horse as he struggled to parry. Carina pulled free her stave and went after Kiara's opponent from behind, beating at his head and shoulders. Carroway sank a throwing knife hilt deep into a guard's chest. Vahanian ran his opponent through and dispatched him with a slash across the throat.

Vahanian made short work of a fifth guard just as Kiara's attacker was thrown from his panicked mount, trampling the downed soldier in its hurry to escape. Tris's opponent bore down on him with single-minded focus, fighting for his life now that his companions had fallen. With a two-handed swing, Tris maneuvered past the soldier's parry, scoring a blow that cleaved through the soldier's neck. The last guard launched himself at Tris with a wild cry. Tris barely got his blade up in time to block the strike. Tris knocked the blade aside and swung into a clean Eastmark kick, sending the guard stumbling into the path of Vahanian's sword.

"Someone's bound to be by soon," Carroway hissed. "Let's get this mess cleaned up."

Kiara was already dragging a body into the thicket at the edge of the road. Tris sent Carina to watch the road for danger as he and the others dragged the remaining bodies out of sight.

"Not a bad kick," Vahanian commented as he wiped blood from his hands. "Not bad at all."

Winded and sweating, Tris calmed his nervous horse. "A little too much practice lately, but thanks."

Carina, shaken and pale, drove off the guardsmen's horses. Kiara, her expression grim, cleaned her sword and resheathed it. Carroway cut down a tree branch and began obscuring the blood on the road, masking the signs of struggle.

"Those bodies won't stay hidden long," Vahanian said, resting his hands on his hips.

"If we strip off the uniforms and take their purses, no one may think much of it," Carina said practically. "There're always bandits on the road when there's festival traffic."

Vahanian looked at her and grinned. "You're starting to think like a cutpurse. I like that in a woman."

Carina ignored the jibe and began pulling off the dead guards' livery. Kiara and Tris joined her as Vahanian and Carroway stood guard. Within a few minutes, nothing remained to identify the dead men as soldiers.

"That might buy us a little time," Carroway said. Carina stuffed the torn tunics into one of her saddlebags.

"It would be a shame to hang for killing a soldier when we came to kill a king," Vahanian said dryly. "Come on. Let's get out of here."

The group grew quiet as the day passed. They ran into no more problems as they neared the palace, doing their best to blend in among the crowds headed for the feast day. Tris's mood swung between anger and sadness as they rode. Under Bricen's rule, Margolan had been prosperous. Margolan boasted a large population of trades-people and merchants whose industry and income lifted them—if not up to noble standards of living—then well above the means of their counterparts in Isencroft, Trevath, and Nargi. Most of Margolan's farmers were freemen, taking pride in the small plots of lands and healthy herds they owned for themselves. Margolan had fewer sharecroppers and indentured servants than in either Trevath or Nargi, where such arrangements were often corrupt and indistinguishable from slavery. That meant that the debtors' prisons were relatively empty; those unfortunates who landed in jail could work their way free if they had the will and health to do so. Margolan's prosperity had also meant that its roads were generally safe from brigands and free of beggars. Bricen's disciplined troops had weeded out the highwaymen and cutpurses, while the acolytes of the Mother and Childe tended to the mendicants, taking in those who had nowhere else to go.

For as long as Tris could remember, the closer one got to Shekerishet, the more prosperous the surroundings had looked. The city was full of wealthy merchants and tradesmen who did a thriving business. Their homes and shops reflected their prosperity. The city had bustled with taverns, shops, and theaters, offering tempting diversions and trinkets for wealthy and poor alike.

All that had changed. As the roads grew more familiar, Tris grieved at the differences he saw. Once-thriving inns were empty. Broken windows went unmended. Farm fields stood abandoned, either burned or still in the remnants of the last season's crops, when they should have been plowed and well into new growth. Some villages were populated only by ghosts, old people, and cripples, those who could not or would not flee.

Beggars lined the roads. Even more disturbing were the reasons for their begging. Before, the beggars might have been old blind men or cagy urchins looking for a few coins. Now the beggars were men and women of every age, bearing the scars of war and violence. Children missing limbs, their faces marred by fire. Disheveled women with small children at their skirts, clutching their tattered shawls around them like the remnants of their dignity as they begged for food. War-crippled men whose eyes reflected horrors of which they could not speak, discarded by an army that took them by force, and then sent back to villages that no longer existed. Tris felt the beggars' eyes on them as they passed. While he knew that the ragged villagers did not recognize him for who he was, he felt the responsibility of the crown more heavily than before. Tris's gambit was the only hope these wretched souls had; he was well aware of how uncertain the chance of success remained.

The city, when they reached it, was even worse.

The palace city had been well known for its welcoming, easy feel. Travelers came from all over the Winter Kingdoms to experience its theaters, music gardens, and the taverns that sold Margolan's famous dark, rich ale. Trade flowed from all corners of the realm, with festivals and caravans stopping on the green outside the city's edge. Before the coup, the city had been filled with languages from every kingdom, from across the Northern Sea or the far-away realms of the Southern Kingdoms, below Trevath's borders. Acolytes and pilgrims came from throughout Margolan to make homage at the Childe's sacred grove and the great shrine to the Mother Aspect.

Now, the streets were sparsely populated. Although Tris and the others stayed away from the heart of the city, the outskirts were bad enough. Residents avoided eye contact, and seemed to skitter for shelter like bugs in bright light. Guards roamed the streets in groups of twos and threes, some with snarling dogs on chains. Those without dogs carried quarterstaffs, bouncing them against their hands with casual malice. In less than a year the city's vibrant spirit had disappeared, and the people on the streets looked hard-worn, dressed in muted colors as if they feared to draw attention to themselves. Shops were boarded up. "Traitor to the crown" was scrawled on the door to one pillaged shop.

In the green along the edge of town, where musicians once played and caravan tents used to flutter stood a huge gibbet. Ten fresh bodies still hung from their nooses, twisting in the summer breeze. Tris had to close his eyes, remembering the dark sending at the citadel. Hanging from posts along the green were other bodies, tarred and encased in a form-fitting wire cage to keep the vultures away. It was clear that in King Jared's Margolan, fear reigned with as strong a hand as the king.

ONLY A DAY remained before the Hawthorn Moon. Tris knew there would be no second chances. He brooded over strategy, considering every scenario. Kiara seemed to sense Tris's mood, riding alongside him in silence. She neither pressed him for conversation, nor avoided it when he sought her out as a respite from his own dark thoughts. She gave no hint to her own fears. Jae was restless, flying on ahead of them then doubling back, as if they could not travel quickly enough to suit the little gyregon. Carroway juggled obsessively any time they were not riding. Carina and Vahanian resumed their verbal sparring. Of them all, only Gabriel did not appear concerned.

"We shouldn't go further tonight," Gabriel announced. The roads had grown increasingly familiar. Tris recognized the rutted highway as the same route along which they had fled nearly a year ago.

"I can't wait to see today's accommodations," Carroway murmured under his breath.

"Our lodging is just around the corner," Gabriel said, nudging his horse onward. Gabriel was the first to clear the bend. When the others joined him, they reined in their horses to stare at the tumbledown building.

"It's the same bloody ghost inn we started at," Carroway said.

The burned-out remains of the Lamb's Head Inn hulked in the shadows. But unlike the night of their escape it now appeared to be no more than it was, the ruined shell of an old tavern, unfit for even beggars.

"My liege," a man's voice called in a hoarse whisper from the shadows of the ruins. From the shadows stepped Comar Hassad, the swordsman's ghost who had led them away from the city on the night of Jared's coup.

"Hello, old friend," Tris said, expending the small bit of power necessary to make the ghost visible to the others.

"We've been awaiting your return, my liege," Hassad's ghost said, bowing. "Much evil has been done."

"I know."

"Follow me," Hassad said, beckoning them to lead their horses to the back of the ruined inn. There, enough of a stable remained to both hide and shelter the horses. When the horses were tended, Hassad showed them to an opening in the inn's foundation that led down into the cellars. Tris longed in vain for a fire, but they ate a cold supper from the supply of dried meats and fruits, fresh cheese and wine that Lars had provided for their journey. Gabriel took his leave, returning a few candlemarks later with a satisfied smile, his pallor lessened.

"The spirits will watch over you," Hassad said. Other ghosts appeared from the mist to join him, standing silent and indistinct in the shadows. "The palace ghosts are still banished from Shekerishet," the slain soldier cautioned. "They've grown angry and impatient for vengeance. I don't know if even so strong a mage as yourself, my liege, can control their fury once Arontala's spell is broken."

Tris could feel the ghosts that swirled unseen around them. They were familiar, ghosts he had known since childhood, the ghosts of Shekerishet. This time the spirits did not come to him seeking intercession. These were the ghosts of his ancestors, of loyal family retainers, and of oath-bound guards who had died long ago in the line of duty. The ghosts came to him offering their support and condolences. If he was able to break the spell that banished the ghosts from the palace, Tris knew they would swarm back on their own accord to seek vengeance against Jared and Arontala. If so, they might help to turn the odds. Just knowing that the spirits supported his quest and pledged their fealty was enough to lift his mood from the fears and nightmares that had troubled his sleep.

"I'll stand guard," Gabriel said.

"I'll leave you now," Hassad said, his form growing less distinct. "The castle ghosts are watching over you. You'll be safe tonight." In the blink of an eye, the spirit was gone.

"Somehow, knowing that many ghosts are hovering over me just doesn't make me feel any better," Vahanian muttered as they picked their way through the littered cellar. Gabriel took up a post near the entrance, just beyond where the moonlight turned to shadow.

"How can it still be this cold in Margolan and it's nearly the Hawthorn Moon?" Carina muttered, wrapping her cloak around her. "I thought only Isencroft was cold this late in the year."

"Let's go over things again," Kiara suggested. "Having a plan makes me feel better." Tris conjured faint hand fire in the windowless basement, enough for them to see each other's faces.

Carroway leaned back against one of the thick foundation timbers and took a bite of his dried meat before he replied. "All right. Once we get some rest, Carina and I leave for the city, using the festival crowd for cover. I don't think we'll have any trouble finding help from the hedge witches. We'll meet up with Helki and the others, and see who they've recruited. That gives us most of the day to look for Alyzza and get the crowd going. We'll be in position before you head for Shekerishet."

"Once we're in the city, we raise as many diversions as we can," Carina chimed in. "If we do our job, the city garrison will be so busy they won't have time to worry about what's going on up at the castle."

"While we drop in on them from above." Tris double-checked the climbing ropes they had brought with them and Vahanian made a final inspection of their cuirasses. Kiara honed their weapons. Vahanian carefully counted the arrows for his crossbow, adjusted the bow's string, and assured himself that each arrow was sharp and straight.

"Let's hope they're not watching the moon when we scale the cliffs," Kiara added edgily.

"Gabriel and Jae can help with a diversion there," Tris replied. "Assuming Arontala doesn't sense me coming before we set foot inside the castle."

Kiara stopped what she was doing to rummage in her pack. She withdrew the spelled cloak and offered it to Tris.

"Take this," she said. "Maybe it will hide your magic just long enough to slip by Arontala."

When they were certain that their preparations were complete, they settled down to rest. Carroway stretched out on a board that gave him some protection from the damp dirt of the cellar floor. Vahanian offered to share a stone slab and his cloak with Carina. Kiara slipped close to Tris on a ruined door that kept them off the hard ground, nestling in his cloak while Jae slept at her feet.

Before long, Tris could hear the measured breathing that told him his companions were soundly asleep.

Gabriel left them at dawn for the deeper reaches of the cellar. When Tris was certain he would not wake Kiara he slipped away, covering her carefully with his cloak. He walked to the wall, where a chink in the foundation permitted the sun to send a weak shaft of light into the basement.

You have done well, Tris, a voice sounded in his mind. Tris recognized his grandmother's voice and wheeled. In the shadows of the cellar he could see the robed woman's outline, one hand upraised in greeting.

Grandmother, he said, falling to one knee. *I've missed you.*

The sorceress' face softened into a smile. *You've learned the lessons required of you.*

Will they be enough? Tris asked.

Bava K'aa's spirit gazed at him, her eyes both wise and stern. *No one can see that. It's for you to determine. Beware the orb. It is the doorway to the abyss. The spirit of the Obsidian King is strong and terrible. I hope that when the spirits are freed, if they survive, that Lemuel may be among them. Serae and Kait as well.*

She paused, her outline growing more and more diffuse as she made a sign of blessing. *The Lady keeps Her own.* And with that her form disappeared, but her words lingered in Tris's mind.

Still kneeling, Tris looked up at the rotting timbers overhead. "Lady Bright," he murmured, "I've sworn my sword to you to bring Jared and his mage to account. Take my life if you must, but let me free Margolan from this evil."

Nothing stirred, not even the rats that infested the cellar. Tris looked at his sleeping companions and felt his throat tighten. It would be a miracle of the Lady's own working if they all lived through this campaign. He had told no one, but the dreams of the dark sending had returned to him, making his sleep fitful. They would need the blessing of the Lady and more than a little luck to live to tell about their adventure.

Mid-morning, Carina and Carroway made ready to head into the city. Carroway checked the pouches at his belt one more time for his fireworks.

"It's time," Carroway said, managing a reckless grin. "Come on Carina, let's give them a performance to remember."

Carina hugged Kiara. Tris clapped Carroway on the shoulder, at a loss for what to say. In turn,

Vahanian bid him farewell and wished him the blessing of the Lady.

"Watch your back," Vahanian warned Carina as he kissed her goodbye. "Good luck."

Even in the dim light, Tris could see the healer blush. "The Lady's hand be on you as well," she murmured. She took Carroway's hand and made her way out of the cellar.

CHAPTER THIRTY-FOUR

CARROWAY AND CARINA made their way into the palace city, hidden by the crowds that came to celebrate the Hawthorn Moon. Above them on the cliffside, the castle Shekerishet loomed dark and watchful. But today the city's attention was not on the palace and its king, but on the revelry that marked the coming of the solstice.

The streets were a solid press of people, crowding to see curbside shows or buy sweetmeats from the vendors that hawked their wares along the thoroughfares. It was obvious that this year, the festival-goers planned to spend as little time in the city with its guards as possible. They arrived in droves late in the day just before the festival's start, and Carroway bet that the crowds would clear out very quickly once the festivities were over. It was a stark contrast to the nearly empty streets just days before. The smells of roasting meat and hearty ale wafted from the makeshift booths, and pilgrim and villager alike eagerly pressed around the carts. The crowd was in a festival mood, despite the guards who lingered at the edge of the town square. Whether the guards expected trouble or merely meant to make their presence felt Carroway did not know, but the feeling of being watched made him anxious for the night's work to begin.

Carroway and Carina made their way through the crowded streets, toward the small tavern where they had arranged to meet Macaria, Helki, and Paiva. Carina hoped that Carroway's friends had been able to recruit more minstrels to their cause. She relaxed, just slightly, when they passed an unfamiliar bard whose song she recognized. It was one of the new songs Carroway and his friends at the inn had been practicing, songs designed to spread dissent. Quickly, Carina glanced over her shoulder, but the guards were on the other side of the square, breaking up a fight between two drunks. Before the guards returned, the dissident bard vanished into the crowd.

"I know them!" Carroway whispered to Carina.

"The guards?"

Carroway shook his head. "The 'drunks.'" They're bards. I'll bet ten skrivven the fight was staged to distract the guards."

Carina smiled. "Sounds like the party is starting without us."

They rounded a corner and found a storyteller surrounded by a small crowd. Two guards lingered at the edge of the group, waiting for the storyteller to say something out of line. But before he reached the climax of his tale, a burst of flame and a puff of smoke started from a merchant's cart at the far end of the block. The two guards sprinted toward the disturbance, where a hunched old woman in a tattered robe was muttering and wringing her hands, talking to herself. The guards tried to extinguish the fire, which seemed to grow larger the more the old woman tried to help. Finally, the guards shooed the woman away. Meanwhile, the storyteller's tale had veered into a dramatic recounting of a peasant uprising, a bloody tale of a corrupt king brought to justice. By the time the guards put out the fire, the storyteller was gone.

"Look there," Carina said, pointing into the crowd at a short, robed figure that ducked around a corner and disappeared from view.

"What?" Carroway asked, peering over the crowd. "I don't see anything."

"Come on," Carina said, grabbing him by the wrist. They pushed their way through the crowd, past a trio of puppeteers and their bawdy show to follow the robed figure. It was the old woman who had been with the burning cart. They caught up half way down the street, and Carina broke into a broad smile.

"It *is* you!" she cried, as the stranger glanced up.

The cowl fell back to reveal Alyzza. The old hedge witch smiled a wide, broken-toothed grin and clasped Carina into a hearty embrace.

"By the Lady, I knew you'd come!" Alyzza exclaimed, greeting Carroway with equal heartiness. "I knew if you were still alive, you'd be in Margolan for the Hawthorn Moon." Her eyes narrowed. "Will the deed be done tonight?"

Carina nodded, glancing around them. "We're to make sure there's enough of a ruckus in the city that the guards are distracted," she whispered. "There's not much time."

Alyzza clapped in glee. "Oh that's fine with me!" the old hedge witch exclaimed. "I haven't raised a real fuss since before you were born. Just tell me what you need, and I'll keep them hopping." Once Carroway told Alyzza about the plot to enlist the minstrels' help, she motioned for Carina and Carroway to follow her, leading them through the feast day crowds toward the Bristle Boar Inn where Macaria and the others waited.

Helki was waiting for them at the bar. When they entered, he rose and walked toward a private room in the back. Without a word of greeting, Carroway and the others followed him, remaining silent until the minstrel closed the door behind them.

"Are you sure we're safe here?" Carina asked.

Helki nodded. "The innkeeper's daughter disappeared when she went up to the palace after the coup. She'd been seeing your friend Soterius. When she went looking for him, she was never heard from again." Helki's expression made clear his distaste. "Our innkeeper bears no love for the crown."

Macaria and Paiva greeted both Carroway and Carina with embraces, and Carroway was heartened to see a dozen other bards and musicians packed into the small room. "This isn't all of us, not by half," Paiva said. "We've been recruiting since we left you at the Sparrow's Roost. There must be five score of us, or more. We've been playing all over town for the last few days." She grinned wickedly.

"Saving our best songs for this evening, naturally. But Lady True! What a reaction there's been, even to the ditties we've sung so far—mark my words, the crowd is angry. With enough ale, they'll be spoiling for a fight!"

"Our innkeeper enlisted a few of his friends around town," Macaria said. "Especially the ones near the guards' posts. The later the night gets, the more they'll fill the glasses, without extra charge. By the Crone! We should have the town drunk and fighting by tenth bells." Macaria laughed as Carroway pulled her close and kissed her on the cheek in glee.

"So it's true what they've told us? Prince Martris is returned to win the throne?" asked one of the minstrels, a dark haired boy who held a fiddle in one hand. Carina looked from the boy to Carroway, and then to the other musicians crowded into the small room.

Carroway stood and nodded. "It's true," he said, all mirth gone. "It's going to be a hard fight. Tris is a Summoner now—maybe the strongest spirit mage since Bava K'aa. But Arontala is powerful, and he'll be drawing on the power of the Obsidian King. It's going to be a battle."

The boy met Carroway's eyes defiantly. "I'd rather die a free man than live like we have been, under Jared's rule. We can't go on like this. If there's a chance to be rid of Jared, then I'm in, and Istra damn the consequences!"

"Istra aside, there are still the guards to contend with. We've been pretty successful at creating diversions so that we can draw off the guards, but it doesn't always work. Kason lost a couple of teeth when the guards roughed him up for the song he sang about Bricen. He was lucky it wasn't worse."

Macaria gave a dangerous smile. "But I could feel how angry the crowd was when the guards broke them up. A little more ale, and I think we can turn this our way."

Carroway nodded. "Don't start anything unless you've got a clear exit. With luck, the crowd will figure out that there are more of them than there are of the soldiers, but the guards still have their clubs and dogs. Let's not get anyone hurt if we can help it."

"Except for the guards," Paiva supplied.

Carroway grinned. "Yeah. Except for the guards."

CHAPTER THIRTY-FIVE

AFTER CARROWAY AND Carina left their base-ment hiding place, the candlemarks passed at a crawl. Tris paced, too tense to rest. They waited out the remainder of the day until evening gave them cover to move. There was no way of knowing whether Carroway and Carina had worked their plan in safety, or whether they had been captured and the venture betrayed. Tris could see the same tension in his companions' faces, though none of them spoke their thoughts. Dusk on the night of the Hawthorn Moon final-ly approached, leaving only a few candlemarks until midnight. Tris checked his weapons again. Gabriel joined them at sundown.

"It's time," Gabriel said, stepping to the door as the ninth bells rang in the city below. The summer night was windless and unseasonably cool. High above, clouds obscured the moon.

Good, Tris thought. *The darker it is, the more likely we can drop in unnoticed.*

Hassad's ghost awaited them. "I can't take you the entire way, my liege, because of the banishing spell. But I can lead you to the best pathway up the mountain."

"I'll take them up the mountain," Gabriel said.

"I want Jared alive, to pay for what he's done," Tris said. "If any hand slays him, it should be mine."

Gabriel bowed his head in acknowledgment. "As you wish, my liege. You may find my... talents... useful in reaching your goal." Even in near darkness, the pallor of his face was a noticeable contrast. "I hunger."

They fell silent, making their way in the shadows at the edge of the roadway. Twice they dodged into the bushes to escape patrols, narrowly evading a confrontation. As the path began a steep incline up the mountain behind the palace, the roadway became less traveled and more difficult. At the road's end, still a candlemark's climb from the peak, Hassad stopped.

"I can't go further," the spirit said. "May the blessing of the Goddess be with you, my liege." He dropped to one knee in fealty.

Tris gestured for the ghost to rise. "You've served this kingdom faithfully. If tonight's workings don't release you, I'll return, by the grace of the Lady, and set your spirit to rest."

Hassad inclined his head in gratitude. "What I served in life I serve willingly in death. Go, and may the hand of the Lady be upon you."

Tris led the others up the rocky slope where no road marked their way. Gabriel picked out safe passage when the moonlight failed them, guiding the party to the peak. Finally they stood overlooking the palace city. Below them, partially carved from the mountain itself, was Shekerishet.

"Here's where it gets interesting," Tris murmured as they unpacked the climbing gear. In silence, Tris, Kiara, and Vahanian secured themselves into their sturdy harnesses and anchored their climbing ropes. Then, with a glance among the three companions and nods to indicate completion, Tris lowered himself over the edge and began to carefully make his way down the cliff face. Below them in the mews Tris could hear the cry of Kait's falcons. Jae circled in kinship, hissing to the captive birds of prey.

Gabriel signaled silently to them, descending to a shadowed place out of sight of the guards. They watched as a small noise attracted the attention of the two guards beneath them. The doomed soldiers approach Gabriel's hiding place. The only sound that traveled up to them was a gasp of astonishment. Moments later, Gabriel appeared from the shadows and signaled them to descend.

"You're one hell of a scout," Vahanian muttered to Gabriel as they reached the stone walkway and rapidly detached themselves from the harnesses.

Kiara moved quickly to the mews and gently set Jae down near the caged falcons. The gyregon hissed and the falcons responded with an answering cry. Carefully Kiara opened the cages and stood back as Jae flew into the air. Tris joined her. They each took up the gloves of the falconers that lay nearby, carefully removing each bird and its hood and launching the falcons into the air from their gloved forearms. The birds soared up to where Jae circled. Most fell in behind him. A few decided to challenge the newcomer, but the sparring was brief and decisive and the gyregon emerged dominant. Kiara and Tris removed the gloves, and Kiara smiled.

"I think we can be sure that the roof is secure," she murmured.

Gabriel stepped forward, beckoning for them to follow him. Even by moonlight, Tris noted that the *vayash moru*'s pallor had decreased, and his lips seemed more full and red.

"Come. The hunt is on," Gabriel said.

By THE NINTH bell on the day of the Hawthorn Moon, Carroway and Carina had made the rounds of the city, finding that word of the uprising had preceded them among the other minstrels, who had added ideas of their own.

Already, the mood of the revelers was beginning to shift. The minstrels' songs took on a harder edge, replacing the maudlin love songs with ballads of heroes who threw off tyrants' yokes, and the great warriors of Margolan's past. Groups of wandering actors played out their skits, but now the tales told of villagers defying corrupt soldiers and maidens rescued from defilement. Guards set their dogs on the crowd, but one of the cart vendors tossed his load of meat pies in the opposite direction, drawing off the snarling dogs, who ran like puppies to snatch up the fallen treats. Angered, the guards started to beat the vendor, but the crowd closed around them, and one man who was as broad as both guards together and a head taller than either of them hefted one of the guards in both hands and hurled him against a nearby wall. The other guard began to run, and the crowd pelted him with garbage as he fled.

By the tenth bell the crowd grew restless, then belligerent. Tales of hardship and oppression resonated within the audience. A dozen villagers climbed the bell tower and tore down the royal banner, setting it ablaze. Cries of outrage against the palace grew more strident.

"Now let's really get their attention," Carroway hissed. He headed toward the guardhouses just beyond the city gates, below the palace. A crowd milled there, mostly alesmen and whores tending to the needs of the guards. Positioning Carina and Alyzza for an easy escape, Carroway strolled among the crowd, ostentatiously juggling several flaming batons.

"You there, let's see you juggle!" called the captain at arms, leaning away from the strumpet beside him.

Carroway obligingly came closer, sending the fiery batons high into the night air. The soldiers gathered around, cheering and clapping. The whore withdrew a coin from her bodice and tossed it at Carroway's feet.

On the pretense of glancing at the coin, Carroway dropped one of his batons into the haystack nearest the guardhouse. The other two flaming batons went flying, one landing on the thatched roof of the outpost, the other landing so close to the drunken guardsman that he and his strumpet were obliged to jump out of its way.

"Stop him!" the captain cried.

"Now!" Carroway shouted. Alyzza flung a handful of pellets onto the ground between Carroway and his pursuers. The pellets exploded into puffs of colored smoke, startling the guards. With a touch of her own, Alyzza summoned a ball of mage fire, giving the smoke an eerie glow and setting the guards back a pace. It was enough of a diversion for Carroway and Carina to lose themselves in the crowd as the fire raged and the guards' attention turned to salvaging their post.

The flames were the signal the rowdy crowd needed. Soldiers tried in vain to keep back the revelers as the mob surged forward. Wielding whatever came to hand, whether broken boards or broom handles, the surly crowd pressed toward the soldiers. The captain waved his sword in vain. More shouts sounded a few streets over. In the distance, another guard house went up in flames.

One of the guards sent an arrow flying. It struck a man at the front of the mob, taking him through the heart. Like a spark to tinder, the crowd's rage ignited. A wave of rioters swept forward. There was the sound of glass shattering as men smashed wine bottles to use as weapons. The night smelled of sweat and ale and of burning straw. To the soldiers' horror, the angry revelers advanced with a howl and did not stop, even when more men fell to the archers' arrows.

Alyzza's hand moved, hidden by the press of bodies around them. The stable doors flew open and a loud noise sent the guards' horses stampeding out the back, fleeing in panic down the streets. She chuckled as her hand traced a sigel in the air. "I've fused the blades together in the armory," she called to Carina. "Let them try to use those!"

Rocks crashed through the windows of the guard house. One of the guards fell with a hunting knife protruding from his chest. The panicked soldiers rushed the crowd, brandishing swords. The mob advanced, beating back the soldiers with staves and walking sticks. Two men came running with the spoils from a looted blacksmith's forge. The rioters took up a cry as metal bars replaced walking sticks and horseshoes flew with deadly aim at the soldiers. Three more guardsmen fell to the ground as the crowd rushed forward, dragging their own dead and wounded out of the way.

The hapless guards, faced with several hundred drunken and increasingly well-armed festival goers, abandoned their burning post and fled. The crowd cheered and pelted the fleeing soldiers with rocks.

"I thought this was just supposed to be a diversion," Carina said as they watched the fire from afar.

"I think there's more loose tonight in the crowd that some ale," Carroway said. "Looks like we touched a raw nerve."

"Aye, but can you control what you've started?" Alyzza cackled as the flames grew higher.

CHAPTER THIRTY-SIX

CAREFULLY, TRIS, KIARA, Vahanian and Gabriel made their way into Shekerishet. Outside the tenth bell chimed, reminding Tris that within two candlemarks' time their quest must be successful or lose everything. Gabriel slipped ahead of them to clear their path and disappeared into the shadows. Tris felt for the pouch at his belt and took a wad of rope vine from it, holding the bit of dried leaves clenched in his teeth as a precaution against wormroot-tainted traps.

Tris stretched out his senses. The absence of castle ghosts left an uneasy void. In their place was a new, dark presence that chilled him.

Arontala, Tris thought, *and the orb*. The dark magic permeated the castle, although Tris could not pinpoint any single place as its locus. He headed for the throne room with every mortal and mageborn sense on high alert, his sword in hand, Kiara and Vahanian behind him.

Tris found his way through the corridors of Shekerishet easily, memories returning as he wound through the darkened hallways. Twice they pressed themselves into the shadows as a servant passed by. Around one corner, they found the still-warm bodies of half a dozen guards, the corpses unmarked except for the bloodless punctures on their necks. Three more guards happened upon them from the opposite direction. Vahanian's crossbow silenced one before he had time to realize he was under attack. Kiara made short work on the second, running him through. Tris swung into a clean Eastmark kick, sending his opponent sprawling, and finished the third with a single sword stroke. They did not bother to hide the bodies, but their pace increased. Tris hoped that Gabriel had made a clean sweep of the area in front of them.

Tris moved carefully, mindful of the traps he had encountered in his training at the citadel. *Surely Jared has protections in place*, Tris thought. *There are enough of his subjects who want to kill him.* Mortal guards could be easily removed by Gabriel without the sound of a scuffle. But the further into Shekerishet they got without springing any traps, the more concerned Tris became.

He's expecting me. He knows I'm coming for the orb. Like a spider with a web. All he has to do is wait.

"I don't like this," Vahanian muttered under his breath. "I don't trust anything that's this easy."

"Do you think we've been betrayed?" Kiara whispered.

Tris shook his head. "Jared doesn't need a spy to guess that we'd come for the Hawthorn Moon. Arontala probably thinks it's too far gone for us to turn it around. Jared figures he'll sit back and let Arontala do the fighting, and come in for his fun once we're beaten."

"It still means we're being set up," Vahanian said, his grip tight on his crossbow. "The question is—when does the trap spring?"

Just before they reached the throne room, Vahanian put up a hand for caution and moved ahead slowly, his attention drawn to a dark pile on the floor. He ventured ahead a step or two, and then waved for the others to follow. Four men in the livery of the king's personal guard lay dead in a heap.

"Gabriel's going to need a week to sleep this off." Vahanian shivered as he looked at the punctures in the dead men's throats.

A few more steps and the doors to the throne room stood before him. Tris paused, stretching out his senses once more. He felt the blood magic that wrapped itself around Shekerishet like a moist shroud, so strong that it seemed to come from everywhere at once. He focused his senses on Mageslayer, and felt the spelled blade thrum with power. The sword itself seemed to pulse, sensing their mission. Tris glanced at Kiara and Vahanian. They nodded, their weapons ready. Trap or not, the night's work would begin in earnest as soon as they found Jared.

Sword in hand, Tris pushed open the great doors. As his hand touched the door a light flared, pulling him into the room through an invisible curtain of power. Behind him, Kiara and Vahanian vanished.

As he crossed the threshold, Tris felt a gut-wrenching lurch. Mageslayer, so full of power a moment before, became dead steel in his hands, its magic gone. Fearing for the others, Tris looked behind him but the corridor was empty. And as he reached out to ward himself, he realized that in this room, his magic was suddenly out of reach.

"I HOPE TRIS has everything under control up there," Carroway breathed as they watched the crowd. The revelers tumbled out of the heart of the city, moving up the hill toward the palace itself. Rioters took up staves and bricks, shouting curses and threats as they backed the overwhelmed garrison toward the city gates.

The bells in the tower at the heart of the city tolled eleven.

"Tris is running out of time," Carina fretted, looking toward the dark shape on the cliffside. Lights burned within Shekerishet's many windows, but nothing hinted of unrest within the great, silent castle.

Carroway shared her worry. There was no middle ground. Come morning, Martris Drayke would be King of Margolan, or he and the others, if still alive, would surely hang.

"We've certainly kept the guards out of the way," Carroway observed as soldiers from the palace streamed toward the city gates and the fire at the garrison. At the approach of the soldiers, the mob drew back, and then surged forward again.

"Disperse!" the captain-at-arms cried. Behind him, a dozen soldiers armed with longbows took the field. "Disperse now, or risk the consequences!"

But the crowd, riled by the minstrels and made foolhardy by ale, pressed forward. A dozen men at the front fell to the flying shafts, and a roar went up from the mob in fury. Before the archers could ready their bows again, the crowd lurched toward them like an angry wave, trampling the guards.

Carroway lifted his head. "Do you hear something?"

"No. What—?"

The sound of hoof beats thundered louder. Alyzza's curse told Carroway that the old witch heard it as well. As they watched, fighters on horseback streamed toward the city gates at a gallop.

"WELCOME HOME," JARED Drayke said to Tris. "What took you so long? Planning to use grandmother's magic to just wink me out of existence?" Jared moved from his place near the tall window, and fingered an amulet beneath his robes, a null magic charm. "Your magic won't work on me, boy. I've a few protections in place, and a sorcerer in my employ. I've spent the better part of a year trying to find you, brother dear. And then I realized that in time, you'd come to me. All I had to do was wait.

"The doorway was spelled for you alone. As for your friends," Jared shrugged. "My mage has use of them. Tonight, we raise the Obsidian King."

"I have no intention of letting that happen," Tris said, advancing steadily, his sword ready. "I came to kill you—and destroy Arontala and his orb." *With or without magic*, he added silently.

"Still the dreamer. How pathetic." Jared took a step toward Tris. "In here, without your magic, you're just the same boy I've thrashed before. I could always whip your ass."

"I've seen what you've made of Margolan, how many people you've killed to get a throne that would have been yours in time."

"In time," Jared spat back. "In time. Only if Bricen couldn't find a way to have me removed from the succession. He threatened that, you know. He threatened to set me aside, and pass the crown to you. And if he'd known you'd become a mage he would have certainly done it. I couldn't allow that." Jared drew his sword. "And so I took matters into my own hands."

"You've destroyed Margolan. You have to be stopped."

"By you, little brother?" Jared gestured toward the window to the courtyard below. "Did you see my garden?" Tris was close enough to see what lay below; it made his stomach churn. Stout, sharpened pikes, braced in the ground, stood in an obscene tracing of the crest of House Margolan. Impaled on each pike was the corpse of a victim.

"It's full now, but there'll be a place for your friends, I guarantee," Jared said smoothly, madness glinting in his eyes. "Some—the strong ones—are able to remain aloft and keep from piercing anything vital for more than a day. Quite fascinating, the dance-like motions, up on their toes—"

"You're a demon, just like Arontala."

Jared shrugged. "Arontala understands the power in death. I see the beauty. And speaking of beauty... I suppose I should thank you for bringing back my bride."

Tris felt his blood rise. "She'll never be yours."

"Oh, I'll *take* what's mine. Maybe I'll leave your body in the room the first time—just to relish the victory." His voice hardened and his face contorted with anger. "And every time I have her, I intend to make her pay for loving you." A smile twisted the corner of his mouth. "Of course, the first brat she whelps will have to die. Can't have a question of paternity when the throne is at stake."

"You're not going to live that long."

Jared raised his sword. "If you want the throne of Margolan, then win it, if you can. The only way to claim your inheritance, boy, is to take it over my dead body." Jared lunged in attack, swinging his heavy sword for Tris's head.

Tris countered the powerful blow, though it nearly tore Mageslayer from his grasp. Jared scythed a dagger dangerously close with his left hand as Tris parried two-handed, beating back Jared's advance. The clang of steel echoed in the throne room as the brothers circled, their swords glinting in the torchlight. Jared's blows fell with the wild strength of madness. A fierce press drove Tris toward the open fireplace. The heels of his boots crunched on the burning embers and he felt the heat at his back.

Tris held Jared off, struggling to remember every trick Vahanian had taught him. Jared let up just for an instant and Tris dove, rolling, with a wicked slash at Jared's heel that scored a deep cut and barely missed hamstringing the king. Jared howled in rage and dove after Tris, delivering a pounding set of strikes that Tris was hard-matched to counter.

"You've been practicing, little brother."

Tris regained his feet and launched the offensive, anger fueling his strength. He delivered great, hacking blows that drove Jared back toward the open window.

The point of Jared's dagger connected with Tris's forearm, slashing deep and giving Jared the opening he needed to turn the attack. This time it was Jared who delivered a sequence of sword blows that forced Tris against the wall by the window, breathless. The stench from the bodies beneath made the night air sickly sweet. Tris felt familiar warmth radiating from the gash on his arm; Jared's blade was tainted with wormroot. He clenched his teeth on the rope vine. While Jared's null charms had already put his power temporarily beyond reach, the wormroot threatened to slow his reactions, something he could not afford. Whiskey had never blunted Jared's skill with a sword; Tris knew from bitter experience that Jared was more vicious drunk than sober.

"You've had an apt teacher," Jared taunted. "Your mercenary friend? No matter. You've shown far more potential than I ever dreamed—challenging the throne, raising an army against me, bedding my bride-to-be."

"I have no desire to kill you," Jared assured him, driving the point of his sword closer, so that Tris pressed against the cold stone of the wall, "at least, not yet. Tonight, the Obsidian King returns to Margolan. He'll need a body to inhabit. Arontala will be that vessel, one with powers already in place. You can be the final meal for the Obsidian King's spirit before he returns in all his power. Perhaps he'll let some bit of you remain to witness the grand event."

Tris worked his fingers up inside of his sleeve for the dagger concealed in a sheath above his wrist. It fell into his palm, and he flicked his hand just as Jared shifted. The dagger embedded itself in Jared's shoulder, not his chest as Tris intended. Jared roared with pain and anger, slashing at Tris with all his might. Tris managed to deflect his wild blows—barely—but the force of one strike tore Mageslayer from his grip and shattered Jared's sword. Tris felt the full effect of the wormroot hit him as the blade skittered out of reach to lie beneath the window. Jared yanked the knife from his shoulder and threw it to the ground. His eyes burned with pain and madness, heedless of the blood that stained his tunic.

Tris dodged as Jared dove for him, upending a table to put distance between them. Jared seized a poker from the fire and swung it wildly, keeping himself between Tris and the fallen sword. Tris looked about for anything he could use as a weapon. He grabbed a pitcher of water from the table and hurled it at Jared's head as Jared vaulted over the table. Tris tried to duck out of the way of the poker, but its glowing tip seared into his left shoulder. He cried out and dove under Jared's swing with a vicious kick to Jared's groin. His foot connected, and Jared howled with pain and rage.

Tris reached the hearth first, grabbing a bucket of ashes from beside the fireplace. He threw the hot ash at Jared as his brother headed toward him at a dead run. Jared narrowly missed the heavy bucket, but the ashes formed a smothering cloud. Jared cried out, throwing his arms up to shield himself.

Tris used the diversion to run for his sword, but something hard clipped him on the side of the head and he fell, blood starting from his temple. A candlestick clattered to the ground beside him. Blinded by the blood that flowed from the gash on his brow, Tris struggled to his feet. Barehanded, Jared dove for Tris and tackled him, landing on Tris's back. Tris felt ribs crack and gritted his teeth as the world around him swam red with pain. Jared, taller and heavier, had the advantage hand-to-hand. Tris gasped as Jared's dagger plunged into his side just below the edge of his cuirass. Jared shifted and a cord jerked around Tris's throat, the belt of Jared's robe. Tris struggled for breath as it tightened.

"Speak, Lord of the Dead," Jared taunted. "Where are your spirits to save you? Where are your mighty spells?" Tris fought for air, trying to gain enough leverage to buck Jared from his back. Jared only laughed, the same cold laugh Tris knew too well from the beatings of his childhood.

"This is too easy," Jared said. "I can't see your face. I want to watch you die, and remember just how you looked when the last breath slipped beyond your grasp."

Keeping the noose taut Jared dragged Tris to his feet, pulling him up against the wall beside the gris-ly courtyard garden. He closed his hand around Tris's throat. Tris could smell the whiskey on Jared's breath as his brother leaned closer, his dark hair framing his face and his eyes alight with triumph. Jared tightened his grip. "You may see the spirits of the dead," he whispered. "But I can see the soul leave the body. It's in the eyes."

As the world around him began to darken, Tris brought his hand up sharply, wrenching at the amulet around Jared's neck. It burned his hand like fire, but he hung on and the strap snapped. Tris hurled the amulet away, feeling the magic that the null amulet had pushed out of reach grow just a bit closer. Jared howled with anger and twisted his wrist sharply, tightening the cord around Tris's neck.

"You think that's the only null charm in this room, boy?" Jared snarled. "I've got more protection than that!"

Tris's vision blurred and pinpricks of light danced in his sight. Jared slammed him against the wall just to the side of the window, and Tris felt something against his boot. Mageslayer, he realized as he struggled to remain conscious. A tendril of power was almost within his grasp. He shifted his boot onto Mageslayer's blade, and felt a tingle of power, faint but present. Tris gasped for air, focusing on Mageslayer. *Protect!*

A burst of fire glowed around him, a blue aura that sapped the small amount of magic he could reach. It crackled around Jared like lightning, throwing him clear with a jolt.

It was all the opening Tris needed. The heel of his boot swung up and connected hard with Jared's chest. The force of the blow took Tris to the floor, still gasping for air. Jared staggered backward, and the low sill of the open window caught him below the knees. Flailing, Jared fell from the window with the full force of the kick, and Tris grimaced as he heard the sickening crunch of Jared's body landing atop his sharpened pikes. He pulled himself to his feet and looked down. Jared's body, impaled by three of the spikes, contorted and bucked as he slipped lower with the weight of his fall. But the

spike that took Jared through the back ended his
struggles. As Tris watched he saw Jared's spirit
writhe free of his broken body, flickering a sullied
light. Tris felt the Formless One's approach even
before the dark presence appeared, so close this
time that Tris threw up an arm reflexively to shield
his face, his soul shrinking back within him in
instinctive fear.

From everywhere at once a cloud descended on
Jared Drayke, as if the shadows themselves were
fluid. From within the whirlwind Jared's spirit gave
one wrenching scream of terror and pain. Then, as
quickly as it came, the shadows were gone. And
with them, Jared's soul.

Tris slumped against the throne room wall and
tore the cord from his neck. *I've got to find Kiara
and Jonmarc—and Arontala*, he thought, staggering toward where Mageslayer lay on the floor. He
fought the urge to pass out, weakened by both the
poison and the pain of the wound in his side. He
wiped the blood from his face with his torn sleeve.
His left arm ached where the poker had burned
him, a deep burn that made it agonizing for him to
move his arm or clench his fist. With Jared's charm
gone, Tris could sense more of his magic returning,
slipping in and out of his grasp as he struggled
against the wormroot that coursed through his
veins. He picked up Mageslayer and felt its power
buoy him, lessening the poison's effect. He found
that he could control his magic—just barely.

Outside the throne room, Tris felt the magic more
strongly, a clue that Jared's charm had not been the
only power-dampening talisman in that chamber.
Using every trick he had learned from the

Sisterhood, Tris fought to lessen the wormroot's effect. He let Mageslayer's power strengthen him, hoping that the sword's protections might also stay the damage from his wounds. Tris felt at the edge of his cuirass, where his tunic was sticky with his own blood. The odds, never favorable, appeared to be getting worse.

CHAPTER THIRTY-SEVEN

A T THE ENTRANCE to the throne room Vahanian
and Kiara hung back a pace, their weapons
ready, as Tris approached the heavy double doors.

Kiara's sword was ready in her hand. Vahanian
notched a quarrel into his crossbow. Tris touched
the doors, and the world around them seemed to
turn inside out. In a heartbeat, Tris and the throne
room were gone and Vahanian was falling through
total darkness, into a hole so deep it had no bottom. Somewhere in the darkness, he heard Kiara
cry out. Then, just as quickly as it began, the
wrenching shift was over. Vahanian found himself
tumbled out onto a hard stone floor, his crossbow
still notched and ready in his hand. An instant later,
Kiara appeared from nowhere beside him. A sense
of foreboding filled Vahanian as he took in the
room around them—a room that could be nothing
other than a wizard's study.

Tapestries covered the walls. Thick candles and torches illuminated the room. One wall was lined with books from floor to ceiling. Scattered over tables and on shelves were a hodgepodge of vials and bowls, stoppered bottles, and unfamiliar tools. Over the mantle, above a darkened fireplace, a nearly life-sized portrait of Jared Drayke glared down with a haughty disdain. As dark as Tris was fair, Jared Drayke still bore a striking likeness to his younger brother. They shared the same high cheekbones, fine nose, and wild mane of hair, though Jared's hair fell in a dark cloud around his face, making the cruel turn to his lips even more pronounced.

Vahanian and Kiara climbed to their feet, weapons ready. At the far side of the large room, laughing at their folly, stood a dark-haired man in the red robes of a Fire Clan mage. Beside him, on a pedestal worthy of the Goddess, was a large crystal orb that pulsed like a living heart.

Moving on instinct, Vahanian leveled his crossbow and sent its arrow flying. With a muttered word, Arontala plucked the quarrel from midair. The mage gave a flick of his wrist; unseen hands slammed Vahanian across the room and against the stone wall, pinning him above the floor. Vahanian cried out as the bones in his right wrist snapped, forcing him to drop the bow. With a sound of dry sticks cracking, his right arm and right leg broke as well. Satisfied Arontala released him. Vahanian fell to the floor, gasping in pain.

Kiara lunged toward the mage with an oath, her heavy sword wielded in both hands. Clucking disdainfully, Arontala gestured and Kiara's sword flew from her grasp. Her spelled dagger fell from her belt, clattering to the floor.

"You've saved me the effort of hunting you down," Arontala greeted them. He looked at Kiara and smiled coldly. "I told Jared we'd find you, in time."

"Go to the demon."

"My dear," he replied with a smile that revealed his sharp eye teeth, "I *am* the demon." He gestured once more, and Kiara struggled against a force that pushed her to her knees. "I think a proper attitude is the place to start."

"Leave her alone," Vahanian growled, struggling to reach his bow where it lay below the large mullioned window.

Arontala twitched his finger, and the crossbow slid just out of reach. "Ah," he said, glancing over his shoulder. "My tomb robber—and my Eastmark captain. Once again, you have the very bad luck to cross my path."

"Go screw the Goddess."

Arontala turned back to the orb. "You're about to witness history. Tonight, the Obsidian King returns!"

"He'll destroy everything in the Winter Kingdoms," Vahanian said, desperate to stall for time. Their plan had gone horribly awry. Without Tris, his fate—and Kiara's—appeared sealed.

Arontala shrugged. "I think not. But if so, the kingdoms will be ours to remake as we desire."

"Tris isn't going to let that happen," Kiara said, struggling against the mage force to hold her head up defiantly.

A mirthless smile twisted Arontala's lips. "Don't be too quick to trust in your champion," he said, turning his icy gaze back to Kiara. "He's likely dead already—or will be, soon."

"I'm going to enjoy your education," Arontala said, taking a step toward Kiara. "You have much to answer for. We've heard about your little... *escapade* on the border. And it's no secret that you've aligned yourself with the traitor," he reached out to stroke her cheek, "in more ways than one."

Kiara spat and the mage grabbed her chin roughly, forcing her eyes to meet his. "By ancient law, a royal betrothal is as binding as wedding vows," he said in a low, cold voice. "Treason and adultery are both punishable by death. But there is an alternative." He jerked her closer to the orb.

"Before he can emerge, the Obsidian King must feed," Arontala said, his fingers brushing against the orb that was only inches from Kiara's face. "I've sent many spirits into the orb for him to draw upon, until they're too spent to be of use. Your will, your spirit, and that arrogant pride will do quite nicely. Oh, he'll leave a remnant, enough that Jared can sire his brats by you, enough to remember what you once were. Enough to suffer for the rest of your natural life. And perhaps, I shall extend that life forever so that you can ponder your loss for eternity."

Arontala seized Kiara by the hair, forcing her to stare into the orb. She shut her eyes, and the mage muttered words in a language that sounded like wind against sand. Against her will, Kiara's eyes slowly opened, unable to avoid the orb's glow. "Enter the abyss," Arontala said, as the miasma within the orb swirled and brightened. "The time has come to feed the master."

* * *

"THEY'RE IN THE king's livery," Carroway observed tersely. Hundreds of horsemen were now at the gates, forcing their way through into the crowd. The insurrectionists stood their ground.

"Stop them before they escape!" shouted the beleaguered garrison commander. "We've got an uprising!"

The captain of the mounted troops lifted his helm and archers leveled their weapons, their aim on the soot-streaked garrison instead of the panicked mob. "There's an uprising all right," Ban Soterius said. "We ride in the name of Martris Drayke of Margolan. Surrender, and we'll guarantee your safety. Otherwise, we're prepared to fight you to the last man." Beside him, Mikhail lowered his hood and drew back his lips to show his eye teeth, making it plain just what a fight that would be.

A cheer went up from the crowd. Carroway swept Carina up in his arms, dancing in a little circle and planting a kiss on her forehead. The garrison commander, his provisions and guardhouses in flames, looked from the drunken crowd to the horsemen, and then to his weary command. With an oath, he gestured for surrender. Soterius's soldiers rushed forward to secure their prisoners.

Carroway grabbed Carina's hand and began to fight his way through the unruly crowd, intent on reaching Soterius.

"Ban!" he shouted above the din. "Ban, Mikhail—over here!"

Soterius began to search the crowd. At the sight of them, he swung down from his horse and ran to greet them, clapping them both into a hearty embrace. Mikhail joined them, grinning broadly.

When Alyzza reached them, the old hedge witch looked approvingly at Soterius.

"Well, well," she said. "So this is what you are. Tent rigger indeed. You wear that armor as if it were made for you."

"Stolen, actually," Soterius said with a lopsided smile. "Stole the whole lot—horses, weapons, soldiers, and livery. Learned it from Jonmarc. Nice touch, don't you think?"

"I gather you found some discontented troops?" Carroway asked. He, Carina, and Soterius stood arm in arm, watching Soterius's soldiers secure the last of the garrison prisoners.

"More than I imagined," Soterius said. "I'll tell you all about it later." He glanced toward Shekerishet. "Tris is up there?"

"With Jonmarc and Kiara," Carina said. "And Gabriel."

"Where now?" Carroway asked as Soterius swung back up on his mount.

"To Shekerishet," Soterius replied, reining in his horse. "Between the soldiers and the mob, we should give the palace guard something to think about."

"To Shekerishet!" The mob took up the cry. The garrison commander looked on haplessly. Soterius's horsemen urged their mounts forward, through the boisterous crowd that cheered their passing and closed ranks behind them. Up the hill toward the palace the mob followed, torches aloft.

At the palace gates the soldiers stopped. Behind them, the mob came to a halt.

"Open the gates!" Soterius shouted, the banner of the Royal House of Margolan fluttering above him in the breeze. "We come in the name of Prince Martris, to overthrow the tyrant!"

To their amazement, the gates swung open. Soldiers and servants poured out, waving white cloths in makeshift flags of surrender. The palace soldiers threw down their arms, and the fear-stricken servants surged toward the mob.

"Save us!" they cried, yielding willingly.

"There's demons loose in there!" one man cried, white-faced in panic. "Naught but the Dark Lady can save you if you go there."

"At least we know Gabriel's been hard at work," Carroway observed dryly. Carina looked around for Alyzza, but the hearth witch had disappeared into the crowd.

"Let's take the castle, men!" Soterius shouted, gesturing forward with his sword. "Prince Martris is in there. Are we with him?"

A resounding chorus of "aye" echoed from the stone walls of the bailey. The crowd surged forward in a cloud of torch smoke, smelling of sweat and horses and ale. The rearguard attempted to quiet the mob and set them to work securing the out-buildings and the outer bailey, leaving the true night's work for the trained soldiers. Some soldiers remained behind to keep the mob under control, while the others began to infiltrate the palace.

"You're safest here," Soterius said, turning back to Carina and Carroway. He held up a hand to still Carina's ready protest. "I know Kiara and Jonmarc are in there, and that both you and Carroway have seen more battles that many a seasoned fighter. But if it's a trick, if Jared and Arontala are waiting for us…" He paused, looking toward the upper floors of the castle cautiously and shook his head. "I'd rather know you two were down here, to lead the last charge."

Carina looked as if she intended to argue with him, but then relented. "All right," she conceded. "Just warn your bow-happy archers that the *vayash moru* are on our side, huh?"

Outside, the city bells began to toll midnight.

Carina and Carroway exchanged worried glances. "Time's up," she whispered. "We've either won or lost... everything."

CHAPTER THIRTY-EIGHT

WITH A BURST of magic to smash the binding spells, Tris slammed open the doors to Arontala's workroom.

"Turn them loose."

Arontala only turned a fraction, as if the intrusion did not merit his interest. Gabriel slipped into the workroom behind Tris.

"I've been waiting for you to join us." Arontala jerked Kiara's head up. "You're just in time. My offering will be given to the Master for one last meal before his reemergence. It's over," he said triumphantly. "We've won."

Tris advanced on the mage, his sword held ready, his eyes only on Arontala. "By the Lady, I won't let you do this." The orb was between Tris and Arontala, with Kiara to one side and Vahanian on the other, against the wall. Tris had no clear shot. Anything he did stood a good chance of hitting the orb or one of his friends, and the wormroot made him doubt the precision of his aim.

"The Lady has nothing to do with this," Arontala laughed. "I am the supreme power in Margolan. My will controls its destiny."

Tris searched with his mage sense. Arontala was well shielded, and Tris knew his own strength was fading quickly. He searched for a weapon, anything he could use to turn an advantage, and he felt a glimmer of power radiating from a wax tablet on Arontala's worktable. The tablet was on a stand, covered with a glass dome. Carved into its surface were runes and glyphs traced in fire. Tris stretched out his power and knew the tablet for what it was— the anchor of Arontala's spell to banish the ghosts of Shekerishet. Never taking his eyes off Arontala, Tris sent a burst of power toward the tablet, shattering the glass and igniting the wax. The tablet exploded into flame.

Arontala cursed and sent a streak of red fire sizzling in Tris's direction. Tris hurled himself out of the way before the red fire struck. The temperature in the room suddenly plummeted, cold enough for him to see his breath. With a gust so powerful that it slammed the window open, the banished ghosts of Shekerishet streamed home, released from Arontala's spell. The windows shattered, sending shards of glass flying against the stone walls. In the fireplace, the flames guttered and danced crazily as the freezing wind swept through the room.

ANGRY AT THEIR banishment, the exiled ghosts of Shekerishet streamed back into the room in a torrent, thick as the spirits in the Ruune Videya forest.

Tris struggled to his feet, trying to hold onto his control as the spirits swept over him and through him.

A... ron... ta... la! the spirits howled, knowing the one who banished them from their home. Tris knew that Kiara and the others could see the spirits; Arontala's face twisted in a hateful grimace. The ghosts swirled around the red-robed mage in a wild vortex.

Tris seized the chance while Arontala was distracted and drew on Mageslayer's power. As he had done in the citadel when he fought Alaine, Tris sought the soul within the dark mage, using all of his power to capture and extinguish that spark. But where Alaine had been mortal, Arontala's undead soul had no blue life thread. On the Plains of Spirit, Tris could feel the dark wizard's soul as he reached for it. But within the undead body, animated by the Dark Gift, the soul was shielded by powerful magic. He stretched out, sure that he could grasp the fleeting spark, and felt a wave of cold raw power throw him back, physically and psychically. Tris slammed against the wall, his head reeling, his senses screaming from the assault.

Arontala's shielding glowed so brightly that Tris's eyes hurt to look at the mage. The angry ghosts threw themselves against Arontala's shields to no avail. Arontala's lips worked, casting a spell that wrote itself in fiery letters on the rock of the castle wall.

Tris could sense the power of the banishment spell; he sent his waning power to counter it. As the spirits howled around them the letters of fire wavered, etching into the ancient stones, burning without smoke or ash. With a terrible smile, Arontala met Tris's eyes. Tris knew that Arontala was gauging how much more he could take.

Arontala gestured and the orb flared with a red light that enveloped Kiara. She arched backward and screamed.

With Arontala's attention focused on the ghosts and the orb, Vahanian's left hand slipped to the knives on his belt. He palmed them, and in quick succession sent three daggers flying toward Arontala. Arontala's attention wavered just for an instant as he struck down the daggers, buying Tris a slim opening.

Blue fire streaked from Tris's left hand to intercept the red glow of Arontala's spell. Tris's aim wavered with the wormroot; instead of striking Arontala, his mage fire struck the growing aura of the orb. The orb pulsed once, almost too bright to behold. Tris had scarcely enough time to dive between the orb and Kiara. He flung up his battered shielding to protect them both as the orb flared like a crimson sun and with a roar, exploded into a thousand scarlet fragments.

Gabriel shielded Vahanian from the explosion that seemed to rock the foundation of Shekerishet itself. Tris held on to Mageslayer, fighting the wormroot in his blood to hold his shielding over himself and Kiara. The blast took him off his feet, and the psychic recoil almost blacked him out. Fresh blood started from beneath his cuirass, and Tris's broken ribs made it difficult for him to breathe as he dragged himself to his feet. Kiara, suddenly released from Arontala's control, slumped to the floor.

Tris felt his shields strain dangerously beneath the waves of power that surged from the shattered orb. Old, raw power washed over him, tainted by Arontala's blood magic. Tris could feel the press of spirits rushing toward freedom—Arontala's victims and the Obsidian King himself—joining the angry palace ghosts that swirled around them.

Arontala cried out. Closer to the orb, he staggered from the blast. The fire of the explosion drove Arontala backward. As he redirected his power to contain the spirits of the orb, his shielding wavered. Tris seized the advantage, striking with Mageslayer.

The blade thrummed with power as it hit Arontala's shielding. Tris hung on with all his strength, gasping as his broken ribs protested. Arontala screamed as the blade reached him, blasting his power against Tris's shields. Tris staggered, his strength fading from the wormroot and the warm rush of blood that oozed from his side.

Instinctively, Tris brought his full power to bear on the sword, drawing on the wavering blue life thread within him, holding on as the pommel of the sword became searingly hot. Suddenly the blade broke free. Tris poured all of his will and strength and magic into the sword's downward motion, cleaving Arontala from shoulder to hip through the heart.

An inhuman shriek tore from Arontala's throat. The mage's body burst into flame. Mageslayer began to melt and Tris dropped the pommel, his hands burned and red. The fire was gone as quickly as it came, leaving a cindered corpse and blackened, twisted sword. Bells began to toll the midnight hour. One... two... three...

Hundreds of shadows swirled in a whirlwind around Arontala's corpse. Spectral visages gathered in the darkness around Arontala's spirit open-mouthed and angry, their gaping eyes and toothy jaws eager for vengeance.

This time the Formless One came as a vortex, a maelstrom that plunged down into infinity beneath Arontala's charred body. Tris felt the pull of its winds and heard its roar. A gust of power raged from the heart of the abyss, seizing Arontala's soul in its inexorable grasp and drawing it into the darkness. The last thing Tris glimpsed was the abyss, folding in upon itself. Then it snapped shut and disappeared into thin air.

Tris struggled to stay conscious. He dropped to his knees, his shielding wavering without Mageslayer's power. He saw the spirits stream from the shattered globe, swirling thickly as heavy fog descended around him. The spirits washed over him, grateful for release, brushing against his mind. By Vahanian's gasp, Tris knew that the spirits were visible beyond his mage sight. Kiara caught her breath sharply as the Orb lost its hold on her and her own shields snapped into place.

From the still-glowing shards of the Orb came a spirit of red flame so bright Tris had to shield his eyes and dampen his mage sight. The Obsidian King rose from the splintered glass. Tris could sense its triumph in release, its anger at being denied its chosen vehicle, its desperation to find a host. He knew that the spirit must have a mage's body to inhabit or die. Tris remembered the vision of the dark sending, of what it would mean should he be taken. He sent all his waning power into his wardings, resolved not to permit that vision to come to pass.

The Obsidian King's power slammed against Tris's shielding. It was a bet, Tris knew, as to which of them was the closest to death. Tris threw all of his power into his shields, resolved to die rather than be possessed. He drew power from the blue glow of his own life thread, though it flickered dangerously; he knew that the Obsidian King was weakening fast. Tris could feel the Obsidian King's panic.

Just when Tris thought that his opponent was at the breaking point, the Obsidian King streaked toward Kiara. Weakened from her ordeal within the Orb, Kiara's shields buckled and dissolved. Tris could hear her soul cry out as the invader forced himself into her mind.

"I... am... back!" a voice rasped from Kiara's body, a mixture of wonder and hideous satisfaction molding her features into a visage not quite her own. Four... five... six... The bells continued their mournful toll, announcing that all had been lost.

Tris staggered as he summoned his power for a final salvo. The struggle with Arontala had drained him badly. Without Mageslayer, the wormroot's poison went unabated. In moments his power would be beyond his control. Blood loss made him lightheaded. He knew that the blue thread of his own life energy was dimming. He looked at Kiara, her face twisted by the spirit that possessed her body, her eyes desperate, and he remembered the torment Alaine and Lemuel endured when their bodies had been seized against their will. The vision of his own possible fate foretold by the dark sending, of a blank-eyed and crippled shell twisted to the will of the Obsidian King, made up his mind. He knew that there was only one way to free Kiara.

You must do what I could not, because you have what I did not.

Bava K'aa's words rang in Tris's mind and he dove toward Kiara, snatching up her fallen spelled dagger. The spell to separate a spirit from the body from the hidden journal of the Obsidian King was clear in his mind. Tris murmured the spell of separation as he hurtled forward, knowing that he could not—must not—think about what he had to do. Tris felt Kiara's soul wrench free from her body and he sheltered it within himself, plaiting her life thread with his own. Weakened as they both were, he could not sustain them both long. Tris listened, heartsick, to the toll of the bells. Seven... eight... nine...

"Forgive me," he whispered as he turned the knife in his hand, and as tears streaked down his face, he sank the blade deep into Kiara's chest.

Dimly, he heard Vahanian cry out and Gabriel gasp. Tris threw all of his remaining power into his shields, holding on to the blade as Kiara's blood soaked his hand and her body sagged against him. It was her scream that pierced the night, as her body convulsed in his arms. The spelled blade, wielded by a mage against both a mage's body and a mage's spirit, struck at the only soul remaining within—the soul of the Obsidian King. In the Plains of Spirit, Tris heard the death scream of the Obsidian King as the dagger rent the soul. Tris felt the ancient life force sunder, saw the dying soul tear free from Kiara's open mouth as her head fell back.

In one last burst of magic, the Obsidian King enveloped them in flames. Tris flung his shields around himself and Kiara, his power and life force strained to the breaking point. An acrid stench rose as the stone floor blackened in a circle around his shields. Gabriel, still shielding Vahanian, cried out as the flare burned his cloak. Then the remnants of the Obsidian King's soul dimmed and went dark, destroyed beyond even the vengeance of the Formless One. Tris sank to his knees, cradling Kiara's body.

Tris sagged forward, too drained to move. Sure he was dying, Tris heard a voice in his mind, close by, as if someone leaned down to his ear. *I will sustain you,* he heard a man's voice say, and he glimpsed the image of a tall man with golden hair and green eyes like his own. Tris felt no fear; he was too weakened from the fight to argue. He gratefully accepted the stream of life energy that made it possible to move again.

"What have you done?" Vahanian cried. Tris tore at the throat of Kiara's tunic, desperate to find the vial on the strap around her neck.

"What his grandmother could not do," Gabriel said. Tris lifted the vial, his hands slick with Kiara's blood, and carefully pulled free the stopper.

"Please," he whispered to the fates as he lifted Kiara with one arm and tilted back her head, carefully forcing the vial between her lips. "Please."

There was no time for second chances, Tris knew. No time to find Carina. The attack and Kiara's struggle with the Obsidian King had drained both of them. Supporting Kiara's life force with his own was burning his waning energy even faster. Tris could feel that he was pulling heavily from the strange mage's power. Only a few moments were left for Tris to return Kiara's soul. Tris knew he could not last much longer. His side was wet with blood, and he felt a growing coldness that had nothing to do with the night air.

It wasn't at all like he thought dying would be. One part of Tris's consciousness watched from afar, growing sleepy as death drew near, knowing that he had never really expected to survive the confrontation. There was no fear, no pain; only regret, and even that was dulled by the knowledge that with Arontala's destruction, Kait's spirit and the other prisoners were free. *I will sustain you*, the stranger's voice came again. Tris felt old, strong power bearing him up.

As the final bell tolled midnight, a faint glow began to envelop Kiara's form. It spread from where the potion entered her body, illuminating her. Tris sensed the strong magic of the glow, magic that bore the unmistakable imprint of his grandmother's power. Where the knife had torn into Kiara's chest the skin knit closed without a scar, faster even than the work of an expert healer. Kiara's body jerked as her heart began to beat again. Tris let her spirit slip from within him, gently loosing the glowing thread from his own. As quickly as it came the glow was gone. Tris wavered, nearly losing consciousness.

"That potion... You gambled with Kiara's life?" Vahanian accused.

"No. With his own," Gabriel said. "He couldn't have held on to her much longer."

Tris watched, barely daring to breathe, as Kiara's eyes opened. She raised a hand to touch his face.

Tris could only nod wordlessly, overcome from the physical strain, the fight, the victory, the loss, and the restoration.

"By the Dark Lady, look!" Vahanian gasped, pointing behind Tris.

The doors to the throne room burst open. Two dozen armed men in the livery of the House of Margolan streamed into the room, their weapons drawn.

Tris staggered to his feet, placing himself between the soldiers and Kiara. *Not like this*, Tris thought. *Dear Lady, not so close just to fail*. Against the wall, Vahanian reached for his crossbow with his left hand. Tris saw that Gabriel was ready to strike, although the odds were against him.

The victorious shout of the soldiers' commander jerked Tris's head up as the captain came running toward him.

"By the Lady, you've done it!" a familiar voice cried. The soldier lifted his helm and Tris saw Soterius, beaming in triumph. He thought that Soterius would clap him in a hearty embrace, but instead, the soldier stopped a pace in front of him and went down on one knee.

"Honor your king," Soterius called out to his men. One by one, they also dropped to their knees in fealty. "Hail King Martris of Margolan."

Tris looked out over the group with a mixture of awe and astonishment. His head still reeled from the battle. The reality of Soterius's proclamation, after months of struggle, hit him like a dousing of cold water. Arontala lay dead at his feet. The crown of Margolan was his. Outside the palace walls, he could hear the cries of the mob. He knew that he should feel more, that he should feel *something*, but the battle coldness still gripped him. He could feel neither relief nor triumph. Now, more urgent concerns took his attention. Tris knew how dim the glow of his own lifethread had become. He drew more heavily on the strange mage's power, struggling to remain on his feet.

"Rise," Tris said, his throat tight. He reached out his hand to Kiara, who inclined her head, too unsteady yet even to kneel. Gabriel made a low bow.

"Don't mind me," Vahanian quipped from against the wall. "But I don't kneel well on a broken leg." Soterius rose. At his gesture, two soldiers ran to improvise a stretcher for the wounded fighter. Vahanian protested, and then resigned himself with a sigh.

Tris leaned heavily on Soterius as the soldier guided him to the windows. He flung them open, stepping with Tris onto the balcony, and the crowd cheered below them.

"Hail, King Martris! Long live King Martris!" the crowd cheered from the bailey. Tris lingered for a moment, long enough for the crowd to see him and for him to acknowledge their cheers. Then he turned, stepping back into the room and out of sight of the crowd. He felt the last of his strength falter and the stranger's power slipped out of reach as the floor rushed to meet him and everything around him turned to black.

GABRIEL CAUGHT TRIS before he hit the floor.

"The king is down!" Soterius cried out, rushing to Tris's side. Tris was pale, his eyes were shut, and his breathing was shallow. The hair on one side of his head was matted with blood from a gash that swelled on his temple, and the contrast made Tris seem even paler.

"Stay with us," Soterius urged, shaking him gently. "Tris, stay with us!" There was no response. Soterius looked up at Gabriel.

"Find Carina," Soterius told the *vayash moru*. "She's in the courtyard, with Carroway. Get her up here as fast as you can."

Gabriel nodded, looking at Tris with a sober expression that only fed Soterius's panic. Then the *vayash moru* stepped to the balcony, and disappeared. When Gabriel returned in a few moments, he had Carina with him. The healer looked slightly shaken as she stepped off the balcony, away from Gabriel. She glanced around the room, confused over who needed her most. Kiara's clothes were covered with blood, but she waved Carina away. Vahanian, his leg at an unnatural angle and his sword arm badly broken, shook his head. Then Carina spotted Tris. With a gasp, she ran to kneel beside him.

Soterius stripped off Tris's tunic, revealing the knife gash on Tris's upper arm and the seeping burn where the poker had struck. But when he lifted away Tris's cuirass, Soterius caught his breath. Beneath the bloodied shirt was a deep side wound.

"Sweet Mother and Childe," Carina said to Soterius. "What happened?"

"Tris put up one hell of a fight with Arontala and the Obsidian King," Vahanian supplied. He turned to the soldier who was trying to move his stretcher. "I'm not going anywhere—not until Tris is patched up." Kiara likewise refused their assistance, moving behind Carina where she could see. She put a hand over her mouth to stifle her cry.

"The energy from the blast when the orb exploded—and the battle—would have been a significant drain," Gabriel observed. Soterius realized that the back of Gabriel's coat was burned and tattered. Gabriel's skin, which had been blackened in places and covered with cuts and gashes when Soterius first entered, was healing before their eyes. As the skin healed, it pushed out the bits of broken glass from the orb. They fell to the floor with a crunch at the *vayash moru*'s feet.

"Speaking of that—thank you," Vahanian interjected. "I don't heal nearly as quickly as you do; I'd be a very dead pincushion by now if you hadn't put yourself between me and that bloody ball!" Gabriel inclined his head in acknowledgement, and returned his attention to Tris.

Carina looked at Soterius. "I'm going to need to draw from someone. We don't have time to wait for Carroway."

Soterius met her gaze. "Use me. Take whatever you need—my life if you must—only tell me what you require."

"Do you trust me?" Carina asked.

"Completely."

"Then open your mind to me, and I'll have what I need."

Soterius closed his eyes and laid his hand on Carina's shoulder. She connected with him and he swayed, then regained his balance. Carina frowned and moved her hands over the knife wound in Tris's side. "Dear Goddess," she murmured. "He's lost so much blood."

Carina slipped into a healing trance, drawing on the energy Soterius lent her. The side wound had pierced no vital organs, but the blood loss was substantial. Wormroot made the healing more difficult. Worse was the drain Carina could sense in Tris's life force, from the injuries, the poison, and the strong magic he had worked despite the wormroot. She could feel his life thread flickering. Tris's skin was gray, and his breathing shallow. A rapid, irregular pulse sounded in Carina's mind and she threw her energy into the healing. Tissue knit and sinews repaired under her touch, but replenishing blood would take time. Carina knew she was racing death.

There was something else, there in the darkness of the healing trance. Another presence, old and strong and essential, a Summoner who was not Tris. The image of a man with golden blond hair and green eyes like Tris's own came to her mind: older, saddened, with a haunted look in his eyes. His power was helping to sustain Tris's life. Carina was sure of it, just as she was certain that Tris was very close to death.

"Don't let go," she whispered, unsure whether she was talking to Tris or to the stranger. "Just don't let go."

TRIS SAW HIMSELF on the Plains of Spirit but the spirit realm felt different, more solid. Tris looked backward, toward his own body. As if from a far distance, Tris heard the cries of the soldiers. Tris saw Soterius, panic-stricken, grasping his unresponsive body by the shoulders, shaking him and calling to him. He wanted to respond, but the power to do so failed him. *I'm dying*, Tris thought. *Or perhaps, I'm already dead.* He felt the palace ghosts, newly freed from their exile, swirling past him and through him, bearing him up with their power, rallying around him.

Do you want to live? The question came in the stranger's voice, and Tris saw the man again, walking toward him. His green eyes bored into Tris's soul. Tris met those eyes, and knew.

Lemuel, Tris said, and the tall man bowed. *So grandmother was right—the Obsidian King did possess you, but he didn't destroy your soul.*

Tris could see the weight of that horror in the man's eyes, and Lemuel nodded. *I foolishly thought I could control power that I should never have sought. The price I paid was possession, and the torment of seeing my own body used for the working of one abomination after another.*

Tris found the courage to ask the question that lay between them. *How is it that your eyes are so like my own?*

I can answer that. Another spirit joined them, and Tris knew his grandmother's presence. He was surprised to see her, not as the old woman he had always known, but much younger, still in her second decade, determination and character in her features.

Bava K'aa's spirit stood beside Lemuel on the Plains of Spirit, and Tris could sense the bond between the two. *In the last days of the Great War, I was captured by the Obsidian King. The armies of three kingdoms and the Sisterhood laid siege to his castle. The Obsidian King wanted to know how to make the elixir that would extend his life. He wanted to be immortal.*

Why didn't he become vayash moru? Tris asked.

Because vayash moru *are beholden to their makers for many lifetimes, until the fledgling gains the strength to survive the destruction of its maker. The Obsidian King didn't want to answer to anyone— not even to the Lady Herself.*

During my imprisonment, the Obsidian King did everything he could to force the secret from me. He thought that if he broke my spirit, and my body, that I would tell him. And he used every weakness that he could exploit. Including rape.

Can you even imagine what it was like, Lemuel said, his expression pained, *to have your body used, against your will, to inflict pain on the woman you love? I had no choice but to witness everything, knowing that it was my body used as his instrument. It made the act that much worse because of it.*

I believe the Obsidian King also hoped to break Lemuel, and destroy him, if from grief alone, Bava K'aa said gravely. *Yet all the while, even during the worst, I knew that it was not Lemuel.*

Lord Grayson rescued me—we three had been friends all our lives. I knew that Grayson loved me and stepped aside for Lemuel. But he would not let me die. When Elam healed me and he knew that I bore a child—your mother, Serae—Grayson swore to wed me and raise the child as his own. He told no one, until the day he died and I made his passage to the Lady. For a lifetime, we kept that secret.

Now do you understand? I couldn't free Lemuel's soul, but I couldn't destroy him, knowing how greatly he had suffered.

Bava K'aa met Tris's eyes. *I knew that magic often skipped a generation. When Serae showed no power, I knew you would be my mage heir—you, whose blood descended from the two strongest Summoners of their age.*

You haven't answered my question, said Lemuel. *Do you want to live?*

In the distance, on the Plains of Spirit, Tris could already hear the soulsong of the Lady, the sweetest thing he had ever heard, pulling him toward his rest. Here in the realm of the dead the pain of his wounds was gone, and he knew the freedom of pure spirit. Below, as if in a distant dream, he saw Carina rush toward his body, felt her power stretch out, struggling to heal him. Holding his spirit to his body was a thin blue thread, sustained not by his own life force, but by Lemuel.

Do you wish to live?

Tris looked to his grandmother, and reluctantly toward the song of the Lady, then back to Lemuel. *Yes,* Tris replied. *I want to live.*

Lemuel nodded, and raised a hand in farewell. *Then this is my gift to you,* Lemuel said. *I will sustain you, until the healer's work is through.*

Tris felt himself return to his body, and darkness.

"How is he?" It was Soterius's voice Tris heard, though he lacked the energy to open his eyes. Every muscle ached. His head throbbed as if it might explode. His side, where Jared stabbed him, felt like it had been filled with hot coals. Lemuel's presence was gone.

"He's resting," Tris heard Carina answer, the strain of the healing evident in her voice. "Alyzza helped me make two more healings. I don't know how long it will be until he comes around. We almost lost him, Ban. I thought we had—and then, I can't explain it. It was like the time Tris helped me hang onto Jonmarc, when he almost died in the slaver's camp. There was something—someone— there with us, holding on to Tris while I healed."

Tris wanted to reply, wanted to open his eyes, but his strength was gone. He surrendered to the blackness that engulfed him in its nurturing folds, content to be alive.

CHAPTER THIRTY-NINE

I T TOOK TWO days and several more healings for Tris to awaken. He found himself stretched out on a bed, Carina asleep in a chair beside him.

"Welcome back," Gabriel said, moving from the shadows near the wall. "We weren't sure you'd be joining us."

Tris managed a weak smile. Carina awoke and moved to bring him water. "I wasn't too sure myself," he managed. "Thank you."

Carina shook her head. "Someday, you'll have to explain what happened," she said, taking his hand. "But right now, I'm glad to have you back."

"Kiara—and Jonmarc?" Tris asked, closing his eyes.

Gabriel chuckled. "Neither one would let anyone touch them until they knew whether you would live. Ban's battle healers took care of them. Kiara is exhausted, but unhurt. Jonmarc is going to take a little longer—I fear you'll have a house guest for the rest of the summer. It will be a while before he can think of using a sword, longer until he can ride."

Tris smiled. "Tell him he can stay as long as he wants."

"Soterius and Mikhail are out rounding up Jared's troops and freeing the prisoners in the dungeons. They've had the help of the palace ghosts. Seems that when your power was out of control, you managed to summon every spirit within a league of the palace—not few of whom were Jared's victims. Between the victim's relatives and the angry ghosts, Jared's soldiers are turning up dead faster than Soterius can hunt them down."

Tris looked at Gabriel. "Will the truce hold?"

"Between my people and yours?" Gabriel asked. "It should. Nothing will be won by breaking the peace, now that those who hunted us have been punished."

Carina cleared her throat. "There's someone waiting to see you." She stepped aside, revealing Kiara in the doorway.

Gabriel made a courteous bow. "Until later," he said, addressing both Tris and Kiara. Gabriel and Carina left the room.

Kiara took a step toward where Tris lay. "Good to see you awake," she said, with a tired smile. Tris held out his hand to her, and she moved closer to sit on the edge of his bed. "You gave us a real scare. Carina and I took shifts. We didn't want to leave you alone."

Although his memory of the battle was blurred by the wormroot, the image of destroying the Obsidian King in Kiara's body was searingly clear.

Tris wondered whether the battle had changed things between them.

"I was afraid you might not forgive me, for what happened," Tris said quietly.

The pain of those memories flickered in Kiara's eyes. "When the Obsidian King pushed his way through my shielding, I wanted to die. I was afraid that you wouldn't—wouldn't be able to stop him, or wouldn't free me. I didn't want to exist like that." She paused. "Thank you."

Tris thought of Lemuel, and of his grandmother's story. "I knew I was dying," Tris said. "If the separation spell and the elixir didn't work, I knew we would be together in the arms of the Lady. But I couldn't let the Obsidian King take you."

Kiara blinked back tears. "I'm just so glad to see you—we were afraid we'd lost you. You took an awful chance."

"Lemuel saved me," Tris murmured, closing his eyes. "Grandmother was right."

Kiara brushed the hair back from his face and leaned down to kiss him. "Hush now. You can tell me all about it later. But Carina will chase me out of here with a broom if she needs to heal you again because of me."

Tris opened his eyes and met her gaze. "Don't go far—promise?"

"Promise." She kissed his hand and released it. "Now get some rest. As soon as you can walk, Ban and Mikhail want to get you crowned and make everything official."

Tris watched her leave the room. He shut his eyes and sank back against the pillow, grateful and amazed to be alive. Everything was going to change; all the duties of kingship that he'd never coveted would be his. His wedding would be a bright spot on a very dark horizon. While Carroway and others could see to some of the essentials, like restaffing the palace, there were many things that Tris knew only he could do as King and Summoner. Trials and tribunals to preside over, as the generals and lords loyal to Jared were captured and brought for sentencing. Working with Soterius to rebuild an army and bring order and safety to the land. Mediating for the *scirranish*, who would require his help to make peace with the ghosts of their murdered loved ones.

Tris could feel the energy of angry spirits bound by the pain they suffered at the hands of Jared and Arontala. He doubted Shekerishet would be livable until he exorcised those troubled souls. He would need to appoint an exchequer to find out how badly Jared had looted the treasury. Equally important, he would need to stave off riots and unrest as winter came; ruined fields meant hungry people. *Now comes the hard part*, he thought. *Cleaning up the mess that Jared made*.

TWO DAYS LATER, over Carina's protests, Tris insisted on getting up. When he managed to make it through a hot bath and a shave without collapsing, the healer gave up her arguments. A fresh outfit replaced his blood-soaked clothing, which Carina sent to be burned.

Kiara was waiting for him in the parlor outside his rooms.

"Keeping a vigil?" he asked as she started. Kiara rose to greet him, then remembered herself and dropped to a curtsey.

Tris took her hand with a pained expression. "Please no," he said as he raised her to stand. "Not between us, Kiara. I don't want your fealty. I want your love."

"Always," she said, reaching out to touch his cheek. He pulled her close to him and kissed her. She rested her head against his shoulder.

"Now that you're up," Kiara said, "Ban will want to get you crowned until there can be a real coronation. Technically, you haven't taken the throne."

"There's something I need to do first," Tris said. "Something I have to settle. Will you come with me?"

Kiara smiled. "Anywhere," she murmured. "To the gates of the Lady herself."

Tris made his way to the family's chambers in the palace and opened the door to Kait's room. The sky beyond the window was beginning to lighten, softening the shadows of his torch, only bright enough to cast a dim light over the room. Tris placed the torch in a wall sconce and walked into the silent room.

He closed his eyes against the tears, held back these many months. He found that he could finally weep for Kait and Serae, the first of the innocents who had blocked Jared's path to power. Bricen was a man of war, accepting the dangers of the throne. But Tris's mother and Kait were inconvenient pawns in Jared's desperate bid. It was for them that Tris had returned, far more than the abstract need for justice in Margolan. In the half-light of the early morning he let his grief find voice, allowing the loss and pain to wash over him and through him, permitting the tears to come until his throat was raw and he could weep no more.

Now, Tris thought, perhaps he could do his mother and Kait one final service.

"I've come for you," he said to the empty air. "I've come to set you free." Tris closed his eyes, stretching out along the spectral plains where the restless spirits walked. He felt the touch of a familiar soul, and then another. He opened his eyes to find Serae and Kait standing in front of him. Weakened as they had become within the orb, they had not been destroyed. Tris tried to retain the presence of mind to work the magic he must do. He used his power to make the ghosts visible to Kiara.

"You've won!" Kait said, beaming with pride. "I knew you could. Look at you, king now and a mage!"

Tris had to swallow again before he found his voice. "You know I wish it had never been necessary. I miss you terribly."

"The Lady chooses our paths," Serae's spirit said, her voice as calm in death as it had been in life. "You serve her well."

"I can let you rest," Tris said brokenly. "If you wish." His own heartfelt desire to keep them close to him went unspoken; it was an imposition he dared not make. "But there's someone I want you to meet. This is Kiara of Isencroft, daughter of King Donelan. My betrothed."

Kait grinned and clapped. Serae extended her hands in welcome to Kiara, stepping forward to give a ghostly kiss on each cheek. Serae reached out and laid her hand on Tris's arm.

"With the crown and a bride, you have all that you require to rule Margolan, my son. You don't require my blessing, but I'll give it to you anyway." The ghost smiled at both Tris and Kiara. Kait threw her arms around Tris. Insubstantial though she was Tris welcomed the contact, glad for the chance to sense his sister's spirit at peace.

"When you were born," Serae said, "Mother told me that it would be you who would wear the crown. I never told anyone, not even your father. I never wanted that burden for you. But she was right. You're her heir as much as Bricen's and my own. You've done well."

Tris sensed the presence of two more spirits, revenants strong enough to make their appearance plain to Kiara. Bava K'aa and Lemuel stood beside Serae, and Bava K'aa embraced her daughter. Serae looked from her mother to Lemuel.

"I heard what you told Tris about the Obsidian King," Serae said. "And while I loved Grayson dearly as my father, I can sense in my spirit that what you said is true."

Bava K'aa nodded. Her eyes held the memory of remembered pain. "I'm sorry for the deception, my dear. It was necessary to save your life—and perhaps mine, as well. And to spare Grayson from humiliation that he did not deserve. Now all is known."

"Will you also go to the Lady?" Tris asked his grandmother and Lemuel.

Bava K'aa nodded once more. "I chose to stay on after my death to protect you, and in the hopes that one day I might be able to free Lemuel. You no longer need my protection, and Lemuel is free.

We're ready to go to our rest. We would be honored if you would make the passing over."

Tris looked down, unable to speak. He willed himself to raise his head and meet his mother's eyes. "Then let's begin," he said in a voice like gravel, squaring his shoulders. He closed his eyes once more, stretching out along the currents of magic, feeling the power rise to his command. He felt the shift in his soul that signaled his presence in the spirit world as well as the world of light. For a few precious moments he gathered his family around him, warm and real to the touch. Then he spoke the words of power that freed them, sending their spirits to rest with the Lady.

"Never doubt that you are the Chosen of the Lady," his mother's voice sounded from afar. "She does not choose her champions in vain."

"Goodbye," Tris whispered. When he opened his eyes again, they were gone. He bowed his head, and Kiara wrapped her arms around him. She waited as he swallowed back the last of the tears. Then she took his hand, and they stepped into the corridor together.

Carroway was waiting patiently for them, leaning against the wall with his arms crossed, grinning widely.

"You don't waste time," the bard jibed good-naturedly. "A throne *and* a queen. Now if you'll just appoint me Master Minstrel..."

Tris slipped his arm around Kiara's waist, wincing as his newly healed ribs protested. "Be careful what you wish for," Tris teased. "You're already in charge of planning both a coronation and a wedding."

Carroway grinned wider. "Suits me fine. I'll help the steward plan the food, and I'll arrange the best entertainment and decorations in the Winter Kingdoms. That's how reputations are made, after all," he said with an exaggerated courtly bow.

"Let's wait until tomorrow to start planning the menu, if it's all the same to you," Tris asked tiredly.

"It's been tomorrow for a while now," Carroway replied. "Carina is with Jonmarc. He won't be going anywhere for a long time. I promised to send orders to the kitchen—if the servants ever return—to have their meals sent up to Jonmarc's room." Carroway grinned conspiratorially. "Maybe there'll be a double wedding, before all is said and done. Ban left orders that you're not to be disturbed until noon, but a line of petitioners is already forming and one or two of your father's old retainers have come out of hiding.

"That makes it possible, and probably wise, to convey the crown later this morning." Carroway held up a hand to forestall any protest. "Mikhail pointed out that kingdoms can be lost on technicalities. You've *won* the crown, but you haven't actually been proclaimed king. He tells me there is protocol for a field coronation—King Hotten was crowned that way, so there is precedent—and we can worry about all the pomp and circumstance later."

Carroway shook his head. "We've got a mess to clean up just restaffing the castle," he went on. "And we have to convince the servants that the *vayash moru* will keep the truce, or they won't step foot back in the kitchen. We'll be eating cheese and salt beef for the rest of our lives."

"I don't know," Tris teased, "all that time on the road kind of gave me a taste for salt beef."

"Trail rations never hurt anyone," Kiara joined in. "Builds character."

Carroway rolled his eyes. "I've had my character built enough for ten lifetimes. Now I just want one of those comfortable court positions where I can write songs immortalizing the king and his lady and become one of the most honored bards of the kingdoms."

"Let me know if you don't have enough material for good stories," Tris said. "I can send you back out for a while with Ban. Or maybe Gabriel would take you in."

Carroway gave him a sidelong glance. "No thanks. I think I've got enough to work on."

Kiara laughed. "You two have got business to take care of. I'll go see how Carina and Jonmarc are doing. Don't worry—I'll be with you shortly."

Tris kissed her and let her go, watching as she headed down the corridor.

Carroway looked at Tris, dressed in a borrowed tunic and trews, and shook his head. "I can see that the first order of business is to get you outfitted like a king and not like a tent rigger. Come with me, and let's see what we can find."

CHAPTER FORTY

Six weeks later, the palace courtyards were again filled with cheering crowds for the formal coronation of the new king of Margolan.

"Carroway really outdid himself." Kiara sat with Tris in the banquet hall after the coronation ceremony.

"Remind me never to make him a dare again," Tris replied. True to his word, Carroway had engineered a fete of grand proportions on short notice, with musicians, entertainers, bonfires, and jousts. Tris protested, to no avail, that far too much had been made of the event.

"Staden's enjoying himself," Kiara added. She glanced toward where the Principality king sat, regaling the others at their table with hunting stories. Berry sat next to him, resplendent in a gown of emerald brocade, looking bored. Royster, still unready to return to his self-imposed exile at the

Library, was exuberantly keeping the noble ladies on the terrace entertained with his stories.

"He's certainly entitled to it," Tris replied. In addition to the reward treasure they had left behind in Principality and Vahanian's gold, Staden and Berry presented Tris with a generous coronation gift of precious gems.

"Harrtuck looks no worse for the wear." The burly soldier came into view, milling among guests and guardsmen who greeted him with cheers and back slapping.

"I almost think he enjoyed himself out with the mercs," Tris said. "He's certainly enjoyed telling stories about the adventure."

Harrtuck had returned a few days before the festivities began, riding from the Principality border after dismissing the mercenary troops. The nights before the coronation had been filled with an exchange of stories. The friends had sat up late, trading news of the last days of the campaign over brandy and the cellar's best dried fruits.

"Now there's an odd couple." Kiara looked across the room to where Sakwi and Alyzza bent together in conversation. Sakwi had been successful in his journey to Eastmark to hold back the Nargi troops. This was the first time since his return that Tris had seen the pair without Royster, with whom the two mages eagerly exchanged lore.

"I imagine Royster will have two more visitors, assuming Alyzza and Sakwi don't move in with him altogether," Tris chuckled.

Jolie and Astir moved comfortably among the guests. If any of the nobles thought amiss of Jolie's presence, they said nothing. Jolie brought gifts for the occasion, with bolts of fine Mussa silk and casks of aged Cartelesian brandy, whose origin Tris decided not to consider too carefully. Maynard Linton joined them; it was clear that Jolie and Linton were long-time trading partners.

For Kiara, Jolie brought bolts of creamy Noorish satins and silks. She gave them to Kiara with an aside that brought a crimson blush to the princess's cheeks. Along the back wall, the innkeeper Lars and his wife Tabethe were dressed in fine clothes. They looked dazed, as if they could not believe themselves guests at the king's coronation. Tris had no doubt that once the designation of "king's favored inn" was widely known, Lars would never again lack customers.

"Damn fine feast, Tris," King Harrol boomed, clapping Tris on the shoulder. "Your father would have been proud." Harrol, Bricen's brother-in-law, was more than pleased to preside over the coronation and present Tris with the crown, bringing with him welcome news that the magicked beasts on Dhasson's borders were destroyed.

"Blame Carroway," Tris grinned. "He's out to build a legend."

Harrol laughed heartily. "He doesn't need to. He can tell your stories until his dying day and never lack for an audience." He looked down at Kiara. "Remind me to tell you some stories of my own, about Tris's fostering, sometime when there's a flask of brandy on the table," he said with a broad wink to Tris.

Kiara gave a wicked grin. "That sounds tempting." If Tris intended to make a rejoinder, it was cut off as the musicians struck up a lively tune. Harrol moved away with a wave, seeking out one of the noble ladies to dance with him as the celebrants crowded the dance floor.

"I haven't seen Carina in a while," Tris said, watching the festivities.

"She's probably out walking with Cam," Kiara replied, her toe tapping to the music. King Donelan, thinking it unwise to leave Isencroft so soon after his recovery, had sent Carina's twin brother as his ambassador. Cam had arrived from Isencroft with news of King Donelan's full recovery. The brother and sister had retreated for many long, private walks, recounting their separate adventures. Cam had also carried a private correspondence for Kiara, within which Donelan granted his unreserved permission to honor her betrothal contract with Margolan's new king. Although she and Tris had announced their betrothal in exile, proclaiming it at the coronation made the celebration even more festive.

"How's Jonmarc putting up with the competition?" Tris chuckled.

"Reasonably well. He hasn't squabbled with Carina in a day or two, so it must be true love. Honestly, those two deserve each other!"

Even the palace ghosts, now returned from their long banishment, were determined to make the coronation memorable. They appeared freely to the guests, and Tris could sense their whole-hearted approval and blessing.

Tris watched the entertainment restlessly. A nearly endless line of well-wishers and boon-seekers formed to greet him and offer their fealty, renewing pledges made to his father and grandfather. But in

the tower on the far side of the palace were the
nobles who had freely assisted Jared, along with
dozens of soldiers loyal to Jared who had been
imprisoned for their crimes. Their trials and, most
likely executions, loomed ahead, an unpleasant part
of assuming the kingship.

Kiara squeezed his hand. "Don't borrow trouble."

"Sorry," Tris said with a smile. "An old habit."

"I have to admit, you know how to throw a
party." Vahanian joined them, making a perfunctory bow. Even with his leg in a splint, Vahanian
managed to stride across the room as if he owned
it. A sling of black silk held his still-healing sword
arm, but the splint on his leg was more difficult to
hide. Vahanian was dressed in black with a dark
burgundy long coat, his swordbelt notably visible.
Tris gladly granted him permission to wear his
sword in the presence of the king, though until
Vahanian's arm healed the gesture was largely sym-
bolic.

"You're going to miss us," Tris said, grinning.
"Although you might have your hands full with
Dark Haven."

Vahanian grinned. "Carina and Gabriel and I've
been making plans; I've had nothing to do but play
tarle and wait for my bones to heal for the last six
weeks. Gabriel made drawings of the manor house,
and we've put a plan together to make it habitable
again. We think we can get the lands profitable in a
season or two. Once the party is over, Gabriel is
going back to get things started between now and
the royal wedding. As soon as I can ride, I'll go up
and see how I can help." He paused. "I've asked

Carina to winter at Dark Haven. She's said yes—if Donelan can spare her."

Kiara grinned. "I can arrange that."

Vahanian smiled. "Who knows? I might even be able to convince all of you to visit." Carina and Cam joined them. Vahanian slipped his good arm around Carina's waist and kissed her. "After all," he added, "celebrating Haunts in Dark Haven might be a whole new experience."

Carina, beautiful in a dark red gown that matched Vahanian's long coat, merely laughed and patted his good arm. "I wouldn't know what to do with my time if you quit making a target of yourself. You're my star patient."

Vahanian turned to her with a wicked smile. "I might be able to suggest some other pastimes," he said and she reddened.

"I'll have to bring my chaperone." Carina looked to Cam, who drew himself up to his full height.

"I can be bribed," Cam said

"We'll talk later," Vahanian said.

"Still doubt the Lady's hand?" Carina asked. "Or are you chalking all this up to gambler's luck?"

"Thinking about being on the receiving end of the Goddess's attention doesn't make me sleep well at night, to tell you the truth," Vahanian replied.

"They say the Lord of Dark Haven *is* favored by the Dark Lady," Carina said mischievously. "Gabriel told me so."

"The last time I felt favored, I almost died," Vahanian said, remembering the illusion in the Nargi camp. "There's something to be said for anonymity."

Carina barely hid a snicker. "Then by all means, go on believing you're anonymous. It's just your phenomenal *luck* at work."

Tris chuckled at the banter. He looked back to the acrobats who tumbled and whirled in the great hall. "Look there," Kiara said, nodding toward the crowd. Gabriel and Riqua stood together against the back wall, resplendent in fine silks and brocades, unremarkable among the guests except for a pallor that was nearly hidden by the candlelight. All of the Blood Council was in attendance except for Uri. While both Tris and Vahanian shared a sense of foreboding about Uri's absence, both refused to worry about it on this day of celebration.

"You add new meaning to the part of the litany about being 'king of the realm, master of the living and the dead,'" Kiara said dryly. "Until now, I always thought that was just a nice overstatement."

Tris grimaced. "I'm still getting used to that part," he admitted. "And the palace ghosts have brought their own list of grievances to be redressed. I have a feeling that once I get down to the work part of being king, I may never get a moment's rest."

Kiara gave him a mischievous grin. "Let me take care of that," she said, placing her hand over his.

Just then the doors to the greatroom opened, and a hush fell over the celebration. A single robed figure stood in the doorway. Dressed in the plain-spun brown robes of the Sisterhood, the figure made its way through the crowd that wordlessly parted to make a pathway to the dais. Tris rose to his feet. The woman's cowl fell back, revealing Sister Taru's face.

"The Sisterhood, too, has a gift for the new king," Taru announced. She reached beneath her cloak and withdrew a gleaming sword. Its grip was beautifully worked, its steel etched with runes that seemed to burn in the torchlight. From the way it laid across her open hands Tris knew it was perfectly balanced, the weapon of a master blade maker.

Tris made his way down to stand before the sorceress. "Welcome, esteemed Sister," he said respectfully. "We're honored at your presence."

"You are the grandson of Bava K'aa," Taru said, offering him the sword that lay across her outstretched hands. "Heir of blood and heir of power. Take her sword to replace Mageslayer. It will serve you well." And in a voice that only Tris could hear, Taru said, "You may find it harbors a vestige of her power, as well as her memory."

Tris accepted the sword, taking it carefully on his open palms. With his touch, the runes along its blade burst into flame that neither burned nor smoked. The audience gasped. When Tris looked again to thank Taru, she had disappeared.

"That certainly took care of any doubts your guests might have had about you being a *real* spook," Vahanian observed dryly.

Tris sheathed the sword carefully, and the runes faded to indistinct tracings. "I'm going to have to ask Royster about that inscription." The musicians struck up their tunes again and the guests resumed their conversation.

Tris looked out over the ballroom; he let his mind wander with the music. It was more than he had hoped just to be alive. Everything around him was starting to change. Shekerishet—and Margolan—

would never be as it had been under Bricen. That truth was sad but undeniable. In time, Tris hoped that Jared's legacy would fade, and that Margolan's wounds could be healed without added bloodshed. It would take a strong king to do that. Tris fervently hoped that he was up to the challenge.

He smiled, looking at his friends amid the mix of coronation guests. Carroway, thoroughly at home in charge of the festivities, was fully enjoying the role of Master Bard. Soterius, now Margolan's youngest general, had earned such deep loyalty from the rebel army that he would be playing an essential part in rebuilding the kingdom's defenses. Vahanian and Carina were headed together to Dark Haven, with its promise and danger. Harrtuck, Royster and Cam—all of them had been forever changed by the quest to unseat Jared. They stepped into a future that none of them could have foreseen.

As the music swelled, Tris's attention returned to Kiara. In just a few months, many of these same guests would return to Shekerishet for their wedding. The thought was exhilarating and unsettling all at the same time. Kiara looked at him quizzically, but before she could speak Carroway slipped up behind them.

"Quit upstaging me with that sword," Carroway hissed, chasing down an errant cupbearer. "Good entertainers are hard to get."

"So are good dancing partners," Kiara said. She made a little bow, and reached out to take Tris's arm. "Shall we, Your Majesty?"

"At your service, milady," Tris replied with an answering bow. "Now and forever."

ABOUT THE AUTHOR

Gail Z. Martin discovered her passion for science fiction, fantasy and ghost stories in elementary school. The first story she wrote—at age five—was about a vampire. Her favorite TV show as a preschooler was *Dark Shadows*. At age fourteen, she decided to become a writer. She enjoys attending science fiction/fantasy conventions, Renaissance fairs and living history sites. She is married and has three children, a Himalayan cat and a golden retriever.

You can visit Gail at:

www.myspace.com/chronicleofthenecromancer

www.chroniclesofthenecromancer.com

Read her blog:

blog.myspace.com/chronicleofthenecromancer

MAIN CHARACTERS

ALAINE
Sister Landis's assistant.

ALLE
A spy and member of the Margolan resistance.

ALYZZA
A half-mad mage who traveled with Linton's caravan as a hedge witch and helped Tris with his first efforts to learn control of his magic.

ASTASIA
One of the *vayash moru* nobles on the Blood Council.

BAN SOTERIUS
Captain of King Bricen's guard on the night of the coup and a close friend of Tris Drayke.

BAVA K'AA

Mother of Queen Serae, grandmother to Tris and his sister Kait. A powerful Summoner, Bava K'aa fought the Obsidian King during the Mage Wars and was responsible for binding his spirit in the orb Soulcatcher. Until her death, Bava K'aa led the Sisterhood, an elite group of mages.

BERRY (BERWYN)

Daughter of King Staden of Principality, she first meets Tris as a captive of slavers, where she hid her identity to lessen her risk.

BRICEN OF MARGOLAN

King of Margolan, father to both Martris (Tris) Drayke and his half-brother, Jared. Killed by Jared and Foor Arontala on the night of the Feast of the Departed (Haunts) along with Queen Serae and their daughter, Kait.

CARINA JESTHRATA

Healer to King Donelan of Isencroft, distant cousin to Kiara Sharsequin and sister to the fighter Cam. Sent to find an elixir to heal King Donelan from a mage-sent illness, Carina and Cam were traveling incognito with Maynard Linton's caravan when Tris and his friends also took refuge with the caravan on their way north to find sanctuary.

CARROWAY

A gifted bard in the court of King Bricen and a close friend of Tris Drayke.

CURANE
A Margolan noble who is among Jared's most loyal supporters.

DARRATH
A senior general in the Principality army. He is an expert tactician, provided by Staden to help Tris plan his strike against Jared.

ELAM
The Sister in charge of the citadel in Principality City, and a close friend of the late Bava K'aa.

FALLON
A member of the Sisterhood who oversees a citadel in northern Margolan.

FOOR ARONTALA
A Fire Clan mage and one of the undead *vayash moru*, Foor Arontala is mage-advisor to Jared of Margolan. Arontala seeks to reawaken the spirit of the Obsidian King from its prison in the orb Soulcatcher and permit the spirit to possess him, incarnating the greatest dark Summoner the Winter Kingdoms has known.

GABRIEL
A *vayash moru* lord who travels with Tris and his friends as their friend and protector. One of the Blood Council.

HANT
King Staden's spymaster.

JARED DRAYKE

Son of King Bricen of Margolan and half-brother to Tris Drayke. As the eldest son, no one questioned Jared's position as heir to the throne. With the help of his dark mage, Foor Arontala, Jared murdered his father and all of the royal family except for Tris. He seeks to destroy Tris and solidify his hold on Margolan.

JONMARC VAHANIAN

A gifted fighter with a checkered past, Vahanian has twice before been brought to grief by Arontala. Harrtuck gets Tris to hire Vahanian as a guide to take the group safely through the northern mountains.

KIARA SHARSEQUIN

Daughter of King Donelan of Isencroft and the late Queen Viata, Kiara is sent by the Oracle of the goddess on a coming of age Journey that takes her into dangerous territory across Margolan. Bound by an old pact, Kiara is desperate to avoid an arranged marriage to Jared of Margolan, to whom she was betrothed at birth.

LANDIS

One of the senior Sisters at the citadel in Principality City.

LEMUEL

A great Summoner and the lover of Bava K'aa. Lemuel was possessed by the spirit of the Obsidian King. Bava K'aa bound the Obsidian King's spirit in the orb Soulcatcher rather than destroy him because she hoped that Lemuel still existed within the Obsidian King's power and could someday be freed.

MACARIA, HALIK AND PAIVA
Three bards from the Margolan court who are close friends of Carroway.

MARTRIS DRAYKE
Known as Tris to his friends, Prince Drayke is the only survivor of the coup against his father, King Bricen of Margolan, except for Jared the Usurper. Grandson of famed sorceress Bava K'aa, Tris learns that he has inherited his grandmother's powerful spirit magic and is a Summoner, a mage who can intercede among the living, dead and undead. Although as Bricen's second son Tris never desired or expected the crown, he realizes that he is the only one who can challenge Jared and bring peace to Margolan and the Winter Kingdoms.

MAYNARD LINTON
A smuggler and long-time friend of Jonmarc Vahanian, Linton ran the caravan which provided cover for Tris and his friends on their flight from Margolan.

MIKHAIL
A *vayash moru* from Gabriel's undead 'family' who served King Hotten, Tris's ancestor, over 200 years ago.

OBSIDIAN KING
The powerful evil spirit of a great Summoner from long ago. His spirit possessed the mage Lemuel a

generation before Tris Drayke's birth. In Lemuel's body, the Obsidian King waged war against the Winter Kingdoms in what became the Mage Wars. He was defeated and his spirit was bound in the orb Soulcatcher by Bava K'aa.

PELL, TABB AND ANDRAS
Margolan soldiers loyal to King Bricen who deserted after the coup and are among the refugees in Principality.

RAFE
A powerful *vayash moru* who is one of the Blood Council.

RIQUA
A wealthy and powerful *vayash moru* who serves on the Blood Council.

ROYSTER
Librarian and Keeper at the Library at Westmarch.

SAHILA
A leader among the Margolan refugees.

STADEN
King of Principality and the father of Princess Berwyn.

TADRIE
A Margolan farmer whose family was rescued from angry guards by Kiara. Now a leader among the Margolan refugees.

TARU
One of the mages of the Sisterhood responsible for Tris's training.

TOV HARRTUCK
A loyal guardsman to King Bricen who helped Tris, Soterius and Carroway escape on the night of the coup. Harrtuck's friendship with Jonmarc Vahanian and their shared past as mercenaries connected the group with Vahanian as a guide.

URI
One of the *vayash moru* lords on the Blood Council.

Book one of the Chronicles of the Necromancer

"Attractive characters and an imaginative setting combine
in an excellent, fast-moving quest novel."
— David Drake, author of the Lord of the Isles series

GAIL Z. MARTIN

THE SUMMONER

Book One of the
CHRONICLES OF THE NECROMANCER

ISBN: 978-1-84416-468-4

The world of Prince Martris Drayke is thrown into
sudden chaos and disorder when his brother
murders their father and seizes the throne. Cast
out, Martris and a small band of trusted friends are
forced to flee to a neighbouring kingdom to plot
their retaliation. But if the living are arrayed
against him, Martris must call on a different set of
allies: the ranks of the dead...

www.solarisbooks.com

 SOLARIS FANTASY

Nowak, R.M. 1973. North American quaternary *Canis*. Ph.D. Thesis, University of Kansas, Lawrence.

Odum, E.P. and Kuenzler, E.J. 1955. Measurement of territory and home range size in animals. *Auk* 72:128-137.

Ohmann, L.F. and Ream, R.R. 1971. Wilderness ecology: virgin plant communities of the Boundary Waters Canoe Area. USDA Forest Service Research Paper NC-63, St. Paul, Minnesota.

Oldemeyer, J.L., Franzmann, A.W., Brundage, A.L., Arneson, P.D. and Flynn, A. 1977. Browse quality and the Kenai moose population. *Journal of Wildlife Management* 41:533-542.

Olson, S.F. 1938. Organization and range of the pack. *Ecology* 19:168-170.

Ontario Department of Lands and Forests. 1970. Wolves and coyotes in Ontario, 14pp.

Osgood, W.H. 1901. Natural history of the Cook Inlet region, Alaska. North American Fauna No. 21, U.S. Government Printing Office.

Packard, J.M. 1980. Deferred reproduction in wolves (*Canis lupus*). Ph.D. Thesis. University of Minnesota, Minneapolis, Minnesota.

Packard, J.M. and Mech, L.D. 1980. Population regulation in wolves. In M.N. Cohen, R.S. Malpasse and H.G. Klein (eds.), *Biosocial Mechanisms of Population Regulation.* Yale University Press, New Haven, Connecticut.

Palmen, J.A. 1913. Bär, Wolf and Luchs in Finnland. *Zool. Beobachter* 54:1-6.

Palmer, L.J. 1938 (unpublished). Kenai Peninsula moose. Research Project Report, Bureau of Biological Survey. Sept.-Oct. 1938, Kenai National Moose Range files.

Parker, G.R. 1972. Biology of the Kaminuriak population of barren-ground caribou. Part I. Canadian Wildlife Service, Report No. 20, Ottawa.

Parker, G.R. 1973. Distribution and densities of wolves within barren-ground caribou range in northern mainland Canada. *Journal of Mammalogy* 54:341-348.

Pedersen, S. 1978. Geographical variation in Alaskan wolves (*Canis lupus* L.). M.S. Thesis, University of Alaska, Fairbanks, Alaska.

Peters, R.P. 1979. Mental maps in wolf territoriality. In E. Klinghammer (ed.), *The Behavior and Ecology of Wolves*, Garland STPM Press, New York, 119-152.

Peters, R.P. and Mech, L.D. 1975. Scent-marking in wolves. *American Scientist* 63:628-637.

Peterson, R.L. 1955. *North American Moose.* University of Toronto Press, Toronto.

Peterson, R.O. 1977. Wolf ecology and prey relationships on Isle Royale. U.S. National Park Service, Fauna Series 11, Washington, DC, 210pp.

Peterson, R.O. 1979. Social rejection following mating of a subordinate wolf. *Journal of Mammalogy* 60:219-221.

Peterson, R.O. and Allen, D.L. 1976. Ecological studies of the wolf on Isle Royale: Annual Report, 16pp.

Peterson, R.O. and Scheidler, J.M. 1977. Ecological studies of wolves on Isle Royale: Annual Report, 12pp.

Peterson, R.O. and Scheidler, J.M. 1978. Ecological studies of wolves on Isle Royale: Annual Report covering 20th year of the Isle Royale studies, 14pp.

Peterson, R.O. and Scheidler, J.M. 1979. Ecological studies of wolves on Isle Royale: Annual Report, 18pp.

Pianka, E.R. 1970. On *r*- and *k*-selection. *American Naturalist* 104:592-597.

Pietrewicz, A.T. and Kamil, A.C. 1981. Search images and the detection of cryptic prey: an operant approach. In A.C. Kamil and T.D. Sargent (eds.), *Foraging Behavior: Ecological, Ethological, and Psychological Approaches,* Garland STPM Press, New York.

Pimlott, D.H. 1960. The use of tape-recorded wolf howls to locate timber wolves. 22nd Midwest Fish and Wildlife Conference, 15pp. (mimeo).

Pimlott, D.H. 1967. Wolf predation and ungulate populations. *American Zoologist* 7:267-278.

Pimlott, D.H. 1970. Predation and productivity of game populations in North America. *Transactions of the IX International Congress of Game Biologists.* Moscow.

Pimlott, D.H. (ed.). 1975. *Wolves.* IUCN Supplemental Paper No. 43, Morges, Switzerland.

Pimlott, D.H., Shannon, J.A. and Kolenosky, G.B. 1967. Interrelationships of wolves and deer in Algonquin Park. *Transactions of the Northeast Wildlife Conference,* Quebec.

Pimlott, D.H., Shannon, J.A. and Kolenosky, G.B. 1969. The ecology of the timber wolf in Algonquin Provincial Park. Ontario Department of Lands and Forests Research Report (Wildlife), No. 87, Ottawa, 92pp.

Pujol, R. and Hilding, D. 1973. Anatomy and physiology of the onset of auditory function. *Acta Otolaryngology* 76:1-10.

Pulliainen, E. 1965. Studies on the wolf (*Canis lupus* L.) in Finland. *Annalles Zoologici Fennici* 2:215-259.

Pulliainen, E. 1973. Pohjoismaiden sudet. *Suomen Luonto* 32:172-173, 223.

Pulliainen, E. 1979a. Erfarenheter av uppfuljning av de stora rovdjuren i Finland. *Viltrapport* 9:60-70.

Pulliainen, E. 1979b. Ecology of the wolf in the settled areas of Finland. In E. Klinghammer (ed.), *The Behavior and Ecology of Wolves,* Garland STPM Press, New York, 84-92.

Pulliainen, E. (in press, a). Comparison of the present land mammal faunas of eastern and western Fennoscandia. *Acta University of Ouluensis.*

Pulliainen, E. (in press, b). The present status and ecology of the wolf in Finland and adjacent areas. In R. Soutar (ed.), *Proceedings of the International Wolf Symposium,* Edinburgh, April 1978.

Pulliainen, E. (in press, c). Predation on the wild forest reindeer in Kuhmo, eastern Finland. In *Proceedings of the 2nd International Reindeer/Caribou Symposium,* Røros, Norway, Sept. 17-21, 1979.

Pulliainen, E. (in press, d). The status, structure and behavior of populations of the wolf (*Canis l. lupus* L.) along the Finland-Soviet Union border. *Annalles Zoologici Fennici.*

Rabb, G.B., Woolpy, J.H. and Ginsburg, B.E. 1967. Social relationships in a group of captive wolves. *American Zoologist* 7:305-311.

Radcliffe-Brown, A.R. 1952. *Structure and function in primitive society: Essays and addresses.* Cohen and West, London.

Radyclyffe, C.R.E. 1904. *Big Game Shooting in Alaska.* Rowland Ward Ltd., London.

Raup, H. 1935. Botanical investigations in the Wood Buffalo Park. *National Museums of Canada Bulletin* 74, Bio. Series 20, 174pp.

Rausch, R.A. 1967. Some aspects of the population ecology of wolves in Alaska. *American Zoologist* 7:253-265.

Rausch, R.A. 1969. A summary of wolf studies in southcentral Alaska, 1957-1968. *Transactions of the North American Wildlife and National Research Conference* 34:117-131.

Rausch, R.A. and Hinman, R.A. 1977. Wolf management in Alaska — an exercise in futility? In R.L. Phillips and C. Jonkel (eds.), *Proceedings of the 1975 Predator Symposium*, University of Montana, Missoula, 147-156.

Rausch, R.L. 1951. Notes on the Nunamiut Eskimo and mammals of the Anaktuvuk Pass Region, Brooks Range, Alaska. *Arctic* 4:147-195.

Rausch, R.L. 1953. On the status of some arctic mammals. *Arctic* 6:91-148.

Rausch, R.L. 1958. Some observations on rabies in Alaska, with special reference to wild Canidae. *Journal of Wildlife Management* 22:246-260.

Rearden, J. 1972. An end to poisoning? *Alaska Sportsman*, May 1972, p. 13.

Reger, D. 1974. Prehistory of the Northern Kenai Peninsula. In *The Native, Russian and American Experiences of the Kenai Area of Alaska*, Proceedings of a Conference on Kenai Area History, Nov. 1974, 27-34.

Robinson, W.L. and Smith, G.J. 1977. Observations on recently killed wolves in upper Michigan. *Wildlife Society Bulletin* 5:25-26.

Roper, T.J. and Ryon, C.J. 1977. Mutual synchronization of diurnal activity rhythms in groups of red wolf/coyote hybrids. *Journal of Zoology* 182:177-185.

Rosenberg, S. 1959. The maintenance of a learned response in controlled interpersonal conditions. *Sociometry* 22:124-138.

Rosenberg, S. 1960. Cooperative behavior in dyads as a function of reinforcement parameters. *Journal of Abnormal and Social Psychology* 60:318-333.

Rosenberg, S. and Hall, R.L. 1958. The effects of different social feedback conditions upon performance in dyadic teams. *Journal of Abnormal and Social Psychology* 57:271-277.

Rosenzweig, M.L. 1968. The strategy of body size in mammalian carnivores. *American Midland Naturalist* 80:299-315.

Rothman, R.J. and Mech, L.D. 1979. Scent-marking in lone wolves and newly formed pairs. *Animal Behavior* 27:750-760.

Rowan, W. 1950. Winter habits and numbers of timber wolves. *Journal of Mammalogy* 31:167-169.

Rowe, J.S. 1959. Forest regions of Canada. Canadian Department of Northern Affairs and Natural Resources, Bulletin 123.

Rowell, T.E. 1974. The concept of social dominance. *Behavioral Biology* 11:131-154.

Rutter, R.J. and Pimlott, D.H. 1968. *The World of the Wolf*. J.B. Lippincott Company, Philadelphia.

*Ryabov, L.S. 1973. Wolf and dog hybrids in the Voronezh region. BMSNRBS, 6.

*Ryabov, L.S. 1978. New facts regarding the wolves and their hybrids with dogs in the Voronezh region. BMSNRBS, 3.

*Ryabov, L.S. 1979. Stray and wild dogs in the Voronezh region. BMSNRBS, 4.

Ryon, C.J. 1977. Den digging and related behavior in a captive timber wolf pack. *Journal of Mammalogy* 58:87-89.

Ryon, C.J. 1979. Aspects of dominance behavior in groups of sibling coyote/ red wolf hybrids. *Behavioral and Neural Biology* 25:69-78.

Samuel, W.M., Ramalingam, S. and Carbyn, L.N. 1978. Helminths in coyotes (*Canis latrans* Say), wolves (*Canis lupus* L.) and red foxes (*Vulpes vulpes* L.) of southwestern Manitoba. *Canadian Journal of Zoology* 56:2614-2617.

Schenkel, R. 1947. Expression studies of wolves. *Behaviour* 1:81-129 (translation).

Schenkel, R. 1967. Submission: Its feature and functions in the wolf and dog. *American Zoologist* 7:319-329.

Schlegel, M. 1976. Factors affecting calf elk survival in northcentral Idaho: a progress report. In *Proceedings of the 56th Annual Conference of the Western Association of State Game and Fish Commissions* 56:342-355.

Schonberner, D. 1965. Observations of the reproductive biology of the wolf. *Zeitschrift für Saugetierkunde* 30:171-178 (translation).

Schotte, C.S. and Ginsburg, B.E. 1978. Continuing development of social organization and mating in a captive wolf pack. Presented at annual meeting, Animal Behavior Society, Seattle, Washington.

Schotte, C.S., Smiley, L., MacDonald, K.B. and Ginsburg, B.E. 1977. Social organization and mating in a developing wolf pack. Presented at annual meeting, Animal Behavior Society, University Park, Pennsylvania.

Scott, B.M.V. 1979. The Vancouver Island wolf (*Canis lupus crassodon*): An initial study of food habits and social organization. M.S. Thesis, University of British Columbia, Vancouver.

Scott, B.M.V. and Shackleton, D.M. 1980. Food habits of two Vancouver Island wolf packs: A preliminary study. *Canadian Journal of Zoology* 58:1203-1207.

Seal, U.S. and Erickson, A.W. 1969. Phencyclidine immobilization of the Carnivora and other mammals. *Federal Proceedings of the Symposium on Laboratory Animals and Anesthesia* 28:1410-1419.

Seal, U.S., Mech, L.D. and Van Ballenberghe, V. 1975. Blood analyses of wolf pups and their ecological and metabolic interpretation. *Journal of Mammalogy* 56:64-75.

Selander, R.K. 1972. Sexual selection and dimorphism in birds. In B.G. Campbell (ed.), *Sexual Selection and the Descent of Man*. Aldine, Chicago, 180-230.

Semenov, B.T. 1976. Izmeneni'a rasprostraneni'a i ceslennosti ptic i zverej fauny Arhangelskoj oblasti. Petrozavodsk (not seen, cited after Danilov et al., 1978).

Severinghaus, C.W. 1974. Note on the history of wild canids in New York. *New York Fish and Game Journal* 21:117-125.

Severinghaus, C.W. 1976. Deer management in the central Adirondacks. *The Conservationist* 30(5):26-27.

Severinghaus, C.W. and Gottlieb, R. 1956. Big deer versus little deer. *The Conservationist* 14:30-31.

Shahi, S.P. 1977. *Backs to the Wall*. East-West Press, New Delhi.

Shahi, S.P. 1979. The Indian grey wolf. *Portland Wolf Symposium*, Portland, Oregon, 12-17 August 1979.

Sharp, H.S. 1978. Comparative ethnology of the wolf and the Chipewyan. In R.L. Hall and H.S. Sharp (eds.), *Wolf and Man: Evolution in Parallel*, Academic Press, New York.

Shiras, III, G. 1935. *Hunting with Camera and Flashlight: Vol. II*, National Geographic Society, Washington, DC.

Sidowski, J.B. 1957. Reward and punishment in a minimal social situation. *Journal of Experimental Psychology* 54:318-326.

Sidowski, J.B., Wyckoff, L.B. and Tabory, L. 1956. The influence of reinforcement and punishment in a minimal social situation. *Journal of Abnormal and Social Psychology* 52:115-119.

Silver, H. and Silver, W.T. 1969. Growth and behavior of the coyote-like canid of northern New England with observations on canid hybrids. *Wildlife Monographs* No. 17.

Singer, F.J. 1975a. The history and status of wolves in Glacier National Park, Montana. Glacier National Park Scientific Paper No. 1.

Singer, F.J. 1975b. Wildfire and ungulates in the Glacier National Park area, northwestern Montana. M.S. Thesis, University of Idaho, Moscow, Idaho.

Skeel, M.A. and Carbyn, L.N. 1977. The morphological relationship of gray wolves (*Canis lupus*) in national parks of central Canada. *Canadian Journal of Zoology* 55:737-747.

Skinner, B.F. 1953. *Science and Human Behavior*, Macmillan, New York.

Skinner, B.F. 1962. Operadum. *Journal of the Experimental Analysis of Behavior* 5:224.

Skoog, R.O. 1968. Ecology of the caribou (*Rangifer tarandus granti*) in Alaska. Ph.D. Thesis, University of California, Berkeley.

*Sludskii, A.A. 1962. Relationships between the predator and its prey. *Transactions of the Zoology Institute at the Science Academy of the Kazakh Soviet Socialist Republic*. Vol. 17, Alma-Ata.

*Sludskii, A.A. 1970. The problem of "predator—prey" in game management in Kazakhstan. *Transactions of the 9th International Congress of Game Biologists*. Moscow.

Smith, C.S. 1978. Summer-fall movements, migrations, seasonal range and habitat selection of the Middle Fork elk herd. M.S. Thesis, University of Montana, Missoula.

Smith, I.D. 1968. The effects of hunting and seral succession upon Vancouver Island blacktailed deer. M.S. Thesis, University of British Columbia, Vancouver.

Smith, I.D. and Davies, R.G. 1975. A preliminary investigation of the deer and elk range in the Tsitika River watershed, Vancouver Island. B.C. Fish and Wildlife Branch Report, Nanaimo, 71pp.

Smith, J.M.N. and Dawkins, R. 1971. The hunting behavior of individual great tits in relation to spatial variation in their food density. *Animal Behaviour* 19:695-706.

Sneath, P.H.A. and Sokal, R.R. 1973. *Numerical Taxonomy: The Principles and Practice of Numerical Classification*. W.H. Freeman and Co., San Francisco.

Snyder, R.L. 1974. Probability matching in foxes. Annual meeting of Animal Behavior Society, Champaign-Urbana, Illinois.

Soper, J.D. 1941. History, range and home life of the northern bison. *Ecological Monographs* 11:347-412.

Soper, J.D. 1945. Report on wildlife investigations in Wood Buffalo National Park and vicinity, Alberta and Northwest Territories, Canada. Canadian Wildlife Service, 71pp.

Spencer, D.L. and Hakala, J.B. 1964. Moose and fire on the Kenai. *Tall Timbers Fire Ecology Conference* 3:11-33.

Spencer, R.F. 1959. *The North Alaskan Eskimo.* U.S. Government Printing Office, Washington, DC.

Spraker, T. and Ballard, W.B. 1979. Unit 13 Brown Bear Studies. Alaska Department of Fish and Game. P-R Project Report W-17-R. Juneau.

Stanfield, R. 1970. Some considerations on the taxonomy of wolves in Ontario. In Jorgensen, S.E., Faulkner, C.E. and Mech, L.D. (eds.), *Wolf Management in Selected Areas of North America.* U.S. Fish and Wildlife Service, Twin Cities, Minnesota.

Stefansson, V. 1919. *My Life with the Eskimo.* New York.

Stefansson, V. 1922. *Hunters of the Great North.* New York.

Stenlund, M.H. 1955. A field study of the timber wolf (*Canis lupus*) on the Superior National Forest, Minnesota. Minnesota Department of Conservation, Technical Bulletin No. 4, 55pp.

Stephenson, R.O. 1974. Characteristics of wolf den sites. Alaska Federal Aid to Wildlife Restoration, Final Report, Projects W-17-2 through W-17-6, Juneau.

Stephenson, R.O. 1975. Wolf Report. Alaska Federal Aid in Wildlife Restoration Program Report, Project W-17-6 and W-17-7, Juneau.

Stephenson, R.O. 1978. Unit 13 wolf studies. Federal Aid to Wildlife Restoration Report, Project W-17-8, Alaska Department of Fish and Game, Juneau, Alaska.

Stephenson, R.O. and Ahgook, B. 1975. The Eskimo hunter's view of wolf ecology and behavior. In M.W. Fox (ed.), *The Wild Canids: Their Systematics, Behavioral Ecology, and Evolution.* Van Nostrand Reinhold, New York, 286-291.

Stephenson, R.O. and Johnson, L. 1972. Wolf report. Alaska Federal Aid to Wildlife Restoration Report, Project W-17-3, Juneau, Alaska.

Stephenson, R.O. and Johnson, L. 1973. Wolf report. Alaska Federal Aid to Wildlife Restoration Report Project W-17-4, Juneau, Alaska.

Stephenson, R.O. and Sexton, J.J. 1974. Wolf report. Alaska Federal Aid in Wildlife Restoration Progress Report, Project W-17-5, Juneau, Alaska.

Studley, J.T. 1912. *The Journal of a Sporting Nomad.* John Lane Company, New York.

Sullivan, J.O. 1978. Variability in the wolf, a group hunter. In R.L. Hall and H.S. Sharp (eds.), *Wolf and Man: Evolution in Parallel.* Academic Press, New York, 31-40.

Sullivan, J.O. 1979. Individual variability in hunting behavior of wolves. In E. Klinghammer (ed.), *The Behavior and Ecology of Wolves,* Garland STPM Press, New York.

Sullivan, J.O. and Paquet, P.C. 1977. Behavior of wild canids. *Proceedings of The American Association of Zoological Parks and Aquariums.* Hill's, Topeka, Kansas.

Swartz, M., Turner, V. and Tuden, A. 1966. *Political anthropology.* Aldine, Chicago.

Tempany, I.R. and Cooper, S. 1976. Techniques for counting bison. In J.G. Stelfox (ed.), *Wood Buffalo National Park Bison Research: 1972-76.* Canadian Wildlife Service, Parks Canada Annual Report.

Tevis, Jr., L. 1950. Summer behavior of a family of beavers in New York State. *Journal of Mammalogy* 31:40-65.

Theberge, J.B. and Cottrell, T.J. 1977. Food habits of wolves in Kluane National Park. *Arctic* 30:189-191.

Theberge, J.B. and Pimlott, D.H. 1969. Observations of wolves at a rendezvous site in Algonquin Park. *Canadian Field-Naturalist* 83:122-128.

Theberge, J.B., Oosenburg, S.M. and Pimlott, D.H. 1978. Site and seasonal variations in food of wolves. Algonquin Park, Ontario. *Canadian Field-Naturalist* 92:91-94.

The Wildlife Society. 1975. Summary of responses to legislation questionnaire. In New York Chapter Newsletter, April 15, 1975.

Thomas, K.P. 1966. Nocturnal activities of the white-tailed deer on Crab Orchard National Wildlife Refuge. M.S. Thesis, Southern Illinois University, Carbondale.

Thompson, D.Q. 1952. Travel, range, and food habits of timber wolves in Wisconsin. *Journal of Mammalogy* 25:37-43.

Thompson, J.H. (ed.). 1966. Figure 9 in *Geography of New York State.* Syracuse University Press, 543.

Tibbs, A.L. 1967. Summer behavior of white-tailed deer and the effects of weather. M.S. Thesis, Pennsylvania State University, University Park.

Todd, A.W., Gunson, J.R. and Samuel, W.M. (in press). Sarcoptic mange, an important disease of coyotes and wolves of Alberta. In J. Chapman and D. Pursley (eds.), *Proceedings of the First Worldwide Furbearer Conference,* 1980, Fosberg College, Fosberg, Maryland.

Trainer, D.O. and Knowlton, F.F. 1968. Serologic evidence of diseases in Texas coyotes. *Journal of Wildlife Management* 32:981-983.

Tristram, H.B. 1866. Report on the mammals of Palestine. *Proceedings of the Zoological Society,* London, 84-93.

Tristram, H.B. 1885. The fauna and flora of Palestine. The Committee of the Palestine Exploration Fund, London.

Trivers, R.L. 1972. Parental investment and sexual selection. In B. Campbell (ed.), *Sexual Selection and the Descent of Man.* Aldine Press, Chicago, 136-179.

Truett, J.C. 1979. Observations of coyote predation on mule deer fawns in Arizona. *Journal of Wildlife Management* 43:956-958.

Tylor, E.B. 1878. On a method of investigating the development of institutions. Journal of the (Royal) Anthropological Institute 18. Quoted from R. Fox (ed.), *Kinship and Marriage,* Pelican, Middlesex, England, 1967.

U.S. Bureau of the Census. 1973. Census of population: 1970. Vol. I: Characteristics of the population, Part 24, Michigan. U.S. Government Printing Office, Washington, DC, PC(1)-A to C24.

Van Ballenberghe, V. 1972. Ecology, movements and population characteristics of timber wolves in northeastern Minnesota. Ph.D. Thesis, University of Minnesota.

Van Ballenberghe, V. 1977. Physical characteristics of timber wolves in Minnesota. In R.L. Phillips and C. Jonkel (eds.), *Proceedings of the 1975 Predator Symposium*, Montana Forest Conservation Experimental Station, University of Montana, Missoula.

Van Ballenberghe, V., Erickson, A.W. and Byman, D. 1975. Ecology of the timber wolf in northeastern Minnesota. *Wildlife Monographs* 43:1-43.

Van Ballenberghe, V. and Mech, L.D. 1975. Weights, growth and survival of timber wolf pups in Minnesota. *Journal of Mammalogy* 56:44-63.

VanCamp, J. and Gluckie, R. 1979. A record long-distance move by a wolf (*Canis lupus*). *Journal of Mammalogy* 60:236-237.

Van der Donck, A. 1655. *A Description of the New Netherlands*. T.F. O'Donnell (ed.), Syracuse University Press, 275pp.

Vehrencamp, S.L. 1979. The roles of individual, kin, and group selection in the evolution of sociality. In P. Marler and J.G. Vandenbergh (eds.), *Handbook of Behavioral Neurobiology, Volume 3: Social Behavior and Communication*. Plenum Press, New York, 351-394.

Verme, L.J. and Holland, J.C. 1973. Reagent-dry assay of marrow fat in white-tailed deer. *Journal of Wildlife Management* 37:103-105.

Victoria, Sister. 1974. Russian experience. In *The Native, Russian and American Experiences in the Kenai Area of Alaska*, Proceedings of the Conference on Kenai Area History, Nov. 1974, 45-82.

Weaver, J.L. 1978. The wolves of Yellowstone. USGPO NPS National Research Report No. 14, 38pp.

Weaver, J.L. 1979. Population history, ecology and status of wolves in northwestern Wyoming. Presented at the Portland International Wolf Symposium, August 1979, Portland, Oregon.

Weaver, J.L. and Fritts, S.H. 1979. Comparison of coyote and wolf scat diameters. *Journal of Wildlife Management* 43:786-788.

Weise, T.F., Robinson, W.L., Hook, R.A. and Mech, L.D. 1975. An experimental translocation of the eastern timber wolf. Audubon Conservation Report No. 5, National Audubon Society and U.S. Fish and Wildlife Service, Twin Cities, Minnesota.

Williams, G.C. 1966. *Adaptation and Natural Selection*. Princeton University Press, Princeton.

Williamson, V.H.H. 1951. Determination of hairs by impression. *Journal of Mammalogy* 32:80-84.

Wilson, E.O. 1975. *Sociobiology: The New Synthesis*. Belknap Press of Harvard University Press, Cambridge.

Wittenberger, J.F. 1979. The evolution of mating systems in birds and mammals. In P. Marler and J.G. Vandenbergh (eds.), *Handbook of Behavioral Neurobiology, Volume 3: Social Behavior and Communication*. Plenum Press, New York, 271-349.

Wolf, L.L. 1975. "Prostitution" behavior in a tropical hummingbird. *Condor* 77:140-144.

Wolfe, M.L. and Allen, D.L. 1973. Continued studies of the status, socialization and relationships of Isle Royale wolves, 1969-70. *Journal of Mammalogy* 54:611-635.

Woolpy, J.H. 1968. The social organization of wolves. *Natural History* 77:46-55.

Woolpy, J.H. and Eckstrand. 1979. Wolf pack genetics, a computer simulation with theory. In E. Klinghammer (ed.), *The Behavior and Ecology of Wolves.* Garland Press, New York.

Workman, W.B. 1974. Prehistory of the southern Kenai Peninsula. In *The Native, Russian and American Experiences in the Kenai Area of Alaska*, Proceedings of the Conference on Kenai Area History, Nov. 1974, 11-26.

Wright, B.S. 1960. Predation on big game in east Africa. *Journal of Wildlife Management* 24:1-15.

Wright, S. 1939. Statistical genetics in relation to evolution. *Actualitees Scientifique et Industrielles*, 802. Paris.

Young, S.P. and Goldman, E.A. (eds.). 1944. *The Wolves of North America.* American Wildlife Institute, Washington, DC, Dover Publishers, New York.

Zar, J.H. 1974. *Biostatistical analysis.* Prentice-Hall, Inc., Englewood Cliffs, New Jersey.

Zimen, E. 1971. *Wolfe and Konigspudel: Vergleichende Verhaltensbeobachtungen.* Piper, Munich.

Zimen, E. 1975. Social dynamics of the wolf pack. In M.W. Fox (ed.), *The Wild Canids: Their Systematics, Behavioral Ecology and Evolution.* Van Nostrand Reinhold Company, New York, 336-362.

Zimen, E. 1976. On the regulation of pack size in wolves. *Zeitschrift für Tierpsychologie* 40:300-341.

Zimen, E. 1981. *The Wolf: A Species in Danger*, Delacourt, New York.

Zimen, E. and Boitani, L. 1975. Number and distribution of wolves in Italy. *Z. für Saugetierkunde* 40:102-112.

Zimen, E. and Boitani, L. 1979. Status of the wolf in Europe and the possibilities of conservation and reintroduction. In E. Klinghammer (ed.), *The Behavior and Ecology of Wolves*, Garland STPM Press, New York.

Zollitsch, H. 1969. Metrische untersuchungen an Schädeln adulter wildwolfe und goldschakale. *Zodogischer Anzeiger* 182:153-182.

*The original reference appears in Russian; these are literal translations.

Index

Wolf (continued)
178, —greatest length, 174, 176, 178, 179, 194, —nasal bones, 197, 198; teeth, 347-349, —canines, 179, 192, —incisors, 192, —molars, 192, 197, 198, 347; toes (foot pads), 181, 182; weights, 14-16, 21, 22, 111, 112, 174, 178, 179, 193, 194, 196, 198, 199, 378

population density: 4, 7, 8, 10, 11, 22, 26, 29, 54, 55, 59-61, 68, 77, 78, 82, 114, 121-123, 136, 144, 145, 159, 236, 411, 412, 414, 434; censusing, 6, 11, 27, 56-58, 60; interbreeding, 359, 360; isolation, 351, 356, 357

population distribution, 55, 182-185, 196

population regulation, 115, 144, 282

population, sex/age structure, 141, 142, 144, 192

population size, 10-12, 112, 120-122, 130, 131, 143, 144, 146, 159, 160, 186, 187, 196, 328-333, 337, 342, 360, 370

population stability, 430

population status: 328-333; decline, 112, 113; elimination, 334, 335, 339-341, 360, 363, 365, 366, 395; increase, 68, 71, 135-145, 169, 178, 334, 342, 379, 380; reappearance, 334, 340, 342, 360, 366, 399

population variation, 122, 174-182, 431

predation, effects of, 43, 54, 124-127, 130, 131, 188, 411-415

predation, kills: 47, 48, 364; competition with bears for, 72-80; days at kill, 49; distance between, 53, 129; influence on movements, 87, 88, 97, 98; proportion consumed, 40, 45, 50; revisits to, 49, 50, 87, 88

predation rates, 27, 36, 39, 40, 48, 52, 78, 79

predation, selective nature of: 125, 129, 136; age-classes of prey, 22, 32, 36, 37, 39, 41, 45, 48, 50, 51, 64, 65, 67, 68, 78, 127, 129, 149, 151, 188; physical condition of prey, 45, 50, 51, 149, 151; sexes of prey, 36, 48, 50, 51, 53, 149, 151; vulnerability, 128, 129, 155, 156, 162, 188, 263

prey (see individual species, also see hunting, predation): food exchange, 103; foraging pattern,

273; influence on population dynamics, 106, 143, 282; pack size, 106

pups: care of, 82, 96, 209, 224, 229-231, 237; development, 81, 198-201, 236; diseases in, 111, 112, 115; feeding of, 81, 232, 233, 238-260, 308, 311, 317-320; grooming, 229, 230; left alone at homesite, 97, 102, 231, 232; maturation, 217, 223, 236; nursing, 100, 224, 229, 230, 235; preference for individual adults, 229, 236; protection of, 101, 102; survival, 235, 282; weaning, 85, 100

range (see also populations): 4, 5, 158, 169, 170, 173, 177, 328-333, 400, 417; discontinuous, 121, 168; effects of dispersal on, 164; reduction, 120, 122, 168, 173

rendezvous sites: 13, 14, 17, 19, 81, 108, 115, 426; characteristics, 20, 23; identification of, 20; periods used, 84

reproduction: 146; abortions, 312; breeding season, 191, 192, 209, 211, 212, 217, 219, 226, 234, 294, 297, 308, 317, 322; estrus, 212-214, 216, 219, 224, 317; limits to, 233, 234; litters, 213, 233, 367, 374, —combining of, 210, 215, 219, —multiple, 74, 214, 215, 218, 219, 223-225, 234-237, —number of, 309, 310, 312, —sex ratio, 191, —size, 30, 32, 59, 164, 191, 216, 224, 229, 236, 282; parturition, 85, 100, 191, 210, 216, 229, 245, 246; potential, 164, 233, 234; reproductive value, 220; vaginal bleeding, 224, 309, 312, 316, 317

scent marking, 213, 308, 311, 313

social behavior: 206, 238, 282-316, 423, 431; evolution of, 82; influence of sex/age/social rank, 282-322; social rank order (dominance hierarchy), 226, 234, 246, 257, 287-322, —alpha female, 85, 86, 88, 91, 100, 212-214, 219, 224, 226, 234, 284, 289-293, 296, 298, 300-312, 314, 316-319, 322, —alpha male, 85, 86, 89, 91, 93-95, 100, 213, 214, 216, 234, 284, 288-294, 296, 298, 300-311, 313, 314, 316-319, 321, 322, 426, 427, 430, —beta male, 213, 214, 216, 289-294, 296-298, 300-310, 318, 322, —dominance (dominants), 102, 211-217, 219, 221, 223, 224, 226-228, 234, 235, 237, 246, 259, 280,